Daybreak in
Indiana

Carol Walls Howell

Carol Walls Howell

*Thank you and
God Bless*

 2022

This is a work of fiction. All of the characters, names, incidents,
organizations, and dialogue in this novel are either the products
of the author's imagination or are used fictitiously.

Scripture quotations are from the Revised Standard Version of the
Bible, copyright © 1946, 1952, and 1971 the Division of Christian
Education of the National Council of the Churches of Christ in the United
States of America. Used by permission. All rights reserved.

LifeRich Publishing is a registered trademark of The Reader's Digest Association, Inc.

LifeRich Publishing books may be ordered through booksellers or by contacting:

LifeRich Publishing
1663 Liberty Drive
Bloomington, IN 47403
www.liferichpublishing.com
1 (888) 238-8637

Because of the dynamic nature of the Internet, any web addresses or links contained in
this book may have changed since publication and may no longer be valid. The views
expressed in this work are solely those of the author and do not necessarily reflect the
views of the publisher, and the publisher hereby disclaims any responsibility for them.

Any people depicted in stock imagery provided by Thinkstock are models,
and such images are being used for illustrative purposes only.
Certain stock imagery © Thinkstock.

ISBN: 978-1-4897-1339-1 (sc)
ISBN: 978-1-4897-1340-7 (hc)
ISBN: 978-1-4897-1338-4 (e)

Library of Congress Control Number: 2017949760

Print information available on the last page.

LifeRich Publishing rev. date: 09/28/2017

PART 1

PART I

Chapter 1

THE WINTER HAD PASSED, AND ALL THE ARRANGE-
ments had been made. Anna Marie Patterson and the two children,
Pat and Tim, would stay on the farm until her husband, Brady, sent
for them. This past winter, Brady and his friend Frank met many
times as they finalized their plans for the trip back to Indiana and
their newly acquired farmland. The men staked out their land last
year on their scouting trip, and both planned to build cabins on the
rich Indiana soil. For the last six months, the men had used a corner
of Brady's barn to store the equipment they would need for their journey. In Indiana, they would clear the properties and build both cabins
before Brady's family moved north from Kentucky to join them.

❈

It was Easter Sunday 1837, and everyone who had ever gone to
church in the little town of Reed's Crossing showed up at church
that morning. Preacher Martin and his wife, Naomi, were excited to
see such a large gathering. Brady sat in the pew with the two boys.
The air was filled with excitement as the choir led the congregation
in four spirited Easter hymns. Preacher Martin followed with an
uplifting sermon, and the morning concluded with two baptisms.
Several families brought baskets of food to share at the usual Sunday
dinner. The weather cooperated; it was warm enough to eat outside,
and that's what several men did. Brady filled his plate, went outside,

and joined Jeremiah, Pricilla's husband. They had been friends now for two years. Pricilla had their first child, Joseph, last November, two months after Anna Marie gave birth to Timothy.

Brady hopped up on a wagon beside Jeremiah and said, "Great meal today."

"Yeah," Jeremiah replied. "This fried chicken tastes real good."

"Remember to save room for dessert. I saw two pumpkin pies inside."

"I guess you'll be leaving soon for Indiana. I'm a little jealous of you striking out on your own to homestead a new farm," Jeremiah admitted.

"Heck, that's nothing to be jealous of. Why don't you come along and get some land for yourself? Frank's coming to my place on Wednesday to make plans for the trip. Bring your family over. The women can visit while we make final arrangements."

Jeremiah let the thought sink in for a few moments. "You know, Brady, I think I'll talk to Pricilla about it. That's a great idea. I could go with you, help you build your cabin, and claim some land in the same area." From the look on his face, Brady could tell that Jeremiah would be joining them.

After the meal, all the church members gathered their food baskets and departed for their homes. Brady told Jeremiah, "Let me know your decision. You'll be a good buddy to travel with."

Jeremiah helped Pricilla and the baby into their buggy. He was getting more excited by the moment as his mind raced at the prospect of going in search of a new homestead. But how would he approach the subject with his wife? Jeremiah waited until he and Pricilla were sitting at the supper table. An oil lamp on the washstand by the wall filled the kitchen with light. A short, fat candle in a small crock in the middle of the table cast a warm, golden glow on their faces.

He held Pricilla's hands across the table and looked into her eyes. "You are so beautiful," he told her. "How can I be so lucky to have you for my wife? I would do anything for you."

Pricilla looked at him and smiled. "What brought that on? I knew when I married you that you loved me and would take good care of me."

He remained quiet for a few moments and looked away. Then he said, "I talked to Brady Patterson today at church." He paused and cleared his throat. "He asked me to go to Indiana with him this spring. I'd help him build his cabin and find a farm for us." He held her hands a little tighter. "I want to do this for us. What do you think?"

"That's a lot of work. Do you really want to farm?" She studied the look on his face. "You've never farmed. Why don't you build a big house with several bedrooms, and we can run our own boardinghouse? It's such hard work trying to make a living on a farm."

"That's not a bad idea. Does that mean you would agree for me to go away for a couple months this summer?"

She smiled approvingly. "You go with Brady and look at the land. Then make your decision. If it's meant to be, it'll work out."

He jumped out of his chair, went to her, and pulled her close. He kissed her passionately. When he released her, they were both breathless. "I'll find out when Brady plans to leave, and we'll make arrangements for you and Joseph." He held her close and stroked her hair. "I can't believe this is happening. It's like a new world is opening up for us."

❁

Wednesday arrived. Anna Marie and Pricilla sat in rockers and visited while the men worked out the final details for their trip north. The mood was serious, and Jeremiah listened intently to Frank and Brady while the three sat at the kitchen table. Frank wrote down last-minute supplies they would need. The men had already stored several items that would be hauled in the wagon that Big Al helped Brady build. Frank had worked with the local blacksmith the previous winter and taken a pair of workhorses, complete with harnesses, for his pay. He learned blacksmithing along with how to make horseshoes and nails.

Jeremiah was overwhelmed with the amount of planning needed for such a trip, but he had a skill the other men didn't have—he could cook! He had cooked regularly in the boardinghouse at Reed's Crossing and enjoyed preparing meals. Baking biscuits was one of his specialties. Of course, cooking outside over an open fire and using a spider pan would definitely be a challenge. But it was one he was willing to tackle.

After an hour, the men agreed they were about ready to leave on their journey. The women heard a roar of laughter, which signaled the serious part of the meeting had ended, and someone had told a joke.

"Brady," Anna Marie called, "are you ready for fresh coffee and a piece of gingerbread?"

"Sure thing," he replied.

"Gingeebed, Mommy, gingeebed," Pat said. Anna Marie and Pricilla laughed.

"Gingerbread for everybody," Anna Marie said. She took the coffeepot off its hook, where it had been brewing in the open fireplace. They all gathered in the kitchen to talk excitedly about the coming weeks. With persuasion from Brady and Jeremiah, the women agreed that they and their babies would live together until it was time to pack up and move. Anna Marie and Pricilla smiled and hugged each other.

Anna Marie told Pricilla, "You can live here with my family. Jeremiah can decide the best time to move you here."

"I'm so glad that we're good friends. Our time will go much faster when we have each other to talk to and share meals and do our needlework. The children will learn to play together. All in all, I think it'll be a good arrangement."

The babies lay asleep on a blanket in the bedroom, unaware of the events around them. Pat didn't realize what changes would take place in his life in the coming months, but he'd learn soon enough that his papa was leaving.

"Jeremiah, we welcome you to the greatest adventure of your life. It'll be a pleasure to have you come with Frank and me. Besides, neither of us can cook worth a darn," Frank said. Everyone laughed.

Brady, Frank, and Jeremiah all shook hands. They decided to leave on the first day of spring, in about two weeks.

❋

The day after the meeting, Anna Marie was close to panic, wondering how she could manage with so much to do in two weeks. She decided to visit her neighbor and friend, Lucy. As soon as she finished putting the vegetables into the stewpot for their noon meal, she took the boys outside to the porch. Then she went to the barn, hitched her horse, Mandy, to the buggy, and brought them up to the front of the house.

"Okay, boys, we're going to visit Lucy this morning." They got into the buggy, and Anna Marie made sure the boys were secure on the seat. She kept Mandy at a steady trot until she reached the Bennings' home. They were greeted by Big Al, hoe in hand, working around a flowerbed in the yard.

"Mornin'," Big Al shouted. "Is everybody all right?"

"We're just fine. I felt like I wanted to visit with Lucy this morning, if she's not too busy."

"Let me take Mandy over to the watering trough. You take the boys on inside the house."

"Thanks, Al." She lifted Pat down to the ground and picked up Tim. Tim flailed his arms and squealed as he felt the excitement of the upcoming visit with the other children. Pat jumped around and yelled out, "Lucy."

Lucy came to the door. "Hello, Pat. Did you come to visit?"

Pat replied, "Uh-huh. I want to play."

"Well, bless your heart. I'm happy to see all of you. Come inside." The three joined Lucy in the kitchen. "This is a surprise. Sit down, and we'll talk." The two women sat at the table as Pat went off to play with Lucy's young children.

"Lucy," Anna Marie started, "Brady had a meeting at our house last night, along with Frank Justice and Jeremiah, Pricilla's husband. They've set their date to leave for Indiana to work on our homestead.

7

They're leaving in two weeks," she said with a stressed tone in her voice.

Lucy reached to hold Anna Marie's hand as she said, "Now, now, no need for you to be upset. You knew the time would come when Brady would leave to work on your new home, didn't you?"

"Yes."

"You need to calm down and tell me more."

Anna Marie inhaled deeply and said, "Well, Jeremiah decided to go with Brady and Frank, thinking that he would look for land. Pricilla and her baby will come live with me."

"That sounds like a good plan. You two young mothers will manage your families together, and you won't have the loneliness that you experienced last year. Right?"

"Right."

"You sit here and relax, and I'll fix us some more tea, then we'll visit, and I'll help you work things out." Anna Marie felt better already. She realized that she really wasn't that upset. She needed to tell Lucy what was going to happen these next two weeks. After all, Lucy had been her best friend since she and Brady were married.

Anna Marie stayed until nearly time to feed her boys their noon meal. She gave Lucy a hug and said, "Thanks for listening to me; you're the greatest. I'll get the boys and be on my way."

"We'll talk again real soon, okay? Be careful going home."

Anna Marie's mood was lighter now as she guided Mandy down the road toward home. It was a reality that she could now face with a surety that she and her boys would survive the next few months as they prepare for the move to a new home and a new life.

That evening Anna Marie sat at the kitchen table with Brady while they discussed preparations for the upcoming move. Brady said, "Jeremiah will come back to Reed's Crossing when we have our home completed; Frank and I will stay and keep working. You'll need help packing up our belongings. I think that you should contact your parents to come, as I'm sure that they'll want to see you and the boys before we leave Kentucky."

"It would be nice to have some time with them," she replied.

"Jeremiah is having two covered wagons built, one for his family and one for us. He'll drive the wagon for his family. You'll need someone to drive your wagon. Do you think your father is up to it?"

"I don't know. Why don't we go visit them? They haven't seen their grandchildren for several weeks."

"Sure thing, we'll go as soon as I can arrange for Big Al and his boys to take care of our farm."

Anna Marie rose quickly and went over to Brady. She sat on his lap and wrapped her arms around his neck. "Brady Patterson, you are the best husband any woman could want. I love you," she told him. He pulled her close and kissed her.

When they parted, Brady told her, "My sweet Anna, you are the woman I chose. For me, you are the most wonderful woman a man could ever want." She leaned against him and laid her head on his shoulder. They sat there and cuddled for several minutes—and then Tim cried out. Brady kissed Anna Marie on the forehead and they both smiled then she rose to check on the baby who had awakened.

"There, there, you're all right," she cooed as she picked him up. When Tim was taken care of and put back to bed, Anna Marie and Brady went to their bedroom. As they lay in bed face to face, Brady stroked Anna Marie's hair and face.

"Beautiful lady, what would I do without you? I can hardly bear the thought of being away from you another summer but I must."

"I know," she replied. "It's to be our future and our life together, a new beginning." Brady and Anna Marie made love together. Many thoughts of the coming weeks whirled around in their heads for some time until they were able to fall asleep.

❋

After church on Sunday, the Patterson family got into their buggy to go visit Anna Marie's parents, who lived thirty miles south of Reed's Crossing in a small community called the Glade. The rolling hills held small farms nestled in the thick Kentucky bluegrass.

Each home seemed to have been strategically built inside a grove of trees for protection from the weather. They passed by a church and small cemetery, which had rambling roses displaying clusters of red blooms. Anna Marie pointed them out to Pat, who, of course, wanted to stop and pick some.

Anna held Tim while Pat sat between her and Brady. A picnic basket was tied to the back of the seat along with a bag that held a change of clothes for the boys. She also included a couple quilts, for the spring air had a little chill in it. They trotted along at a steady pace for an hour when they decided to stop to rest the horse and step out of the buggy for a short break.

"Pat, would you like a sandwich to eat?" Anna Marie asked.

"Uh huh," he muttered and nodded.

"I'd like one of those," stated Brady. Anna Marie reached into the picnic basket and got sandwiches for the three of them. Pat took a couple bites of his, and he couldn't stand still any longer. He ran around the trees and bushes that were close by. He stopped when he spotted two wild turkeys. The tom had his feathers fanned out as he strutted around the hen. The strutting continued for several minutes.

"Look, Papa," Pat said excitedly.

Brady walked over to Pat and knelt down. "Those are turkeys, son," Brady told him quietly. The turkeys heard the talking, and they turned their heads toward the two. "Don't be too noisy; it will scare them away." Pat and Brady observed the turkeys together for several minutes. Anna Marie, carrying Tim, walked over to view the ritual going on in the woods.

"Seeing this go on in nature is so special," Anna Marie remarked. Brady spotted a turkey feather lying at the edge of a bush and picked it up.

"Look here, Pat." Pat quickly turned from watching the turkeys toward his father. "I found a turkey feather. Would you like to have it?"

"Sure," Pat answered as he reached for it at the same time. Pat smiled as he took the feather and began examining it. He looked around and saw another one and picked it up. "For Tim," Pat said.

"We better go; we still have several miles to travel," Anna Marie said. The four got into the buggy and started down the road. Within minutes, Pat and Tim were both sound asleep.

It was now late afternoon as the buggy went over the last hill before reaching its destination. Anna Marie felt excited inside as she viewed the home that she grew up in. Brady guided Mandy up to the hitching post, which stood under a large maple tree a short distance from the house. Mandy began drinking as soon as she was tethered. Anna Marie's parents, Ben and Lydia, came out to the porch to greet their family.

"It's so good to see you," Lydia said happily. She hugged Pat first. "My goodness, you are getting to be such a big boy," she told him.

Anna Marie stood there holding Tim. "Oh, let me hold little Timmy," Lydia said as she reached for him. Tim let Lydia take him into her arms. He squirmed and reached for her hair. "You little rascal, you can't pull my hair!" she said as she nuzzled him and made him giggle.

Ben walked down off of the porch and went to greet Brady. The two men shook hands. "Nice to have you come visit," Ben told him. "Come on inside and wash up a bit. Lydia has a nice meal ready for all of us."

"It's good to be here. I'm ready to rest," Brady replied. Lydia poured mugs of hot tea and gave Pat a glass of milk. They all sat around the kitchen table laden with a pork roast and several bowls of vegetables.

"Mother, did you fix my favorite dessert?" Anna Marie asked.

Lydia placed her hand on her cheek and looked thoughtful. "Let me think." She paused a few moments. "I remember now. Could that be brown Betty?" She smiled lovingly at Anna Marie and winked. As she walked over to the wooden stand beside the dish cabinet, she said, "Yes, I believe I did make one of those."

Brady patted rhythmically on the table, drawing attention to him, and said, "It's my favorite too," he declared.

Anna Marie said, "Sure, all desserts are his favorite!" After everybody had a good chuckle, the five of them chatted and told

11

stories until bedtime. Pat had curled up on a rug, holding the toy horse he had brought with him. Brady went outside and took care of his horse and buggy. When Brady finished bedding Mandy down, he returned inside. He picked Pat up and carried him to the small bed in the extra bedroom. Brady and Anna Marie were tired but happy to be at Ben and Lydia's for a visit.

❋

Morning arrived bright and sunny with crowing roosters and chirping birds. Brady had gotten up long before Anna Marie awoke. He dressed and went outside to walk around in the fresh morning air. He looked toward the barn and saw Ben coming out of the barn with a pail of fresh milk.

"Mornin'," he called out.

"Mornin'. I didn't expect to see you out this early," Ben remarked.

"Oh, I'm up early every morning. It suits me to greet the morning sun."

"I agree. My pa always said, "Get up and start the day early; people die in bed!"

Brady chuckled. "That's true," he agreed.

"We best go inside and check if the coffee is ready." The men went into the kitchen. Lydia was bustling around like she was fixing breakfast for the duke and duchess of England. The cook stove was hot, and the sausage cakes were sizzling in the iron skillet. Lydia was cutting the dough for the biscuits and placing them into a baking pan. Ben filled the mugs from the large tin coffee pot. Anna Marie, carrying Tim, came into the kitchen while the men were enjoying their coffee. Pat's little feet pitter-pattered along behind them.

"Did everyone sleep well?" Lydia asked.

"I slept like I did as a child," Anna Marie answered.

"That's good to hear. I didn't hear the children during the night either."

"No, they slept all night without any problem."

"Breakfast is ready," Lydia announced. "Let's eat."

As the morning meal ended, everyone became suddenly quiet. Brady and Anna Marie looked at each other as if saying, *Is this the time?* Ben and Lydia noticed the curious look on their faces.

Anna Marie spoke. "I have something to tell you."

"Well, go ahead," Ben replied.

"Brady and I are moving to Indiana this summer. He will be leaving shortly with Frank Justice and Jeremiah Whitmore, his longtime friends. I'll need help later on when it comes time for me and the boys to move."

Brady spoke, "Frank has already arranged for a covered wagon. Jeremiah is coming back for his wife, Pricilla, and they'll also be moving with us. Is there any chance that you could go with Anna Marie and drive the wagon for her?"

Ben and Lydia were in shock at first, but that soon changed to acceptance along with smiles and good wishes. They both agreed that they would arrange to help Anna Marie, and Ben would drive the wagon for her. Lydia would help with the two boys and the meals. Anna Marie and the family stayed the day and another night visiting. They left Tuesday morning laden with fresh bread and preserves to share along the way. The stay at her parent's home was enjoyable for Anna Marie, but she was ready to return to her and Brady's home. She knew her place was with her husband and children and the life they had made together.

❖

The next ten days flew by with all that Brady had to do in preparation for his journey back to his Indiana acreage. The weather had cooperated, and he was able to sow grass seed for the summer hay crop. The crop was intended for Big Al and his boys in repayment for caring for the farm and his family. He mended the fences around the barn and chicken lots.

Early on the last day before he was to leave, he and Anna Marie went by Big Al and Lucy's home. After sharing a hot drink and a biscuit, Brady and Anna Marie told them that they were going on to Reed's Crossing.

Lucy said, "You two need some time alone today. Let me keep the little ones until you come back this way. It'll be good for all of you."

"That's very kind. It'll make it a little easier to get the last-minute things done," Brady told her. "Thank you."

He took Anna Marie into town so she could get sewing items or anything else she would need during the weeks that he would be gone. He also longed for her closeness, to be alone with her away from anybody or anything else. They went to the mercantile and the post office, then they went to the boardinghouse. They immediately saw Jeremiah and Pricilla sitting together at a table.

"Hello. Come on over and sit with us," Jeremiah invited. "Would you like something to eat?"

Brady looked lovingly at Anna Marie, as he admired her beauty. "We all need to eat, don't we?" he answered.

"Tell you what," Jeremiah told him, "this meal is on the house. We've got pot roast cooked today and cheesecake for dessert." Knowing that Jeremiah was going to be his cook for some time on the journey, Brady poked fun at Jeremiah. "It'll probably be the best meal I'll have all summer!" Jeremiah's face turned red, and he replied, "I'll make sure you get the bony piece of meat every meal!" Everybody laughed.

Anna Marie asked Pricilla, "When do you think you'll be able to move over to my place?"

"I think that I'll stay here at the boardinghouse in the spare room for a little while. It won't be too long. My little Joseph has had a tummyache and I want to be sure that he's feeling good when I come."

"That sounds all right. I'll probably come into town next week, and I'll pay you a visit."

"I'll look forward to that. We'll have a lot to talk about."

The rest of the daytime hours went without any problems, quite ordinary actually. Brady and Anna Marie left town, stopped by Big

Al and Lucy's home, chatted a little, and then took Pat and Tim back home with them. They had sandwiches, leftover baked beans, and milk for their supper.

Anna Marie was starting to get an empty feeling deep inside. She undressed Pat and washed his hands and feet before putting him to bed. Tim needed to be cleaned up from head to toe, as he had gotten dirty crawling around for much of the day. Brady kept himself busy checking and rechecking his lists that he had made for his trip. He had even gone out to the barn two different times while Anna was caring for the boys.

The work was finally done, and Anna Marie stripped off her clothes and washed herself, then put on her clean nightgown. Brady had a quick glimpse of her as he saw her put on her nightgown. He took a big breath and held it for a moment as he drank in her beauty. His body began to stir with emotion. He went to her and drew her as close as possible. They were lost in the moment.

He murmured to her, "I'll wash and come to you." He kissed her as if it were his last. She went into the bedroom, pulled the covers back, lay down, and waited. When Brady came to her, they lay in bed with their arms wrapped around each other. It would be the last night they would sleep together for most of the summer. After the lovemaking, Brady slept, drawing in deep breaths. Anna Marie stroked his muscled body. Oh, how she loved this man. Tears filled her eyes, ran across her cheeks, and onto the bedcovers. Anna Marie knew that she was a much stronger wife and mother now than she was a year ago. Many pioneer women learned to survive when their husbands were gone, and she knew that she would be strong for her family. Breathing deeply, she brushed her tears away and sighed. *Tomorrow is the day,* she thought. She smiled to herself; she would be ready.

Chapter 2

May 7.

THE SUN HAD BEEN SHINING NOW FOR TWO HOURS. Frank had hitched the workhorses to the supply wagon, tied his horse onto the back, and climbed up on the driver's seat. He looked over toward Jeremiah and Pricilla, who were holding each other as they said goodbye, and he could tell it was hard for them to part.

Brady went over to the boys, gave them a squeeze, and then he walked over to Anna Marie. He held both of her hands and looked lovingly into her beautiful green eyes. "Don't worry, sweetheart. Frank and I will have our cabins built, and we'll all be together in no time. You'll see," Brady assured her.

Anna Marie's voice choked as she tried to talk. "I know this is something you have to do. The boys and I will be all right, but please take care and don't get hurt. I need you."

Brady hugged her and gave her a parting kiss. "I love you," he said softly. Then he turned and went to his horse, checked the saddle, and mounted. Brady and Anna Marie had said their "good-byes" in private last night. She was excited for all the possibilities waiting for herself and her family but knew there would be a lot of hard work ahead, and she was not looking forward to being without Brady for another summer.

Frank hollered out, "Okay, let's get started. Jeremiah, mount up; it's time to move out!"

"Coming," he replied. He gave Pricilla one more parting kiss and then walked over to his horse. Pricilla picked up Joseph and held him close while streams of tears fell down her cheeks.

Brady said to Frank, "Are you sure we have everything? Did you check our list?"

He hollered back, "What do you think I was doing while you men were kissing your ladies?"

Brady laughed and replied, "You got me. I was busy! Guess we're set."

Jeremiah rode up beside Brady. "I'm ready when you are."

"Okay, Frank, let's go," Brady stated.

Frank snapped the reins on the backs of the horses, and the wagon moved forward. Even though the wagon bore a heavy load, the horses pulled it with ease along the path. Pricilla and Anna Marie watched intently until the men and all that accompanied them were out of sight. They looked at each other and their children and the world around them. It was still the same, except they knew that they were on their own for the next few months. The full impact of this would not be felt until later.

"Let's go sit on the porch for a while," Anna Marie said to Pricilla. "It's such a beautiful spring day." The two sat on the porch rockers and planned for Pricilla's move to the Patterson farm. Pat entertained himself out in the yard with his toy horse, and Tim played with Joseph on a quilt that Anna Marie had laid on the porch. The two women visited until nearly noon when Joseph began to whimper and fuss.

Pricilla spoke. "I think it's time to go back to the boardinghouse. Joseph still has something upsetting him." She went to her horse and buggy. "I'll see you next week when you're in town," she told Anna Marie.

"Yes, you will. I hope Joseph gets better soon," Anna Marie replied. She waved good-bye and watched Pricilla's buggy disappear out of view.

She turned and went back beside Tim, who was still playing on the quilt. He flailed his arms and legs excitedly and reached out as if to say, "Pick me up, Mama." It worked, and he quickly found himself in his mama's arms. She held him very close to her breast, and without warning tears flowed uncontrollably down her face as she sat on the rocker. Pat looked at his mama, went over to her and Tim, and put his hands on her arms.

After a few moments, he patted her and said, "You all right, Mama?" stating what his mama had said to him many times.

That brought a smile to her face, and she said, "Yes, Pat, I'll be all right," and she bent over and kissed him on the cheek.

"When is Papa coming back home?" he asked.

"It will be later this summer. You help me with chores and with Timmy. We'll get along just fine."

"Okay, Mama."

Anna Marie gave him a squeeze, and a few more tears crept down her face.

The three of them stayed on the porch and watched the clouds as they floated along in the sky. They discussed what the shapes and forms might be. They saw a bird fly from tree to tree and make an occasional swoop down to check the grass for worms or bugs to eat. They were at peace, but more than that, they were a family, bound together.

❋

The following week was normal for the Patterson family. The weather was typical for spring. Anna Marie had Big Al and his two older sons come over to dig up her garden spot. She planted the early vegetable seeds, hoping for fresh vegetables later this summer.

On Tuesday, May 13, after breakfast and chores, Anna Marie hitched Mandy to the buggy. She and her boys went into Reed's Crossing. They went directly to the boardinghouse to see Pricilla and found it wasn't busy. As soon as they entered, they spotted Pricilla sitting at the kitchen table holding her son, Joseph.

Pricilla spoke cheerfully, "Good morning, Anna Marie. I was hoping to see you. Come, have some hot tea."

"Thanks, I'd enjoy that. Joseph looks like he is feeling good." He was standing on the floor while holding onto his mama and jumping up and down.

"He's much better."

"Have you decided when you would like to move to my place?'

"Yes. I'd like to come out the day after tomorrow. Would that suit you?'

"That sounds perfect. Do you need any help?'

"No. Jeremiah had already made the arrangements for two of his friends to help me. We should be there shortly after noon."

"I can hardly wait," Anna Marie said anxiously. The two women chatted away about their children and their husbands. After an hour had passed, Anna Marie saw customers coming in for their early noon meal and decided that she needed to leave. She said her good-bye and took her children to the mercantile. She gathered the items she needed in short time, got them to the buggy, and started for home.

Pricilla had given her some sliced sweet bread before they left. Anna Marie drove the buggy out of town and decided to give the boys some to eat. They ate the treat so quickly that it made Anna Marie smile.

A weather front lurked on the horizon. The wind blew forcefully, and dirt was swept up in the air. Suddenly, a big gust swirled in front of the horse and buggy, and the dust hit all three. The two boys began crying and rubbing their eyes. Anna Marie pulled the horse and buggy over next to a grove of trees. She took her handkerchief and wiped both Tim and Pat's faces. When the boys seemed to be better, they continued on down the road. Again the wind blew dust all over the travelers. Both boys whimpered as they rubbed their faces.

They approached the Bennings home, and Anna Marie decided to make a stop. She pulled up to the hitching post at the side of the house. She lifted Pat out of the buggy and then picked up Tim. The wind blew so strongly that Anna Marie nearly tripped on her skirt as she walked up to the front door. She rapped urgently. Just as Big Al opened it, a burst of air blew against all of them, nearly knocking Anna Marie against the door jam.

"Come on inside, young'uns, out of that darn wind," Al stated with a tone of authority.

"Thanks, Al, I'll be glad to," Anna replied. She carried Tim, with Pat holding her hand, and they quickly entered.

"Mama, my eyes hurt," Pat whimpered. Lucy walked into the room.

"Come over here, Pat. Let me see your eyes," Lucy said. She took a clean handkerchief from her apron pocket and took Pat upon her lap. She dabbed his eyes carefully, then wiped at his nose. While Lucy was caring for Pat, Anna Marie soothed Tim and then breast-fed him.

"There, does that feel better?" Lucy asked Pat. He nodded his head and muttered, "Uh huh."

"That's my good boy," she said as she hugged him. She put him down, and he walked away.

"How are you doing?" Lucy asked Anna Marie.

"I'm getting along well. I talked to Pricilla at the boardinghouse. She plans to move to my place in two days."

"I'm glad to hear that. You know, Al and I worry about you and the boys when Brady isn't around. Do you or Pricilla need any help?"

"No, I don't think so. Pricilla has two men to help her move. I think that we'll get along just fine." Anna Marie ended up staying at the Bennings' for lunch. As they ate, they visited about raising their children.

Lucy told this story about Matthew. "When Matt was a boy about seven years old, he would catch bugs or butterflies or anything else that crawled or jumped around. Well, one day he brought his bug box into the house. That particular time he had collected grasshoppers. It sat for most of the day in the corner where he played. He took it out by the barn and left it for the night. The next day he went out to check to see if they were alive. Sometimes he would set them loose, or else he would try to feed them and keep them alive for several days. A few days later, I found two dead ones under the kitchen wash stand. I said to him, 'Matt, I found two dead grasshoppers in the house today when I was cleaning. Do you know anything about them?' His eyes twinkled as he smiled, and he answered back, 'There's two more!'"

Lucy giggled and said, "I looked and looked, but I never did find them."

Big Al said, "You know, boys will be boys. I collected worms when I was a boy. Mother never knew where they would be crawling around. His eyes twinkled, and he laughed heartily. They all had a good chuckle.

Anna Marie soon decided it was time to go home. She took her boys and said her good-byes. The weather had improved, so they didn't encounter further distress with blowing dirt.

☀

Brady, Frank and Jeremiah were making progress as they journeyed north. They traveled about twenty-three miles the first day. The loaded wagon wasn't a hard pull for the two workhorses as the roads had been traveled enough that the ruts were worn down smooth. They had spent the first night on the southern edge of Lexington. They took time to stop there for additional ammunition. They discussed the possibility that there may still be angry Shawnee Indian bands around. The second day, the men rose at sunrise and had a quick breakfast of coffee with jerky and bread, and then started up the road. They talked about the difficulty of following the Kentucky River and, consequently, went on a more traveled road northwest. They passed by many farms and small settlements where several farmers and their wives were working their fields and gardens. The men stopped late that afternoon at one of the farms, which lay along a small stream. Frank unhitched the two horses from the wagon and led them to the water. Brady and Jeremiah dismounted their horses and did the same. It was a hot, humid day, and the men were sweltering wet. The farmer watched the men in the grove of trees over beside the stream. He mounted his horse and rode over to see who they were.

"Howdy fellas, how air ya?" he asked.

"Howdy," Frank replied. "We're takin' a little break from the road; been ridin' all day long."

"Where're you from?"

"Our place is south of Richmond. We're on our way to new farms in Indiana."

Brady and Jeremiah walked up. "Howdy," Brady greeted. "Are you the farmer we saw over there?" he asked.

"Yep, my wife and I have a few acres here we try to make a livin' on. We don't have any young'ns yet."

"You know, there's lots of time for a family," Brady said. "I've got two small sons back home."

"You're a lucky man."

"You're right. Soon as we build a cabin, we'll be movin' to some fine farm ground. Would you mind if we spent the night here on your place?"

"That's all right, but maybe we should introduce ourselves. My name's Joshua Simons."

The three travelers each stated their names and shook hands with Joshua.

"I bet you guys could stand a home-cooked meal. The wife has the stew pot cookin' full of meat and vegetables," he told them.

"That's mighty kind of ya, but not necessary," Jeremiah stated.

"You know, we don't get to talk to many people out here. We'd enjoy your company."

The three travelers looked at each other and agreed to accept the offer. They met Joshua's wife, Willamina, but he called her Willie. She was a slim woman with dark hair that flowed down her back. Her face had high cheekbones and distinctive eyebrows above her dark, twinkling eyes. She had quite a lively nature about her. Before the men left to make up their bedroll, Willie brought out her dulcimer. She then proceeded to play and sing a few Appalachian folk songs. She sang and played with a feeling for music that the men had never heard. Joshua leaned back in his rocker and beamed as he listened to her music.

As they sat, completely focused on her artistry, Willie's music seemed to soothe the men. When she stopped, the men were quiet for a while, and then they applauded.

Brady spoke to her. "I enjoyed both the meal and your music. Thank you. My wife, Anna Marie, is also a singer. I'm sure you two would enjoy music together." Frank and Jeremiah joined in complimenting her.

As the men started to leave, they again thanked the two for their hospitality. It didn't take them long to bed down the horses and crawl into their blankets. The night was calm and, except for the hooting of two owls in the nearby trees, they slept well.

❋

The next three days went well with the men. The horse-drawn wagon kept up the pace. It was late afternoon when they neared the approach of the ferry landing on the Ohio River. Jeremiah stayed with the horse and wagon as Frank and Brady walked down the riverbank. They found that the last ferry had already left for the opposite side. Frank and Brady recognized that nothing had changed from the previous year when they were there, same situation with the mules— the stench, the flies, the mud, all of which were still disgusting. They talked to the owner of the ferry and found that it would return about nine thirty the next morning. The men talked about where to spend the night as they returned up the bank toward Jeremiah.

"What's the plan?" Jeremiah asked.

"We can't leave until midmorning tomorrow," Frank replied. "We need to decide where to camp tonight."

"Well, we need drinking water, and I wouldn't mind a swim to wash off the sweat and road dust," Brady stated.

"I agree with that," Frank said. "Let's find a level place for the wagon in one of the river coves." The men decided that was a good idea. They proceeded along a lesser-used road that followed the uneven riverbank. They plodded along for a while at a much slower pace than they had held on the main road. They finally found a level, grassy area where they could make a campfire and lay out their blankets. As evening approached, some clouds floated around in the west, partially covering the sun.

Frank took care of the horses as Brady toted a pail of water up from the river. Jeremiah didn't waste any time gathering wood and starting a fire. He went to work filling a pot with stew meat and potatoes. As the meal cooked above the flames, the men decided to go down to the river's edge and wash up.

The cove they had chosen created some sort of a feeling of ownership while secluded from the rest of the world. Perhaps it was the sun's glow hitting the ripples of the river, the warm breeze brushing against their faces, and their having reached a milestone, the mighty Ohio River. They felt their blood pulsing through their bodies. It was the feeling of accomplishment.

The men descended the riverbank laughing and joking. They peeled off all their clothing down to their long johns and cautiously stepped into the water, using their feet to feel the way along the bottom. Acting like young boys, they immediately began splashing water on each other. They laughed as they frolicked until Jeremiah looked around and spotted a snake in the water nearby. The snake swirled the water not far from the men.

"Oh, my God, look over there!" Jeremiah exclaimed. "There's a snake."

"Head for the riverbank right now!" Frank hollered. The men quickly changed their spirit from carefree to serious. They kept watching the snake as their legs plunging forward at a panicked pace through the water. The three men were out of breath when they ascended the riverbank and walked back to the campfire.

"Do you think that snake was poisonous?" Jeremiah asked.

"A plain water snake is harmless, but if it's a cottonmouth, its bite could kill. If you come across a copperhead or a timber rattlesnake, then you have a problem. They are very poisonous," Brady told the men.

"Do you think there are any of those around here?" Frank asked.

24

"We need to stay alert and cautious. As you know, many different animals live near water and in the woods. The fire helps keep us safe, but we can't take any chances," Brady said.

Jeremiah decided to find more firewood to stoke the campfire for the night. He walked toward a grove of trees and began picking up pieces of dead wood. He had his arms nearly filled when he saw something moving in the grass and leaves about six feet away. He reached for another chunk, and he heard a swish and saw the brown snake watching him. Jeremiah jerked his hand back and the snake moved toward him. He froze in his tracks; his first impulse was to run, but he couldn't. He wasn't sure, but by its coloring, it looked like a rattlesnake, as its color blended in so well with the leaves and twigs lying on the ground.

"Brady," he shouted, "I've got a problem, bring a gun over here."

Brady heard the urgency in Jeremiah's voice. He grabbed his rifle and ran toward the direction of the call for help. At first Brady didn't see the problem.

"Over there, can you see the snake right in front of me?" Brady spotted it. "Don't move," he quietly spoke. He carefully aimed and fired. At that very moment, Jeremiah stepped back as the snake writhed in the grass in front of him. It had been hit. Jeremiah turned toward the campsite as Brady shot the snake again.

Frank watched anxiously as Jeremiah rushed into the camp. He dumped his armful of wood near the campfire and began telling Frank about his close call with the reptile. Brady arrived a couple minutes later. The men agreed to sleep as close to the fire as possible that night. They had experienced enough episodes with snakes for one day.

The men aroused as daylight appeared in the eastern sky accompanied by the twittering and chirping sounds of the woods. Frank fed the horses while Jeremiah punched at the campfire and placed small pieces of dried wood on it to get it to flame. The men enjoyed their morning coffee and rehashed the previous evening.

Jeremiah said, "I don't care to spend another night here. I'd rather spend the night sleeping with a sick calf than fret about snakes

25

crawlin' all over me." When he said that, all three men laughed uncontrollably. They agreed that Jeremiah was lucky to be alive.

They hitched the workhorses to the wagon, cleaned up the camp, and started back toward the ferry. As they traveled along, Frank looked over toward the trees and spotted a tom turkey. Frank halted the horses and wagon. "Stop here, I see a turkey over there, and I'm going to shoot him. We'll have something fresh to eat if I can shoot him."

Frank grabbed his gun and walked stealthily into the woods. The men heard a shot, and within minutes Frank reappeared with one arm holding his rifle and the turkey dangling from his other. He had a big grin on his face as he placed the large bird on top of the loaded wagon.

"Well, the cook finally has some fresh meat to fix for supper," Jeremiah said, speaking in a teasing voice.

"Yeah, well, let's see if you even know how to roast a turkey," Frank retorted.

"All right boys, I think we'll all be enjoyin' a good meal tonight. Let's head on to the ferry," Brady told them. Frank urged the horses pulling the wagon, and the three headed toward the river.

The men arrived at the ferry site long before the ferry returned from the other side. They unsaddled the horses and put them in a shaded area where they could graze. The air was humid, and the stench of the manure caused the flies to swarm around everybody. The men sat on the ground upwind from the smell. They watched an older man and woman riding on a buckboard approach the ferry area. It was apparent that they had their belongings with them. They tethered the horses and proceeded down the riverbank. They were shabbily dressed from head to toe. Their hair was unkempt, and their faces reflected a life of hard work. After a short time, the two came back up the bank to their buckboard. They meandered over toward the three men.

"Care if we join ya?" the man asked.

"Come on and rest in the shade. Are you crossing the river today?" Frank asked.

"We caught a big bunch of animals in our traps this last winter. We hope to sell them there hides in Madison," the man answered.

The woman reached into the large pocket of her apron and pulled out a corncob pipe and a sack of tobacco. She proceeded to stuff some tobacco into the pipe. The men were somewhat taken aback, as they had never witnessed a woman smoker. She then put the pipe into her mouth as if smoking it. She took it out and laughed and said, "Kinda hard to smoke tobaccy without a fire to light it!" Taking the pipe from her mouth, she mocked the smoking manner by puckering her mouth. Everyone laughed as she strutted around, bending her arm back and forth and tossing her head with her pretend smoking.

"That's about enough showin' off for now, Polly! You best sit down," her husband, Duff, told her. She gave him a disgusted look but complied with his suggestion.

"She gave us a good laugh. We all need that from time to time," Brady said.

"Well, she sure enjoys actin' up and havin' fun," Duff replied. "You know, we've been together since we were young. We ain't been lucky enough to have any babies; we jes' have each other. She goes right with me, and we work side by side, no matter what we do."

"Yeah, I'm a good worker and a good cook too," Polly stated. She got up and walked over to Frank's wagon. "I see you've got a dead turkey. When did you kill it?"

Jeremiah answered, "I shot it about an hour ago. After we get over the river and settle for the night, I plan to roast it over our campfire."

"You ought to clean that bird. If you wait until nighttime, with the hot sun on it all day, it'll go bad." She took the turkey out of the wagon.

"Now Polly," Duff called out, "that's not yours to decide what to do."

"She's right," Jeremiah stated. "I'll get busy right now." He walked toward Polly. "Hand me the turkey."

By the time the turkey had been gutted, the men realized that the ferry had arrived. They saw the passengers from Indiana coming up the riverbank. Frank hitched his team up to the wagon for travel, as did Duff and Polly. They all processed down the bank and waited until the time for the ferry to make its return to the Indiana side of the Ohio. The sun had heated the air and everything at the riverbank. The stifling smell from the mules had been stirred around by the breeze from the river. Gnats and flies swarmed, irritating on the animals and the travelers. On occasion, a horsefly would bite one of the horses, which caused the horse to kick and whiney. The group anxiously waited to board the ferry as they held their horses tightly.

At last the ferry captain gave the signal. Duff and Polly went first, then Brady, Frank, and Jeremiah, all with their horses and wagons. At the last minute, two well-dressed women arrived, each on well-groomed mares, and asked if there was room for them. The captain agreed that there would be if the others wouldn't mind being a little crowded. All agreed. A very full ferry was ready to cross the big Ohio River.

The ride across went fairly well—no rushing waters as they had experienced before. One incident took place when a horsefly bit the horse of one of the well-dressed women. The horse kicked one of the horses belonging to Duff and Polly. That started a chain reaction by causing their buckboard to jolt, and the whole ferry rocked back and forth for a few minutes. The two women almost lost their footing, each grabbing the nearest man to hold her balance. The faces of the men turned bright red as the women shrieked. By the time the boat settled down, their embarrassment turned to laughter. The rest of the crossing went well.

The passengers and their animals arrived at the river shore and, when the ferry was secured, they all went up the riverbank. The two fancy-dressed ladies mounted their horses and rode along their way. Duff and Polly waited for the three men to make it up the bank.

Polly asked the men, "Where do ya plan to rest tonight?"

Brady answered, "After we pick up some bacon and feed for our horses, we'll find a place outside of town to rest for a while."

"Do ya care if we join ya? We won't go back across the river afore tomorrow."

Brady, Frank, and Jeremiah looked at each other. "Guess that'll be all right," Frank answered. "I would surely 'preciate it," Polly replied. She secretly hoped that she and Duff could eat a portion of the wild turkey that she knew they would cook soon.

"You go sell your hides, and we'll get our supplies. When you are finished, go to the north side of town and wait for us. After we all get back together, we'll search out a good place to camp. How does that sound?" Frank asked.

Duff and Polly both nodded their heads in agreement. With that decided, they all went about their business. Brady, Frank, and Jeremiah decided to find a place to eat in town. They were already weary of fixing their own food, and what they had for breakfast had been digested long ago. They found a café about midway down the main street where they were able to have a satisfying meal. They then went about the task of getting their needed supplies.

By midafternoon, the three men headed northward. A short way out of town, they spotted Polly and Duff, sitting on the grass beside a grove of oak trees. Frank noticed Polly smoking her corncob pipe, and Duff had a jug sitting on the grass beside him. The grove of oak trees actually looked like it would serve well as a place to spend the night. Even though they wanted to cover more territory before stopping, they had to deal with the two that seemed to have latched onto them. The three men quietly agreed that they didn't want the company of the two strangers any longer than today.

Jeremiah placed the wagon safely away from the road and unhitched the horses, which he tethered nearby. He then gathered wood for the fire to roast the turkey. Frank walked over to Duff and said, "Hey there, Duff. Having a drink are ya?"

"Yep, I am. I figure that I worked all winter for those hides in the cold and snow, and, by golly, I deserve to lean back and have me a jug a whiskey."

"I hope you don't intend to drink all that tonight," Frank stated.

"I just take a snort now and then." Duff laughed.

"We don't take too much to drinking," Frank stated and walked away.

Polly asked Jeremiah, who was almost finished cleaning the turkey, "When you skin that turkey, could I have the tail feathers? I could use those purdy feathers to make somethin'."

"Let me see how it looks when I get it done. I'm sure there'll be feathers for whoever wants some."

Three hours later, the turkey was roasted along with potatoes that were laid beside the fire to bake. Everyone began gathering around the fire area preparing to eat. Duff, toting his jug, staggered toward the group. It was apparent that he had drunk enough that it had affected him. As he bent to sit down, he lost his balance and teetered forward.

"Careful there, old fella," Frank spoke as he grabbed Duff by the arm and helped him sit. "You best put that jug away for the night. Let me put it over in your wagon; it's no good for you." Frank took the jug and carried it off.

Polly scolded Duff. "I've told you before to leave that there whiskey alone, but you won't listen to me." She cuffed him on top of his head and moved away from his side. The three other men grinned at each other in amusement.

Soon they all had eaten their meal. Duff lay down by the campfire and instantly went to sleep. Polly went to the wagon and came back with their bedding, covered Duff and stuck a folded towel under his head, and then sat beside him. She stuffed tobacco into her pipe, lit it with a burning twig, and calmly smoked. Meanwhile Brady, Frank, and Jeremiah went to check on their horses away from the campsite. They talked quietly together.

"We need to make a plan to get away without Duff and Polly going with us," Jeremiah said.

"I agree," stated Frank. "What do you think, Brady?"

"I think that the best plan would be to leave early tomorrow morning. When they wake up, we'll already be gone."

"Yeah, that sounds good," Jeremiah agreed. "I'll stay up until Polly goes sound asleep, then I'll hitch up the horses and move the wagon up the road where I'll sleep the night. When you two wake up, saddle your horses, and ride to where I am."

"We'll make a few miles before they'll even know we're gone. That'll be a relief," Frank said

So the plan was made and executed. Jeremiah sat up with Polly until she succumbed to sleep. He left her a handful of turkey feathers and quietly went about hitching the wagon and moving it away.

Frank and Brady arose an hour or more before dawn, saddled their horses, and quietly led them northward a quarter mile before mounting them. They found Jeremiah and woke him. Within minutes the three were once again bound for their new farms. Their hearts were pounding with excitement. You would think that they had carried out a mission of great importance.

After they had ridden a few hundred feet, the three men burst out laughing. They laughed uncontrollably for some time. Jeremiah remarked, "I can see Polly now, looking around, completely confused and wondering what happened to us." He laughed harder. "She's probably walking around, smoking on her pipe, and smacking on ole Duff."

"Yeah, and he'll be so fuzzy-headed from his whiskey drinking, he probably won't remember where he is," Frank said, and roared with laughter.

Brady said, "They'll climb up on their buckboard and start back to Madison—no free coffee, turkey, or anything." Brady let out a whoop. "I hope we don't meet another Polly or Duff. Yee-haw, boys, we're on our way to our new homes."

Chapter 3

MAY 15. IT WAS AN IDEAL, SUNNY SPRING DAY WITH A few clouds passing overhead. Anna Marie had spent the previous day cleaning and rearranging the room for Pricilla. She had made an egg, potato, and onion dish for their evening meal. She was anxiously waiting for Pricilla's arrival.

Pricilla, with the help of Jeremiah's friends, finished packing the wagon. She sat on the seat of her buggy with her baby lying next to her feet. The trip to Anna Marie's home wasn't long. Pricilla, Joseph, and the men with the loaded wagon turned onto the lane leading up to the Patterson cabin. She saw Anna Marie and the boys waiting on the porch. She waved and called out, "Hello, we're here." Anna Marie waved back enthusiastically.

The next couple hours were hectic, to say the least, as Pricilla's buggy and the wagon were being unloaded. Pricilla and Joseph were officially moved in to their room. Pat and Tim played until they both fell asleep on a rug, each holding a carved horse, their favorite toy. Anna Marie and Pricilla talked and laughed through the evening as they worked on their needlework. They soon decided they were exhausted, so they said their good nights.

❋

The two families blended together quite well. The boys would play without fussing or whining as they passed the days by playing with blocks of wood and their toy horses. The two mothers would place quilts on the grass in a shady portion of the yard where they all would sit together to watch the squirrels chase over the yard and scurry up and down the trees. With Big Al's help, Anna Marie planted her vegetable garden. She and Pricilla both tended it by hoeing out weeds and watering plants. They all concluded if the right amount of rain falls, the garden should grow and produce plenty of fresh vegetables.

May 25. A routine had been established with the women and children. Big Al and his two older boys went to check on the Patterson ranch often and helped the ladies whenever they could. Once a week, Anna Marie and Pricilla would go to Reed's Crossing for supplies. They would check their mail and stop by the boardinghouse for tea.

Pricilla and Anna Marie attended church each Sunday with the Bennings family, often staying for dinner with them. On the first Sunday after Brady, Frank, and Jeremiah left for Indiana, they were at the Bennings' enjoying the food and conversation. After the children had finished eating, the older children went outside to play. Lucy and Al told about their marriage and their honeymoon trip.

Big Al began, "Lucy and me got married in June in southern Kentucky at her mother and father's home. All our families and friends were there. After the wedding ceremony, we had a big meal outside. There were tables full of food. Her ma had baked two big cakes, and my ma brought a large bowl of fresh-picked strawberries. After everybody ate their fill, we had a dance out in the barn. Lucy's brothers and her pa had worked for days cleaning out the old straw bedding and manure. They put fresh dried grasses on the floor and put stacks of straw around for people to sit on. My pa played the fiddle, and his brother played the banjo. My grandma Nellie sang as she played songs on the dulcimer."

Lucy looked lovingly at Big Al and said, "It was a wonderful wedding day. Everybody stayed and danced and laughed late into the night."

"About nine o'clock, a ruckus started," Al continued. "One of Pa's friends had brought a jug of moonshine, and he was sharing it with some of his buddies. They got pretty well drunk and started

33

arguing and picking a fight. Pa told them to take their fight outside of the barn. They started punching each other as they went out the barn door. Next thing I knew, two of the men landed in the horse trough." Al paused to laugh. "My Pa told them, 'You fellers best go home now. We don't want any more fightin'." They were dripping wet. We all laughed as we watched them leave, water squishing in their boots with each step. The rest of the night we danced and danced."

Lucy laughed and admitted, "We were so tired after all the excitement of the day that we went to bed, kissed each other good night, and went sound asleep." They all laughed about that as Lucy and Al turned beet red.

Al continued, "The next morning after breakfast we packed a bag and left in my buggy for a trip to Beattyville to do some fishing on the Kentucky River. I had friends that lived there, John and Libby Shaw. We stayed several days with them. John and I would go fishing every morning after chores and breakfast. We'd come back with our catch and clean them, and each time the women cooked the fish and made my favorite, hush puppies. I can still remember how good that food tasted."

"One evening it looked cloudy, like it might rain, so we put the buggy in the barn. The next morning when we went to do our chores, a skunk was lying on the buggy seat. We didn't see it until it was too late, and that ornery animal sprayed on both of us before you could say jack rabbit!" Everyone laughed and laughed till they couldn't laugh any more.

Lucy added, "You can't imagine how bad those two smelled!" She shook with laughter.

"That was quite a wedding story," Anna Marie stated as she giggled.

"My wedding was dull compared to that," Pricilla added. The two women stayed and visited a little longer, then gathered their children and headed back to the Patterson farm. It was one of many memories the two women would recall in the weeks to come.

May 27. Brady, Frank, and Jeremiah arrived at the home of preacher man O'Reilly. It was late afternoon when they rode up to find him working with a hoe in his corn patch. The old fellow looked the same as last year, and it took him a few minutes to recognize Frank and Brady. He walked slowly, using the hoe as a walking stick, and met the men at his house.

"Well, I'll be a cockeyed rooster!" O'Reilly said with gusto. "You young fellas came back." He stuck out his hand to shake theirs. "Welcome back. Who's your friend with you?"

Brady said, "This here is Jeremiah Whitmore. He's going with us to get land for his family."

Jeremiah said, "I heard about the roasting ears you raised last year. Too bad they aren't ready today!" Jeremiah laughed.

"You boys are spending the night here, aren't you?" the preacher asked with expectation.

"Guess we can. We have to sleep somewhere," Brady replied.

"How're you getting along, old-timer?" Frank asked. "Have the church ladies been takin' good care of ya?"

Preacher O'Reilly answered, "Yep. They bring pies and fancy baked goods and give to me. It's a wonder I'm not as big around as I am tall," he joked. "How about you fellas? Has the Lord been good to you?"

Brady answered, "It couldn't be any better. The wife and I have another son now; we named him Timothy."

"That's a blessing, two sons in your home. I'm anxious to meet your family."

The three men spent the evening and night with Preacher O'Reilly. They talked and laughed and told stories until they were tired out. The next morning, they arose when the glow of the sun reached the treetops. Preacher O'Reilly already had a pot of coffee boiling and a large kettle of oats just about ready to eat.

After breakfast, as they prepared to leave, Preacher O'Reilly grabbed each and gave them a hug and a handshake. "Sure was good to see you boys. If you come by here again, be sure to stop and see me," he spoke with the voice of a father. "None of us know how many days we have left on this earth, so you boys take care of yourselves," and then he added an Irish blessing:

"May the road rise to meet you. May the wind be always at your back. May the sun shine warm upon your face, the rain fall soft upon your fields, and until we meet again, may God hold you in the palm of His hand."

The men saddled their riding horses, hitched the workhorses to the wagon, and then started down the road. Preacher O'Reilly waved until the men were out of sight.

The men traveled with added vitality after having enjoyed the visit at the preacher's home. They noticed a bank of dark clouds coming toward them from the west, and the wind seemed to be whipping up. They began to discuss where they could find shelter. They were concerned about all their supplies and tools getting soaked with rainwater. The last good-sized town that they passed through was Seymour, but they weren't sure where the next one was. They stepped up their pace. They needed to find a place that would offer some protection.

After nearly two hours of riding, it seemed that the weather was definitely turning worse. The black clouds were closer, and they saw flashes of lightning and heard the roar of thunder. They came upon a small town named Bedford. They went down the main street at a slow pace, keeping their eyes open for a place to stay out of the upcoming storm. It was then that Frank spotted a blacksmith shop located inside a livery stable. He rode up to the large opening where the blacksmith stood pounding on his anvil.

"Hello. Guess you know a storm is heading this direction. Would it be possible for me and my friends to bring our horses and wagon inside for a while?"

"I may have to crowd your horses. Let me see if I can move the horses around that I already have stabled. I'll be right back."

The blacksmith went toward the back of the stable while Frank waited. The men heard more violent lightning and thunder, and felt gusts of wind blowing. Brady grabbed his hat and steadied his horse. Big drops of rain began falling.

Jeremiah called out, "We need to do something quick!" About that time lightning struck a tree not far away, and the workhorses both reared up and jerked the wagon.

"Whoa, there," Jeremiah called out to the horses, "easy now."

The blacksmith returned to where Frank stood waiting and told them, "I made room in the back. Go ahead and take your horses to the two open stalls and pull your wagon over here inside." Frank motioned to Brady and Jeremiah to come on inside. They didn't get the animals and wagon in any too soon, as the rain began pouring down. All of the horses in the barn were restless, making whinnying sounds and striking the stable boards with their hooves. The storm went on and on. The blacksmith closed the large entrance, but the worn doors still let rain blow inside, and the dirt floor became wet enough to be slick and gummy to walk on.

At last the storm let up. The three travelers decided to leave the horses and go somewhere to find some food before continuing their trip. The men paid the smithy to give water and oats to the horses. The men returned to pick up their horses and wagon and wasted no time getting back on the road. Traveling wasn't easy as the men dealt with driving their wagon through the large water puddles that had collected in the low spots between the hills. There were times that the horses had to pull hard to keep the heavy load moving.

"How far do ya think we'll get today?" Jeremiah asked.

"We've got at least four hours of daylight left, so we might make another ten miles, that is if nothing goes wrong," Frank replied.

The three came to the place in the road where you go either north or south around the woods. They turned northward as they had the year before. As the sun began to reach far into the western horizon, the men began to look for a place to rest for the night. They found a suitable spot a couple miles up the road where the ground was fairly level and a small rivulet provided a water source for all their needs.

Jeremiah got the campfire going for the night without too much work. The horses had been watered, fed, and tied close by, and the men were able to settle down to eat and rest.

Frank asked Brady, "Aren't we close to the road where we saw the black bear last year?"

"Are black bears around here?" Jeremiah asked as his senses became alert.

"You better believe there are," Brady replied. "We helped fight off a bear that was trying to attack a young Indian boy." He proceeded to recall the whole episode as he told Jeremiah all about it.

"Now I don't know if I'll be able to sleep any at all tonight wondering if there are bears coming into our camp," Jeremiah stated.

"The best thing that we can do is to make a hot fire and sleep close to it. Don't forget to keep your rifle close at hand. Chances are slim that one will come," Frank spoke assuredly.

The night passed without further alarm or disturbance, and the men slept soundly. All three arose feeling refreshed and ready to push forward on their journey. Within a short period of time, Jeremiah had coffee and hoecakes ready to eat. He surprised them by offering a jar of molasses to go with them.

"Jeremiah, those hoecakes hit the spot. You may qualify as a good camp cook yet!" Frank joked.

Brady added, "I agree. If he can keep up with the challenge, he'll be ready for a chef's hat!"

"You're very funny! With you two as friends, who needs enemies?" Jeremiah retorted, and then threw the last hoecake in their direction. They all laughed together as buddies do.

The men cleared the camp, hitched up the team, and soon were on the final leg of their journey. They rode all morning until the sun was high in the sky, and then they stopped to rest the horses and themselves. Jeremiah drove the loaded wagon off the road toward a shaded area. He felt a big jar and realized that one front wagon wheel dropped down into a large hole. The right front side tipped down and nearly threw him off his seat.

"Whoa, horses!!" he shouted. Frank and Brady immediately realized something was wrong as they rode quickly over toward Jeremiah. Jeremiah got off the wagon and looked at the wheel in the hole as the other men dismounted. The three stood there, assessed the damage, and shook their heads in disbelief. The jolt had cracked the wheel enough that the bottom four wheel spokes popped out, and two were broken. That wagon wasn't going anywhere!

Jeremiah removed his dusty hat, slapped it against his thigh, and asked in a disgusted voice, "What do we do now?"

Frank unhitched the two workhorses, took them to a shady area and fastened them to a low-hanging tree limb. Frank and Jeremiah sat down together on the cool grass under a large tree and drank deeply from their canteens. Each man swiped his brow and cheek with his shirt sleeve in an attempt to remove the sweat and dust that had collected during the day. The unforeseen accident with the wagon seemed to have taken the zest out of all three. Frank rested his back against a tree trunk and sat quietly, both hands on his head. Brady stood and stared down at the broken wheel. Jeremiah got up and walked around, regretful about the whole accident. A few minutes passed, and then he picked up a sizable tree limb and cracked it against the closest tree. The loud popping sound caused the others to jerk and turn quickly toward Jeremiah.

He hollered loudly, "Fellas, we can't just sit down. Let's figure out how to fix this problem now!"

Brady spoke, "You're right." He turned to face Frank, "Help me take the wheel off of the wagon. We have to try to rebuild it." The two men first had to raise the wagon and brace it in place before trying to remove the broken wheel. Once this was accomplished, they took it off and managed to move it under a shade tree. Frank knew he had to locate a piece of hard wood that would bear pressure, so he set out to find it.

Brady found a chisel and began cleaning out the pieces of the spokes still left in the wheel. A while later, Frank returned with enough wood that he and Jeremiah could go to work on their project.

Frank sat on a stump, and by using his skinning knife, he worked several hours carving on the wood to make the spokes. The carved spokes were now ready to put into the wheel. Brady had some wire that he used to reinforce the cracked wooden wheel, and in no time the refurbished wheel was back on the wagon. The men filled that devilish hole with rocks and chunks of wood, which would enable them to pull the wagon out. The men hitched the horses, pulled the wagon to the road, and with determination continued onward toward their destination.

Chapter 4

MAY 30. THIS WAS THE DAY THAT THE CHURCH congregation had voted to have a fish fry. Anna Marie and Pricilla were busy preparing food to go with the meal. The mothers dressed their children for the day, and changes of clothes were stuffed into a bag, the usual preparation for a trip. As they climbed into the buggy, they noticed high clouds floating around in the sky. Big Al had agreed to show the men of the congregation where to catch the fish. Considering all the times that Al had fished in the Muddy, he was the natural one to be the guide.

The fun day and picnic, first outdoor social gathering this spring, was being held on the bank of the Muddy River only a thirty-minute ride from the church. After the Sunday morning church service, several families traveled together for a fun afternoon of play and food. Al took them to a nice sandy area where the children could play and located a level grassy spot for the women. The river appeared to be calm. A sandbar was located at a curve in a shallow part of the river, and it grew out about twenty feet. The children were emphatically instructed not to go there.

The men and older boys, carrying their fishing poles and bait, walked along the riverbank as Al led them to his favorite fishing spot. The women spread their blankets out under a shade tree while the children began playing games. The mothers became deep in conversation and didn't notice that despite their warnings, the children had gone to play on the sandbar. The boys and girls removed their shoes and kicked their feet in the water and watched it splash.

Millie, the six-year-old daughter of Lucy and Al, announced with certainty, "I'm goin' to walk all around the sandbar." Before Mae, her eight-year-old sister, could tell her not to do it, she had already started.

Mae yelled, "Millie, get out of the water right now! You're not supposed to be there." Millie had a big smile on her face while she marched in the river. She ventured out a little farther, where the water was at the level of her knees. Suddenly, she stepped down into a deep hole, fell, and went under the water. Mae saw her fall and went to help her. Millie tried to stand but fell back again into the water. Mae yelled, "Mama, Mama, come here quick. Mama, help!"

Millie came back up, spitting and sputtering, gasping for air, and slipped and fell once more into the river. All the women were running toward the sandbar. Pat, sensing danger, stood up, began crying and ran toward his mother. Lucy ran as fast as possible and, when she finally reached where the children were, she was breathing hard as her heart pounded with fear.

Mae cried out, "It's Millie, Mama, she fell into the water!" Lucy looked and looked until she finally spotted her. She stepped into the river, slipped a little and lost her balance but managed to grab Millie's limp body. She tugged her back onto the sandbar, held her close to her body, and squeezed her midsection.

"Breathe, Millie, breathe," Lucy pleaded.

Anna Marie said, "Lay her face down and push down on her back. She has water in her lungs."

About that time, the men arrived. They had heard all the commotion and hurried down to where everyone was gathered. Big Al went to Millie. He spoke urgently, "Millie, it's Pa. Take a breath." He pushed on her back repeatedly. There was no response. He grabbed her feet and held her upside down. Water dribbled from her mouth as her lifeless body dangled from his grip. Finally, he laid her down. She had drowned.

Lucy knelt down, pulled her child to her breast, and wailed, "My baby Millie, don't die. Please, Millie, come back." She and all the women and most of the men and children were sobbing. Big Al took Millie from Lucy's arms and carried her to their buggy. Lucy collapsed with sorrow. Tears streamed down the faces of her two oldest boys as they helped her stand. They walked her up the riverbank and over to her blanket.

The church fish fry and fun day had ended. The happiness of only moments before had disappeared. It was as if a ferocious thunderstorm had pushed the sunny skies far over the horizon and left a dark cloud of deep sadness hovering over the scene.

Each mother and father gathered their children and their belongings. Slowly and silently, each family left for their separate homes. Preacher Martin and his wife, Naomi, went with Big Al and Lucy to help with the funeral arrangements. Anna Marie and Pricilla, with their children, had followed the Bennings along the road and watched them turn onto their lane. The two mothers and their children were all very quiet the rest of the way back to the Patterson farm.

☀

June 1. It was midmorning, and nearly all the residents of Reed's Crossing were gathered at the church cemetery. The day was windy with large clouds floating across the sky, casting ominous shadows over the church yard and cemetery. Flanked on each side by their two older sons, Big Al and Lucy stood stooped over, bent with grief. Mae clung to her mother's side and her fourteen-year-old brother, Peter, gripped his papa's shoulder. Anna Marie and Pricilla stood beside the Bennings family. Each held a bouquet of wild flowers to place on Millie's grave.

Preacher Martin gave the eulogy for Millie. He said: "It's tragic for anyone to lose a child. Millie has been a wonderful blessing to her family and the church members. She had a love for life that reflected in her beautiful smile. I remember the summer when she was four years old. Our now departed Mrs. Hester Updike dropped her cane when she tried to get up into her buggy. Millie saw it fall, and as quick as a wink, went over and picked it up. She said, 'Here's your cane, lady, you'll probably need it.' Millie smiled a big smile, then she looked at me, and I nodded my head in approval. Mrs. Updike leaned over and patted Millie on the head and said, 'Thank you. You're a sweet child.' Millie ran back to the church step with the same smile on her face and a sparkle in her eyes."

Preacher Martin reassured the family that all children will have a place in heaven. He quoted scriptures where Jesus said, "Suffer the children to come unto me."

After the funeral, everybody went into the church building. Many had brought food for the noon meal. Lucy was grieving so that she couldn't eat. Pat went over to her and crawled upon her lap and patted her arm. After a while, he slid down and went over to sit beside Mae. One by one, the people began gathering up their baskets and left for home. A short time later, Big Al and Lucy decided they should go home.

Anna Marie and Pricilla took their children to their buggy. Once again they proceeded to follow their sorrowing friends down the road. The clouds had gathered and now covered the sky, blocking even the slightest ray of sunshine. A rainy mist fell on the tear-stained faces of the mourners. The buggies slowly made their way home. The sadness of the last three days pressed down on each family.

☀

Anna Marie and Pricilla visited the Bennings family at least twice a week during June. The women shared many cups of tea along with recipes of fresh-made fruit or vegetable dishes. At last, Lucy was able to smile and even giggle with her friends. Losing Millie would never be forgotten, but the pain of the loss was becoming gradually diminished and somewhat controllable. There were a few times when

Big Al joined the women at the table for tea and a piece of dessert. His worried, gruff voice was becoming calmer, and he could smile and chuckle.

Mae was the one in the family that couldn't seem to accept the fact that her sister, Millie, would never return home. She would sit cross-legged on a braided rug, hugging her doll and singing to it. Lucy had even heard her call the doll Millie; that really concerned her. Lucy spoke to Anna Marie and Pricilla, and it concerned them.

Anna Marie said to Lucy, "Why don't you let Mae go home with us today to stay a few days? She can play with our boys, and maybe it will take her mind off of Millie."

Lucy looked surprised, and then she smiled, nodding her head, and said, "You know, I like that idea. It would get Mae away from the house. I think it's worth a try."

"Great! Go tell her and pack a bag of clothes." Within minutes, Mae was riding down the road in the buggy, smiling, with Anna Marie and the others.

Chapter 5

THE PATCHED-UP WAGON WHEEL HELD UP DURING the last leg of the trip. The weary men stopped at the home of Foster and Beulah Browning. The place looked as it did the year before. Foster was busy as usual, working on a set of wagon wheels. He looked surprised when he realized who had ridden up. Both Brady and Frank walked over and gave Foster a hearty handshake.

"Good to see you young whippersnappers. How have you been?" Foster asked.

"We're both good," Brady replied. He turned toward Jeremiah and said, "This here is Foster Browning. He and his wife, Beulah, helped us locate our acreage last year and were kind enough to let us stay here in his barn while we staked our claim."

Jeremiah extended his hand to Foster and said, "I'm Jeremiah Whitmore. Any friend of Frank and Brady is a friend to me."

"Thank you, same here." Foster replied, "I see you brought a wagon full of tools and supplies. Guess you're plannin' on puttin' up a building."

Frank spoke, "Jeremiah came along to help us, but he's also interested in a small piece of land. He wants to build a boardinghouse."

"You can work that out with Beulah," he replied. "She keeps the land records." About that time she came out hollering, "Hello and welcome." She went on and on about how glad she was to see the men. "I'll fix you a good hot meal tonight," she announced with sparkling eyes.

Frank noticed that Foster hobbled as he walked over beside her. Frank asked, "I see you're limpin'. What's wrong?"

"I got me a case of the gout," he replied. "Some days are better than others."

❋

So, the work on the farms began. Brady, Frank, and Jeremiah, and sometimes Foster, worked at building Brady's cabin first. The men borrowed Foster's wagon to haul logs out of the timber. Each evening the men came back to the Brownings' place bone tired and dirty. They cleaned up best they could at the well out behind the house. They were fed Beulah's best food; whether it was pork hock and beans, fried chicken and taters, or mulligan stew, the men relished it all. Usually when they finished eating, the men would go out and sit on the porch with a cup of hot coffee to enjoy the cool of the evening and to rest.

Foster would get wound up tellin' a tale. The men never knew how true the story could be, but, nonetheless, they all had many a good laugh. An example of one of his yarns was one about two mules that he got through a trade.

"I had just finished making a four-wheel wagon for this fellow named Kermit. Kermit was a short, fuzzy-faced, frizzy-haired fellow around forty years old who lived by himself close to the woods. He had two coon hound dogs and a few nanny goats, which he milked. Kermit seldom came into the settlement, staying to himself, earning him the nickname Kermit the Hermit. When Kermit came to pick up the wagon, he informed me that he would have to owe me. Well, as you might well know, that wouldn't suit.

"I told him, 'You have to pay or the wagon stays right here.' Kermit wasn't too pleased, so he said, 'Tell you what. I've got a pair of right fine mules I'll bring over. You can use 'm or sell 'm. If you don't get 'm sold, I'll buy 'm back when I get the money. That'll work, won't it?' I wasn't in favor of having traded for two mules, but I finally agreed.

"The next day, Kermit brought the animals over and tied them to the hitching post in the horse lot. He informed me, 'The tall mule with the right ear half off is called Buck. The other mule with the cut lip is named Nipper. Both of these mules are good, hard-working animals. You harness them up to a wagon or plow, and they'll go all day.' He spoke in a slow, drug-out manner.

"So Kermit took the new wagon and went home. Later on that day, I decided to take them mules into the barn for some hay. I untied Buck from the hitch and started leading him toward the barn door. Next thing I knew, he kicked both his hind legs up high in the air, and when his hind legs came down, his front legs and head flew up, and me along with them. Boom! I came down on the ground, lost my grip on the rein, and that consarned mule bucked all the way around the horse pen. Then he went over and stood by the barn like he was waiting for a servant to open the door for him. I thought to myself, *what sorta deal did I make?*"

Jeremiah, Frank, and Brady all laughed hard and slapped their thighs as they pictured Foster bein' tossed around. Foster continued, "That wasn't the end of it. I led Nipper to the barn with no trouble. When I bent over to put out feed for both mules, Nipper tried to bite my rear. Then, I knew how he got his name!" By this time all the men were bent over with laughter.

Foster continued, "The very next day I tied those two mules to the back of the wagon and took them back to Kermit. I told him, 'Pay me now, or I take my wagon back.' You know what? He went into his cabin and brought out the money he owed me. That fuzzy-haired rascal just wanted to get rid of those two pesky mules, and he tried to pass them off to me." The laughter continued for a while. They talked on till nearly dark when the men's eyelids, heavy with sleepiness, indicated that it was time to rest their tired bodies.

☀

It was now the end of May. Brady had planned to build his one-room cabin with partitions for the bedroom, kitchen, and front room. There would be a loft in the attic where the children would sleep. He hadn't realized how many logs he would need; it seemed an overwhelming number. The days had passed by quite routinely as the men cut logs, trimmed and shaped them. The corners of the cabin were solidly in place, as were the cross supports, beams, and rafters for the roof.

The rainstorms started on May 30. The first rainy day, the men ate, played cards, and rested. The second day they were becoming restless. After breakfast, they went to the porch and watched the clouds roll by while the rain coursed down. As the men sat and talked, they saw horses pulling a covered wagon coming along the road. The pouring rain obscured their view, but as they kept watching, they saw a man and woman with a child seated between them. The wagon halted, and the driver stepped down and walked over toward the porch. He was soaking wet from his hat to his boots.

"Howdy," he spoke. "Is there any place here about where my family could find shelter?"

Foster stood up, stuck out his hand and said, "Hello, young fellow. My name is Foster Browning."

"Good to know you Foster. My name is Luke Hennessy."

"Take your horses and wagon to that lean-to over by the barn and bring your family over here out of the rain."

"I'll go for my wife and son and be right back. Thank you." The three travelers came to the porch, shivering wet. Luke quickly introduced his wife, Lorelei, and son, Shawn. Beulah had been making pie crust in the kitchen when she heard all the voices coming from outside. She quickly cleaned her hands and went to the front door.

Seeing the three visitors soaked by the rain, she excitedly said, "Land sakes, do come inside. Why, you're dripping wet! You need some warm, dry clothes. Let me see what I can find for you." They went inside and followed Beulah into the kitchen. Before searching for clothes, Beulah managed to find enough cups and poured three cups of hot tea and set out a bowl of sugar cookies for her guests.

Beulah fussed over Shawn by insisting he chose a large one. The men came into the kitchen to join the others.

"Where were you headed out here?" Beulah asked Luke.

Luke replied, "We heard there was land out here that we could settle on. Neither one of us has any close family; our folks died from typhoid. We didn't realize how hard it would be to start out on such a journey in a covered wagon."

"Your family needs a dry, warm place to stay until the rain passes through. Lorelei, you can sleep here in the house, and the men can sleep on a blanket out in the barn," Beulah suggested. Luke and Lorelei looked at each other and nodded in agreement with Beulah's offer.

The Hennessy family stayed with Foster and Beulah during the rainy spell, which lasted nearly four days. Luke and Lorelei had talked it over and told Beulah that they would like to homestead in the area. She and Foster decided to let them stay until something could be worked out. Luke worked with the other men. They struck an agreement to work together to clear the land and build homes. Lorelei and Beulah had become close friends as they worked together cooking and cleaning. Shawn would go with the men regularly and often took his fishing line so he could fish in the small creek located nearby. When he gave his catch to Beulah, she would go on and on about him being a great fisherman. She would cook the fish and made sure that he got the first piece. Sometimes she would secretly give Shawn extra cookies or a piece of pie. He would take his treat and eat it behind the large maple tree in the back yard.

Brady's home was being built much faster now with an extra man working alongside. The cabin walls were finished, and soon the roof would be completed. Shawn and Foster together gathered enough rocks for a fireplace. Foster had Shawn help dig clay from the creekbed, which they would use to caulk between the rocks. This would assure that the smoke would draw out the chimney rather than fill up the house.

✺

June 30. Brady and Jeremiah decided they needed to have some time off from the weeks of hard work, so they left at daybreak for Seymour. There were several reasons for the trip—food supplies, rope, horse feed, and other items—but mainly to send letters to their wives. An unspoken truth was that they were homesick. Luke was able to see his wife and boy every day. Watching Luke hold his wife was enough to cause Brady and Jeremiah to experience strong emotions and desires. They drove the horses hard all day and arrived at Seymour late that evening. They didn't have enough money for a hotel room, so they slept with their horses in the church yard.

The next day the men located the post office and mailed the letters. They went directly to the mercantile and picked up the goods they needed, and then packed them into the wagon. Just as Brady and Frank crossed the street toward the café, they stopped abruptly, astonished at what they saw. They couldn't believe their eyes. There was Jim, Little White Feather, and Running Fox. Little White Feather was still as beautiful as ever. Her long black hair, accented with beads and ribbons, flowed loosely down her back. Her face glowed with happiness.

Frank hurried over to Jim and grabbed his shoulder, and the two shook hands heartily. Frank said, "Good to see you. You look pretty good for a black bear hunter!" and he laughed heartily at him.

"You too, you old sodbuster!" Jim razzed back to him. "What in thunder are you two doing back here in this neck of the woods?"

Frank turned as Brady approached and said, "We're homesteading farms west of here. We came to town to pick up supplies." They both turned to Little White Feather and Running Fox. "Good to see you both," Brady greeted them as he shook hands with Running Fox. "You're growing up, young brave," he stated.

"My eyes are happy to see you," Running Fox replied. "How was your journey?" he asked.

"It was good when you consider it all," answered Brady.

51

"Let's go where we can visit," Jim suggested.

"Good idea," Frank agreed.

(It was last year when Brady and Frank, accompanied by Jim, made their first trip north from Reed's Crossing. Jim had been seriously hurt when he tried to save Running Fox from a bear attack, and he was the one who got injured. The grandmother of Running Fox healed Jim. Her daughter, Little White Feather, helped care for him. The two were attracted to each other, and Jim had remained with the two women and the boy.)

They all went to a café close by where they sat and visited nearly three hours. Jeremiah listened as the others told stories of the other men's adventures. There were times when all the men's joyful laughter was quite loud, causing the others who were sitting nearby to give them annoyed looks. Finally, it was time to part with their friends, and they reluctantly said their good-byes.

Frank told Jim, "It's good to see that you and Little White Feather are now as one. She's still as beautiful as she always was."

"We were married by her mother with an Indian ceremony. We hope to have a child together. She and her family are my family now."

"I'm happy for you both," Brady added. "You're a lucky man." They all shook hands and parted.

Jeremiah and Brady made sure that their horses were watered before they began their journey home. They knew they wouldn't get far by sundown, but they figured sleeping out for one night would be all right. As they lay on the damp ground, a chilly breeze blew over them. They heard the night sounds and felt the stings of the pesky mosquitoes. They hadn't rested well, which caused both men to be out of sorts by the time they got up the next morning. Jeremiah retrieved some hardtack and crusty bread to go with their coffee while Brady gave oats to the horses. Soon they were ready to leave. The two traveled several miles without talking, quietly observing the countryside as they remembered their surprise meeting with Jim and the others. Brady recalled his memories of the past year and their struggles. He was pleased to see that Jim's misfortunes had turned out well for him.

The men stopped under a few trees located beside a small stream at about noon to give the horses rest and let them drink. The men knelt down beside the horses at the water's edge. They splashed water on their arms and faces in an attempt to wash off the road dust, which had clung to every exposed, sweaty pore of their bodies. The July sun was so hot that the men felt as seared as if they had stood close to a roaring campfire. Brady gave the horses an extra portion of oats as they rested to ensure that the animals would keep their strength for the miles yet ahead of them.

Their trip back dragged along as the heat poured down relentlessly on both men. The horses were lathered with sweat when they plodded into the Browning barn about an hour after sunset. Brady unhitched, watered, and fed the spent animals, then brushed their dirt-covered, sweaty bodies. In no time, the men had their boots off, and they were on their bedrolls, resting their bone-tired bodies.

Chapter 6

MID-JULY. MAE WAS STILL LIVING WITH ANNA MARIE.
It was amazing how well she had become more like herself. It was
probably because Pat, now two years old, could be like a big sister
to him. When Big Al and Lucy came to visit one day, they observed
Mae playing and giggling while she played with Pat. The four adults
sat at the kitchen table and visited while they enjoyed cold biscuits
and honey with cool clover tea.

Lucy remarked, "Mae looks so happy. How can I ever repay you
for helping her?"

Anna Marie waved her arm in such a way to indicate "forget
it." She said, "You and your family are dear to me, just like kinfolk.
You know the Good Book says, "Love your neighbor as yourself."
We love you and your children. It's been said "time heals," and Mae
is healing."

"So true," Big Al agreed. Lucy reached for her hanky and wiped
tears from her eyes. Al looked lovingly at her and patted her hand.
Anna Marie and Pricilla both observed the love between the two.

Lucy asked, "Would you two mothers like to go with me to Reed's
Crossing today? Al has already agreed to stay with the children and
let us spend some time together." Anna Marie and Pricilla smiled at
each other.

"I should take Joseph with me," Pricilla remarked. "You know
I'm still breast-feeding him."

"It would probably be best if I took Tim. He's also drinking mama's milk," Anna Marie added. Within a short time the three women, with Tim and Joseph, were in Lucy's buggy and on their way. When they arrived, they tied the horse in front of the mercantile store. Anna Marie had a full basket of eggs to sell and another sack of yesterday's picking of green beans. The mercantile owner was pleased to get the eggs and fresh beans. Anna Marie felt proud to have contributed something toward the purchases she would make. They left with their bags of dry goods and placed them in the buggy.

"Have you heard from your husbands?" Lucy inquired.

"No," they each replied.

"Why don't you go to the post office and check if you have any mail?" Lucy asked.

Pricilla spoke, "I think that's a good suggestion." The two friends walked across the main street and entered the post office building. To their surprise, each one had gotten a letter from her husband, posted about ten days prior. Anxiety pulsed through their bodies. Pricilla handed Joseph to Lucy as she quickly opened the envelope.

Jeremiah's letter had been written on course, brown paper. It read as follows:

Dearest Pricilla,

I miss you awful. I feel I've been away from you a year. Frank and I work hard every day cutting logs and building on Brady's cabin. We'll soon have it finished, and then we'll start on Frank's. Should have it done this fall. We'll live with him this winter. The folks we're staying with are good, likable people. I'll come for you and Joseph next month. I can't wait to hold you in my arms. Love to you and Joseph.

Jeremiah

Pricilla sat on the bench in front of the mercantile where she read and reread the letter. She said to herself, *Jeremiah, I miss you awful, too.* Pricilla had only been apart from Jeremiah no more than a few hours, never this long. She wiped the sweat from her brow and dabbed the tears from her eyes with her lace hanky. She watched Lucy talking to Joseph. Both were smiling. Caring for Joseph was the one thing keeping her intact this summer.

Anna Marie held her letter tightly as she sat Tim down in the buggy. She walked to the corner of the mercantile into a more private, shady area. She removed her bonnet and tucked it in the fold of her arm, then proceeded to open the letter. It, too, was written on the same brown paper as Pricilla's. Brady wrote:

My dear Anna Marie,

How I wish you were here now living with me. I miss you and the boys so much. We've all worked hard every day, and our home will soon be ready. Jeremiah is leaving at the end of July to go back to Reed's Crossing. Get word to your folks and prepare for the trip up here.

I can't wait to see you and hold you close. Having you here would complete my life. I'll love you forever.

Brady

When she finished reading the letter, she held it close to her heart, closed her eyes and breathed deeply. She thought, *Brady, my love, if I could only be near you in this moment.* She felt excitement pulse through her body as she recalled moments of intimacy.

She opened her eyes the instant she heard Tim cry out.

Lucy hollered, "O my God!" Tim lay on the road crying at the top of his voice with blood streaming from rock cuts on his forehead and face. He had tried to climb out of the buggy and fell out, head over heels. His wailing drew the attention of all around. Anna Marie ran toward her son, her right hand clutching Brady's letter, her bonnet lying on the ground. Joseph, reacting to Tim's crying, erupted into his version of dismay.

Pricilla quickly took Joseph into her arms to sooth him. Lucy picked up Tim, with his flailing arms and his tearful, bloody face, and handed him to Anna Marie as she rushed toward the buggy. Anna Marie used her lace hanky to clean his face. The cut on his forehead was deep. She pressed the cloth firmly on his wound. It took several minutes to calm the two youngsters.

Lucy blamed herself for the mishap. "I should'a paid more attention," she spoke apologetically.

"Don't you go blaming yourself," Anna stated. "I'm the one who walked away from the buggy. Brady's letter was all I could think about."

"I wasn't watching either," Pricilla admitted.

"Maybe you should take him over to the doctor's office so he can bandage Tim's head," Lucy suggested.

Anna Marie nodded in agreement. So, the ladies, with their two little boys, went across the street. Tim wiggled around as his forehead was being treated and wrapped. "Tim will have a scar for a while," Doc told her.

"Thanks for your help. Next time I come to town I'll bring you some fresh vegetables from my garden," Anna Marie told him. You know, we are moving to Indiana to a new farm next month."

"Here, let me give you a few bandages and some iodine to take with you."

"Thank you, Doc. You're very kind," she told him as she held Tim.

"Well, now, boys will be boys," Lucy said. "Let's go have a cup of tea at the boardinghouse. We'll all calm down."

The three ladies drank their tea together. They saw other friends that they enjoyed visiting with, especially Naomi, Preacher Martin's wife. The minutes flew by as they chitchatted away. They all decided that they needed one of the huge sweet rolls that the boardinghouse now offered. Anna Marie and Pricilla's babies fell asleep on their laps. The women realized that the afternoon had passed quickly, and they soon returned to the Patterson farm. Mae, Pat, and Big Al were sitting in the yard under the shade of a huge, old maple tree. Al laughed and Mae giggled as she helped Pat try to do somersaults. She would kneel down to help him, and he would go sideways every time. Anna Marie and Pricilla joined the fun time. The afternoon ended with all the adults enjoying bacon and lettuce sandwiches while the little ones ate bread and jelly with milk.

Chapter 7

AUGUST 1. JEREMIAH RODE AWAY FROM THE Browning place shortly after sunup. Clouds partially covered the eastern sky, and a light wind blew from the west. Perspiration had already begun to roll from his brow, an indicator of extreme heat and humidity, which he and the other men had endured for many days. He kicked his horse to a medium fast trot and held him there for several miles before taking a rest break. This was the pattern by which Jeremiah intended to travel during his entire trip back to Reed's Crossing.

He arrived at Madison the third day at noon. He ate at a familiar café before going down to the river. Approaching the river's edge, he could see the Ohio River was calm. Jeremiah used the extra time to water and feed his horse, which was tied under a shade tree. Jeremiah's horse was constantly switching his tail as he tried to ward off the biting flies. Jeremiah took a breath and coughed when he rode past the mules and their strong-smelling manure piles. He and two other couples waited about an hour to board the ferry. He smiled to himself as he recalled the meeting with Polly and Duff, grateful that they weren't around. Thankfully the ride across the river was uneventful.

As soon as the ferry docked, Jeremiah mounted up, glad to be on Kentucky soil with hopes that he would cover several miles before stopping. As evening approached, he located what he thought would be a good place to bed down for the night. He tied his horse to a sturdy low limb in a grassy area and removed the saddle and saddlebag. After gathering dry wood pieces, he started his campfire and laid out his bed roll. He took some sugar cookies out of a bag, which were left from the noon meal, and began munching, enjoying his sweet treat. Some sugar crumbs fell on his blanket, but it didn't matter to him. His eyes soon became heavy, and he lay down.

Jeremiah fell into a deep sleep. He awoke abruptly during the night with stinging bites. He threw off his covers and brushed frantically on his skin. The darkness wouldn't reveal his attackers that he felt crawling on his feet, legs, and the back of his neck. He removed his pants and shirt, grabbed a short, burning piece of wood from the campfire and held it over his blanket. He could see it was covered with ants and then noticed that he had made his bed beside a large anthill. After making sure he had brushed all the ants off of himself, he shook his blanket fervently and laid it aside. He took the burning piece of wood and held it down over the anthill. Finally, he sat down on his blanket on the opposite side of his first bed site and tried to settle down. He threw more dry wood on his fire, poked at it to get it to flame, and then once again lay down to sleep.

Jeremiah awoke at dawn to flashes of lightning and the sound of roaring thunder. The wind blew so hard that it whipped the limbs of the trees and bushes around him. His horse whinnied and scraped his hooves on the ground as he pulled on his rope. Jeremiah felt groggy with his lack of rest, thanks to the ants. He got up, pulled on his boots, and began rolling up his bedroll. He had no more than fastened it on his saddle when the rain began pouring down. He was half-soaked by the time that he remembered he had a jacket stored in his saddlebag. He pulled it out and hastily put it on. Unconcerned about leaving the campfire, he pressed southward with the rain pounding down on both horse and rider.

After what seemed like an undeterminable length of time, he spotted an old, run-down barn built behind what appeared to be a small, fallen-down cabin. The rail fence that had enclosed the barn was mostly on the ground. When he rode close to the barn, rats scurried from the accumulation of leaves, tree limbs, dried rabbit carcasses, and various other bits of debris that were piled around the rails. Jeremiah had no choice but to go inside the barn if he wanted some protection. He dismounted and walked in the mud to the half-open door and cautiously pulled it open. The smell of dirty, moldy grasses filled his nose and lungs. As he took a few steps inside, cockroaches and spiders scurried into corners and under pieces of wood. This was not a place that he would purposely choose, but he decided it would be all right for a little while. He took the saddle off of his horse and tied him away from the door. *What a place to have to stay,* he thought. *First an anthill, now this!*

Jeremiah stayed in the barn, and at noon he was still damp from his early morning soaking. *I need to make a fire to dry off, but I can't take a chance doing that in this place. Maybe I can figure something out.* In only a few minutes Jeremiah realized he could clean the dried grasses and wood chips from an area and dig a pit in the dirt floor for his fire. He took a large knife from his saddlebag and began the task. The packed dirt was quite hard, no doubt due to the horses and cows that had walked over it hundreds of times through the years. He knew the hole needed to be deep. He chopped and stabbed with determination, managing to remove chunks as he worked. At last the hole was deep enough that a small fire would be safe. Lighting the wood pieces, dried twigs, and grass inside wasn't a problem. Within minutes the flames rose, producing the welcome heat. The lightning and thunder continued, and he knew the rain wasn't going to let up.

Jeremiah thought as he worked, *I missed July Fourth, Independence Day. I don't guess there was much celebrating going on around here. I wonder what Pricilla's doing. At least she won't be in a place as bad as this! Dear God, I miss her and Joseph. I was hoping to be with her within two days; now I know it'll be longer.* Just then the wind blew a spray of rainwater on him through the cracks of the walls. Drops of water fell constantly from the holes in the roof, and at times it streamed in the corner close to where his horse was tied. Jeremiah was not looking forward to spending the night, considering what may creep around there in the dark.

He was startled when suddenly the barn door opened, and a small-framed, bearded man looked inside. Jeremiah jumped up and took a step backward.

"Good day to ya," the man said.

"Howdy," he replied.

"Care if I join ya? I'm soaked to the skin. I don't mean any harm."

"Guess not, long as you're not a killer or thief," Jeremiah answered.

The man sloshed his way in, holding the reins of a dapple gray mare. "It's not fit for man or beast out there," he stated.

"Maybe you should tie your mare away from my stallion. They might not get along."

"Sure enough," he agreed. He tethered her on the opposite side and came back to the fire pit. "I saw the smoke from the road," he spoke. "I couldn't figure why there would be a fire in the old barn, so I decided I would take a look see, thinking I could use a little heat myself and maybe dry out a bit."

"I'll see if I can fix us a pot of coffee," Jeremiah offered.

"Ah, that would be very kind of ya, laddie." The men sat around the fire, drank their coffee, and told about their lives while the storm carried forth its fury.

"I have to ask, with the way you talk, ere you Irish?" Brady asked.

Gentry grinned widely and replied, "Begora, I truly am, through and through. My father and mother came from Ireland to this country and landed in Virginia about 1800. I was born five years later. When I grew into manhood I married my sweet Sarah Leanne, and we moved to Kentucky." Gentry was enjoying telling his story, so he continued, "Life was hard for both of us." Gentry swallowed hard and brushed a tear aside. "She tried so hard, but she got weak. We never had any children. Last winter she got sick and didn't seem to have the strength to get well."

"I'm really sorry," Brady told him. "I know it's hard, but you have a lot of life ahead of you. Stay strong and keep your good spirit, and you'll be sure to have a happy life."

"Thank you for the good words. You could be my Irish brother, Brady Patterson."

They shared food from their saddlebags, which was enough to get them through the night. They visited a while longer while Brady shared about his family and future plans. It had become dark early, due to the heavy clouds, which made their surroundings become more uncertain. The two could hear strange sounds of scratching, squeaking, and rustling—nothing large. They unrolled their blankets, one on each side of the fire, their guns within reach. Surprisingly, they slept.

When the men awoke, the rain had ceased. The morning sun pierced through the leftover clouds sending rays of light through the cracks of the old barn. Jeremiah couldn't be happier. He and Gentry had their morning coffee and prepared to leave. They led their horses outside so they could drink from the water puddles.

"'Tis a much better looking day, my friend," Gentry proclaimed in his distinctive Irish voice. "It'll be a good travelin' day for sure."

Jeremiah agreed as he gave his horse some feed. "Let's have sunshine as we go our separate ways. I've been rain soaked enough to last me a long time," he proclaimed.

"It's true enough," Gentry agreed. He stuck out his hand and said, "Many thanks for sharing your shelter with me. I'll not forget your kindness. I hope we meet again another day under better circumstances."

"If you come by my place, you'll be welcome," Jeremiah said. The men mounted up and bid each other good-bye. Gentry headed north and Jeremiah rode south, both men feeling lighthearted and refreshed.

❄️

It was a hot summer day on the first Sunday in August on the Patterson farm. Anna Marie and Pricilla had been looking forward to this day for some time, as they were weary of the routines on the farm. The women loaded their food and boys into the buggy and went into Reed's Crossing to the church picnic and celebration. Naomi,

Preacher Martin's wife, greeted them with a hug when they arrived and said, "So glad you came."

"We're happy to be here," Anna Marie replied, "and I'm sure Pat will enjoy playing with the other children."

"Where do we put our pies?" Pricilla asked.

"There's a table set up in the church," Naomi answered. "Give them to me, and I'll take them inside for you."

The day was enjoyed by all as they ate, visited, and played games. Big Al and Preacher Martin kept the children busy with contests. The men had the job of judging all the pies baked by the women. They decided that they had the most rewarding job of the day because they got to taste all the pies. The winner of the best pie was the preacher's wife, Naomi. Everyone laughed as Naomi presented herself with the prize that she had made.

By midafternoon most of the people and their children were ready to leave for home. Pat was sweaty and dirty from all the activities. Anna Marie and Pricilla gathered their food baskets and children, got in their buggy, and headed back to the farm.

Pricilla spoke up, "When do you think your parents will come up to help with the packing?"

"I'm not sure, probably the middle of the month," Anna Marie answered. "Jeremiah should be coming this week, don't you think?"

"If he left when he planned, it could be any day now. I'll tell you the truth, I can't wait to see him."

"I feel the same way about Brady but I'll have another month or so before that happens. One good thing, we'll all be together soon."

"You're right. I'm so glad we're friends," Pricilla told her. The two families rode back to the farm content and pleased.

August 4. It was a hot summer evening. Brady and Frank sat with Foster, Beulah, and the Hennessey family on the front porch. Each one relished a piece of fresh cherry pie that Beulah had made that morning. The men had worked most of the day in the hot sun and decided to quit early. Their faces and arms had turned a deep brown from the many hours of exposure to the weather.

"How far do you think Jeremiah has gone?" Foster asked.

"Hard to say," Frank answered. "If he had good weather and no bad luck, he should be halfway or more."

"Do you suppose Polly and Duff are still around the ferry?" Brady said as he laughed.

"I feel sorry for him if they are," Frank answered, chuckling. Brady proceeded to tell the others about Duff and Polly and how they had snuck off early of morning and left the two asleep.

"No doubt those two would've followed us all the way here if we hadn't gotten away," Brady told them.

"That Polly wanted everything," Frank interjected, "and Duff only wanted his jug of liquor." Foster and Beulah joined with Frank and Brady as they laughed, recalling the whole episode.

Foster, Beulah, and Lorelei soon went inside to prepare for bed. Frank, Brady, Luke, and Shawn sat quietly and watched the moon rise up in the sky. They heard the calls of whippoorwills coming across the meadow. A few fireflies blinked their lights in the quiet air near the house. The men enjoyed seeing Shawn run around trying to catch them. Within a few minutes, Luke called for Shawn to head for the barn, and the two left Frank and Brady sitting on the porch.

Brady, breaking the silence, spoke, "We've been gone from home nearly three months now. I sure miss my wife."

"I'm sure you do," Frank agreed. "We'll have your house finished soon so she can move right in when she gets here."

"Thanks to you and the others and the Lord's blessing, we'll do our best to get yours built before cold weather."

"That's what I'm hopin'. You know, I think I'm ready to find myself a good woman."

"You don't say! I was beginning to wonder about you," Brady chuckled.

"I guess workin' on your home got me to thinkin' about bein' alone in my place. Next spring I plan to look around for a gal who will have me."

Brady slapped Frank on the knee and said, "That's the catch, finding someone who'll put up with you!" Both men laughed and shook their heads.

"I'm ready to head for the barn and get some rest. How about you?"
"I'm past ready. Let's go."

❖

August 8. Jeremiah had spent the night on the outskirts of Richmond. Since he had left the old barn two days ago, he had made good travel time. He was so anxious to get home and see his Pricilla that his heart hammered in his chest, and he broke into a sweat. As he urged his horse down the road, he prayed silently, *Lord, please let Pricilla and Joseph be all right. Lead me home soon.*

❖

It was a normal day at the Patterson farm. Anna Marie and Pricilla were out in the garden gathering fresh vegetables, pulling weeds as they worked. Joseph had been playing in the yard, entertaining himself. He came running up to his mother saying, "Kitty, kitty." He motioned for her to go with him.

"Oh, my gosh!" Anna Marie exclaimed. She took him by the hand and said, "Come away from here right now. Those aren't kitty cats; they're skunks!" The skunks started walking toward them.

"Hurry Pat, we need to go into the house." They rushed back around to the garden. Anna Marie shouted to Pricilla, "Get inside the house as quick as possible."

Pricilla had a quizzical look on her face and just stood there. Anna Marie said again, "Inside, quick, there are skunks out here!" The women went into the kitchen and closed the door as the skunks came around the corner of the house. After a few moments, the women realized the front door had been left partially open. Pricilla made a move to go close it, but the skunks had already begun parading into the house, just like they owned it!

"Oh, look what came in the front door!" The women lifted their children into their arms and went back outside, leaving the

66

kitchen door open. They went around to the front of the house and stood under a large tree in the shade. They looked at each other, and Pricilla spoke, "Can you believe this? A family of skunks just took over our house." They sat on the grass and both broke out in uncontrollable laughter. Tears streamed from their eyes as they realized the ridiculous situation. Pat laughed with the women and crawled around in the grass.

They hadn't noticed a horse and rider coming down the lane toward the farm home. Suddenly, he was right beside them. The women jumped up, and they both realized at the same time that it was Jeremiah. He dismounted, dropped the reins, and grabbed Pricilla in a big hug and swung her around. When he finally let her go, he picked up Joseph and swirled him around, making him giggle. "What a big boy you are. You've grown so much," he said.

Jeremiah realized he hadn't even spoken to Anna Marie. "I apologize," he said. "I didn't even say hello to you. How are you?"

"I'm just fine," she smiled and answered.

"What were you both laughing about?" he asked.

They both giggled again. "You see, we were evicted a few minutes ago by a skunk family," Anna Marie told him, hardly able to contain herself. "They were outside; we ran in the back door of the house. They came in the other door, so we went back outside and let them have the house." The women couldn't hold it any longer. They were laughing so hard that they rolled on the grass and wiped tears from their eyes. Pat ran around happily saying, "Kitty, kitty, kitty."

Jeremiah spoke, "Ladies, your knight has arrived to save you from the evil skunk family." He went to the garden and took some green beans and carrots from the garden, then walked to the kitchen door. He took his knife and sliced the vegetables up into little pieces and placed a few at the entry of the door. He then started dropping the pieces in a little trail leading away from the house. He went around to the front door and looked inside and saw the skunks wandering around. When they went into the kitchen, he stepped into the front room to prevent them from coming back into the rest of the house. In a few moments, they found the vegetables. Slowly, but surely, the intruders followed the trail of food outside. It wasn't long until the striped "kitties" meandered farther away and disappeared into the woods.

It was a joyous evening for everyone. Jeremiah enjoyed watching the little boys play as the three adults told all that had taken place the past weeks. Pricilla glowed with happiness as she watched her husband. Jeremiah told Anna Marie, "Your home is almost finished. We can begin gathering what we need for the journey north. Have you notified your parents?"

"Not yet; I was waiting until you came back. I'll get a letter to them as soon as possible," she replied. "I'm sure they'll be able to come here within days of receiving the news."

"I'll go into town and see about our covered wagon. The smithy said it would be ready for us about now."

"I'm so excited to go to Indiana," Pricilla said in a high-pitched voice.

"So am I," Anna Marie echoed.

Chapter 8

ANNA MARIE'S PARENTS OPENED THEIR LETTER August 15 with the news that Jeremiah had come back from Indiana. They had been making plans to go to the Patterson farm for some time. Lydia had a trunk packed and only needed to add last-minute items and prepare some food for the trip. Lydia scurried around the house gathering this, putting away that, and asking Ben questions over and over. Ben finally said, "Lydia, for goodness sake, slow down and take a deep breath." He gave her a reassuring hug and kissed her on the forehead.

"You're right. I was anxious to leave the house just right."

"It's perfect now. Let's relax and rest for the trip."

Two days later, they closed the doors, stepped up into their buggy, and left. They weren't worried about their place, as they had arranged for their neighbor's recently married son and his bride to live there until they returned.

August 17. Activity on the Patterson farm had picked up considerably. It would put one in mind of a family of squirrels harvesting nuts for the winter. Every nook and corner of the house and barn had been sorted and packed with meticulous care. Anna Marie's parents had arrived safely the day before. Lydia had delegated herself as caretaker of Pat and Tim. Big Al came for the few head of livestock and all but a cage of six chickens, which would make the trip to Indiana. Jeremiah placed the two covered wagons close to the house, making them easily accessible to load.

Two days later, shortly after sunrise, Jeremiah and Ben fed and watered Mandy, Anna Marie's mare, and the two teams of horses, then proceeded to hitch them to the covered wagons. Big Al and Lucy came to the farm to help with the final loading. Mae tagged along. With the time that she spent with Anna after Millie drowned, Mae felt much closer to her.

Ben helped Jeremiah lift each of the heavy, wooden barrels of water and placed them on a special plank which had been fastened to the back of each wagon. They then tied a rope around each one and ran the rope through loops of rope which had been nailed to the wagon bed. Al hitched Anna Marie's horse to the Patterson buggy and tied her to the porch post. A sense of protection came over him as he checked the horses' legs and hooves. He felt as if he was losing his own daughter and her children.

Anna Marie and Pricilla gathered their last bit of food and placed it into their wagons. Tears began flowing down Anna Marie's cheeks. Lydia placed Tim in the buggy and climbed in beside him. Pat was still running around enjoying all the activity going on that morning.

Lucy hugged Pricilla first and then turned toward Anna Marie. They embraced each other tightly for several moments. The words of good-byes refused to be said. It was a tearful parting. Finally Anna Marie managed to say, "I will miss coming to your home with all its busyness, good food, and laughter, but most of all, your advice. I'll write you when we reach our new home."

Jeremiah helped Pricilla and Joseph board their wagon. He climbed up on the seat and reached for the horse reins. He looked lovingly at her, put his arm around her shoulder and gave her a quick kiss. They both smiled happily.

Big Al had picked Pat up and held him as he walked over to Anna Marie. He held her to his burly chest, unable to tell her good-bye but managed to say, "God bless you and your family. I pray that no harm comes to you." Anna Marie cried openly and gave him a kiss on the cheek. Mae ran over to the three and grabbed Anna Marie around the waist.

"Take me with you," she cried with tears pouring out of her eyes. Anna Marie knelt down and pulled her close. "Now, now, your mother needs you. You're her only daughter, and you have a lot to learn from her. You'll always be very special to me. I hope that one day when you get older, you will come visit us at our new farm." They hugged warmly. "Hold out your hand." Anna Marie took Mae's hand and placed a doll on it that she had made for her. It had brown yarn hair and green button eyes. Its dress was made of green satin-like material and trimmed with yellow lace.

Mae had a surprised look on her face when she saw the doll. "Thank you. She's beautiful. I'll never forget you."

The two hugged one last time. "I must go now. I'll always remember you too."

Anna Marie's father went to her and put his arm around her shoulders. "Dry those tears," he said. "This is a happy time in your life. Another chapter in your life is waiting for you and your family. Now, let me see your beautiful smile." He patted her softly on the cheek, and she nodded affirmatively and grinned. She took her handkerchief and dabbed at her eyes.

"You're so right, Papa. Surely today will be a journey toward a new life."

Ben untied Mandy and handed Anna Marie the reins. He hollered to Pat, "Come on, boy, let's ride this big wagon together." Pat ran toward his grandpa. Ben grabbed him with his strong arms and put him on the seat, swung himself up on the wagon seat and grabbed the reins.

Jeremiah said loudly, "Is everybody ready to go?" They all agreed. "Then wagon's ho and Indiana, here we come!" Jeremiah took the lead followed by Ben and lastly Anna Marie and Lydia. They all waved good-bye to Big Al, Lucy, and Mae as they rode up the lane.

The heat of another hot August day pressed down on the travelers and their horses. They kept a steady pace until midday when they stopped to rest the horses. They all got off of the wagons and buggy to have something to eat and rest. It was a welcome break. They weren't accustomed to sitting on the hard, uncomfortable seats for long periods of time. They walked on the soft grass under the cool shade of the grove of trees. Pat ran around the trees looking for turkey feathers but didn't find any, so he picked a handful of wild flowers and took them to his mother.

The men took some buckets to find water to give to the horses. Within an hour, all had eaten and rested. Feeling somewhat refreshed, they resumed their trek northward. Groups of puffy clouds drifted across the sky and blocked the sun a short while, giving everyone some relief from the heat. Another rest stop seemed necessary at midafternoon as everyone had become tired and worn early the first day. After a short rest, the group agreed to push on for a couple more hours. Finally, the men chose a camp site that offered some protection with a small stream alongside where they would spend the night.

Jeremiah took Pat with him to pick up sticks for firewood and then proceeded to build the campfire. Pat was attracted to the fire as he watched Jeremiah stir the wood, which caused the popping and cracking and sent sparks flying into the air. Pat picked up a dry stick, and when nobody was watching, he poked the fire. The end of the stick caught fire. He carried it around while it was burning, quite enjoying himself. Anna Marie and Pricilla were preparing the evening meal as Pat walked up and said, "Look mama, see my stick."

Anna Marie immediately quit her work and snatched the stick from her son before you could've said "jackrabbit." She stuck the stick into the dirt and rubbed it until the flame was out.

"It's very bad to play with fire," his mother told him. "You could burn yourself or somebody else." Pat began to cry. She held him as she wiped his tears with her apron.

Pricilla commented, "Lucky Pat didn't get hurt or set something on fire."

"You're so right," Anna Marie agreed.

They all ate their meal and talked about their day. As the sun was setting, Lydia and Ben were the first to decide to go to bed. Pat had already fallen asleep. Since he would be sleeping with his grandma, Ben carried him to the covered wagon while Lydia made up their bed. Ben took his bedroll and lay down beside the campfire.

The excitement of leaving home and the rigors of the first day of travel had been stressful on everyone. Anna Marie took Tim to the wagon Jeremiah had driven. Pricilla, carrying Joseph, followed, and the two young women cared for their babies and then quickly made their beds. Jeremiah checked on the horses, tended the fire, and rolled out his blanket opposite of Ben.

All became quiet. An occasional hoot of an owl echoed through the air, but it went unnoticed by the weary travelers, deep in sleep.

❂

August 20. Ben and Jeremiah were awake at daybreak. Jeremiah fed the fire dry wood pieces, stirred it back to life, and set the coffee pot on the lapping flames. Ben tended to the horses. Within minutes, everyone was up. The early morning sun rays greeted the group with beautiful colors and promise of a fair day. The young mothers cared for their children as Ben and Jeremiah made sure that the horses were harnessed correctly. As soon as they ate breakfast, everyone climbed into their wagon. Ben stepped up beside Pat and yelled out, "Let's go," and he snapped the reins on his team of horses. As everyone followed along, Anna Marie felt especially anxious to being closer to her man.

Lydia held Timmy. She liked to call him that, while Anna Marie handled the buggy. The two chatted for a while, then Lydia started singing a hymn, and soon Anna Marie joined her. As they sang, it seemed to make the time and the miles go faster.

The group traveled steadily for a full three hours before stopping for a rest and a drink of water. Anna Marie took some of her sugar cookies out of a bag for everyone. They ate their cookies while they walked around, which exercised their backs from the hard wagon seats. Pat especially enjoyed a chance to run around and explore. They stopped for only a short while, and then once again they were heading north. The plan was to ride another three hours before taking a longer break for a noon meal.

The wagons rolled on a few miles when they encountered a few steep hills. They went over one that was especially challenging. When they reached the top, they realized it was going to be treacherous going back down. The wagons wanted to go faster than the horses pulling them. Looking ahead, they saw a large draw at the bottom of the two hills. Evidently heavy rains had washed the road out, and the crevice was deep.

"Hold tight to your reins!" Ben shouted. The horses struggled to hold back the push of the heavy-laden wagons. "Hang on, Pat," he told his grandson.

Pricilla let out a shrill yell and held Joseph tightly. Sensing danger, Joseph began to cry. Lydia said loudly to Anna Marie in her mother-like tone, "Please be careful, we don't want to wreck the buggy." The drivers struggled with the horses, but all managed to arrive at the bottom of the hill safely, even though the three women were left a bit shaken up.

Ben and Jeremiah got off their wagons and walked over to Anna Marie and Lydia. "Our wagons won't be able to cross here; it has washed out much too deep," Jeremiah stated. "We'll have to find another way."

Ben helped Anna Marie move the buggy to a safe place, then proceeded to unhook her horse and saddled it. Jeremiah mounted his horse, and the two men rode back up the steep hill in search of a better route to drive the covered wagons. As they descended the other side, they looked at the lay of the land.

"It looks like we're going to have to backtrack to find a way around the wash," Ben said.

"That'll put us behind, but what choice do we have?" Jeremiah replied.

Ben noticed a break in the tree line around the south side of the hill. "Look over there," he said as he pointed. "There seems to be a path through those trees."

"Let's go check it out," Jeremiah responded. The two men kicked their horses into a canter, and they rode over to the possible route—there surely was a usable pathway. They slowed down and then proceeded through the wooded area. They rode on until they determined that they had, indeed, reached the same road that the wagons were traveling beyond the impassable wash. They rode back through the woods and realized that many of the trees had low-hanging branches, which would have to be cut in order for the covered wagons to clear without causing damage.

The men rode back to the two women and the children and explained that they had found a way around. "We'll have to do some work to make sure that the wagons can get through, but at least we'll be able to continue our trip," Jeremiah explained.

Ben hitched Anna Marie's horse to her buggy, and the two covered wagons and the group went back over the large hill. As soon as they arrived at the wooded area, the men decided that they would spend the night there. The teams were unhitched and then tied in a shaded area where they could graze. A few hours of daylight were still left, so Jeremiah and Ben took their axes and rode into the woods.

The women decided to help by gathering the firewood. Lydia volunteered to take care of the two babies. "Come go with me," Anna Marie said to Pat. "We're going to pick up sticks." Pat clapped his hands excitedly. He was ready to be where he could run around. He helped with the sticks for a while and then became more interested in seeking other things in the woods. To his delight, he found two blue jay feathers.

They soon returned to the wagons, and the women prepared the evening meal. The men returned tired and hungry. They sat quietly and ate their meal, and then afterward fed and watered the horses. Everyone, exhausted from the trip, went to bed as soon as the sun faded in the west.

☀

After coffee and corncakes, the men went back to work in the woods. They had made progress but had many more limbs to cut. A few hours later, they returned to the camp.

"Ladies, we have good news. Ben and I think that we may be able to get through the woods with the wagons. We'll eat, and then we'll hitch up the horses and be on our way."

Within a short time, the group had headed down the path and through the woods. Except for stopping only twice to clear tree branches, the covered wagons managed to make it to the good road, past the big hills. The travelers were all of good spirit, renewed from a good night's sleep and the prospect of covering a long distance. They went several miles that day and stopped east of Frankfort. Jeremiah rode ahead, checking if there would be a bridge across the Kentucky River that would support the big wagons. When he came back, he reported that they would have no trouble crossing the river.

Ben suggested, "Let's stop here for the night. We need to rest the horses." All agreed as they began their usual routine of preparing to stay. They pulled off of the road to a level spot for the wagons, unhitched the horses and tethered them to nearby trees. The evening was quiet. Very little breeze stirred the humid summer air. As night settled across the Kentucky River Valley, the mosquitoes began their buzzing and biting ritual, making a good night's sleep impossible. The children cried themselves awake several times from the stinging bites.

Everyone rose early the next day and not in the best humor. A cloud of fog encased the valley, which caused the smoke from the campfire to hang low around the area. The group finished their breakfast, hooked the horses to the wagons and the buggy, and were soon on the road. They approached Frankfort, awestruck by the beauty of the river and the size of the city.

"There's the big bluff up there," Jeremiah announced as he pointed. "That's where Brady and I were last year."

"Oh, my!" Lydia exclaimed. "Look at that Anna Marie. What a sight!"

"It's beautiful here. Maybe we could stay a little while," she said.

The travelers arrived at the bridge. Ben and Pat went over first, followed by Jeremiah and his family. Anna Marie, Lydia, and Timmy crossed last. Ben drove his wagon until he found a churchyard, and he guided them to stop in the shade of some large trees. The two men helped the women and children off the wagons, who proceeded to spread small coverlets on the thick grass where they could sit. Pat, happy to be free to run around, began checking the area.

Ben walked over to Jeremiah and said, "What do you say, should we go pick up some supplies?" Ben drove Anna Marie's buggy, and Jeremiah mounted his horse. They immediately left to go seek places to shop for their needs.

While the men were gone, the women busied themselves by feeding and caring for the children. They saw a man and woman approach from the other side of the church. All three looked at each other quizzically; however, their apprehension was short-lived when the man spoke.

"Hello, ladies. My name is Delmar Delaney. My wife Bella and I bid you welcome. I'm the minister of this church. Could we help you in any way?"

Anna Marie spoke, "Thank you, Mr. Delaney. We are resting here as our menfolk have gone for supplies."

"Would you care for a refreshing cup of tea? I would be happy to make it for you," Bella asked. Anna Marie looked at Pricilla and Lydia, who smiled back, indicating a yes. "That would be kind of you," Anna Marie answered.

"Good. I'll be back shortly." Bella turned and went toward her house.

"How about I water your horses?" Preacher Delaney offered.

"We would certainly appreciate that," Lydia said. "You know, the heat has been hard on animals and people alike."

Later on that afternoon, the men returned and quickly loaded the fresh provisions into the two covered wagons. Preacher Delaney and Bella reappeared. He introduced himself to the men. He asked, "Where might you be headed with your families?"

"We're going to Indiana, where we have secured new homesteads," Jeremiah replied.

"I hear there's good farm ground there."

"That's what we're counting on. Ben and Lydia will be returning to Kentucky after we get settled."

"We hope that you'll be safe during the rest of your journey. May I offer a prayer for you and your families?" The travelers nodded in approval. After the prayer, they all bid good-bye.

Della gave Pricilla and Anna Marie each a loaf of fresh bread. "God be with you," she told them.

"Thank you, and God bless both of you," Pricilla told her. Anna Marie and Lydia both hugged her and thanked her. All the travelers boarded their wagons and buggy and continued onward toward Indiana.

Chapter 9

ALL THE MEN HAD COME IN FROM THEIR DAY'S WORK and ate their supper heartily, complimenting Beulah highly about her cooking skills. She had washed the dishes and had a pan of peelings and scraps that needed to be thrown out. After drying her hands on her apron, she went out the kitchen door toward the fence. It had been a good day. She slowly walked toward the fence, happiness enfolding her. She gave the table scraps a hefty toss and lost her balance. She fell down, and her head hit hard on the fence post and landed in the tall grass.

The others sat on the front porch and visited about the day. Foster nodded off, took a short nap, and woke up half an hour later. He said, "I think I'll go in and get me another cup of coffee." He went inside and noticed the kitchen was quiet. "Beulah," he hollered. No answer. "Beulah," he said again as he went toward the back door. He didn't see her.

He went back to the porch. "Have you seen my Beulah?" he asked everyone.

"No," not since supper," Brady replied.

"She's not in the house. Help me look for her," he stated. Everyone got up and began the search. Knowing that she wasn't in the front part of the property, they went to the backside. As Foster went back toward the fence he spotted her on the ground.

"Oh God, she's down over here!" he cried out. He knelt down and saw the blood on her head. "Beulah, Beulah," he called, "can you hear me?" She didn't respond.

Frank arrived at Foster's side first, grabbed her by the wrist, and felt for her pulse. "She's still alive," he announced. He saw the blood. "She must have hit her head when she fell. We should try to get her inside." Frank, Foster, Brady, and Luke carefully picked Beulah up, carried her inside, and laid her on her bed. Lorelei had already gotten a water pan and cloth to clean the wound.

A few minutes after Lorelei cared for her by placing a cold cloth on her wound, Beulah began to stir. She reached for her head and moaned. Lorelei gently took her hand and said, "Be careful; you've hurt yourself." Beulah went back to sleep. Foster sat at her bedside, too upset to talk; he only looked lovingly at her, his hands folded under his chin. He sat there all night.

Everyone arose from their sleep by dawn's light and went to check on their friend. Foster was asleep in the old rocker. He jumped when he saw them in the room.

"How's she doing," Brady inquired.

"All right, I guess. She slept all night," Foster replied. Brady took her hand and checked her pulse. She was still alive. About that time, Lorelei came into the room, went to Beulah's side, and rubbed her forehead with a damp cloth. Beulah opened her eyes and moaned. Lorelei noticed blood had soaked her pillow.

"She's awake," Lorelei announced. Foster immediately went over to Beulah's side and knelt down. He held her hand and stroked her arm.

"Beulah, can you talk?" She moved her head and looked into his eyes. He patted her hand gently. "Beulah, say something," he said softly, pleadingly.

"My head hurts. What happened?" she asked.

Foster told her that they found her after she had hit her head by the back fence. Lorelei gave her a sip of water. She licked her lips and muttered, "Thank you." By midmorning, Beulah was asking to sit up.

❖

It was several days before Beulah was able to stay up a few hours a day. Besides her head concussion, the fall had bruised her left shoulder and arm and wrenched her back. She had trouble recalling simple things each day. If Foster asked her, "What did you eat for breakfast?" she couldn't remember. The fact was that Beulah would never be the same as before.

Lorelei took over all the household chores, and the men were impressed with her cooking. She had made hot biscuits with nearly every evening meal and served them with a sweet sauce from whatever fruit was available at the time.

❖

Brady's new home was completed enough for his family to move into, so the men had begun cutting logs for Frank's cabin. They had worked until early afternoon when they decided that the temperature outside had surely reached ninety-five or one hundred degrees. Exhausted, they quit and went back to Foster's place. When they arrived, they went to visit with Foster, who was working under his favorite shade tree, putting the finish on a new buckboard wagon.

Foster spoke up, "I'd like to go to Columbus to try to sell this wagon and the extra set of wheels that I have finished." As the men visited, it was decided both Foster and Frank would drive a buckboard there, and they would bring supplies back. Brady and Luke were to stay with the women and the boy. The two men left early for Columbus. Foster drove the new buckboard, which held the new wagon wheels, while Frank followed along driving the buckboard, which would carry the purchases. Their plan was to return in three days.

❖

The trip from Frankfort to the Ohio River had been routine, hot and dusty. The two covered wagons and Anna Marie's buggy had reached the ferry crossing after noon. By this time, the entire group was worn out from the trip. The searing heat from the sun had caused sunburns, sores, and rashes on the travelers. They decided to camp by a cove on the Ohio where they could bathe and wash some of their clothes. They would cross the river tomorrow.

The thick, shady cove was a welcome relief. The men unhitched the horses and led them down to the water's edge. After they drank their fill, Ben and Jeremiah tethered them in a grassy area. The three women spread quilts in the shade for all to sit and rest. Pat ran around barefoot picking wildflowers. He was on his way back with a handful to give to his mama.

Pat suddenly screamed loudly and came crying to Anna Marie. She quickly stood up as he ran into her arms. "My foot, Mama," he cried. She looked and saw a red, swollen spot. She observed what appeared to be the stinger of a bee. She used her fingernails and pulled it out. She told him, "You were stung by a bee. Now it will get better," she soothed. She held him, and his crying quieted down to a whimper as the stinging subsided. "Be careful where you step now. We don't want you to get hurt again."

"Yes, Mama," he answered. He crawled off of her lap to return to play.

Jeremiah and Ben went over and sat with the women in the cool shade. Jeremiah decided to gather wood for the evening fire. He called, "Pat, come help me get the sticks." They came upon what appeared to be an old campfire spot close by. *I wonder who camped here before,* Jeremiah thought. "Always look before you reach into the grass," he said to Pat. "We need to be careful when we pick up sticks."

"Okay," Pat replied. Sure enough, as they walked around in the wooded area, Jeremiah spotted a snake.

He went up to Pat and pointed, "See over there—that's a snake. It could bite you, and it would be very bad. Never get close to a snake!" Pat, who was quivering, grabbed a hold of Jeremiah.

"You'll be all right. Stay close to me." When they had their arms full of firewood, they returned to the camp.

Jeremiah announced to the others, "We need to be alert because we saw a snake in the woods."

Pat chimed in, "See snake; snakes bad." The adults agreed as they chuckled at Pat's earnestness.

Ben said, "We need to be especially watchful if we go down to the river. No doubt there are snakes in and around the water."

Lydia suggested, "Let's all go down together to wash and be sure to take guns or knives for protection." They all agreed.

Before evening, the group had been down to the water's edge and had done their washing. The men took fishing lines with them in an attempt to catch enough fish for a meal. The first catch by Ben was a large turtle, which they returned to the water. They changed their fishing spot, and within fifteen minutes each man had pulled in a good-sized fish.

"Those are keepers!" Ben remarked. They continued their self-appointed job, which rewarded Jeremiah a huge catfish and Ben a largemouth bass.

They all went back to the wagon site when the three women finished their washing. The men proudly carried their fish back to the camp. After the men had cleaned them, the women enthusiastically began preparing the fresh fish. They rolled each piece in cornmeal and stuck it on skewers made from scraped, clean sticks. Ben poked at the campfire and revived the flames. As Pat watched intently, he joined the activity by bringing sticks to his grandpa Ben.

By bedtime, everyone had eaten their fill of fish and bread along with a pot of cooked beans. The men slept close to the fire, weapons within reach, for fear that a snake might decide to crawl into the camp.

※

Daylight broke through a mostly cloudy sky. Ben and Jeremiah led the horses down to the river and let them drink. Lydia took it upon herself to stir the fire and add some wood, and soon the water began to boil for coffee. Anna Marie sat in the covered wagon where Pat was sleeping and fed her baby. Suddenly, a shriek came from Pricilla as she bolted out of Anna Marie's wagon with Joseph clinging tightly to her neck. Anna Marie heard her chickens squawking.

"What's wrong?" Lydia asked Pricilla. "Lands sake!" she answered. "There's a rattlesnake crawling on the chicken crate.

The men had already started up the riverbank when they heard Lydia shout, "Ben, Jeremiah, come quick!" In no time they had tied the horses to a sapling and came running.

"What happened?" Ben asked, breathing hard from the run. As soon as Pricilla told them about the snake, both men picked up a rifle and cautiously approached the back of the wagon. They saw the snake, trying to poke its head into the chicken cage. Its tongue flashed in and out of its mouth as the rattle shook on its tail.

"It's a timber rattler!" Jeremiah yelled.

"I see," Ben answered back as he lifted his rifle and put the snake in his sight. "This will be tricky, but as soon as he raises his head, I'll take a shot."

The women jumped when they heard the shot. There was a scuffle and another shot. Ben hollered out, "Got him. He won't bother the chickens anymore." The whole group gathered around the back of Pricilla and Jeremiah's wagon and viewed the camp invader as it lay on the ground. Pat clung to Ben's leg.

Ben bent over the snake and showed Pat the snake's tail. Giving the tail a shake, Ben took out his knife and cut the rattle off as Pat watched with great interest. "After it dries I'll give it to you," Ben said.

The group soon finished breakfast, loaded up, and were on their way toward the ferry crossing. They soon learned that only one covered wagon could cross at a time, as the ferry wasn't big enough for both. They were then told that the ferry had about an hour wait on each side of the river before each crossing. Jeremiah and Pricilla let all the others cross first; consequently it took several hours for all three drivers to make the trip. Finally, all the travelers had crossed the Ohio River and arrived safely on the Indiana shore.

The Kentuckians passed through Madison on their northward trek when, at the far edge of town, they came upon a man and his wife peddling fresh garden vegetables. Out of curiosity, or perhaps enticement, Ben and Jeremiah stopped and walked over to check the offerings. The men looked at the variety of fresh produce and visited with the sellers, John and Mattie.

"Where 'bouts are ya headed?" John inquired.

Jeremiah replied, "We're goin' north to settle on a new homestead."

"How long have ya been on the road?"

"It's been several days now; probably will be a couple weeks more before we get there, barring no bad luck"

"We live 'bout three miles up the road. If you need a camping spot for the night, you're welcome to come to our farm."

Ben and Jeremiah looked at each other, gave a nod, and accepted the offer. They went back and told the women about the invitation. The wagon drivers waited until they could follow their hosts to their home.

John helped build a blazing campfire. He went into his barn, brought out a large iron kettle, and said, "We'll roast a pot of sweet corn for supper tonight." John hung the big kettle over the fire on an iron bar, held up on each end by a forked post. Ben and Jeremiah helped shuck the corn while Lydia helped Mattie peel and cut potatoes and onions to fry with some bacon chunks. After the main meal, Mattie brought out an apple cake and fresh cream for everyone. Even though all were stuffed, they made room for the cake. John told the men they could sleep in the barn, and they didn't hesitate to accept.

During the night, the travelers awoke to lightning and loud claps of thunder. Ben and Jeremiah quickly went to the wagons and helped take the women and children to the barn for safety. Just as they made it inside the protection of the building, the skies seemed to open, and the rain poured down. The two babies cried loudly, having been disturbed during their sleep. Pat clung tightly to his mother while she tried to console both he and Tim. Lydia spread the blankets on a hay pile that she had fluffed in an attempt to make it comfortable for sleeping. The storm continued for another hour before the adults could rest.

Dawn arrived, revealing a clear sky and cooler temperatures. Gone was the oppressing heat of former days. Even though the rain had left the ground muddy, the refreshing air had lifted the spirits of everyone.

Chapter 10

AS PLANNED, FOSTER AND FRANK RETURNED THE evening of the third day. Foster had sold his buckboard and wheels for a fair price and came back with supplies plus a basket of red apples and a smoked ham. With the help of Luke and Brady, the wagon was quickly unloaded, horses fed and stabled.

Foster was anxious to see if his wife was all right. He went into their home and found her in bed, leaned back on several pillows, eyes closed. He called out, "Beulah, my love, I'm home. Her eyes fluttered and then slowly opened. She took a moment to recognize him and then a small smile formed on her lips.

"Do you know who I am?" he asked. She nodded a yes. He bent over and kissed her cheek. "I want you to get better," he whispered into her ear. He took her hand and placed a lavender satin ribbon in it that he brought for her in Columbus. She immediately wrapped her fingers around it and looked into his eyes as a slight smile appeared on her face.

Lorelei came to the bedroom door and said, "She should rest." Foster patted his wife's arm and left her side. They both went outside where everyone else stood under a shade tree. The cool air that blew in the day before had refreshed everyone.

The group was quiet, almost somber. Foster looked at each one. "Do you think Beulah will get better?" he asked.

"She needs time. That was quite a blow she had on her head," Frank answered. "People survive this type of thing all the time. No reason to think she won't," he consoled.

"That's right," Luke added. "Give her a month, and she'll be back in the kitchen baking cakes and pies." That brought a smile to Foster's face, and his eyes sparked with hope.

"Boys," Brady said with urgency in his voice, "tomorrow we better work hard on Frank's cabin. Next thing you know, winter will be on its way, and we need to have his place ready."

When the men arose the next day, they were more spirited than usual. They ate a hearty breakfast and, true to their intent, left to go work on Frank's cabin. The rafters had been secured. The next job would be to start working on the roof. Smaller logs had been split and piled up that they would use. There would be problems if some of the logs were too short; however, they could be pieced, tapered, and wedged to fit as snugly as possible. The men worked diligently all week long. Luke and his son would go to the small creek and bring buckets of clay each day and press it into the joints of the logs.

Beulah was beginning to show signs of improvement. Even though she didn't remember much of what had happened to her, her mind seemed to be functioning better. She spent more time out of bed and came to the kitchen table for her meals.

Foster would come into the house and say, "Beulah, my love, where are you?" She would answer, "I'm still here, alive and kickin', but not fallin'." He would wrap his arms around her and slowly spin her around, then both would hug and laugh. Their joy spread throughout the household. Lorelei continued doing the household chores, and Beulah enjoyed letting her do the work. Beulah had worked so hard for so long; she felt like a queen as she sat and rocked and smiled contentedly.

＊

Shortly after breakfast, the newfound friends, John and Mattie, stood alongside the covered wagons bidding good-bye to the Kentucky travelers. The women all hugged as the men shook hands and wished each other a good life.

"God bless you folks for your kindness," Jeremiah told them. "You be sure to come see us if you get the chance."

"When you get your place all ready, write a letter our way. We just may take a special trip next spring to come see your new farm," John told him.

"Sure enough, you got a deal." Anxious to continue their journey, the men, women, and children boarded their wagons and buggy and waved farewell, snapped the reins on the horses, and away they rode.

The sky was clear, and the cool air promised an excellent day for travel. The horses were rested and frisky; they nearly pranced down the muddied road. As per their past schedule, they rested an hour at lunchtime, stopped midday to water and rest the horses, then continued on until early evening. They kept this pace for four days until they realized it was Saturday. Tomorrow they would rest in honor of the Sabbath. They came upon a sign that read, "Welcome to Seymour." They rode into town and spotted a church set back from the road, nestled in a small grove of trees.

"What a perfect place to spend the night," Pricilla said loudly.

"Whoa, hoss," Ben yelled out. Jeremiah pulled the reins on his team, and Anna Marie halted Mandy. The men dismounted their wagons. "Suppose we could hold up here tonight?" he queried.

"Let's look around," Jeremiah suggested. They found a horse trough and hitching posts. Around back was a well where they could have water to fill their barrels. Now they needed to see who to talk to for permission to stay. About that time, they were approached by a bearded, middle-aged man wearing a dark-brimmed hat and white shirt with a dark vest.

"Welcome. I'm the pastor at this church. What can I do for you people?"

"Hello," Jeremiah and Ben each said. "We were wonderin' if possibly our families could spend the night and tomorrow here while we rest a day? We've been traveling for some time," Ben stated.

"I don't see any problem with that at all," he said, smiling. "Where are you from?"

"We left middle Kentucky around two weeks ago. We're traveling to our new farmland farther north from here. We have only a few days of travel left."

About that time, the women and children approached. Ben introduced Lydia and Anna Marie; then Jeremiah introduced Pricilla and Joseph.

The preacher tipped his hat and said, "It's a pleasure to have you fine people in our town. We worship at nine o'clock. You're welcome to attend, and I hope you like the old hymns; our congregation truly enjoys singing."

❄

Attending Sunday church in Seymour became a time to remember. The preacher stood at the pulpit, extended his open arms, and said, "Welcome everyone. We are blessed today to have visitors all the way from mid-Kentucky worshiping with us today. These folks are on their way to begin a new life on land that they are homesteading in our state."

"Now, will the musicians, our Appalachian family, come forward and celebrate this Lord's Day with joyful praise?" A tall, lanky man carrying a washtub one-string bass, and his wife with her dulcimer, approached the front with their two children a few steps behind. The girl, appearing to be about twelve and bashful, had her dark hair in braids, which fell down her back. She carried a small washboard under her left arm. The boy, probably fifteen, tall like his father, walked proudly with both hands holding a banjo. For at least twenty minutes, they played as everyone sang along with the familiar melodies. Some members of the congregation stood up, clapped their hands, and sang at the top of their voices.

Unsure of themselves at this unique worship service, the Kentuckians found that they were drawn into the joy they heard in the music. They joined in the singing and clapping, and some tapped their toes as the music soaked into their very souls. It was so moving that, had there not been a sermon, surely all attending that day could have left inspired.

When the musicians sat down, the people quieted. The preacher stood at the pulpit, his gaze fixed skyward, lifted his hands, and began to pray. He then proceeded to give his sermon in calm reverence. He ended his message by stating, "Let us live by the Golden Rule, which tells us to love our neighbors as we love ourselves." The musicians led the people as they all sang "Amazing Grace."

"And now," the preacher prayed, "may the Lord watch between me and thee while we are absent one from another."

The people rose and began chatting. Most of the congregation went to welcome the visitors. Slowly, they all made their way out to return to their homes. The preacher told Ben, Jeremiah, and the women, "If you need any help, let me know."

"Thank you. You've already shown kindness by allowing us to stay here." Ben replied.

☀

The Kentuckians returned to their campsite and ate lunch. Anna Marie and Pricilla laid the babies and Pat down for a nap. The adults spread their quilts out under the shade of a large tree and lay down to rest. A breeze swept through every so often, which helped to keep the heat of the day pushed away.

Toward late afternoon, Ben and Jeremiah started filling the water barrels, which were fastened on the wagons. As they packed the fresh water to the barrels, they noticed the preacher and his wife

91

arrived, along with the Appalachian family, their arms carrying what appeared to be baskets full of food.

"Hello, friends," the preacher spoke enthusiastically. "We come as good neighbors, bearing gifts of food, good will, and blessings." Ben and Jeremiah went over to the visitors and shook their hands.

"Welcome to our camp," Jeremiah said. "We don't have any chairs to offer you a seat."

"I can fix that. We'll go into the church and bring out a table and chairs for everyone," the preacher told him. The men immediately went to work at their self-appointed task. Meanwhile, the women all gathered on the blankets.

"It's so good of you to come visit us," Lydia exclaimed. "The world is full of so many nice people," she declared.

"If we can't help our Christian friends, who can we help?" queried Orphia, the Appalachian woman. "I know by experience that traveling from your home with children for so many miles is exhausting. I've done that, and it isn't easy."

"No, it isn't, but soon we will reach our new home," Anna Marie said.

"We can endure many hardships as long as the Lord is with us," Lydia added.

"That's *so* right," Orphia agreed. "When we moved, I kept telling myself every morning, we're one day closer to our final stop; at last the day arrived when we reached our destination. I can look back on it now, and I realize that it wasn't that bad."

Orphia spoke up. "Look, the men have a table and chairs for us. Let's go get the food out of the baskets, and we'll eat." Everyone gathered together. A large pan of fried chicken was sitting in the middle of the table surrounded by dishes of boiled potatoes, sliced tomatoes, and cooked cabbage. Being rested from his nap, Pat ran around excitedly until Anna Marie called for him to come to her.

The preacher stood and said, "Let's bow our heads and give thanks." He prayed, "Our heavenly Father, we thank you for this food and these people gathered here today. We ask you to bless each one with health, happiness, and your guidance in our lives. We pray that you will be with these families who are making this journey to their new homes. Give us all strength to live our lives according to your will. Amen."

It turned out to be a wonderful evening. Everybody ate and visited and laughed then they moved their chairs into a circle around the campfire that Jeremiah had started. The family from Appalachia began singing. They sang funny songs, sad songs, and ballads, songs which told stories. The words and tunes were much different than the Kentuckians had ever heard; even so, they tried to sing along.

The moon rose above the trees and cast a warm glow down on the group. They looked up and became quiet, in awe of its beauty, almost prayerful for several minutes. The only sounds to be heard were the chirping of crickets and sounds from other small creatures.

The preacher arose from his chair and said softly, "I do believe our God is with us this evening. Good friends, it is time to say good night. Rest well, and may God bless you as you continue your travel tomorrow." As if on cue, they all hugged or shook hands, and each one quietly left.

Chapter 11

BRADY'S ANXIETY CONCERNING HIS FAMILY MADE him nervous and difficult to be around. He had received a letter that told him Jeremiah had made it home. That was over three weeks ago. Brady knew the trip back would be slower and much more difficult considering they were coming with two covered wagons carrying three women and three children. As Brady remembered his first trip, his mind conjured up so many scenarios of events that *could* go wrong that he wasn't sleeping much at night. He would wake up, drenched in sweat, as he envisioned creatures going into their camp, growling and tearing at the wagon covers. Wolves would jump in with Anna Marie and bite her arms. He once dreamed he saw a snake crawl under the bedcovers beside Pat. *How much longer will they be?* he thought. *They could've rolled down the banks of the Ohio right into the river. Oh my God! I may never see them again!* Brady would wake from his nightmares, get out of his bedroll, go outside, and walk down the road, as if he might see them coming toward him.

One morning about daybreak, Foster walked out to the porch and found Brady sitting with his head bowed and cradled in his hands. "You're up early, friend," he remarked. Brady slowly lifted his head but remained silent.

Foster couldn't help but notice Brady's mood. "Something bothering you?" he asked.

Brady stood and looked down the road. "Wish I knew where they were," he said. "It's got me wonderin' if they're all right." The wrinkles in his forehead and dark circles under his eyes reflected his lack of sleep and his worrisome state of mind.

"So that's why you've been like a barefoot boy who's been walkin' in a thistle patch! You ain't been yourself for some time now. Now, you know Jeremiah will take good care of your wife and sons. Why, they even have her papa along, and you know he'll protect her with all he's got."

"Yeah, I know, but I can't help it. I've been worried, and it's been eatin' on me."

Foster placed his hand on Brady's shoulder. "You've gotta right to feel uneasy, but the chances are they are doin' just fine. Come on inside, and we'll find some breakfast."

Beulah was in the kitchen acting like her perky old self. She was even humming. Foster and Brady looked at each other in disbelief at the way she was moving around. Lorelei sliced a loaf of bread and had made a big pot of oatmeal. Beulah went to the cupboard and took out a small stone jar that held some honey and placed it in the middle of the table. The conversation at the breakfast table became lively with Beulah joining in and even joking a little. Foster's eyes simply twinkled as he watched her.

Frank, Luke, and Brady packed the wagon and headed over to work on Frank's cabin. The sky was overcast, and the westerly wind blew briskly. The men made sure to secure their hats as they left. They worked steadily all morning. The heat and humidity felt like a storm was brewing, and, sure enough, just as they stopped to eat their noon meal, the thunder rolled, and before long the rain poured down. Luckily, the roof and sides were completed, and they were well protected. When the men realized the wind was blowing rain into the cabin, they hurriedly covered the cabin door and left for home.

❋

Two nights of rest at the same place was good for the travelers and their horses. The men had watered and fed the horses at daybreak, and then Jeremiah punched at the slumbering coals left from the evening before. He pumped a bucket of fresh water and then moved quickly to get the coffee made. He set out jam with bread and butter and some apples for their breakfast. Ben decided to grease the wagon wheels before they hitched up the horses.

Jeremiah's heart pounded as he felt the excitement. He knew home was now about three days away. As everyone boarded the wagons and buggy, Jeremiah stood close so they could hear him speak.

"Folks, we've had quite a good trip for the most part." He had a big grin on his face. "Baring bad luck," he paused, "we should reach our new farms in three to four days." Everyone cheered and laughed at the good news. Instantly, as if a fairy appeared and waved a magic wand, everyone's mood sparkled.

Jeremiah shouted loudly, "Ho," and waved his arms, which meant "let's go." The horses seemed to feel the urge to move at a more spirited gait when the reins smacked their backs. Anna Marie and her mother chatted together most of the morning. They remarked about how the land seemed to lay flatter with only soft, rolling hills, and that it should be better for raising crops. Lydia thought eighty acres was too much land for Anna Marie and Brady to farm; at the same time, she was proud of them and all they were doing.

The group had made two stops to rest and refresh themselves, and their spirits were still running high when they stopped late that afternoon. The evening became quite windy, causing the covers on the wagons to flop hard against the wooden staves; moments later they heard the thunder rumbling. The horses became restless and began to whiney.

Ben said to Lydia in a hushed voice, "It seems a storm is coming. I'll go talk to Jeremiah." He walked over by the campfire. Ben saw him look skyward, where they both saw a black cloud moving their way. Sheets of lightning flashed across the horizon.

He crouched down beside Jeremiah and said, "It looks stormy. Do you think the wagons will be safe for us?"

He replied, "If the wind gets stronger, we could be in trouble. It's pushing hard against our wagon, and I'm not sure the cover will hold up. Should we move it closer to the trees?"

"That's not a bad idea," Ben agreed. "Let's tell the women and get moving," Jeremiah stated.

Jeremiah went for a horse team as Ben went to tell the women. The horses seemed to intuitively realize a bad storm was near. They reared and made throaty sounds as they took short, dance-like steps while Jeremiah led them to be hitched to the wagon. A big thrust of wind blew through, which caused the men to almost lose their balance.

"Ho, now!" Ben said as he soothed the horse. They hitched Anna Marie's wagon first, circled around the campfire and stopped by a large oak tree, then tied the reins to a sturdy branch. The children became upset and began crying. The women, with their children, climbed into the secured wagon.

The men hurriedly brought the second team to Jeremiah's wagon. The lightning cracked, thunder rolled, and the wind blew harder. Before the team was hitched, straight-line wind blew so forcefully that the men could hardly stand. At that moment, Jeremiah saw his wagon crash over on its side.

"Oh my God, look! Your wagon blew over," Anna Marie exclaimed to Pricilla. The men struggled as they took the team over beside the other horses and tied them securely. They looked around at Anna Marie's buggy lying on its side, the wheel on top wildly spinning around. At that point, the two men climbed into the covered wagon with the women and children. There was barely enough room for everyone since the wagon was already packed full. The wind ruffled the feathers of the chickens, which had hunkered down in their pen. The rain continued to pour down well into the night before it stopped. Needless to say, the Kentuckians didn't get much rest that night.

As the morning sun rose, the air became hot and steamy. The men's boots splashed and squished as they walked through the soaked ground. They checked the horses, which had endured the storm unharmed. They were able to upright the buggy without difficulty.

Because all the wood was soaking wet, they couldn't start a fire. The travelers made do with bread and jerky. Everyone decided to walk over to assess the damage to Jeremiah and Pricilla's wagon.

Jeremiah took one look and said, "We'll have to unload everything before we can set it upright, then we'll be able to see the damage." Pricilla stood beside Anna Marie and shook her head in unbelief as she tried to accept the damage the storm had done. Tears streamed from her eyes as the exhaustion, paired with the distress from the loss of property, had drained her whole being. She looked at Anna Marie, who immediately sensed her dismay and took a hold of her arm. "You need to stay strong. My father and Jeremiah will be able to repair whatever is needed. Think about it; we don't have much farther to go. We'll be there soon; you can count on that! I'll watch Joseph while you and Jeremiah empty out your wagon."

"Thank you. I'll start as soon as he's ready." Anna Marie went back to her wagon, where she and her mother made plans to fix the next meal.

Ben and Jeremiah unloaded the heavy items while Pricilla gathered dishes, pots and pans, and other small items. She came across two oil lamps with broken flues, her mother's woven basket with a broken handle, and a large, heavy glass pitcher that was cracked and chipped, probably unusable. It was quite a chore for the three to remove everything and place each item on the soaked ground without causing more damage.

When they had finished, Ben and Jeremiah had to decide the best way to upright the wagon. Jeremiah located two long ropes. He tied one securely to the side of the wagon that was on top; the other end would be fastened to the saddle horn of Ben's horse. The other rope would be fastened in like manner and work as a counterbalance, tied to Pricilla's horse. As Ben's horse slowly pulled one direction, Pricilla's horse would steady the wagon in order to prevent the wagon from landing too hard when it hit the ground. In a few moments, the job was complete with no further damage. The three could now see what must be done to assure that the wagon would be trail-worthy again.

Three of the staves that held the heavily woven cover had snapped in two; two others were cracked. As they checked the wheels, they saw that the back wheel wasn't setting straight. Looking closer, the pin that held the wheel on the axle had broken off. They all agreed that the damage could've been much worse. Lydia had come over to the wreck site to help Pricilla deal with the soaked bedding and clothes. They were thankful that the sun was shining and warm. They draped the wet items on the bushes or threw them over some low tree branches, trusting that the heat from the sun would dry them.

The men worked diligently the remainder of the day, and by suppertime the wagon was ready to roll once again. The Kentuckians' spirits had been renewed, and it was reflected that evening as they sat around their campfire after their evening meal. They began telling stories and laughing.

If anyone asks me, "What was the funniest thing that happened on your trip, I'll laugh and say, it was probably the day the snake crawled into the wagon and tried to get the chickens," Pricilla said with a funny voice.

Anna Marie added, "Sure, you jumped out of the wagon, screaming, which let everyone know how much fun you were having!" Lydia and Anna Marie laughed so hard that they bent over as they spoofed the event.

"What I enjoyed the most was seeing the Ohio River and then crossing it on the ferry," Ben said.

Lydia interjected, "Yes, it was exciting, but I feared for my life at the same time."

Anna Marie spoke up. "The river was so big and beautiful. I'll look forward to crossing it again one day."

"Remember, everyone, that beautiful river can be very treacherous when Mother Nature is exercising her wrath with stormy weather," Ben reminded the group.

"I hope I don't have to cross when that happens," Lydia commented. All agreed with her. As the fire lowered, their eyes became heavy with sleep. One by one, they said their "good nights" and sought out their beds. The rest of the night remained calm.

Chapter 12

BRADY SAT ON THE PORCH BENT OVER, HIS HEAD being held up with the palm of each hand as his elbows rested on his knees. He had awakened before dawn, disturbed and anxious. The day slowly came to life as the rays of the sun began to light up the world around him. He *had* to do something. It was one of those urges that pleaded and throbbed throughout one's body. Indians would probably say, "The Great Spirit calls me to go, and I must answer."

Brady went into the kitchen and informed his friends of his plan to ride east. He quickly ate breakfast and readied his horse for the trip. His heart pumped excitedly as he was driven with anticipation. He rode at a gallop for the first mile, and then realized he needed to slow the pace for the sake of his horse, and they settled into a steady trot. His senses remained alert as he absorbed all the sights and sounds of the countryside.

He caught sight of a red fox moving quietly through the trees on his right. Brady watched with interest the animal's movements as he wove around the bushes and tree saplings, stopping often to sniff along the ground, as if he might find the scent for his next meal. Suddenly, a small flock of blackbirds squawked overhead as they took flight out of the large elm tree that grew beside the road. The noise they created caused Brady's horse to toss his head and sidestep. "Easy, boy," he said as he patted the horse's neck.

The man and horse rode about fifteen miles and then stopped to rest. Brady led his horse to a large water puddle a short way from the road. As the horse drank, Brady removed his hat and splashed the cool water on his face then walked under the shade of a tree to cool down. Brady sat on the ground while his horse grazed a bit.

He rested a short time in the shade and then decided to lead his horse back to the road. His eyes looked toward the curve in the road that lay ahead. At first he thought he was hallucinating, causing him to rub his eyes. *My God, that's two covered wagons! Could it be ...?* He mounted up and rode at a gallop toward them. Within minutes they met.

At first sight, Ben whooped loudly, "Whoa, boys" and stopped his horse team. Brady rode up and shook Ben's hand. "You're a sight for sore eyes," Ben stated.

"Welcome. Am I ever glad to see you," Brady said.

He saw Pat sitting there beside his grandpa. He dismounted and took Pat into his arms and gave him a big hug. "Hello, boy, remember your pa?" he asked. "I've missed you," and he squeezed him again, then set him back on the wagon seat.

Brady walked back to the next wagon, which held Jeremiah, Pricilla, and Joseph. Jeremiah jumped down, and the two men shared a manly hug. "I told you I'd get your family here safe and sound," Jeremiah told him.

"It's so good to see all of you. I just knew you'd make it," Brady declared.

Brady spoke to Pricilla. "Are you and Joseph all right?"

"Oh, yes, we're much better now since seeing you. Your wife, Tim, and Lydia are right behind us," Pricilla said to him. She paused, "Well, go on and see her!" Brady nearly ran to the buggy where she sat.

When Brady came into Anna Marie's sight, she yelled out, "Brady is that really you?" She began climbing down from the buggy seat, and he grabbed her before her feet touched the ground. He wrapped his arms around her and held her tightly. When he released her, he saw tears flowing from her eyes. He touched her cheek and said, "Don't cry. Everything's gonna be fine. You're almost there." He kissed her briefly. He kept his arm around her waist as he turned to Anna Marie's mother. "Hello Lydia," he said. "How are you?"

She smiled and replied, "I'm doing just fine now that we're here. We're all so happy to see you."

"I can't explain how glad I am to see all of you." He looked into Anna Marie's eyes. "I've hardly been able to sleep, worrying about everyone. I'll go talk to Ben and Jeremiah to check about how much traveling they want to do today." He gave his wife another quick kiss, then rode up toward the men.

"Do you plan to keep going now? We're about fifteen miles from our destination," Brady said.

"Sure, there's a lot of daylight left. We'll go as far as we can," Ben and Jeremiah agreed together. "One more night on the road, then the trip will be over. What do you say? Let's go!" Jeremiah stated.

Ben hollered loudly, "*Wagons ho,*" and snapped the reins on his team. Brady went back, mounted, and rode his horse alongside of Anna Marie and Lydia.

❋

September 3. Before noon the next day, the Kentuckians arrived at the Browning residence. Beulah was sitting in the rocker on the porch and watched the wagons pull up and stop. Brady had Anna Marie drive her buggy up to the hitch near the house.

"Land's sake," Beulah hollered, "look who's here." She stood up and waved at everyone. Brady helped Anna Marie, who was holding Timmy, and then Lydia down off the buggy and walked them to the porch.

"Mornin', Beulah," Brady spoke. "This is my beautiful wife, Anna Marie, and her mother, Lydia." He took Tim and said, "Here is my youngest boy, Tim." Pat ran up beside his pa and grabbed his hand. "This is Pat. Pat, this is Beulah. She's a very nice lady."

"Hi," Pat timidly said.

"Well, look at you. What a fine young boy you are," Beulah told him.

Jeremiah couldn't wait to see Brady and Beulah. "Come with us, Ben," he said. He quickly helped Pricilla and Joseph down from the wagon, and they walked over to the others. Jeremiah made his introductions as the women all hugged and chattered.

Lorelei heard all the talking from inside the house and went to see what was happening. She came out the door, quite surprised to see that the wagons had arrived at last. Beulah immediately introduced Lorelei to the new arrivals.

Speaking to the women, Beulah said, "Let's all go inside. My goodness, you must be plumb worn out!" As they started to go into the house, Ben said, "We better decide where to set the wagons for the night and take care of the horses."

Brady guided the wagons beside the barn, where the men unhitched the horses, stabled and watered them.

☀

Foster and Frank, along with Luke and his son, had worked all day trying to finish the inside of Frank's cabin. Today they had finished the walls between the front room and the bedroom. Foster had made the frame for one bed and built a shelf in the bedroom. When the sun began its slide down toward the western horizon, the men, quite worn down by now, decided to quit and head back.

The bumpy ride back to Foster's home finished taking the last bit of energy left from the workers. As the men approached their home destination, they observed the two covered wagons boldly standing together at the side of the property. Frank's eyes widened as he yelled out, "They're here! Oh, my God! They really made it!"

Foster said, "Are you sure that's your Kentucky friends?"

"I'm positive. They've arrived." He snapped the reins on the horses and said, "Giddyap, boys, let's roll." The men forgot how tired they had felt only moments ago as they rushed up the road. The four hopped off their horses and went directly toward their friends. Frank and Jeremiah hugged like long lost brothers, slapping each other on the back saying, "It's so good to see you."

The women were laughing, still euphoric with the reality that the trip had ended, and they had actually arrived. They heard the joyful noises coming from the men who were outside, and they went out to join them. The reunion continued until the babies began crying, a signal for the women to go inside. The men used this time to brush the horses down and placed clumps of hay in the manger, which the horses eagerly began eating.

The evening meal had been prepared, eaten, and cleaned up. They all sat and listened to the many stories the travelers told about their trip. Bedtime arrived at last. Preparations had been made to allow all the women and children to sleep inside the house.

Brady's desire for Anna Marie was overwhelming. He wanted her beside him. Before they parted that evening, he led her outside away from the house. He held her close and kissed her longingly. "Tomorrow we'll take the covered wagon to our new home. I can't wait to show it to you," Brady told her. He stroked her hair as he held her so close he could feel her breath on his face.

"Brady, I missed you so. Promise that we'll always be together," she said. He kissed all over her face and then said, "I promise."

He led her over to their covered wagon, and they climbed inside. Anna Marie's hands trembled as she unbuttoned her dress. Brady's desire for her was intense. They lay down together. Control was abandoned, and the loving was beyond description. They clung to each other, two hearts beating as one. Brady lay next to her, curled around her back, feeling more content than he had felt for weeks. Anna Marie felt secure and complete, feelings that had eluded her during his absence. She rolled over toward him and clung to his strong body.

Brady held Anna Marie's face and said, "You should go back to the children, right?" She nodded her head affirmatively. They proceeded to put their clothes on and sauntered back to the house, hand in hand. He gave her a kiss good night and then went to the barn, where he would sleep alongside Jeremiah, Frank, Ben, and Luke.

Everyone was up with the first streaks of light. Joseph and Timmy were very uneasy in their new surroundings. They cried and fussed while their mothers tried to calm them. That left Beulah, Lydia, and Lorelei with the breakfast work. The babies settled down after they were fed and cleaned up. It was hectic with all the people crammed in the Browning home trying to eat their breakfast. An hour later, the Patterson family was ready to go to their new home.

Brady could hardly wait to show Anna Marie the homestead. He and Jeremiah went out and got the team ready to hitch up to the covered wagon. Pat followed them around like a puppy dog, managing to get in their way often.

Pricilla and Jeremiah followed Anna Marie and her children out of the house. Frank said to them, "If you want, you can ride on Foster's wagon and go with us to the new farms."

Pricilla looked at Jeremiah and said, "Oh, yes, let's go."

"Why not," he replied. Pricilla squeezed Jeremiah's hand as they smiled at each other.

Soon Brady and Anna Marie, with Pat and Timmy, were going down the road to their new home. Frank followed behind Brady with Pricilla and Jeremiah. The wagon lumbered along, and the riders could feel every bump on the rough dirt road. After all, the wagon was built for hauling tools or lumber and such, not comfort. The group went over the last hill when the homestead came into view. It was a picture—the new cabin placed a short distance from the road, farm ground framed with several varieties of trees that grew along the banks of the stream that meandered south of the field, turned, and then traveled on the west side.

Brady halted the horses in the shade of one of the larger trees he left when he had cleared the land. He helped Anna Marie and the boys down from the covered wagon. Brady looked at Pat and said, "This is your new home. Do you want to see it?"

"Yes, Pa," he answered.

Brady took his hand and walked him toward the front. Anna Marie, carrying Tim, followed behind, as did Frank and the others. They stepped up on the few boards that Brady had nailed together for a porch. He walked up and opened the front door. Anna Marie had tears in her eyes as Brady put his arms around her and kissed her cheek. She handed Tim over for him to hold. She slowly looked at each room as she began to absorb the cabin, her new home. "Brady, I can't believe this is ours. It's perfect."

Frank, Jeremiah and Pricilla walked inside. "You've built a beautiful home," Pricilla said. She walked to the kitchen where Anna Marie was checking her cupboard and shelves. "This is *so* exciting. I'm happy for both of you." She gave Anna Marie a squeeze around the waist. Pat went back and forth as he explored each room.

In a little while Jeremiah said, "Are you ready to start unloading your wagon?"

"Yeah, I guess we better get started," Brady replied. The men worked for several hours until the job was finished. Frank, Jeremiah, and Pricilla returned to the Browning residence.

This would be the first night Brady, Anna Marie, and their boys would spend together in their new home. Life as it was is now history. From this day forward, their lives will be fresh and new with all the daybreaks in Indiana.

❋

Ben and Lydia rose the next day, ate their breakfast, and soon after hitched a horse up to Anna Marie's buggy. With Jeremiah as their guide, they rode off toward Brady and Anna Marie's new farm. Lydia was especially anxious to see their home.

"Good morning, Anna Marie," Lydia said when they met her at the front door. "We couldn't wait to come see you and help wherever we can."

Lydia gave both her parents a hug and said, "Thank you. Come on inside." Lydia set a fresh loaf of bread on the table that Beulah had sent for her. She and Ben both could see the strain from the trip was taking its toll on Anna Marie, even though she was smiling. Pat came running and gave both grandparents a hug. Timmy laid on a quilt over in the corner and played with his wooden horses.

Brady entered the kitchen with a pail of fresh milk. "Hello folks," he spoke. "Mornin', Jeremiah. Mm, I smell something good."

"I made biscuits," Anna Marie replied. "Would you like one with hot tea?" Within minutes, everyone was seated at the kitchen table enjoying the food.

The rest of the day Lydia helped Anna Marie by caring for the two boys and preparing the meals. Anna Marie busied herself going from room to room putting things away. The two women talked about rugs and curtains and other homemaking ideas. Meanwhile, Ben and Brady continued working outside, cutting trees for the lean-to and an outhouse. The small branches and chunks were piled up for firewood.

Ben and Lydia continued helping for another ten days, then made the decision to return to their home. It was a difficult parting for both families. They all realized that it would be months, maybe years, before they see each other again. It was mid-September when they started toward Kentucky, retracing the same road they had traveled nearly three weeks ago.

Chapter 13

TWO MONTHS HAD NOW PASSED. IT HAD BEEN ONLY A month ago that the leaves along the creek had boasted red, yellow, and orange leaves. Now those leaves lay in dry, swirled bunches, driven by the cool winds, a prerequisite of the coming winter. Squirrels ran about as they diligently searched among the hickory and walnut trees for nuts to store away.

Timmy walked around and around in the new home. Anna Marie had received a long letter from her mother telling about their trip home and that they were all right. Brady had enclosed the lean-to so his cow and horses would have good shelter from the winter weather. It wasn't very big, but it would have to do for now. Brady, Jeremiah, and Foster had all worked on Frank's house until it was livable, and now Jeremiah and his family will share his home for the winter.

Beulah had taken another fall. She hit her head again quite hard and suffered several bruises. She cannot function as well as before and spends most of her time sitting in a rocking chair and looking out the window. Luke and Lorelei now care for both Beulah and Foster. Their son, Shawn, has learned to make wagon wheels, so he was able to carry on Foster's business.

Next week will be Thanksgiving. The three women, Anna Marie, Pricilla and Lorelei, had decided they would all go to the Browning home and spend the day. The husbands planned to hunt for the meat, a turkey or deer, for the feast.

❋

On Thanksgiving eve, cold, cloudy weather arrived, and the first snowfall came during the night. Pat looked out the window and saw the white all over the ground and became excited. "Look, mamma, snow!" and he squealed with joy. He remembered what snow was from last year—walking in his boots, falling down and laughing, making snowballs, and watching rabbits hopping around in jerky patterns.

Anna Marie had made a large pan of white beans with bacon, a bowl of sauerkraut, and her favorite, chocolate cake with chopped nuts on top. She was sipping on a cup of hot tea as she packed the sauerkraut into a basket, and suddenly she felt queasy. She sat down and rubbed her stomach. *What is happening?* she thought. *I don't want to be sick on Thanksgiving Day.* About that time Brady came into the house from his morning chores.

"What's wrong, Anna?" he asked.

"I'm not sure. I was packing the food to take to dinner, and all of a sudden I got a sick feeling in my stomach."

"Do you feel like going over to the Brownings' today?"

"Oh, I think I'll be all right in a few minutes." He knelt down beside her and looked into her eyes. "I want you to tell me the truth. Are you going to be all right?"

"My stomach feels better. I'm sure it's nothing."

After Brady heard this, he and his family proceeded with the plans of the day and went to their friends for dinner. It turned out to be a happy time for everyone. Beulah ate at the dinner table with everyone, enjoying the food and appearing to be somewhat more alert than before. After the bountiful meal, the women went into the front room to visit and care for the children as the men sat around the kitchen table and shared hunting and fishing stories. As late afternoon approached, the friends began gathering their coats and leftovers and said their good-byes. They bundled up in their warm clothing, got into their buggies and proceeded homeward.

By December 1 the weather had warmed enough to melt the snow. Brady came into the kitchen to eat his breakfast. He looked around and couldn't see Anna Marie. "Where's Momma?" he asked Pat. "Outside," he replied.

"Outside—why?" Papa asked.

"I don't know," Pat answered.

Brady went back outside. Anna was stooped over, clinging to the house. Brady ran to her side. "Anna, what's wrong with you?"

"I'm not sure. I started cracking raw eggs into a bowl, and all of a sudden I got so sick."

Brady put his arm around her waist. "You've been getting sick two or three times a week. What's wrong?"

She looked deeply into his eyes and quietly told him, "I think I'm going to have a baby."

His eyes sparkled as he held her head with both hands. "My sweet wife, I love you." He kissed her and stroked her hair.

"Are you ready to come back inside now?"

"Yes," she said quietly. I think I'll be all right now."

☀

December. Early on Saturday, Jeremiah, Pricilla, and Frank arrive at the Patterson farm. Anna Marie and Pricilla had decided to get together to make Christmas cookies while the men went to cut wood. There were many trees down in the timber that would be available to harvest. The Indiana winter always called for a big supply of firewood. Brady had bought a kitchen stove earlier this past fall, to the delight of Anna Marie. She hadn't mastered the oven, so today will be the day to try to conquer it. Pricilla's boy Joseph, now called Joey, and Timmy, both about the same age, were enjoying playing together. Of course, the boys had eaten cookies, which had boosted their energy level, so they were running about and squealing loudly.

By the time the men came in for their noon meal, the aroma of rabbit stew and fresh baked cookies permeated the whole cabin.

Frank came through the door first followed by Jeremiah and Brady. Frank said, "Wow! I don't know what you women have been cooking, but it smells great!"

Pricilla remarked sassily, "Go wash your dirty paws if you expect to sit at our table." All the men comically raised their arms up and bent their wrists as if they were dogs, and headed toward the wash bowl. Anna Marie and Pricilla began giggling at the sight, and then everyone joined in on the silliness of it all.

☀

The women took a break from cooking after the noon meal. As soon as they got the three boys to take a nap, they both sat down in rocking chairs for a rest. They were enjoying a cup of tea and confessed that they were both tired. Anna Marie spoke. "At least I'm not sick today."

Pricilla got a concerned look on her face and responded by saying, "What do you mean?"

Anna Marie realized she had let the cat out of the bag. "Well—uh, guess I may as well tell you—I'm going to have another baby."

Anna Marie saw a big smile on Pricilla's face as she laughed and said, "That's wonderful. When do you think your baby will come?"

"I think next June."

Pricilla replied, "You know what? I'm having another baby about the same time!" Both women laughed joyfully.

Anna Marie said, "Well, I guess that's what happens when we're reunited with our husbands after being apart." They both giggled. The two sat and rested for nearly an hour, sharing their lives as it was back in Kentucky compared to what it is now. They decided to make one last batch of cookies, so they would have enough to share at the gathering on Christmas Eve.

The men returned an hour later, cold and tired but in good spirits. Anna Marie had made sure that coffee was ready to drink when they ate the freshly baked cookies.

"Mm, these cookies are delicious," Frank remarked as he reached for a second one.

"I agree," said Jeremiah.

"Me too," came from Brady. "A good hot drink when I come in from the cold really warms me."

The men weren't talking much as they enjoyed their refreshments.

Jeremiah suddenly spoke. "You know, it seems that it won't be long until more and more people will be coming to this part of the country. I think we need to be thinking about the future. Our families are growing, and soon we'll need a church and a school."

At first everyone remained silent, taken aback by Jeremiah's seriousness. His statements were quickly followed by light chuckling laughter as they all agreed. They began to realize they were all part of the forming of a town.

Frank stated, "By golly, my friend, you're right! We're going to make history!"

Brady spoke up. "It'll take time and a lot of hard work from all of us."

"We could use the church for both worship and teaching our children until the population grows," Anna Marie suggested. "Sunday would be church day, and Monday through Friday could be for school."

"I suggest that next spring when it warms up that we try to cut some logs and set them aside for the church building," spoke Jeremiah.

"I'll go along with that," Brady said.

"That sounds like a good idea," said Frank. "I think I'll have another cookie with that decision," he said as he laughed. "You know just thinking about cutting logs takes a lot of energy."

"We may run out of cookies before Christmas," Pricilla said jokingly.

Within the hour, the men had rested. It was time for Frank, Jeremiah, and Pricilla, along with baby Joey, to return to Frank's cabin.

Midafternoon on Christmas Eve both families and Frank went to the Browning residence. Lorelei and Shawn had made new candles, one for each one attending the meal and worship service. Foster had made special candleholders for the children. He and Shawn had walked around in the woods and gathered bittersweet boughs and pine cones. Lorelei had decorated each bough with small red ribbons and placed them around to make the house festive. The aroma of apple-cinnamon tea, which was simmering on the cookstove, drifted throughout the house.

Beulah sat in her rocking chair as usual. Her eyes were intent on the three large candles surrounded with cedar branches that were placed in the center of the fireplace mantle. Their constant flickering seemed to have her in a trance. She responded to the greetings offered by the visitors, but no one was sure if she realized what was happening. Beulah hadn't forgotten how to knit, so a bag of yarn sat by her chair at all times. During her good times, she would put her hand into the bag and take out a ball of yarn and her knitting needles. She then proceeded to knit row after row of stitches until she became tired.

Foster was openly happy to have everyone there in his home. "Welcome, welcome," he called out when they arrived. He gave a gentle hug to the women and a hearty handshake to the men. Laughter and joyfulness began to fill the atmosphere throughout the house. At first the three little boys looked slowly around the house, but within minutes they started running and playing. Beulah stopped watching the candles as the children caught her attention, causing a big smile to appear on her face.

"Hi," she called out, "hi, little boys," waving her hands.

Foster stopped in amazement as he watched. He walked over to her, knelt down, and took her hand in his and stroked it gently. She looked straight into his eyes as she continued smiling. He could see the fine wrinkle lines crinkling at the outside corners of her eyes.

He still adored this woman. "You look happy today," he said to her. "Are you feeling good?" She nodded her head. "I'm happy too," he said to her. As he stood up, he kissed her hand, then her forehead. As he looked around, he saw that the other adults had observed this loving moment.

Lorelei was especially touched by the scene that she had just observed. She walked over to Luke, and he wrapped his arms around her waist. Jeremiah took a hold of Pricilla's hand and said, "The Bible says, ' a man is to leave his father and mother and be joined to his wife, and the two shall become one.'"

This quiet moment was abruptly interrupted by the shrieks and giggles coming from the boys as they continued their playing. Foster spoke up, "I think it's time for our Christmas Eve meal." The women went back into the kitchen area and continued to prepare the meal. Soon it was ready, and they all gathered around the table. Each adult shared a short prayer expressing thanks for their many blessings.

It was a truly blessed time that the friends had shared that Christmas Eve, one that they would remember throughout the years.

Chapter 14

MID-JANUARY 1839. ANNA MARIE AND PRICILLA BOTH are now close to halfway into their pregnancy. During the times that they were together, it looked as if Anna Marie was carrying a much larger child than Pricilla. She had difficulty going about her normal daily chores. It felt like this child was more active, moving constantly. She hadn't experienced this hardship with the first two children until the last month before they were to be born.

Every day Brady had been out in the cold wintry weather caring for the livestock. The water would freeze in the horse trough, which had to be chopped out. He carried the ice chunks into the house and thawed them in a big pan on the cookstove and then carried the warm water back out to the trough. He had to do this chore morning and evening. He no longer had to care for their chickens. He knew they wouldn't survive the first winter without a proper place to roost, so they had been butchered and eaten.

Today Brady entered the kitchen, and a whoosh of cold air followed him inside. He hung his hat on its hook and walked directly to the cookstove to warm up. Anna Marie was sitting at the kitchen table sipping a cup of hot tea. Brady removed his snowy boots and moved to a chair. She saw the little puddles of water form as snow melted off of Brady's shoes onto the kitchen floor, but she didn't say anything to him. Timmy came into the room and saw the water. He immediately sat down and began smacking it with the palms of his hands and made it splash all around. Pat saw Tim playing and decided to get in on the fun. The two parents laughed at the boys as they spread the water all over themselves, but they made no attempt to stop their play.

"Are you in for the night?" Anna Marie asked.

"Not quite. After supper, I'll carry in another armload of wood, but that's all I need to do," he replied. "How are you feeling now?"

"My stomach feels sore from the baby's kicking. I find myself sitting down more."

"Maybe I should take you to a doctor to check you."

"Let's wait and see if it gets any worse."

"All right, but I want you to stay healthy," he stated.

❂

February 10. The winter weather still had a firm grip on the country. A blanket of snow remained on the ground, covering every tree, bush, and fence post. The dead milkweeds and thistles appeared as flowers with their crown of white. As Anna Marie looked over the countryside, she regarded it as a winter wonderland, a picture painted by a great artist. Clouds that hung in the sky began blocking the sun, leaving a thick, foggy appearance in the air. Today the temperature was only a few degrees above the freezing mark. It began to rain a very cold rain. Brady and Anna Marie both knew this would make it more difficult to care for the animals and bring in the water and firewood.

By midafternoon the cold rain had frozen on everything. Large icicles began to form on the roof edges. The slick ground made it hard for Brady to walk from the house to the animal shed, especially when he toted the buckets of warm water for the cow and two horses. He was running out of hay to feed the animals. He predicted he might have enough hay and straw for ten days. *What was I thinking when I moved my family farther north,* he thought. *It's not fair to them. I'm only a man that can do so much—I need to do more.* About that time, Frank and Jeremiah rode up on their horses.

"Howdy stranger. We thought we'd ride over and check on you and your family," Frank said. "How's everybody here at the Patterson place?"

"We're doin' pretty good, I guess. Why don't you come inside, and we'll visit," Brady told them.

The two riders led their horses into the shed and then followed him into the kitchen. The men took off their wet boots and set them on a rug beside the door. They immediately felt the heat radiating from the stove as it warmed flesh and bone. The aroma of a large pot of stew simmering wafted throughout the house. Anna Marie rested in her rocker with her legs propped up.

Jeremiah said to Anna Marie, "Hello. How are you today?"

"Well, it seems I can't work very long at a time, and then I have to sit and rest. To tell you the truth, I feel like I have a kangaroo inside me instead of a child," she answered.

"Don't take me wrong, but you do look larger than Pricilla," he commented. "When this weather clears up, maybe you should have Brady take you into Seymour to be checked by a doctor."

"We've talked about that. My feet and legs are swollen, and I can hardly walk around now," she commented.

"You be sure and take good care of yourself," Jeremiah told her. She nodded affirmatively.

"I think there's some coffee in the pot; come join me," Brady said to the men. They sat around the kitchen table where they visited and joked for a good hour.

When it was time to leave, Frank and Jeremiah offered to help carry firewood inside for the night. Brady accepted without hesitation. The temperature had dropped below freezing, and the uneven ground was now covered with ice. The men walked to the woodpile, located on the east side of the small shed, and filled their arms with the cut logs. They often slipped on their trek, but they helped fill the wood box located inside the corner of the kitchen.

"Thanks, I appreciate your help," Brady told them.

"You're more than welcome," Jeremiah replied. "By the way, I talked to Anna Marie. She seems overly tired with the baby she's carrying."

"Yeah, she is," Brady confirmed.

"You need to seriously consider taking her to a doctor," Frank said.

"I know, but the weather is really bad."

"How about checking with Foster? I think I saw a sleigh stored in the back of his barn," Jeremiah told Brady.

"I may check first thing in the morning. Talk to you tomorrow," Brady told him. "See you then."

The men went for their horses and rode off toward Frank's cabin. Brady went inside the home and related their conversation to Anna Marie. She agreed that it was a good idea. The plans were now set in motion.

The next morning, Brady left right after breakfast for the Browning home. The extreme cold made Brady shiver down to his bones. It was so difficult for his horse to walk on the rough, icy road that the trip took at least twice as long going the few miles to see Foster.

Of course, Foster was quite surprised to see Brady. They talked, and, sure enough, he had a sleigh. They dragged it out of the barn and checked it over. It seemed to be in sound condition. Foster rubbed oil all along the wooden runners and hitched it to Brady's horse.

"There you are, friend. You best take your Anna to Seymour today." Foster looked Brady directly in his eyes and said, "Every day you wait is another day of suffering for your wife." Brady shook Foster's hand and nodded in agreement, then left immediately for his home.

Brady rode to his home and told Anna Marie to get ready to go with him to Seymour. There was urgency in his voice. She understood his concern, and at the same she felt relief. He then went directly to Frank's cabin and related his decision. He was there a short while, until Jeremiah and Pricilla could get ready to go with him. Pricilla and Joey climbed onto the sleigh, and Jeremiah mounted his horse, then they all went back to Brady's cabin. Pat and Timmy were excited to see Joey, and the little boys began playing immediately. Anna Marie had dressed warmly, packed some sandwiches, grabbed two quilts, and was ready to leave.

"We'll take good care of your boys, so don't worry. Stay a few days if it is necessary," Jeremiah assured both Brady and Anna Marie.

"Thanks. You're good friends," Anna Marie told them. The two women hugged, and Pricilla handed her a jug filled with hot tea. Brady took Anna by the arm and helped her out the door and onto the sleigh. They all waved as Brady snapped the reins, and the sleigh moved away from the house.

Despite the cold air, Anna Marie felt warm inside, almost giddy. Her face radiated with joy. Perhaps it was the idea of being alone with her husband, relieved of the care of her two young boys. Maybe it was the excitement of riding on the snow and ice in an old sleigh, but it was dream-like to her. As Brady carefully guided the sleigh down the road, Anna Marie watched the ice patterns on the bushes and trees glistening in the morning sunlight. She felt young and free as she held onto Brady's arm. It was a quiet, wonderful time.

They stayed on the road for nearly three hours and then decided to give the horse a rest. Brady guided the sleigh into a wide clearing. He poured some water into a small pan and gave to the horse. He and Anna Marie sipped on the jug of tea and ate their sandwich.

Brady wrapped his arms around his wife. "Have I told you lately how much I love you?" he asked.

"I recall you said it last night," she replied and smiled. He kissed her and caressed her cheek. "You are *so* beautiful," he said as he gave her another quick kiss. "We better keep going. We have a long way to go." He clicked his tongue and lightly flipped the reins, and the sleigh started moving again.

Even though they were traveling on rough snow and ice, the sleigh seemed to be gliding along very nicely. As the sun made its way across the sky, the hours flowed on, and time called for another rest. Brady guided the horse down the lane near a farm home.

"Whoa, horse," he called, and they came to a stop a short distance from the front porch. Brady helped Anna Marie down off the sleigh, walked her to the front porch, and rapped on the door. After a few moments, a middle-aged man with a full beard appeared before them.

"Good Lord, what are you two doing out here in this kind a weather?" he asked.

"We're on our way to Seymour to see a doctor, and we've been on the road all day. Could we come in to rest awhile and get ourselves warmed up?" Brady inquired.

"Come on in. We'll be glad to oblige you." They entered the farm home. The warmth from the blazing fireplace wrapped around the two travelers. Until this moment, they hadn't realized how cold they had gotten.

"My name is Victor, Vic for short. This here is my wife, Lodema." He pointed to the medium-framed woman with gray-streaked hair that was sitting in the rocker. She laid her darning needle down and stood up. She brushed her hands on her apron and said, "My goodness, take your coats off. You must be worn out."

Vic helped hang their coats and scarves on the pegs next to the door. Brady spoke up and said, "My name is Brady Patterson, and this is my wife, Anna Marie. Thank you for your kindness." The farmer and his wife immediately observed that Anna was with child.

"Would you like some clover tea?" Lodema asked them. "You're probably cold to the bone."

"That would be very nice," Anna Marie replied. She groaned and rubbed her belly as she sat down next to the fireplace.

After Brady stabled his horse, the four sat and visited the next hour away. Brady shared that he and Anna Marie had moved to Indiana the past fall with their two small children, and now they are expecting another child in June. Lodema told that they had three grown children that were married now and living elsewhere. She then revealed that she had been a midwife to several women. Brady and Anna Marie looked at each other, no doubt thinking the same thing—they may have to call on her later for help.

As the sun began setting, Vic spoke. "You folks are welcome to spend the night. We have an extra bedroom, and it's too late in the day to leave for Seymour."

"What do you want to do?" Brady asked Anna.

"Actually, it would be good to rest here tonight," she replied.

Brady turned to Lodema and told her, "Thanks. We accept your invitation." She stood up and said, "I have some cooked bacon, a pot of beans, and a freshly baked pan of cornbread that we can eat. We'll have some supper shortly."

Following their meal and more conversation, Lodema showed Brady and Anna Marie their bedroom. Anna Marie thanked Lodema for her kindness, and she began preparing for bed. Brady went out, checked his horse, and gave him some oats and water. Minutes after his return, they both were sound asleep.

Everyone arose early the next morning. The house was toasty-warm as Vic had made an extra effort to keep the fire going strong all night long. Anna Marie and Brady both had rested well. The women drank tea, and the men had their coffee. Lodema had prepared a hearty breakfast of porridge with biscuits and berry jam.

"Lodema, your biscuits and jam are very tasty," Anna Marie remarked.

"I agree," echoed Brady. The four sat at the breakfast table and exchanged portions of their life. A bond was being formed that, no doubt, would last.

Following their meal, the two travelers wrapped themselves for the cold weather and prepared to continue their journey.

"Many thanks again for your hospitality. We'll not forget how you favored us with food and shelter," Brady told the couple.

Vic replied, "You be sure and take care of the lady and get her to the doctor safely."

"I'll do my best," Brady replied as he shook hands with Vic.

Brady harnessed the horse and hooked him to the sleigh. Lodema hugged Anna as she was leaving. "You stop back by and let us know how you are, okay?"

"I'll plan to do that," Anna Marie assured her. Brady took Anna by the arm and helped her onto the sleigh. They waved at their new friends and resumed their trip to Seymour.

❋

The weather this day was a carbon copy of the previous day. Sunshine sparkled on the ice crystals and hoar frost. With every exhale, a steamy cloud left their nose or mouth like a puff of smoke. She and Brady looked at each other, first smiling, then laughing, childlike. They felt young and free—the whole world ahead of them. It was all so very good.

The miles seemed to fly by. Anna Marie and Brady laughed and planned their future together. They reminisced about the past, like the time he shot the fox that had been killing their chickens. Brady had sold the fox fur to buy Anna a tea set for Christmas. Anna squeezed Brady's arm lovingly.

Suddenly, as they trotted over the top of a large hill, they saw a man standing beside a cart crosswise of the road with a broken wheel. Brady shouted out loudly, "Whoa, horse; whoa, there." The horse hardly had his footing, much less be able to slow down a moving sleigh going downhill. A crash seemed inevitable. Brady shouted, "Hang on, Anna!"

The sleigh swerved back and forth, bouncing over icy bumps that caused Anna Marie to holler, "Do something, Brady; we'll turn over!"

By some miracle, the horse guided the sleigh around the stalled cart, through a ditch, and brought it to a stop at the bottom of the hill. The man standing there was trying to figure out what to do. Brady climbed off of the sleigh and approached the farmer. "Looks like you have a problem here," he said.

"Yeah, my dad-blamed cart broke a wheel. Bad luck seems to follow me around. I don't know what to do next," he replied.

"I see you've got some chickens here. Where were you going?"

"The winter weather took all the feed I had for the chickens. I even took them warm water every morning, yet they quit layin' eggs. The wife cooked a couple hens, and then I decided to take a crate of them to town to trade for food. I had to do something."

Brady said, "It's too cold to stay here. Why don't you put your crate on the back of the sleigh, and you can ride with us into town? We'll try to get your cart to the side of the road for now."

"That sounds like a good idea." The man chuckled, "I'm stranded out here the way it is."

Right away the two men worked with the horse to drag the cart off the road. They then tied the man's horse to the back of the sleigh. Within a relatively short time, the chore was completed, and the three were on their way to Seymour. They chatted as the sleigh made its way down the road, and within an hour or more they reached their destination. Brady let his new-found friend off at the livery stable and bid him farewell.

"Thanks for your help. You and your wife take good care. One day I hope to return the favor," the man stated.

"I'm just glad I came along and was able to help out," Brady replied. "See you later."

Brady proceeded to take Anna Marie to a café, seeking a warm place and a hot drink for both of them. Not realizing how cold she was, Anna Marie sat and shivered, but with time she slowly warmed up. The two sat and talked about their life and the new baby that was coming. They went ahead and ordered a meal; after all, it was nearly noon. The child that Anna was carrying suddenly became very active. She put both hands on her belly and groaned.

"Are you okay?" Brady asked.

"Sure, but this baby really knows how to punch and kick," Anna told him.

When the waitress came with their food, Brady inquired where the doctor's office might be. She gave them easy directions, and they found that they weren't too far from there. As soon as they ate their meal, they went directly to the doctor's office. The doctor had just finished with a patient.

"Hello, I'm Dr. Parrish. How may I help you?"

Brady said, "As you can see, my wife is carrying a baby, and we want you to check her."

"Well, come into my examining room," Dr. Parrish said to her. He turned to Brady and said, "We won't be too long." Brady waited patiently.

After checking Anna Marie, Dr. Parrish said to her, "I believe you have more than one baby. I felt two heads, and I think you're going to have twins. I want you to take good care of yourself. Get plenty of rest both during the day and the night and don't overdo yourself. You should try to drink more milk and water every day. Other than that, you are healthy, and you should give birth without any trouble."

Anna Marie was taken aback to think that she would have two babies instead of one. *How will I ever manage two babies at one time?* She and the doctor left the examining room to where Brady was waiting.

"How's she doing?" he asked the doc.

"She and her babies are doing fine." The doc chuckled.

"What do you mean, babies?" Brady asked.

"I believe your wife is going to have twins."

"Holy cow! Are you sure?"

"I'm pretty sure. I felt two heads."

Brady was overcome. He instantly hugged Anna Marie and then said, "Thanks, Doc. I'll take extra care of her." Brady paid the doctor for his help, then he and Anna Marie left.

Brady took the sleigh by the mercantile store and picked up some supplies. He also bought three sticks of candy for the little boys left at home. Anna Marie picked out some yarn, thread, and some cotton material to make baby clothes. They also bought big bags of sugar, flour, and oats, maybe enough to last until better spring weather.

They went back to the café and got hot tea for their jug and some food to take along with them on the return trip back home. Now they were ready to go.

❋

It was midafternoon. Vic was outside breaking the ice in the horse trough and throwing the chunks into a bucket. The sun was shining, and its warmth was melting the ice from the rooftop. The water dripped down the already formed icicles and turned them into huge stalactite-looking forms. Vic looked up and recognized Brady's sleigh coming up the lane toward the house. The ground had become quite slippery, and, as he waved his arm enthusiastically, he lost his footing and fell firmly on his rump right into a newly formed, ice-cold water puddle. He began laughing as he struggled to stand up. Brady had stopped the sleigh and immediately went over to help him.

"Let me give you a hand," Brady stated. Vic and Brady were both laughing as he slowly stood up.

"Did you hurt yourself?" Brady asked. "Naw, only my pride," he said as he brushed his soggy britches. "Let's go inside. I'll put on some dry clothes."

"I'll help Anna down from the sleigh, and we'll be right in," he answered. Anna Marie carefully stepped out of the sleigh with Brady's hands firmly holding on to her. They walked up the porch steps and through the front door.

"Good to see you back," Lodema told them. "I'm anxious to hear about your doctor visit. Come, sit down and tell me." Anna Marie sat in a rocker near the fireplace. She placed her shawl on the back of the rocker as her body welcomed the heat from the fire. Lodema watched and waited for the news.

Finally Anna started talking. "See how big I am at about six months along? There's a reason." She paused. "I'm having twins."

Lodema's mouth fell open, and she gasped. "Twins—really? That's wonderful. A double blessing for your family, that's what it is."

"I certainly hope so. I'm going to need some help when it's time to deliver."

"I'm willing to help," Lodema told her. "Remember, I've helped several mothers."

"Vic, did you hear that? Anna and Brady will be having twins."

"No kiddin'. Ain't that somethin'? Congratulations to both of ya," he exclaimed. He reached out and shook Brady's hand.

"Lodema, I would gladly have you for a midwife, but we don't live very close together, and I won't be able to travel much," Anna stated.

"Tell you what; I'll try to see you often to keep up with how you're doing. Maybe we'll both know when your time is close."

"If you want to do this, we'll work something out. You've made me feel better knowing I'll have someone to help me."

Lodema reached and patted Anna's hand. "Don't worry a bit; you'll do fine," she assured her. The four friends had supper together and visited until bedtime. Anna Marie rested well that night, even with all the activity from her unborn babies. The next morning brought another day of warm, sunny skies and melting ice. Muddy puddles replaced the hard, slippery ice. They all knew that they would have another month of winter weather until they would welcome spring.

The next morning, Brady and Anna Marie once again waved good-bye to their now good friends. The air was very cool but not freezing cold as it had been.

❖

By now it was late afternoon when the horse-drawn sleigh approached the home of Foster and Beulah. The couple climbed off of the sleigh and went up to the door. Anna Marie, feeling exhausted from the trip, welcomed a chance to rest. Lorelei met them at the door. She let out a happy squeal and hugged Anna Marie.

"Please, come on inside, and sit a while," she said. Foster and Beulah looked up from their chairs and smiled broadly.

"By golly, look who's here!" Foster stated. "What in the world are you two doing out in this cold, slick day?"

"We have been to the doctor to have Anna Marie checked." He paused and looked lovingly at his wife. "We're going to have twins."

Beulah suddenly appeared to awaken. "Lands sake, is somebody having twins here?" Everybody snickered quietly as they looked at Beulah.

"Do you remember Anna Marie and Brady," he asked her. She replied yes. "They will be having twins later this year. Isn't that nice?" Foster told her.

Lorelei suddenly spoke up with an urgent tone in her voice. "What is wrong with me? I haven't even offered you anything to eat or drink. I'll be right back with some refreshments for you."

As Lorelei was serving tea and sweet rolls, her husband and their boy, Shawn, came inside from working out in the barn. After shaking hands, they all sat together and visited around the kitchen table.

Lorelei remarked, "You're fortunate to have so many babies. Luke and I haven't been able to have any more. We're thankful for our son, Shawn."

Brady joked, "We may be happy to loan you some of ours one day." That remark brought laughter to everyone.

Soon it was time for the Patterson couple to make the last few miles to their home. They bid farewell to their friends with a promise to come back for another visit.

※

Brady helped his wife off of the sleigh and walked her through the kitchen door. The home was buzzing with activity. Pricilla said, "Boys, look who came home!" The boys squealed and ran full speed toward their mother and father. Brady quickly grabbed them by their arms.

"Whoa, easy, fellows," Brady told them. "Let's let your mother sit down so she can hug you good." Anna Marie went over and sat in her rocker. She leaned over and gave Pat and Timmy a hug and a quick kiss on the cheek.

"I missed you two," Anna told her boys. "I'm home, and I'll be here for a long time."

Chapter 15

IT HAD STARTED RAINING THE FIRST PART OF MARCH, and it wouldn't let off. It was either raining or cloudy every day for three weeks. The ground had soaked up all the moisture it could possibly hold, which created water puddles in low places, everywhere a man or animal placed a foot. Brady sloshed around on the saturated earth day after dreary day, getting himself, his boots, and his jackets muddy. That fact alone made extra work for Anna Marie, especially regarding laundry. Keeping the clothes clean for two little boys who crawled around on the floors as much as they walked on them created enough dirt. When you add in the mud and dirty water that dripped off of Brady's boots, she was constantly wiping on the floor with her cleaning rags.

One day Anna had a bright idea—teach the little boys how to wipe up the floor. She would make a game out of it. She had Pat and Timmy come over to her where she sat a lot of the time, in her rocking chair.

"Boys, I want to play a game with you. Here are two cleaning rags." She held them up. "Whenever your daddy comes in for his meal, you both hurry to the kitchen door. Then when he hangs up his jacket and sits down in his chair, you both race to see who can clean up the floor first. Do you understand?"

They both agreed. She smiled and gave each boy a rag and a hug. The boys went about their playing for a while, and then their father entered the door. They both looked at their mother, and she smiled and nodded to them. They quickly grabbed their rags and watched him hang his jacket and walk to his chair. The boys immediately went to work, both giggling, and wiped up the floor from the door to where their daddy's feet rested on the floor. They looked up at him with a glowing look on their faces.

"Hey, boys, you did a fine job of wiping the floor," he complimented.

"We're playing a game," Pat announced, "to see who could wipe the floor the fastest."

Anna Marie was dipping food on the plates and setting them on the table. "Who won the game?" Brady asked her.

"They were both so fast I think it was a tie. They'll have to try again at suppertime, don't you think, Papa?"

"That's a good idea. You boys play that game again at suppertime. I'll watch you very carefully," their Papa said.

"Okay," Pat replied.

Anna Marie and Brady looked at each other with a knowing smile. She knew he understood all about the game. They all sat together and ate their meal.

☀

Finally, the last week of March came. Winter was over. Spring-like sunshine brought southerly winds, which, thankfully, began drying the land. To Anna Marie, it felt good to be outside and feel the warm breeze blowing gently against her face. As the clouds moved away, both Anna Marie and Brady felt their spirits lift, and both were happier. Anna Marie was in an especially good humor because their new friends, Vic and Lodema, were coming for a short visit tomorrow. She had invited Pricilla and Jeremiah to come over and have supper with them. She was looking forward with great anticipation to having other women to talk with.

Brady had decided to work on making the barn lot bigger so he could buy more milk cows as well as two beef calves for food. He knew it would take a lot of work, but he had to figure out a way to increase his earnings. He would crop most of his land and leave room for his livestock. Frank came over to help him set posts for the rail fence. They made good headway on the project that morning. After lunch, the men decided to move some fence posts, which had been piled along the edge of the timber, and bring them up beside the small shed. They took the horse and wagon down to the pile, loaded several posts and went back to the fence site. Brady unhitched his horse and put him back inside the barn and returned to the wagon.

Frank jumped onto the wagon and began rolling the posts off toward the ground. Brady stood alongside the wagon and watched as the large logs fell. Frank slipped and fell backward. The impact of his fall caused the remaining logs to jar loose and roll speedily toward Brady. By the time Brady realized the possibility of danger, the logs were plummeting toward him and hit his legs and feet, knocking him down with such force that searing pain traveled from his ankles up to his hips.

Anna Marie and Pat had stepped outside while Timmy was having a nap. They both saw the logs roll off of the wagon and knock Brady to the ground. He wasn't moving.

Frank was the first to get to Brady. "Hey buddy, are you all right?" Brady moaned. Frank began pulling the heavy logs off of him.

Anna Marie and Pat arrived beside the two men. Brady looked up into Anna Marie's eyes. She saw the pain on his face. "Did you break your legs?" she asked him.

"I can't say for sure. My legs feel like they're on fire."

Once Frank had removed the remaining logs off of Brady's body, he said, "Can you move your feet or legs?"

Brady groaned as he tried. Frank took a hold of his boots and said, "See if you can wiggle your feet." Frank felt some motion. He ran his hands along Brady's legs, feeling for a break. He didn't feel any.

"Do you think you could get up off the ground?" Frank asked him.

"Help me to sit up first," Brady replied. Frank took a hold of his hands and helped support Brady as he pulled himself to a sitting position. "Whew!" Brady whispered.

"Let's get you inside the house," Anna Marie told him.

With Frank on one side and Anna on the other, Brady managed to make it inside their home and sat down in a rocker. Tears welled up in Pat's eyes as he went over and stood beside his papa.

"I think we better take his boots off and check his ankles and feet," Anna Marie suggested.

"Yeah, good idea," Brady agreed. Frank knelt down, gently pulled his boots off, and ran his hands over both legs. Of course, Frank wasn't a doctor, but he didn't think there were any broken bones.

"My friend, you must have the luck of the Irish with you today. You'll be bruised and sore but nothing more." Frank gave him a friendly pat on his shoulder.

"Thanks for your help. Guess our work on a fence will have to wait awhile," Brady said. The two men shook hands, and Frank left, saying, "I'll come back later and milk your cow and do your chores." Anna Marie told Frank how thankful she was for his help.

As soon as Frank went home, he told Pricilla and Jeremiah what had happened. Jeremiah agreed to go with Frank to the Patterson farm and help as long as Brady was laid up. Pricilla knew Anna Marie and Brady were having company the next day, so she decided to go early with the men so she could be helpful.

As the day moved along, Anna Marie noticed that Brady's legs were swelling. She said, "Brady, we have to get your legs up!" She quickly put a pillow on one of their kitchen chairs and helped him lift his legs upon it.

"There now, that should help," Anna Marie told him.

Brady hardly slept that night because of the throbbing pain in his legs. By morning, dark bruises covered both legs from his thighs all the way down to his toes. Anna lightly massaged both legs before breakfast; she didn't know what else to do for him.

Frank, Jeremiah, Pricilla, and Joey all came over in time to help do the morning chores. Joey began playing with Pat and Timmy. Pricilla, also large with child, did what she could to help Anna Marie. Her baby was due to arrive three to four weeks before Anna Marie was expecting her twins. The two women chuckled at each other as they clumsily worked around the kitchen together. Pricilla was aware that two visitors would arrive today sometime. She insisted that she would make the cake and Anna Marie could concentrate on the rest of the meal.

The hours flew by. The women worked away making food and caring for the boys. At one point in the afternoon, Pricilla put the children down for a nap while Anna Marie rested in her rocker. About three o'clock that afternoon, Jeremiah saw a horse and buggy approaching the Patterson home. Vic and Lodema saw Jeremiah and waved at him, thinking that it was Brady. Jeremiah walked toward the halted buggy.

"I'm Jeremiah, friends of Brady and Anna Marie. You must be Vic and Lodema. Welcome." He stepped to help Lodema off of the buggy. He continued, "Brady and Anna Marie are both inside. Brady had an accident, and he's sorta laid up for now. "Lodema, you can go on inside while Vic and I take care of the horse and buggy."

Lodema carried her valise, tapped lightly on the door, and then went inside. Anna Marie hadn't noticed that she and Vic had arrived. She had a surprised look on her face, which quickly broke into a big smile.

"Lodema, I'm so glad to see you. I hope you had a good trip," Anna Marie said.

"I'm happy to see you too," she replied. She then noticed Brady sitting with his legs elevated. "What happened to you?" she asked.

"I was standing in the wrong place when we were unloading some posts. They rolled off the wagon and landed on me! Thank goodness I didn't break any bones," he stated. About that time, Jeremiah and Vic came into the house. Vic immediately looked at Brady, went over and shook his hand. Jeremiah had already related to Vic what had happened.

"Hello, my friend. I see you're inside resting while your neighbor does your work," Vic said laughingly. "I'd say you're a lucky fellow."

"Yep, I agree. The Good Lord was lookin' out for me. Good to see you here. You folks sit down and make yourselves at home.

The rest of the afternoon passed as they all visited and shared their lives with many stories. They enjoyed the food that had been prepared earlier. The men got busy doing the chores while the women cleaned up the kitchen. At sundown, Frank, Jeremiah, and Pricilla, with Joey, left for their home. The same ritual continued for the next several days while Brady was unable to do his work.

During those few days, Anna Marie and Pricilla became close friends with Lodema. She reminded them of Lucy Benning, who lived back in Reed's Crossing, Kentucky. (Lucy had helped deliver Anna Marie's two boys.) Lodema agreed to be the midwife for both of the women, if possible.

❁

March 31. Vic and Lodema were leaving tomorrow if the weather stayed good for travel. Vic was known to be a trickster by those who knew him. Since tomorrow was April Fool's Day, Vic was hatching a plan to trick somebody. He had thought about it into the afternoon. Then the opportunity presented itself. He came upon a grass snake sunning itself on the south side of the animal shed. The snake appeared sluggish, probably because it had just came out of hibernation. Vic grabbed the snake by the tail and, quick as a wink, snapped the snake like a bullwhip, which broke its neck. The snake was dead. Vic looked around and found an old cloth sack, and he dropped the slithery carcass inside. He chuckled to himself as he anticipated Brady's reaction to the prank he was planning.

April 1 arrived. Everyone sat at the table waiting for the men to return to the kitchen when the chores were finished. Knowing that Vic and Lodema were to leave today, Pricilla and Joey had come along with Frank and Jeremiah to bid them good-bye. They all were enjoying a lively conversation as they sipped their coffee. The three little boys sat on the floor and played with their toys, squealing and laughing together.

At last Frank and Jeremiah opened the door and came inside. They hung their coats on the hooks beside the door and went to get a cup of tea.

"Where's Vic?" Brady asked.

"I'm not sure. He said he had to go get something," Jeremiah answered.

"What could it be? I'm ready to eat, how about you men?" Brady asked.

About that time Vic entered carrying the cloth bag. His wife, Lodema said, "Land's sake, *where* have you been?"

"I've got something in here for Brady and Anna Marie for their supper tonight." He made a grand gesture as he handed the sack to Brady.

"You didn't have to do this," Brady remarked. Vic could hardly keep from bursting out into a huge laugh.

Brady opened the bag and stuck his hand inside. As soon as he felt the scaly serpent, he knew exactly what it was. He let out a big yelp and threw the bag, with the dead snake spilling out across the kitchen floor. The women jumped and screamed with him. Vic broke into uncontrollable laughter, as did Frank and Jeremiah. The little boys stopped their play and quickly went to see what the fuss was all about.

Lodema grabbed Vic's arm and said, "You ornery thing, why did you do that?"

Vic, still enjoying his joke, said to Brady, "April fool!"

"You should be ashamed," Lodema scolded, and then she giggled, with Anna Marie and Pricilla joining in the laughter. Brady, still stunned from the prank, finally looked up and smiled broadly.

Vic went over and picked the snake up and put it back into the bag. "You'll not likely forget this day for a long time," he said to Brady as he patted him on the shoulder.

"You're so right," Brady said. "Remember this. Always be ready because what goes around comes back around." Vic rolled his eyes and shrugged his shoulders as if to say, "So what?"

✷

As Vic and Lodema prepared to start their trip back home, Anna Marie said, "When will we see you again?"

"Since spring has finally arrived, it will be easier to travel now," Lodema stated. She looked at Vic hopefully and said, "We'll try to come back toward the end of this month."

Frank, Jeremiah, Pricilla, and Joey made a special effort to be there to bid the new friends a safe journey. "We've enjoyed meeting you both," Jeremiah told them. "We'll look forward to seeing you again."

Pat had bonded with Lodema so much that when he heard she was leaving, he ran to her, grabbed her hand, and said "Dema, Dema, don't leave." She bent over, picked him up and gave him a good squeeze. The other little boys ran up to Vic and Lodema and hugged them enthusiastically. .

Vic told them, "You boys mind your ma and papa."

"We will," the boys chorused together.

Pricilla handed Lodema a bag of food for their travel, and the two hugged. Frank and Jeremiah shook hands with Vic. Brady had hobbled to the door. "Remember, I owe you one!" he said as he waved when they climbed into their buggy and started down the lane.

Vic laughed and said, "You can try." He laughed as he snapped the reins.

Chapter 16

IT WAS APRIL, THE FIRST SUNDAY AFTER EASTER
Sunday. Brady had recovered from his accident and was able to do his work. It was a glorious, wonderful day outside, which persuaded Anna Marie to take Pat and Timmy for a walk in the warm, sunshiny air. The grasses in the yards and pastures were like green velvet. Wild violets had sprung up in a sunny spot near the water trough. Several robins hopped around pecking at the grass checking for worms. Wrens busied themselves carrying dry grasses and small twigs to nests located on the branches of the tree beside the cattle fence. Anna Marie was so filled with joy and happiness that she could hardly contain herself. She had accepted that this truly was the home for her and her family.

Word had been passed around to all the families in the surrounding area that all the residents and their families would meet. The order of business would be to erect a building that would serve both as a place of worship and a schoolhouse. Weather permitting, the meeting and carry-in meal would be held today in the yard of Foster and Beulah Browning. About eight families were expected to attend, a total of nearly sixteen adults and thirty-five children.

Following a bountiful meal, the children entertained themselves by playing hide-and-seek while the adults proceeded to plan the future of their community. The property across the road was owned by Morgan and Eileen Donahue. They had lived there since they were married in 1820. They were willing to donate one acre for the building site. The men agreed that each family would try to provide several logs so that the construction of the building would begin by June 1.

Several of the women had been sitting together visiting and catching up with their family news. Beulah, who seldom talked, sat quietly and listened to the conversations. She smiled and laughed with the women and their stories. After the men had made their decisions concerning the building, the ladies said their good-byes and began gathering their children. Beulah stood up and started toward the front door of the house. She went outside and began walking at a slow pace, lost her balance, and fell face-first. She hit her forehead on the edge of the front porch and rolled on her side. She wasn't noticed at first as most of the people were getting ready to leave.

Pat called out, "Mama, look. She fell down."

Anna Marie quickly turned and saw Beulah lying on the ground. "Oh, dear Lord!" she yelled out. "It's Beulah." Foster and several others ran over to see about her.

"Beulah, sweetheart, open your eyes. Look at me," Foster called out. He squatted down and cradled her in his arms. She had blood pouring from her forehead and running across her face. Tears began to flow from his eyes as he held her unresponsive body. Frank checked for her pulse, but he couldn't feel any. Frank looked into Foster's eyes and slowly shook his head no. By this time, several people had formed a half circle close to Foster and Beulah. Quietness filled the air over the group as Anna Marie, Pricilla, and many others began to weep.

Luke and Lorelei came upon the scene. Lorelei said softly, "Foster, let the men carry her into the house. We can't leave her outside." Foster nodded his head in agreement, and several of the men managed to lift her up and carry her into the house. Lorelei led the men to the spare bed, where they carefully put her down. Luke walked with Foster, helping him with his balance as they went inside. He sat bent over in his favorite chair, elbows on his knees, with his head in his hands. Foster's tears poured down his cheeks, and long sobs came from deep inside as he struggled with the loss of his longtime companion. Luke, Brady, and Frank quietly sat with Foster. Lorelei, Pricilla, and Anna Marie together used warm water to clean the blood from Beulah's face and then covered her. Luke and Lorelei's son, Shawn, helped out by playing with the small boys.

Time passed by slowly. At last, Foster calmed down and sat up in his chair. "Well, I have some decisions to make," he spoke. "I need to arrange her funeral. Boys, there should be enough cut boards out in the barn for a box to bury her in. I refuse to just wrap her in a blanket and stick her in the ground."

Frank said, "We'll all help."

There was a rapping on the door. It was Morgan and Eileen Donahue. Frank invited them inside, and they walked over to Foster's side.

Eileen told Foster, "We're so sorry for your loss. Morgan has something to tell you."

"Friend, if you want, you can bury Beulah next to the acre for the church and school. We need to start a cemetery for our community someplace. It may as well be there," Morgan offered.

Tears once again filled Foster's eyes. He shook Morgan's hand and simply said, "Thank you."

As evening approached, Brady said, "Anna Marie, the boys and I need to go home. I'll come back over in the morning after chores to help you." He shook Foster's hand.

"Same goes for me," Jeremiah said. "I'll come with Brady." He gave Foster a pat on the back as did Frank, and they all departed for the day.

❂

It was a labor of love but one of the most difficult tasks the men ever did in their lives. Foster and Luke were already in the barn sorting through the boards when Frank, Jeremiah, and Brady arrived. There wasn't much talking between the men. The only sounds were those of boards clunking and hammers tapping that floated from the working area near the barn into the area that Foster calls home.

Morgan and Eileen came over before noon. Eileen took a freshly baked cake inside the house while Morgan went to see Foster working nearby. "Mornin' fellas," Morgan greeted. "How're you getting along there?"

Foster looked straight at him and said, "We're getting along all right. We should have a proper box for Beulah finished today. We're workin' slow and careful so it'll be tight."

"I came to have you go with me to pick out your wife's final resting place. Me and my children will gladly dig it for you if you'd like," Morgan told him.

"All right, I'll go now," Foster agreed. The two men slowly walked across the yard and the dirt road onto the Donahue property. Morgan directed Foster upon a rise in the meadow close to a large hickory tree. They stood quietly there together. Foster had to grit his jaw together to keep his grief at bay. He gasped as a flood of tears ran down his face, knowing his decision was so final. "Yes, this will be the perfect place for her. It'll give great joy to her and me both. If I should breathe my last during your life, it would please me to be laid close beside her."

Morgan gave him a brotherly hug and said, "It will be so." The two men returned back across the road. Foster told all the men, "Come inside the house, and we'll eat and rest together awhile."

Lorelei had made a fresh pot of coffee, which the men enjoyed while she dipped up the bowls of vegetable hash she had made. A plate of cornbread and a jar of honey had been placed in the center of the table. Lorelei was glad to have Eileen there with her for companionship. After the meal, Eileen cut pieces of cake and served everyone. The mood in the kitchen seemed nearly normal—then Foster spoke.

"We will have the funeral tomorrow morning at ten o'clock here in the yard. I need for someone to go around and notify our friends. Lorelei, you and Eileen can go through Beulah's clothes and dress her up proper, if you will." Both women nodded in agreement.

Foster turned his head and slowly looked at each one at the table. Time halted, and then he spoke as if an edict had been issued. "That's settled. Now, let's get back to our job at hand."

❋

Tuesday 10:00 a.m. All the friends and neighbors of Foster and Beulah were gathered on the lawn. The box was placed on the back of a wagon, and a quilt that Beulah had made lined the box. Beulah, dressed in her best, lay in it, a pillow under her head. A bouquet of fresh flowers had been placed beside her body. Foster, Lorelei, Anna Marie, Pricilla, and Eileen all sat on chairs in front of the wagon while the rest stood in a semicircle around behind. Morgan stood in front of the group with a Bible in his large, rough hands. Morgan was at least six feet tall. He had a red complexion, and his hair, also red with gray streaks, came down to his collar, thick and bushy. He started to speak words of compassion to those who came to mourn the passing of their friend. He read a psalm from the Bible, related its teachings, and told how Beulah had lived a good, faithful life.

Morgan finally spoke as if a poetic spirit had come from within. "Beulah will be on the rise of the hill beside this hickory tree where she will have the cool shade of summer and protection from the cold wind of winter. She'll hear the songs of the birds each spring, and, as they nest and raise their babies, she'll watch them as they learn to fly in the summer. When summer passes and frost fills the air, the hickory nuts will drop, and the squirrels will scurry around as they gather their winter store. Colored leaves will fall gently around her, warming the earth, preserving everything until the next cycle of life."

It went through Anna Marie's mind that if you couldn't see Morgan and could only hear him speak, you wouldn't believe such gentleness and kindness would come from this ruddy-looking man. When the eulogy ended, he went over to Foster, helped him up, and escorted him for a last look at his departed wife. All the others followed in a line for a final look at their friend.

Frank and Jeremiah climbed up into the wagon, nailed the cover on the box, and then gently flicked the reins on the two horses' backs. They drove it over to the prepared grave site as the others walked behind. It took six men to remove the box from the wagon and lower it into the grave. Foster and several in the group let go of their emotions and cried openly. Morgan repeated to the group about what a wonderful resting place this would be for Beulah. They all nodded in agreement.

Brady and Luke stood on each side of Foster. "Let us walk you over to your home now," Luke told him. Foster agreed. All of the mourners accompanied them back across the road as the others scooped dirt over the box.

Several of Foster and Beulah's friends had brought food. They ate and shared quiet conversations. Many stayed into the afternoon to help console him. One by one they began to leave for their own homes and family needs. By late afternoon, the only people left were Luke, Lorelei, and Shawn. They sat on the porch facing the hill where Beulah was laid and watched as daylight dimmed, and night began to fall.

Foster turned to Luke and Lorelei and said, "You can stay here with me as long as you would like. You can learn my trade, and some day it will be yours. You're like family to me."

They looked at each other, smiled, and nodded. "That's a generous offer. We'll be glad to stay. Thank you," Luke told him. Lorelei went inside and brought out fresh hot tea for everyone. Shawn lit a lantern and hung it on the peg by the door. A few stars began twinkling in the night sky as the croaking of the bullfrogs from a nearby pond resounded through the air. The four sipped their tea, acutely aware of the void they were feeling.

☀

Foster began to heal from his loss as the last two weeks of April passed by. Luke and Shawn had used spades to dig up the garden spot. They managed to plant corn and green bean seeds and hilled up the ground for Irish potatoes. They would have to turn over more sod later to plant the squash seeds they had saved from last year. Foster had been working on building a fancy buggy that would seat two in front and two in the back. He was having difficulty with the boards fitting well together and achieving the smooth quality that he wanted. Luke and Shawn walked over beside him and sat down in the shade to cool off. Foster was mumbling to himself.

"Are you having problems, friend?" Luke asked.

"I can't get these gosh-darned planks to fit right," he replied. "There's got to be an easier way to do this job."

About that time Frank rode up and dismounted. "Afternoon," he greeted. "What's goin' on these days?"

"Foster seems to be having a problem cutting the boards to fit right on his new buggy," Luke stated.

"Have you ever heard of a saw mill? Last time I went for supplies, a fellow in the mercantile was telling that there's one over in Bloomington. It's built over beside a stream. They use the water to turn a wheel, which powers the machine that turns the blade. They can saw a bunch of logs in a day's time. Maybe you should go look at it," Frank suggested.

Luke spoke up. "Why don't you and I both go look at it? If we could figure out a place to put one, we could have our own sawmill."

"You know, I've come to realize that I can't make a living on my small farm. The stream that runs down beside my place might have enough flowing water power to support a mill wheel," Frank replied.

"Well, when do you think we could go see about it?" Luke asked.

"Most anytime suits me."

"Let's go day after tomorrow?"

"That would probably work all right," Frank answered. "Let's meet after breakfast at the crossroads west of here a couple miles."

"I'll be there. Guess I better tell Lorelei," he said as he shook his head and laughed.

Foster sat with his head a little cocked with a curious look on his face as he listened to the conversation. When it ended he spoke up with an edge on his voice and said, "Now that you boys have worked out what you plan to do in two days, how about helping me? I can't wait until your sawmill is up and running to finish this buggy."

The unforeseen outbreak of annoyance startled both Luke and Frank—then they started laughing. They laughed uncontrollably, bent over, and sat on the ground. They both pointed toward Foster as they laughed more. Foster realized how he had spoken to the men. He threw his hammer to the ground and knelt down as the contagious laughter lassoed him into its spell. At last, all three regained control of themselves.

"If you really want help from two experienced woodworkers, it will cost you two large cups of coffee with milk with the possibility of a fresh cookie. That's the deal," Frank said seriously.

"Okay, you got it," Foster meekly replied, as if two crooks were threatening. He knew differently.

Using wood planes and files, Luke and Frank worked at shaping the wooden planks to give them a better fit on the buggy floor. It took time, but the job was accomplished. Foster shook the hands of both men, laughed, and said, "Come on, it's time to fulfill the charges you required." The men exchanged pats on their backs and walked toward the house.

❋

Frank and Luke went to look for the saw mill in Bloomington located several miles east. They asked directions from a couple and managed to find it. They talked with the men who worked there and spent hours watching, even helping part of the time. They were impressed with how well it worked. Right then and there they decided that they wanted to have their own sawmill on Frank's farm. They knew when their mill began working it would change the future for all the community.

❋

May 14. Brady and Anna Marie were outside planting their spring garden when they saw Jeremiah ride up and hastily dismount his horse. He hurried over to them.

"What is it?" Brady asked.

"It's Pricilla. She's not feeling well. I don't know—she might be having her baby," he answered nervously.

"You go on back home and don't worry; I'll go get you some help." Brady saddled his horse and stated, "I'll ride over to Morgan and Eileen's place and see if she'll come back and help Pricilla. There's no time to ride to get Lodema to help."

Anna Marie told Brady, "I'll finish covering these seeds and then go back inside the house." Brady mounted up and rode off. Anna Marie was concerned and restless about Pricilla. She knew that she was too big and awkward with her own pregnancy to try to hitch up the horse and buggy to go see her, so she went inside and sat in her rocker. Pat and Timmy were playing on the floor with empty thread spools, a small ball of yarn, and some flat pieces of wood. The boys were rolling the spools over the floor across a line of yarn, a sort of race game they had invented. They giggled happily as they played. Time flowed slowly, like a winter icicle melting drop by drop.

Anna Marie didn't realize that she had fallen asleep. When Brady entered the house, the boys cried out "Daddy, daddy!" It startled her so that she jumped, and the rocking chair jerked with her.

"I'm so glad that you're home," she told him. "How's Pricilla?"

"She's definitely having her baby. It's too early to say, but I believe she's in good hands. How are you feeling?" he asked.

"I'm a little tired after working in the garden, but I'm all right." Anna Marie rose from the rocker, let out a holler, and grabbed her belly. She slid down on the floor. Brady rushed over to her. "Anna, sweetheart, what's wrong?" Pat and Timmy stopped their playing because their full attention was on what had just happened.

"A sharp pain hit my stomach. Take me to the bed; I need to lie down." Brady steadied her as she walked, crouched over, into the bedroom. He stayed a few minutes with her and then said, "I need to go milk the cow. I won't be long. If you need me, send Pat to the barn." She nodded her head.

Brady had uneasy feelings about what may be happening. He nearly ran as he hurried to complete the evening chores. He started back toward the house when the wind gusted and nearly threw him off balance. He hadn't noticed that clouds had rolled in overhead and covered the sky. As he made it to the kitchen door, rain pelted down.

☀

Both Morgan and Eileen had gone to help Pricilla. Morgan watched over Joey and played games with him. Pricilla, now in full labor, was moaning loudly.

Morgan spoke to Jeremiah, "Do you think it would be better for Joey if I took him for a horse ride? He doesn't need to worry about his mother."

"That's a very good idea, go ahead." Morgan decided to take Joey over to the Patterson place. As he started toward the Patterson farm, he noticed the sky had become cloudy, and the breeze had picked up. They spotted turtles crossing the road in front of them. "Look Joey, there's two turtles crossing the road. They must be looking for some water to swim in." Joey giggled. About that time a few drops of rain fell on their faces.

"We better hurry over to Pat and Timmy's place," Morgan said. He gave a quick kick to the horse, and off they galloped. He saw Brady rush inside the house as the rain began to pour down. Morgan guided the horse to shelter, grabbed Joey, and then ran toward the house. Morgan didn't bother to knock, and both were soaked by the time they were inside. Brady turned and saw who it was.

"It must be important for you to come over in the rain," Brady said to him.

"No, not really," Morgan replied. "Joey's mother was having hard labor, and I thought it best to get Joey out of the house."

"I agree, but I'm not sure it will be any better here," he stated.

145

"Why?"

"I think Anna Marie may be in labor also. Her babies may be coming early."

"Now isn't that something?" Morgan stated.

Pat, Timmy, and Joey played the race game with the old spools for a long time. Brady paced back and forth from the bedroom to the kitchen where Morgan sat. The two men drank coffee and visited. Anna Marie's labor was intensifying. After a couple hours, Brady said, "I hate to ask you to leave, but would you go back and see how Pricilla is doing? We may need your wife here after a while."

"Sure. I'll get Joey. He's probably ready to go home by now. I'll send Frank over here to be with you. This is quite a predicament isn't it?"

"I can't believe it myself. Anna Marie wasn't due to give birth for about three weeks. I guess babies come when they're ready," Brady said as he rubbed his forehead.

The men looked outside to check the weather and saw that the rain had moved on, leaving cool air and water puddles behind. After Morgan and Joey left, Anna Marie's labor pains eased up. She sat up in bed. All the family drank a glass of milk and ate bread and honey together in the bedroom. Brady decided that would have to be their evening meal.

It was now about nine o'clock in the evening. Anna Marie rested, having only twinges of pain. Frank rode up, knocked on the door, and went inside.

"What's the news from Jeremiah?" Brady asked.

"Pricilla just gave birth to a healthy baby girl. "She and the baby are doing all right. How's Anna Marie?"

"She's resting but I'm sure that the babies are on their way soon." Anna Marie let out a yell. It startled both men. Brady went to her.

"Anna, sweetheart, how are you?"

"You need to get me some help as soon as possible." Frank heard what she said.

"I'll go get Eileen right now." With that, he hurried out of the door.

Frank jumped on his horse and urged it to a full gallop. The night was quite dark. The floating clouds only allowed glimpses of the moon and stars. Frank's senses were at least four times more alert. The night noises of owls and tree frogs seemed amplified when they reached his ears. What seemed like miles of riding were actually minutes by the time he arrived back at Frank's cabin. He quickly dismounted and ran inside the house.

"How's Pricilla and her baby?" he asked breathlessly.

"They're both going to be just fine," Eileen replied.

"That's real good because you're needed at the Patterson home. Brady and Anna Marie think that her babies are coming earlier than expected. She's having irregular labor pains."

Jeremiah said, "Who woulda thought that both women would have their babies on almost the same day?"

Frank chuckled and said, "I'd say it was sympathy pains because Pricilla was married to you!"

"Really? And I thought you were my friend!" Jeremiah retorted, and then laughed with him. "At least I found a woman who wanted to be with me. What's your excuse?"

"All right, you got me back. I'll find the right gal soon enough."

Morgan's eyes checked Eileen's. "I'll take Eileen over to help Anna Marie. She needs you both instead of me hanging around. Maybe I can help Brady through the night."

"Sure, that's all right. Let us know how things are in the morning," Jeremiah told him. Eileen wrapped a shawl around herself, and the two left in their buggy. It didn't take long, and they were at Brady's kitchen door. They rapped a few light taps and went inside. It was quiet. Evidently the two little boys were asleep, so they crept to the bedroom door. Brady was sitting in a rocking chair, resting with his eyes closed; it had been a tiring day. Anna Marie glanced at the two from her bed, and Eileen went to her side.

"How are you doing?" Eileen asked with a subdued voice.

"This is so different. I have pains for a while, but then they stop. I hope my babies are all right," Anna Marie told her.

147

"I'm sure they are okay. I'll stay with you and help you through this." Eileen proceeded to gather towels and washcloths. She had Morgan bring water into the bedroom. Brady roused with the activity taking place, got up, and went to the kitchen.

Morgan turned to Brady and said, "Looks like we'll have a long night here together. Let's sit and talk. Do you have any coffee?"

"Sure thing, I'll fix us a fresh pot. Come over to the table. Tell me some things about your life," Brady suggested.

When the coffee had perked, Morgan added some milk, took a couple swallows, and then he began to tell about when he was growing up.

"I had this friend who was nicknamed Buck. We were both about fifteen years old. He was smaller than me but the way he was put together, he was wound up like an eight-day clock that never ran down. I don't know how his name came about unless he was bucked off of a horse when he was young. He had a knot on the back of his head where his hair grew around and stuck up with what we called a rooster tail. His mother would call out, 'Bucky, you be careful tonight and don't get into trouble.' 'Aw, Maw, I won't,' he'd tell her."

Morgan began to laugh. "I remember one evening Buck and I decided to go fishing and stay out all night and sleep beside a campfire on the riverbank. I had a good-sized knife that I kept in a shield that hung from my belt. Buck carried a smaller, sharper knife, which he could use to clean a fish for our meal. What fish we didn't eat we strung twine through their mouths and gills, and then put them into the shallow part of the water. I had gathered some dry wood and started the fire. I used my knife to sharpen the sticks, which we stuck through the fish to hold over the fire. Buck and I thought we were very grown-up.

"After we ate, we sat close to the campfire, talked, and told stories. We planned to stay up late, but our eyes grew heavy. We both crawled into our bedrolls laid out close to the campfire. The fire snapped and crackled as the flames lapped on the dry twigs. I could hear the water splashing on the riverbank and the bullfrogs croaking back and forth at each other. Sleep overtook both Buck and me.

"Sometime during the night, I woke up and felt something near my face. My eyes popped open, and I was star'n' right into another pair of big, dark eyes. It was a raccoon. He jerked his head back, hissed, and reared back on his hind legs. I sat up so fast that it ran, and I hollered, 'Buck, wake up!'

"Buck jumped and yelled at the same time: 'What the heck!' Those feisty creatures scattered in every direction. We quickly looked around our camp area and realized they had been feasting on our catch of fish. Pieces of fish had been torn, chewed, and spit out all around us. Gnats, mosquitoes and big, black flies the size of your thumb—buzzing and biting all over our camping area. What could we do? There's no way we could go back to sleep that night.

"Yep, we rolled up our blankets and collected our gear. We slowly walked back home. It was a long time before we were brave enough to go fishing by the river again."

"That's a good one," Brady told him. "Most of us know what it's like when we fish at the river." The men chuckled together.

The men continued to visit quietly. There were occasional moans and squeals that came from the bedroom that would cause the men to turn their attention toward that direction.

Brady put a loaf of bread on the cutting board in the center of the table. He walked over to the bedroom door to check on Anna Marie. He made eye contact with Eileen and asked, "How's my wife?"

"She's doing all right," Eileen responded.

He walked over to Anna's bedside, held her hand, and said, "How's my sweetheart?" Anna smiled and replied, "I'll be all right." He kissed her gently.

"Looks like this will be a very long night," Eileen said.

"Let's go into the kitchen," Brady told her.

She went into the kitchen, had a cup of hot tea, and ate bread, butter, and honey with Morgan and Brady. It was near midnight, and the three were beginning to wear down as they waited for Anna Marie to give birth.

Morgan sat in the big rocking chair, laid his head back, and fell asleep right away. Eileen and Brady went into the bedroom together to be with Anna Marie. Suddenly Anna Marie grabbed Brady's arm and squeezed hard as she let out a loud yell. "Oh Lord!" she exclaimed.

"Try to relax," Eileen told her. "Your babies will come soon. Brady, you best go in with Morgan. I'll call if we need you."

Two more hours passed by, interspersed with sounds from Anna Marie. Brady wanted to stay awake, but his eyelids became heavier and heavier until, finally, he succumbed to sleep. He had stretched out on the rug in front of the fireplace, his head resting on his folded jacket.

Glimpses of the morning sun appeared through the trees on the horizon. The twittering of awakening birds could be heard inside the house. Anna Marie was near to time to deliver her babies. "Oh Lord, help me!" she called out. Then, a moan turned to a shriek. Brady ran to the bedroom door.

"Anna, are you all right?" He heard Eileen talking.

Eileen told her, "This is the time—push. Yes, that's right, push."

Anna let out a fierce yell as the first baby made its appearance in the world. Eileen called out, "Brady, come to the bedroom and bring a cloth and warm water in the wash pan." Needless to say, both men came to life immediately. Brady was so excited that he nearly dropped the pan of water as he hurried into the bedroom. He heard a smack and a newborn baby cry.

Eileen had cut the umbilical cord with a pair of scissors and handed Brady the baby. "Now, you wash this precious baby girl off and tie this cord, then wrap her up in a towel," she instructed. Anna Marie was still in labor. She let out another chilling scream and the second baby made its appearance. Another smack and cry sounded out.

"Morgan, as soon as I cut her cord, you take this second baby girl and clean her up just like I told Brady," Eileen said. "I'll take care of Anna Marie. She's very tired now. Those little girls will want to be fed in two or three hours; meanwhile, you fellows take care of them while their mama rests."

"Look what you got, two beautiful baby girls! That's something special," Morgan told Brady. They took the babies into the front room, carefully holding the precious newborns. Both Brady and Morgan rocked slowly as they looked lovingly at the tiny bundle in each of their arms. Eileen lay down on the bed beside Anna Marie, and they both slept.

As Eileen predicted, both babies started crying to be fed after two hours. Anna Marie sat up in bed as milk began to fill her breasts. Eileen placed pillows behind her back and went to have the two men bring the newborns in for their first feeding. Brady stayed in the bedroom with his new family. Morgan and Eileen went to the kitchen to make breakfast. By afternoon, Brady and Anna Marie were discussing what to name the twins.

Anna said, "You know how I've always loved flowers, so I would like to give the girls flower names."

"That's all right with me. What do you have in mind?"

"There are several choices: rose, daisy, violet, pansy, lily, or lilac, to name a few."

"I like Lilly and Rose," Brady stated. "Let's figure out what would be the best." By suppertime they came up with the names. They didn't care for Lilac Anne so they picked Lilly Anne and the other would be named Lila Rose.

Anna Marie looked lovingly at her new babies and said, "Now I have two beautiful flowers living right here with me."

Brady said, "Yes, and I have three beautiful ladies living with me." He leaned over and kissed his wife and stroked the faces of his new daughters, Lilly and Lila.

Eileen stayed to help for several more days, and Morgan returned home to care for his place. Frank and Jeremiah came over to help Brady and see about Anna Marie and the twins nearly every day. Conversation revealed that Pricilla and their baby girl, which they had named Jennifer, were both doing well. Jeremiah laughed and said, "We're already calling her Jenny."

☀

So it was that the next month was quite busy. Morgan and Eileen came often to help Brady and Anna Marie. The babies were doing well but caring for the two boys and the twins were already taking a toll on their parents.

"Eileen, I need your help. I don't have enough milk for the babies. What should I do?" Anna Marie asked.

"You can use cow's milk, but you must first heat it to a low boil, take it off the stove, and let it cool. You then skim off the thick milk scum that formed on the surface because a little baby can't digest it. When you need to use the milk you just warm it in a cup."

"I can do that!" Anna replied. "Eileen, you know so much and have been a great help to me. Since my mother isn't here, you are the next best thing." The two women shared a hug and a smile.

Chapter 17

JUNE 1. SINCE RETURNING FROM BLOOMINGTON, Frank and Luke had worked feverishly at preparing the ground and waterway for the saw mill. The creek held the water from a series of several waterways that ran southward and converged together. When thunderstorms came through the area, the water sources created a large flowing stream. It would surely have enough force for the mill. The men dug out the bottom and sides of the creek bed to make room for the water wheel to turn freely. Foster had helped with the design and would assist with its assembly at the mill's site. Frank and Luke left today to return to Bloomington to get bolts and whatever else they would need for their project.

The two men had been traveling over two hours when they decided to stop for a brief rest for themselves and their horses. They halted beside a farm home which had been long established and was in pristine condition. A rail fence surrounded the flower gardens and home, all which had been well tended. There was a porch across the front upon which sat large pots of flowers, and, beside one, two white cats sprawled lazily on a rug, soaking in the warm sunshine. The men took their horses into the shade where they grazed while the men drank from their water jug and ate a couple biscuits left from breakfast.

All of a sudden, a horse and buggy came galloping down the road at breakneck speed. The woman riding in it was trying to control the horses but wasn't having any success. She was hollering, "Whoa, boys, whoa," and was pulling on the reins as hard as she could. Frank and Luke shared a quick look and immediately jumped onto their horses and chased after the runaway buggy. It took some time for them to catch up. Luke, who had longer arms, managed to grab the reins close to the horse's neck then pull him to a halt. Luke continued to constrain the horse as Frank dismounted and hurried toward the lady in the buggy. When he looked at her he held his breath at her beauty and was nearly speechless. Finally he managed to say, "Are you all right?"

"I'm a little shaken, but I'll be okay. Thank you for helping me," she replied politely. She looked directly into his eyes and smiled. Moments passed while he gazed into her eyes, unable to speak as if he was in a hypnotic state.

Luke spoke up, "Hello, Frank, are you here or lost in the clouds?" Frank came back from his trance, removed his hat, and brushed it against his legs, as if suddenly he felt the need to dust it off.

"I'm glad you're all right, uh …, Miss. My name is Frank Justice. I'm pleased to meet you, uh …" His eyes were fixed on her light brown hair, which flowed in waves and curls down on her shoulders. Her pixie-like, innocent-looking face had a smile that totally melted him.

"I'm Maureen Nielson."

Frank nodded and said, "Hello, Maureen. This fellow here is Luke Hennessy. We're going into business together real soon. We're building a saw mill on my place down the road."

"Nice to meet you, Miss," Luke greeted.

"A sawmill, now *that's* very interesting. I'd say you'll need to spread the word in order to get enough logs to keep your mill busy."

"That's very true. Not only are you about the prettiest gal that I've ever met, you're also very smart. If you don't mind me askin', where do you live?"

"Oh, I live just back down the road, the house with the fence around it with the pretty flower gardens."

"Would you let me drive you back home?"

"Alright, I'd like that."

"I'll stay here along the road and wait for your return. No need for me to escort you two," Luke chuckled.

Frank tied his horse's reins to her buggy. "See you in a little while, partner," Frank told him.

While his horse grazed on the cool green grass, Luke sat beside the road with thoughts about his and Lorelei's future. *I want to make a better living for my family. My gut tells me that the plan for the saw mill is the right thing. I believe our future is here in Indiana. We like the people around here, and I'm pretty sure Lorelei won't want to leave her friends. How can we make it work? Jeremiah and his family are living with Frank while Lorelei and my family live with Foster. To keep from riding back and forth from Foster's home to Frank's, I should be living close to the mill. I need to come up with a plan.* He watched his horse munch the growth under the shade tree and thought, *Chester my pal, you live your life each day and don't worry about what's next. If only my life was so simple. But, I'm a man predestined from the beginning of creation to work and care for my family, and with God's help, I will do just that.* Time crawled by. While all these thoughts were swirling through his mind, Frank rode up to his side and halted abruptly, causing Luke to suddenly jump up on his feet.

"Damn, Frank, you nearly trampled me down!"

"Mount up dreamer, we've got to get down the road."

The men arrived in Bloomington, bought the hardware they needed and once again visited the men with the working sawmill. They visited a short time as they picked up tidbits of information and then started back home. They slowed their gait as they approached the home with the flower beds and the white cats. Luke gave Frank a questioning look meaning, *"Do we stop or not?"* Frank thought a moment, shook his head back and forth and said, "Later." The men urged their horses and galloped on down the road for home.

It was a couple weeks later when Luke got his nerve up to talk to Lorelei and Shawn about living with Frank. "I've been thinking, since I'll be working the saw mill with Frank, maybe we should move in with him. You know, Jeremiah and Pricilla could live here and, if

Foster will agree, they could add rooms and start their boardinghouse right here. What do you think?"

"Give me a little time to take this in. You know I'll live anywhere you want to live. That arrangement might work better for you, but what do Jeremiah and Pricilla want?"

"Actually, you're the first to hear my plan. I haven't talked to Foster either; that's next. He's outside working now. We'll talk to him after supper tonight, but only if you and Shawn both agree." Lorelei looked at Shawn, and he nodded his head affirmatively.

"I still need to come over and help Foster make wagons and wheels," he stated.

His dad replied, "Sure thing, son, if you want. I think Foster would welcome you at any time."

Evening arrived; supper had been eaten. Lorelei went about cleaning the kitchen while the others sat in the front room. She soon joined them and sat down in a rocker, ready to rest before picking up her needlework. Foster took a knife out of his pants pocket and then reached for his whetting stone. There were a few quiet moments, and then Luke spoke up and spilled the whole plan. He anxiously waited for a reaction or reply of some sort. Foster sat with his eyes focused downward and scraped the blade of his knife with a slow but intent rhythm. The knife whetting continued rasping a sound that seemed to fill all the space of their world. The three Hennesseys looked at each other. Their eyes flitted back and forth in anticipation.

Foster stopped his scraping, smiled, and looked over to Shawn. "Shawn, my young friend, what do you plan to do if your parents move out of here?"

Being startled by the first question from Foster, he replied, "Of course I'll go with them and do all I can, but I'd like to come back and help you."

Foster smiled. "I'd like that." He looked at Luke and Lorelei and said, "You folks are as near family as I have around here. I understand why it would make sense to locate up there at Frank's place. You go ahead and make your arrangements with Jeremiah and Pricilla, and if they agree, then they are welcome to join me here. We could build onto this old place. Heaven knows it could use some sprucing up."

"Thanks Foster, you've been so good to let us live here. You'll always be special to us," Lorelei told him.

"We'll talk with Jeremiah and Pricilla and see if they will agree to the switch. You know they have two children now to take care of; it might get a bit noisy for you," Luke stated.

"This old house has room for all of them. After all, seeing little ones grow up keeps a person feelin' young," he replied.

Luke stood up, went to Foster and shook his hand heartily. Lorelei and Shawn's faces beamed with joy. Lorelei stood up and said, "That calls for some hot tea and a sugar cookie for everyone!" Much of the rest of the evening was spent in conversation about the myriad of changes that could take place in the upcoming future.

The next day Luke talked with Frank at the mill site, and they discussed the idea of Luke's family moving in with him and Jeremiah's family going to live with Foster. Frank listened and thought a moment. "Since you and I are partners in this sawmill, that makes sense." He scratched his head and stated, "Isn't it funny the twists and turns life throws into our path of life? A year ago we didn't know each other, and now we are good friends and partners."

"Yep, you're right. Put'er there, partner!" The two shared a handshake. "Let's make it work!"

When the men finished their work later that day, they went back to Frank's house. Jeremiah was outside scattering feed in the chicken pen. "Luke and I have something we need to talk to you about. Do you have time?" Frank asked.

"Soon as I water the cows I'll talk." Frank and Luke sat on a couple logs in the woodpile and waited.

Having finished his chore, Jeremiah strode up to the men and sat on a sawed-off tree trunk. "What's on your mind fellows?" he asked.

Luke spoke up and related the whole plan to him. "I know you and Pricilla have your mind set on having a boarding home like you used to have. Foster is willing to go along with the new arrangement if it is agreeable with all of us."

"Let's go inside. We'll sit at the kitchen table and all talk this over." They went inside. Pricilla was surprised to see all the men. They all spoke and sat down. Pricilla made up a fresh pot of coffee and brought out an apple cake she had made earlier that day.

Jeremiah said to her, "Come over and sit with us. We have a plan; that is, an arrangement that we need to discuss with you. We need your approval to make it work." Pricilla had a puzzled look on her face. She thought, *What in the world do these men have on their minds that could be this important?* The four of them sat quietly, each one waiting for the other to begin. Jeremiah took Pricilla by the hand. He slowly related the reasons for the move and explained that everyone else was in total agreement, and they needed her approval for it to happen.

She immediately smiled and said, "Of course I agree." She looked directly into Jeremiah's eyes. "Isn't this what we wanted from the start?" He nodded and gave her a quick kiss on her cheek.

"That's settled. All we have to do is decide when all this will take place. Let's say a week from today, weather permitting. That'll give everyone time to gather their belongings," Jeremiah stated.

☀

And so, moving day arrived. The weather was perfect, and what was supposed to be simple became inundated with mishaps from dawn till dusk. Luke loaded one of Foster's big wagons with his family's belongings. Jeremiah still had the covered wagon from his trip to Indiana that he and Pricilla filled with their possessions.

Pricilla had made breakfast. Joey helped put the dishes into the dishpan and dropped one, which broke, and in turn broke another in the dishwater. She had to dump the dishpan and start over. She picked up the baby, and while she was working around, the baby belched up milk all over her dress. She called for Jeremiah to come hold the baby while she changed her clothes and rinsed the mess off of her soiled dress. She told Joey to pick up all his toys, put them in a sack, and take them outside. He took them out as told, but he dumped them in the dirt at the edge of the garden and started playing with them. As she and Jeremiah managed to load the wagon, she found Joey there in the garden, crawling up and down the rows. He had also picked up some worms and put them in his dad's upside-down straw hat, which happened to be placed on some fresh chicken manure.

"Joseph," Pricilla yelled loudly, "what are you doing? You're all dirty!"

He looked up and said, "Mama, I'm playing with my toys."

"Come over here right now," she told him. She attempted to brush the dirt off of his pants and shoes. "Get your toys, and we'll put them into the wagon." She smiled at him and ruffled his hair; she couldn't be mad at him.

"Are we about ready to go?" Jeremiah asked. "Let me take one last look through the house," Pricilla told him. She came back out, and he helped her climb onto the wagon.

"If we've left anything, we can always come back and get it," Jeremiah told her. "After all, we're not moving that far away from here. He flicked the reins on the two horses, and they started down the road. They came upon Brady and Anna Marie's home. They saw Brady and gave a wave. He walked past the house toward them and signaled them to stop.

"You must be moving today. Need any help?"

"I'd say an extra hand wouldn't hurt if you've got time," Jeremiah replied.

"I'll let Anna Marie know, and I'll be right along."

Jeremiah urged the horses onward. He turned the wagon east on the main road toward Foster's place. He and Pricilla talked and laughed as they reminisced moments of their married life. Suddenly the horses became restless and began snorting and going in sideways motions. The wagon jerked the passengers, and a box fell off of the wagon, spilling its contents along the dirt road. "What is it," Pricilla cried out.

Jeremiah managed to get the horses to halt, and he jumped off the wagon to check out the situation. He saw a snake had crossed in front of the team and was going into the tall grass. A short ways into the brush along the side of the road Jeremiah spotted a nest of half-grown rattlesnakes. He reached into the wagon and took out his gun and began firing into the nest. He wasn't sure if he actually killed them, but he wasn't about to walk toward them to check it out. He found a large rock and placed it near the site of the snakes to mark where they had been. He would check there another day. Jeremiah helped Pricilla down off of the wagon to help gather the spilled items. When they had gathered everything, they climbed back onto the wagon.

Jeremiah said, "Well, that was just what we needed today, wasn't it?"

Pricilla squeezed his arm and said, "Nothing was harmed, and it all ended well." She looked lovingly into his eyes and smiled.

Joey looked around, wide-eyed, not understanding what had happened. He patted his mama on the arm and said, "Mama, Mama."

"Everything's fine; your papa took care of it," his mama replied and gave him a hug. He returned her hug and clung to her a few moments, then sat down. The last couple of miles of their trip went quietly and quickly.

Brady rode up beside them about the time they pulled up to their new place of residence. The whole scene was one of movement: family members talking and laughing, doors swinging open and closed, boxes being carried out and placed on the wagon, horses snickering and snorting. The neighbors across the road, Morgan and Eileen, came over to volunteer their help. Working together to load up one wagon and unload the other became a festive event for all. It would remind one of a family gathering at Thanksgiving or Christmas. There was no roast turkey and dressing or fruit cake, no roaring fire in the fireplace and no tracking in the knee-deep snow, but the fellowship of friends being cultivated would last for many years.

The switching of residents in the home of Foster Browning had been accomplished. Luke, Lorelei, and Shawn drove away toward Frank's cabin. Brady followed along. It didn't take long to get the three settled into their new home as Brady and Frank helped empty the wagon. Frank shook hands with Luke and said, "Welcome friends. I've got some pork and potatoes roasting in the kettle that we can eat whenever you're ready. Shawn, you'll have to sleep on a pad on the floor till we get you a bed made, hope that's okay with you."

"Aw, that'll be good 'nough," he answered. Frank patted him on the shoulder and said, "We're gonna get along just dandy."

By the close of the day, all the families involved with the switch had settled down. Their lives had now taken new directions.

PART 2

PART 2

Chapter 18

Six years later, 1845.

CHANGES HAD TAKEN PLACE IN AMERICA. JAMES Polk had been elected president of the United States in 1844. His presidency was one of many accomplishments, which included settling the boundary dispute of Oregon with Canada and the acquisition of the land of California.

America was moving forward in many areas. A few years ago a man named John Bartleson gathered sixty-nine men, women, and children and left the Independence, Missouri, area on the first organized wagon train to go west. This opened up Oregon to the rest of the nation, California soon followed.

The railroad brought changes to the country. Improvements were being made to the steam engines that powered the locomotives and the riverboats. The Maysville Road through Lexington, Kentucky, was being built to serve as a link to a nationwide transportation network. It would eventually connect the National Road to the north with the Natchez Trace to the south and the Ohio with the Tennessee River systems.

Farmers were helped with the invention of the improved plow by John Deere, a blacksmith of Illinois, and Cyrus McCormick, who perfected the mechanical reaper.

The religious group called the Shakers now lived from Maine to Indiana. Books were being written, such as one by William H.

McGuffey, which emphasized cultural and moral standards and preached patriotism. This had a great influence on American life. Many Americans disagreed with the idea of slavery, which, in turn, was causing unrest among the people.

❈

Frank had courted and married Maureen. Two years later, they became proud parents of a boy, Colin. Frank and Luke had enlarged the cabin to make room for two families. Since Frank now had his own family, Luke realized that he needed to build his own home, so he staked a claim on a separate acreage for a future home for himself and Lorelei. The success of the sawmill proved to be a good business, and it provided enough logs to build onto the house. They had also had the logs that Brady used to add more bedrooms for his increased family.

Jeremiah and Pricilla now have a two-year-old little girl, Jenny. They named her after Pricilla's mother. She had blonde hair, which lay in curls around her neck. Everyone was drawn to this pretty, spirited toddler. Joseph, eight years old, often gave Jenny rides on his pony, and he was very protective of her. The boardinghouse was working well. Several more people had settled in the area. The increase of travelers that passed through kept them busy most days serving meals and cleaning the spare rooms.

Foster had aged and, as life naturally offers, he didn't work the long days as he had before. His hands were crooked with arthritis, and his worn-out legs made it necessary to walk with a cane. Luke and Lorelei's son, Shawn, now nineteen, had taken over most of the wagon and wheel business.

Shawn enjoyed hunting and fishing when he could find the time. During the winter months, he would hunt wild turkeys or deer with his papa. Once they killed a young black bear. They worked together and skinned the hide off of the bear, then they cut the tender meat from its back to make stew. When they returned home, Shawn proudly presented the bear pelt to his mother. At first she was repelled by it. After thinking a while, she decided it would make a nice rug to place in front of the fireplace. Of course, the raw skin would have to be salted down to cure. Later the dried, rough hide would have to be worked and rubbed to soften it.

Pricilla's heart was saddened every day as she watched Foster walk across the road and up the hill to visit his beloved Beulah's grave. The pain of his loss hadn't faded. When the weather was too cold or stormy, he would sit on the porch and gaze toward the burial site. Pricilla would see the tears well up in his eyes and trickle down his weathered face. When someone loses their loved one, people tell them that time is the great healer, but Foster still ached for his love.

☀

It was a perfect June afternoon. As the sun was slowly fading in the west, Brady and Anna Marie were sitting together on their front porch. They smiled as they watched Pat and Timmy race their ponies up and down the road. Pat, now nine years old, and Timmy, seven, were growing up. It had become clear to Brady that Timmy was the weaker of his sons. He did, however, notice what a horseman he was becoming, often winning his race. Brady thought, *Later in time this ability may prove to be a valuable asset.* Tim was the son who had colds and coughs every winter. When the boys wrestled and played rough, Tim was the one who came to the house with the skinned knees or the bloody nose.

Brady recalled the time that he took the boys down to the pond where they often fished and swam. When they weren't fishing, the boys would grab onto a rope that was tied to a tree limb that hung out over the water, swing back and forth, and then drop into the water, making a big splash. There was one time Timmy tried to flip over backward. When he let go of the swinging rope, he didn't make the full rotation, hit his shoulders on the pond bank, and his head snapped back and hit a rock. He was knocked out for a short time, and then a large knot swelled on the back of his head. Brady quickly picked him up and hurried toward the cabin, with Pat following behind, hardly able to keep up with his pace.

When they reached their home, Pat ran ahead and opened the door. The look on Anna Marie's face was one of shock and horror all at once. "Quick, put him on the bed!" she told Brady. She ran for a pan of cold water and a cloth. Timmy was awake but couldn't comprehend what had happened. His mother soaked the cloth, folded it, and placed it on the large bump on his head. Timmy moaned and reached to rub his head. Anna Marie took his hand and told him that he had a big bump on his head, but he would be all right. They all stayed and talked with Timmy until they were assured that he was out of danger. Brady helped him sit up and walked him into the front room where he could sit on a chair. As Brady continued to watch the youngest boy he thought, m*y son, life won't be easy for you.*

The twin girls were now five years old, talkative and curious. Lila Rose resembled her father with her bright hazel eyes and sandy-colored hair, which was usually braided. She wasn't much for having her hair fussed with, and she didn't mind getting dirty; matter of fact, she often followed the boys around and joined into their mischief. Lily Anne was a picture of her mother. She had wavy auburn hair, which had wispy curls on each side of her face, and green eyes, the kind that someday would melt a young man's heart. She enjoyed helping her mother in the kitchen. Her favorite job was to work the biscuit dough and flatten it with the rolling pin. Then her mother would hand her a small tin cup to cut out the biscuits and place them on the baking pan. Lily had two dolls that Anna Marie's mother had sent her. She played house with them most every day, and when she went to bed each night, the dolls shared their own pillow beside her in the bed.

✸

Anna Marie sat with her needle and thread. She had taken the boy's torn britches and some patching material with her and sat in the rocker beside the west window. Her life as a wife, mother, and homemaker had filled every moment of every day since she had married Brady. Anna Marie put her mending down on her lap. She looked out the window and gazed out across the meadow. She saw a pair of geese and their offspring walking in a line across the field toward a water hole on the back side of the property. It amused her, this ritual that took place every year—the parents teaching their goslings where to go find the water. She watched a male redbird that had perched himself on the top of the lilac bush. He kept looking here and there, pausing to whistle periodically. She thought, *surely there's a bird nest buried inside.*

While the minutes passed by, she allowed her mind to wander over the events of her life. Her throat tightened, and she felt the tears fill her eyes. She had never let herself acknowledge the point of how truly homesick she was for her family.

It was six years ago when Anna Marie had traveled, escorted by her parents, from her home in Kentucky, to join Brady on their new farm in Indiana. Oh, how she longed to see her mother and father. Of course, they hadn't seen her twin girls. They would be amazed at how much Pat and Tim had grown. She and her mother had corresponded as often as possible, but it wasn't the same as being together. By this time, her tears were streaming down her face, and she wept softly.

Lilly and Rose walked into the room unnoticed by their mother. They quietly walked over to her, one daughter on each side, touched her hands and looked into her face. They had never witnessed her this way. Anna reached for her kerchief and quickly dabbed her eyes and nose.

"Mama, why are you crying? Are you all right?" Rose asked.

Anna forced a big smile and drew the girls closely to her and said, "I'm just fine. I was sad because I miss my mother and father. They live far away. Do you understand?"

"How far do they live?" Rose asked.

Anna Marie told the girls, "Come and look out the window. If you rode in a buggy and went over that hill and kept going, it would take many days to get there. It would be a long, hard ride. You wouldn't get to play or sleep hardly at all."

"Well, maybe they could come and see us," Lilly said.

Anna Marie laid her sewing aside. She took both girls on her lap and hugged them close. "We all could be happy if your grandparents could come and stay with us awhile. Do you want to see them?" she asked.

"Yes, yes, Mama," Lilly answered as Rose nodded in agreement.

"We'll talk to your papa later, and see what he has to say. Now you girls go on and play."

✳

A few days later, and it was blackberry season. Anna Marie had checked the patch a few days ago, and the berries were turning color. She needed to get them before the birds had their feast. Anna Marie put sunbonnets on the girls, and they made their way south of the house. She led the way through the tall prairie grass, making a path for them to follow. Both Lily and Rose carried a tin can that Brady fixed with a handle.

When they reached the patch, Anna Marie told the twins, "These bushes have sharp stickers, so you need to be careful as you reach to pick each berry. Hold on to the can so it won't spill out. Remember, we need two cans of berries to make a pie."

"I'll be careful," Rose told her.

"Me too," said Lilly.

She then showed them a place to pick where the berries hung low. She walked down the patch a little ways not far from the girls. The three had picked a short while when she heard Lily call out a loud "ouch," then an "oh, no." Here she came crying. She held out her hand, which had a big briar stuck in her middle finger, and then she

170

held up her empty can. "Mama, I spilled my berries," she sorrowfully admitted while tears streamed down her face.

Anna Marie removed the sticky culprit and then hugged her tenderly. She told Lilly, "It'll be all right. Go back with your sister and see if you can find more to pick."

Lilly smiled and said, "Okay, Mama" and started back toward Rose.

The summer sun was getting hot, and the bees and bugs began to swarm around the bushes. The girls were swatting frantically when suddenly Rose let out a scream. Anna Marie jerked, gripped her pail, and immediately headed toward her girls. Rose was crying and holding her neck.

"Rose, what happened?"

"I got stung, mama."

"Let me see," her mother told her. Anna Marie moved Rose's hand and saw a lump from the sting, already turning red. She carefully reached down and pulled the stinger out.

"Maybe we should stop picking for today. What do you think?" she asked the two girls.

"Yes, please," Rose agreed. "I don't want to get stung again."

"All right, pour your berries into my pail, and I'll carry them to the house. Follow me back down the path."

It was about ten thirty a.m.when they were back in the yard of the house. Brady walked over to them and looked at the berries Anna Marie carried. "They look very nice. You girls did a good job and, I'm ready for a berry pie," he stated.

"Look, Papa, a bee stung my neck. See," Rose showed him.

"And I got a sharp sticker in my finger," Lilly added to the story.

Brady wrapped an arm around the two and said, "You three have had quite an exciting time this morning, haven't you?" The girls nodded in agreement and ran on into the house.

"Brady, after our lunch, the girls and I have something to talk over with you."

"Now, what have you three cooked up?" he quizzed. Anna Marie just smiled in a coquettish manner and walked away.

❋

After their noon meal, the whole family sat around the table and shared their morning. Brady was noticeably quiet as he waited for Anna Marie or the girls to let him in on their secret. Finally he spoke. "Does anybody have something special that they can tell me now?"

Anna Marie said to Lilly and Rose, "Should we talk about Grandma and Grandpa?" They both giggled and shook their heads yes.

Anna looked at Pat, Tim, and then at Brady. "We've been here for five years now, and the girls haven't ever seen their grandparents. I doubt that Pat and Tim remember what they looked like. The girls would like for me to write to them and see if they could come for a visit."

Brady chuckled. "Is that all? I think that's a great idea, don't you boys? The boys may have to give up their beds and sleep on the floor or in the barn!"

"Yeah, we'll sleep in the barn. That'll be fun," they happily agreed.

Lilly and Rose clapped and laughed. They climbed off their chairs and ran to their father and hugged him, one on each side. "I thought you and your mother had cooked up something serious," he told them as he laughed and gave them a squeeze.

With a big smile beaming all across her face, Anna Marie announced, "Well, girls and boys, I better get busy and write a letter."

❋

Nearly three weeks after the letter was written and mailed, it arrived at the Kentucky post office. Of course it was a few days before her ma and pa went into town, and Ben checked to see if they had any mail. When Ben picked up the letter and gave it to Lydia, she was so excited to hear from Anna Marie that she shook as she opened the envelope. She read it out loud and became out of breath when she finished. Her eyes sparkled as she looked at her husband, a pleading type of look. He reached up and pulled at his hat and looked skyward. A few empty moments passed by. Lydia stood there and watched hopefully. He turned his head back her direction with a huge smile flashed toward her. He wrapped his big, muscular arms around her. She felt the long-time bond between them and knew they would make the trip. While in town she wasted no time searching out paper and an envelope to return a letter. They sat on a bench where she hastily penned that they definitely would come. "We can't wait to see all of you. Lord willing, we'll see you soon as possible."

☀

August 15. The heat was unbearable. Everything in sight was brown. It hadn't rained for a month, and the grass crackled as Anna Marie walked through the yard to gather her laundry. The leaves on the trees had turned from bright green to a dull yellow-brown, and many had fallen from the branches. Frank and Luke had been forced to shut down the sawmill until rainwater once again rushed down the creek with enough force to turn the mill wheel.

Brady now kept all the livestock in the barn during the extreme heat of the afternoon. The chickens were penned close to the shade on the north side of the building. They walked around with slow, measured steps, their beaks open as they gasp in the hot air. They had twenty laying hens. Brady decided that they would butcher two a week to cut down on the need for their water and feed. Later they would let a few setting hens raise some baby chicks to replenish the flock.

Brady, with help from Pat and Tim, had been hauling buckets of water three times a day from the shallow waters of the creek, which was barely enough for the household needs and the animals. They would probably have to sell a couple horses if it didn't rain soon. Luckily, Brady, Frank, and Luke had cut and piled the pasture grass while it was green. They believed they had enough feed for their horses and cows to last through winter, barring a catastrophe. Now, they were already using the winter store. The corn crop was another story. The drought came when the corn kernels were supposed to fill, consequently, the harvest would likely not turn out well.

✦

Sunday morning arrived, and everyone had gathered at the church for worship and socializing. As usual, food was brought and shared for their dinner. The heat wasn't as noticeable that day, as some clouds had drifted over and blocked the harsh, burning rays of the sun. It seemed to have lifted everyone's spirits. The children ran around and played games while the grown-ups sat and rested in the shade, sharing their past week's happenings.

Suddenly, there appeared a large buggy, a fancy one with a cover for the top and sides. It came to a halt close to the church along where the other buggies were tethered. As soon as the man and woman got down from the buggy, Anna Marie gasped for she knew—it was her parents.

"Brady, look—it's Ma and Pa!" Brady and Anna Marie immediately hurried toward them.

Ben announced to Lydia, "Its Anna Marie and Brady. They're here at the church."

The two women embraced each other emotionally as tears ran down their faces while the men shook hands and patted each other on the back.

Anna Marie said to her parents, "I'm so glad to see you."

Her pa replied, "It was a long, tiring trip, but it was worth it to see you and your family." He held her about her shoulders and gave a squeeze.

Brady said to them, "Come on over and meet our friends. If you are hungry, I'm sure there's enough food for you."

"All right," Ben replied. He reached for Lydia's arm to help her walk. Now Ben and Lydia weren't old by any means, but the trip had made them quite tired. Within minutes, all four of the Patterson children appeared. The joy from the family reunion flowed out among all the people present.

As soon as they had eaten and rested a bit, Brady decided it was time to take everybody back to their farm. Nobody seemed to have noticed that the clouds had thickened until a brisk wind blew and began shaking the tree limbs, and small whirls of dust danced about. The horses began to whiney and take small, nervous steps.

It didn't take long for the group to make the short trip back to Brady and Anna Marie's home. The weather changed when the air cooled, and the wind speed became steadily stronger. About the time they arrived at the cabin, raindrops began falling. Anna Marie, her mother, and the children went on inside while Ben and Brady stabled the horses. They carried the clothes bags inside just in time before the heavens opened up, and the wonderful rain came down.

Brady laughed and said to Ben and Lydia, "If I'd known it woulda rained when you came to visit I'd had you here a long time ago!" They all joined in with his laughter. Anna Marie went to sit in one rocker while Lydia sat in the other, Lila Rose on one side and Lily Ann on the opposite.

Lydia squeezed the girls and said, "I'm so glad we came to see you two," she paused and looked around, "and all the rest of you, too."

"We're glad you're here," each girl told her.

Ben, Brady and the two boys sat at the kitchen table together. They all visited together until time for bed. The boys remembered that they would sleep in the barn, and they were excited for the adventure. Brady had them get their blankets and pillows, and then he and Ben each picked up a lantern and walked them outside.

Chapter 19

UNKNOWN TO THE PATTERSON HOUSEHOLD, THREE runaway slaves had found refuge overnight in a corner of the barn. Isaac, Liza, and their son, Jonah, had escaped from a cotton plantation in northern Alabama. They had been hiding in the woods a quarter mile away. They had watched the two buggies with their passengers come up the road and turn up the lane beside the cabin. They saw the women and children hurry into the cabin. After the men stabled the horses, fed and brushed them down, then carried the clothes bags inside the kitchen, the runaways went inside the barn.

The three runaways were so hungry that they searched through the barn and found the bags of horse feed. The dry oats tasted bland, but they were grateful to fill their bellies. Liza was especially tired and hungry, as she was large with child. They hadn't had a good meal for two days. Isaac found some dry grass which had been stored in the barn. He spread it out in the far corner behind several saddles and layered it like a bed to rest on for the night.

The night was filled with sharp cracks of lightning followed by heavy rolls of thunder. The two boys took their blankets and pillows and spread them out next to the grain bags. Both boys and the animals were restless as waves of heavy rain pelted against the barn. Pat and Tim didn't fall into a deep sleep until the early-morning hours.

As morning dawned, the storm had calmed. A heavy cloud cover blocked the hot rays of the sun and allowed a steady rain to fall on the thirsty land. Both Pat and Tim's eyes popped open when they heard the thump of the latch on the barn door. The horses tossed their heads about and whinnied as they shifted around on their legs. The boys jumped up from their straw bed.

"Look, its Papa and Grandpa Ben!" Timmy exclaimed as he hurried toward them.

"How'd you sleep?" Grandpa Ben asked.

Timmy rubbed his eyes and answered, "Not so good. The lightning, thunder, and rain were really loud."

"Best get used to it," he said with a smile, "you'll be out here till we leave." Tim nodded in agreement.

Brady told Pat and Timmy, "Go ahead and feed the horses; after while we'll turn them and the cows out to pasture." Ben gave hay to the two cows while Brady milked them. They soon left the musty smell of the barn carrying the milk buckets as they splashed through water puddles back to the cabin.

The steady, life-giving rain continued for the next few days. Everyone was relieved to have the water for their crops and animals. Isaac and Jonah would sneak out at night, go to the garden, and take some vegetables. They were careful not to take too many, as they didn't want to do anything to draw attention. They had been taught that stealing was wrong, but the fact was they had to eat to keep up their strength. Their plan was to move farther north as soon as the weather cleared. Isaac and his family agreed that being on the run couldn't compare to living the life of a slave.

☀

Two days later, Anna Marie sent Timmy outside to fetch onions to go with their supper. The sun had just slipped past the horizon, and the shadows had gotten longer and darker. It was still drizzling rain, and as he neared the garden, he thought he saw something move at the far side over beside the tomato plants. He stooped down behind some tall grass and watched quietly.

A few minutes passed by, and he saw what looked like a dark-skinned boy holding something, but what? Timmy's heart began to pound. He crouched even lower. The boy started walking toward him. What could he do? When the boy came upon Timmy, he was startled, and they both yelled.

Tim stood up and asked, "What are you doing here?"

Jonah replied meekly, "I know it's wrong to take from your garden. It's for my ma and pa; we're hungry."

"Where are they?"

Jonah hesitated.

"You better answer me, or I'll get my pa!" Tim told him emphatically. Jonah looked around. His mind raced as to what to say or do next. He decided to tell the truth.

"They're up there in the barn. We've been there ever since it started raining. We ran away from the plantation where we worked as slaves and came north to be free."

"You mean you're all runaway slaves?" Timmy's eyes got big, and his mouth fell open.

Jonah nodded. He pleaded, "Please don't tell. I promise we won't hurt anyone."

"My name's Tim," he said.

"I'm called Jonah."

"I ain't ever seen a colored boy before. Are you black," he paused, "everywhere?"

"Ever'where," he replied.

"I need to get some onions, and then we'll go back, all right?"

Jonah waited, and then the two headed back. "When will you leave?" Timmy asked.

"Don't know. Prob'ly soon," he answered. The two walked the rest of the way in silence, neither knowing what would be next. Timmy wanted to be able to find out more about this stranger, but it would have to wait.

"You better wait in the shadows until I go inside so my family won't notice you," Timmy advised. Jonah understood. His heart pounded with fear as he stayed low and motionless behind a tree and watched his new friend go through the cabin door.

Tim entered the kitchen quietly and put the onions down beside where his mother was working. He kept his secret all evening. He thought about Jonah and his family out in the barn and couldn't wait for tomorrow.

Jonah entered the barn with the fresh tomatoes. He wasn't sure what, if anything to tell his ma and pa. They sat down together to eat their meager meal. Jonah's large, dark eyes shifted back and forth as he watched his parents. He became self-absorbed in his own thoughts. As the wind began blowing forcefully, it caused whistling and creaking sounds inside their hideaway. He was nervous about tomorrow and decided to wait before telling his secret.

※

Tim's eyes popped open at dawn. He was so anxious to see his new friend that he hurriedly ate his biscuits and eggs while he listened to his parents and grandparents chatter. Pat tried to have a conversation with him, but Tim only responded with grunts or a shake of his head.

"You must be sick today. You're just too quiet," Pat remarked.

"I'm all right. I've got a lot on my mind," he replied.

Pat laughed and said, "Sure you do; you're such a thinker!" Rose and Lilly giggled as they watched their brothers banter.

Tim suddenly asked his grandpa, "Grandpa, have you ever seen any black people?" This unexpected remark got everyone's attention. Lily and Rose both looked over to Tim with wide eyes.

"Well, yes, I have, many times. Kentucky is home to blacks that work on the big farms down there."

"Are they all slaves?" Tim asked as he pursued the subject.

"Probably so," he answered. "They don't have enough money to have their own farms."

"Are they bad people?"

179

"They're people just like you and me, both good and bad. You don't know until you get acquainted. I'd say they do what they can to survive like anyone else."

His pa asked, "Timmy, why are you talking about all of this? Did something happen to cause this sudden interest?"

He felt his face flush, then replied, "Of course not. I just happened to be thinking about it."

Pat smacked Tim lightly on his shoulder and said, "I always knew you had something wrong with you." He and the girls all chuckled together.

Brady spoke up. "If you're done eatin', you boys go on and check your horses."

"Yes, Pa," they each replied.

"Ma, could I have more biscuits to take with me?" Tim asked. She nodded, and he reached into the bread basket and grabbed a handful, then he immediately left the kitchen. She knew nothing about who would eat those biscuits. His sisters looked at him wide-eyed and resumed their giggling.

The two young men left the house and strode toward the barn. "What ya gonna do with them biscuits?" Pat asked.

"Can't say right now," Tim answered. "I'll probably get hungry again before noon." Pat didn't understand the mystery of Tim's actions. The two went ahead to feed and water the horses. Tim stayed alert as he watched to see if Pat noticed anything unusual in the barn. They soon finished the chores. Tim took one of the horse bridles and started going through the motions of cleaning it. Pat looked at him quizzically and left the barn.

As soon as Pat left, Tim let out a big sigh of relief. He slowly turned around to see if the black family was there. He saw nothing. His heart pounded rapidly. He walked to the far corner stall of the barn, and there they were, all crouched down under a blanket. As soon as Jonah saw Tim, he jumped up and threw the blanket back.

"No, Jonah, no!" his mother yelled. "What are you doing?"

Jonah turned toward her, "It's all right Ma. He's my friend."

Isaac spoke sternly, "Boy, you better watch out what you say."

Tim said to all of them, "Look, I brought you some of Ma's biscuits. They're really good. My family doesn't know about you." He handed them to Jonah.

Isaac said, "Now what'll we do? We can't stay here."

"Pa, please, we can't go yet," Jonah begged.

"It's too dangerous being here. We've come too far, and we don't want to go back."

"I won't tell, honest," Tim told him. "You can stay as long as you want."

About that time they heard the barn door open. They all crouched down, hardly breathing. Jonah cowered beside his mother and quivered with fear. Since he and his family ran away from their owners, he had been afraid of being caught. He was sure that his family would be sent back or worse and that his pa would be punished with the whip.

It was Grandpa Ben who stood in the doorway. Tim jumped up to go see him. As he hurried toward the barn door, he fell over a board, which caused him to pitch the harness into the air. It flew over toward the blanket that covered his new friends and hit Jonah on the head. Jonah hollered.

"What in the world was that?" Grandpa Ben blurted out loud. Tim froze in his tracks like a statue.

"Timmy, what's going on in here?" Tim couldn't speak.

Grandpa Ben started walking around inside the barn, his eyes keen on his surroundings. His voice belted out loudly, "Is there someone in here?"

"It was probably Buttercup, our barn cat," Timmy suggested.

"That wasn't a cat! Come out, whoever you are!" he announced.

Jonah crawled out from under the blanket, stood up, and lowered his head (as he had been taught to do for his slave owner). His insides quivered with fear. When Ben saw that he was a black boy, he knew why Timmy had asked him those questions at breakfast. Ben immediately toned down his mannerism. He knelt down near him.

"I won't hurt you," he said calmly. "What's your name?"

"I'm called Jonah, sir." He didn't look his inquisitor in the eye. Ben could see him shaking.

"Look up at me, please. I just need to talk to you." Jonah lifted his head and faced Ben.

"Why are you here in our barn?"

Jonah looked all around as he thought about what he should say. "Uh, uh, I ran away from home and needed to have a place to sleep," he answered slowly and quietly.

"Well, Jonah, you must be hungry and thirsty."

"Yes sir."

"Come with me to the house."

"Oh, I can't do that. It's not right."

"Sure it is. Come on now."

Timmy put his arm around Jonah's shoulder and said, "Come on; it's all right. You'll be okay." The three headed for the barn door and left.

Meanwhile, Isaac and Liza slowly lifted the blanket. Liza groaned with the effort as she tried to stand. Isaac got a hold of her arm to help her. They didn't even speak to each other for long moments. What to do raced through their minds. It seemed they had nothing to fear from the farmer that befriended their son, but they had learned from experience not to make a hasty judgment.

Isaac spoke, "We can't stay here any longer. We must move on. Do you agree?"

"I feel tired and weak. I don't know how much farther I can go in my condition."

"You're not getting enough food to keep up your strength. Tomorrow I'll go out and, somehow, get us some meat."

❋

Jonah didn't know what to expect as he walked inside the cabin. He was raised that it wasn't proper to go into the home of the boss. He felt as if his flesh and bones were drawing up, crunching his insides, trying to make him smaller.

Lydia and Anna Marie were the first to see Timmy with his black friend. They stopped their chores as their eyes widened with amazement. Ben spoke up. "Look what we found in the barn—a young, hungry boy. His name is Jonah. Would you happen to have some food for him?"

Lydia answered quickly, "Come on and sit here at the table, and I'll get a plate of food for you."

Ben left the boys in the hands of the women, and he went back outside to tell Brady about the morning events. Rose and Lilly had heard the talking in the kitchen, left the bedroom, and went into the kitchen. Jonah jumped when the two girls rushed into the room. When they saw him, they both stopped and stared, unable to believe their eyes. Neither had ever seen a black person.

Anna Marie placed a plate of food and a glass of milk in front of Jonah. He looked at Timmy as if asking approval. Timmy told him, "Go ahead and eat." He picked up a spoon and ate quickly. The twins watched, as they hadn't seen anybody scoop up food and eat it so fast. As soon as he finished his food he said, "Thank you, ma'am."

"You're very welcome," Anna Marie replied.

The three boys quickly went back outside.

Yesterday Anna Marie had suggested to Brady that the family would enjoy a meal of fresh fish. Ben found him south of the house digging worms.

"We need to talk," Ben announced with urgency. Brady stopped with his spade half full and looked quizzically at him.

"I came to tell you that we have a young black boy eating in your kitchen! I found him talking with Timmy in the barn just a few minutes ago."

"You don't say!" Brady exclaimed.

"Yep, says he ran away. I'm guess'n he's with someone, but I didn't look any further. I didn't want him to get scared and run."

Brady took his spade and worm can, and the two walked back toward the house. They saw Pat, Tim, and the young stranger standing together outside. Pat and Tim were touching the black arm which belonged to Jonah. He quickly jerked his arm to his side as a scared look sprang forth across his face.

Ben spoke calmly as he looked at the youngster, "Don't be afraid. This is Timmy and Pat's pa. His name is Brady. Brady, this young man is called Jonah. Could we all have a talk together?" The question hung in the air, suspended in time.

Brady spoke in a soft, controlled voice, "Jonah, we'd all like to hear about your escape and how you got here." Jonah stared at the can of worms as he searched for words. He didn't want his ma and pa caught.

"I ... uh ... I ... I had to go in the dark ...n ... n ... I was scared. Master, he had hound dogs runnin' loose. If they'd see or smell me, master, he'd find me 'n' I'd get a whippin'.'"

Both Tim and Pat got wide-eyed as they listened. "Tell some more," Tim urged.

"Well, I put on my old coat and grabbed a cover. I waited till t'was all quiet, and master was sleepin'. I opened the creaky door real slow, careful not to make a sound, and I ran out. I ran hard as far as I could. I finally stopped to rest on a tree log. My heart sure was beatin' hard!"

Tim asked, "Wasn't you afraid out there all by yourself?"

"Real scared," he replied.

"Why did you leave without your ma and pa?" Brady asked. Jonah looked over toward the barn and back, and then he gulped. "You sure you're all alone?" Brady continued to quiz. Jonah looked at Tim. He reacted and looked down toward the ground.

"Timmy, do you know anything about all of this?" his pa asked. If there was one thing Tim knew, it was that he'd better tell the truth. He paused, then looked at Jonah, and told him, "We've got to tell him about your folks."

Tim looked directly at his pa and said, "Truth is Jonah and his ma and pa have been sleepin' in the barn since it began rainin'. They haven't had much to eat, and his ma is real big. She probably can't go much farther."

Ben looked directly at Jonah. "Is Timmy tellin' the truth?"

"Yes, sir," Jonah answered, with his head bowed down.

"I understand; you're protecting your family. Don't worry, you're not in trouble. We're goin' to help you. Now, you go into the barn and explain everything, and ask your folks to come out and meet us. We'll be here waitin'. Okay?"

"Yes sir." He turned and walked toward the barn. Brady decided to go inside his home to inform Anna Marie and her mother what he had learned about the young stranger. He immediately returned back outside.

It was one of the hardest things that Jonah ever had to do. He paused at the barn door to gather his strength, and then he went inside. A short time later the three emerged from their sanctuary. The father, Amos, had hardened lines imbedded in his face, which indicated no fear as he approached the two men. He had endured enough misfortune and punishment during his lifetime of thirty years that when he came face to face with adversity, he approached it head-on. He walked straight toward Brady and Ben. Liza followed close behind him. It seemed that walking was a struggle for her, but her composure was in control as she held her head erect. It was obvious to the men that she would soon give birth.

"Hello, I'm Ben." He extended his hand to shake as a gesture of friendship. Amos returned the greeting. "I'm Amos."

"This here's my wife, Liza. I'm sorry if we were intruding on your place; we meant no harm. I know our son told you we were trying to go north and the rain forced us to find shelter."

Brady extended his hand to Amos and said, "I'm Brady Patterson. This is my farm. I hold no ill will against you or your family." The two men shook hands.

Anna Marie, Lydia, and the twins came out the kitchen door. The two women observed Liza's condition and looked knowingly at each other. "She must be close to delivery," Lydia said in a hushed voice. "Let's invite her inside to rest." Anna Marie nodded in agreement. The two walked over and stood beside this anxious, yet composed, woman.

Lydia said in her kindest voice, "You must be tired. Would you like to come to the kitchen and rest?" The women walked with Anna Marie and Lydia on each side of Liza. When they arrived at the kitchen door, Liza was hesitant to enter the home.

Anna Marie reassured her, "It'll be fine; no harm will happen."

The women went inside, sat down together, and chatted about things only women can talk about. Liza even giggled as the women made their connection. Meanwhile the men did likewise. They discussed hard work, horses, crops, and the fact that something always has to be fixed. Amos clearly wanted to help on the farm where ever he could, and it was agreeable with Brady.

That first evening together proved challenging. It was decided that all the men and boys would spend the night in the barn sleeping on the grass hay. Liza slept in the boy's room. For her, it was the first good night's sleep in many days.

Chapter 20

A WEEK HAD PASSED SINCE THE TWO FAMILIES HAD accepted the black family. Ben, Brady, and Amos worked well together. Amos proved to be strong with an inborn knowledge of how to do or fix whatever came up that needed attention. The men became more acquainted to the point of true friendship. When evening approached, and the chores were finished, they went to the kitchen for a refreshing drink of hot coffee or cool milk and chuckled as they recounted their day.

Pat and Timmy were truly enjoying having another boy around. They spent much of the time showing Jonah their secret hiding places and paths around the farm. Lila Rose and Lilly Anne stayed to themselves, as they weren't sure about the whole situation with the new family living there. They would go outside and stay where the boys couldn't see them and observe how the boys did things together.

Liza's time to give birth was close. She was only able to work while seated at the kitchen table. Meals for eleven people now required more food preparation time, so she was either making bread, peeling vegetables, or doing some other kitchen task.

It was now mid-August, and the daylight hours were still quite hot. After sunset, the heat lessened, and the adults would sit outside on the porch as they enjoyed the relief from the day's work. The youngsters still filled with energy, played tag or some other made-up game. The twins usually ran around for a short time, unable to keep up with the boys, and went back to the porch with the adults.

Brady spoke up. "Ben, we're going to have to go for supplies soon. I'd like to go in a couple days. What do you say?"

"That sounds good, but I have to tell you that Lydia has mentioned that she will be ready to go back home soon. We need to go back before the rainy fall weather begins."

Brady remarked, "Would she want to go with us to shop for something?"

"I'll ask her later," Ben answered.

It was at the same time that Liza made a grunting sound, grabbed her stomach, and hollered, "Oh Lordy!" Naturally everyone turned their attention to her as a long silence filled the air.

Amos stood up and moved quickly to her side. "What's happenin' woman?" He took a hold of her arm.

"Amos, I think the baby's ready."

"Let's go to the porch and rest," he said to her. Everyone eventually made it to the porch.

The quiet of the night was only interrupted by the sounds of the wind rustling the dry leaves and the occasional shrill sounds of the tree frogs. Jonah went over to his mama and spoke with a quiver in his voice. "Mama, what's wrong?"

She raised a hand to touch his and replied, "Nothing's wrong; it's time for me to have a baby brother or sister for you. You go along now. I'll be just fine." He bent down and hugged her. She responded by kissing him on the cheek. Being reassured, he walked back to sit with Pat and Tim.

The mood relaxed, and once again the previous lighthearted atmosphere resumed. The women discussed what sort of dessert to bake the next day as the men told tales of the big fish they had caught, laughing at the tall tales. Ben suggested that they should go fishing again soon. Clouds floated across the sky and covered the moon, which often created dark, eerie shadows. The boys hid behind the trees and shouted out "boo" when another walked by with an attempt to scare them.

Twenty minutes had probably passed when Liza let out a loud yell, and she grabbed her belly. Jonah's eyes got big as Lydia and

Anna Marie went over to her. Lydia spoke, "Come, Liza, you need to go lie down." She nodded. Amos took her by her arm and waist and escorted her inside to the bedroom.

The women tended Liza through the evening and into the night. Ben went to the barn with the boys to keep them calm, but Amos and Brady spent the night together. They talked about life's good parts and bad parts but decided that all in all their life was worth the living. Amos began to open up and tell about his past.

"Liza and I grew up together as little kids, living on the same farm. The chil'n could play till they reach seven before they worked learnin' to pick cotton. We'd take buckets of water out to the mamas and papas to drink two times each mornin' and two times for the afternoon. Even the small buckets full of water were heavy for youngsters to carry! You know, those cotton fields got mighty hot if you stay out there workin' all day. My folks came in from the fields all dirty and worn down. We'd carry a bucket of water for them to drink their fill, and then they'd wash their arms and face off in the same bowl of water. We'd eat potatoes, turnips, greens, and tomatoes from the large farm garden. Master'd give us grits, cornmeal and flour, and one dozen eggs a week. On Sundays he'd give each family a hunk of meat, which, if we didn't eat too much, would last a couple more days of the week. My mama never ate much meat 'cause she wanted us chil'n to have it. She'd say, 'Amos and Juleen can have more.' She didn't think we knew what she was doin', but we did."

Brady asked, "Can you read or write?"

"I can write my name, and I know my numbers. We had no cause to learn to read. All we knew was work. Master thought I was smart enough with numbers that I'd go with him to help him figure if he was bein' cheated by some of the traders. He'd give me and my family new shoes every year after the crops were done and a bundle or two of cloth so Liza could make herself a new blouse and skirt as well as shirts and pants for me and our boy."

About that time, Liza let out a bloodcurdling scream that made both men jump up from their chair, causing Amos to knock his mug of coffee over, sending the brown liquid all over the table.

"Is she all right? What's happening?" he blurted out. Large beads of sweat covered his face.

Lydia stepped out of the bedroom and said, "I know you're worried. The baby's not here yet, but it won't be long." Brady grabbed a dishcloth and wiped at the spilled coffee, then the men sat back down.

Brady inquired further about what plans Amos and his wife made for their future. "Tell me, Amos, where do you plan to go from here? Do you have anybody to help you?"

"No, sir, I don't."

"You can't wander around with your wife and two children. You need a place to live and a way to support them, right?"

"I surely do," he replied.

"I know what I'm about to offer you isn't much, but how about we build on to the barn to give you and your family a place to stay together? Later we'll figure out a better solution."

"That's a mighty fine idea, but how's the others gonna feel about it?"

"You know my family accepts your family. About others, I don't think there'll be a problem 'cause we haven't had any black people around. No one around here owns slaves. I don't even know anyone who believes in slavery."

"I know for sure my Liza and the new baby won't be able to do much for a while. Let me talk this over with her tomorrow."

"Good enough," Brady agreed.

Hours passed. Both men dozed in their chairs and roused occasionally with noises from the bedroom. It wasn't until the light of the morning when the sun streaked across the sky that Liza gave birth to her baby girl. Amos and Brady heard the loud shriek, a spank, and the first cry of the newborn. Lydia came from the bedroom to tell Amos that Liza had given birth to a daughter.

"Wait a little while. I'll tell you when to go see her and your little girl," she told Amos.

Brady shook his friend's hand and said, "Congratulations. Daughters have a way of getting right into your heart," he warned with a chuckle.

It was about three days until Amos and Liza could agree on a name for their daughter. They decided on Marianne, a sort of backwards Anna Marie. When they told her about the name, she was surprised and pleased at the same time.

☀

Ben, Brady, and Amos decided it was time to make a trip to town for supplies. Amos drove the wagon while Ben sat beside him, and Brady rode his horse. It didn't seem unusual to the people who watched them come into town. They naturally assumed that Amos was their slave. The three men went together into the stores as the supplies were picked up and packed into the wagon.

When it came time to eat, the three went into the café and sat down together. Some of the people stared at the men with raised eyebrows, and a hush came over the room. Never before had a black man sat down to eat with the while people in this town. At first, Ben and Brady didn't notice the calm. Amos was the first to speak up. "I think I should go outside." He stood up.

"Hold on," Ben said. "Sit back down." He sat.

Two tough-looking men, who had been seated next to the wall, stood up. One was large-framed with big muscles, with long, unkempt hair hanging beneath a black, dusty hat. He had a deep scar on his left cheek, and two fingers were missing on one hand. He looked like he was mad at the world. The other one had long hair on his head and face with spittle matted on his scraggly, red beard. He wore a gray, tattered shirt that reeked of body odor. They strutted over toward Brady's table. Their eyes squinted as they focused on Amos.

Brady stood to face the men. In an effort to be friendly he said, "What can I do for you men?"

191

"You can take your nigger out of here. He shouldn't be eatin' with us," the big man answered.

"This man isn't my slave; he's my friend. We work together," Brady informed him. "He eats with us back home, and he can eat with us now."

The second man puffed up and shook his fist and yelled toward Amos, "Your kind needs to eat outside with your own kind; now git up and git out!"

Ben stood and said loudly, "Now see here; he has as much right to eat here as anybody. Why don't you turn around and go finish your meal?"

One of the two waitresses ran to get the owner. Several customers headed out the door as they were anticipating trouble. It happened that the owner of the café was an open-minded fellow, but he certainly didn't want his place of business torn up.

Meanwhile, the dirty man took a swing at Ben, and he ducked the blow. The muscled man began punching toward Brady. Each man had taken two or three blows by the time the owner came upon the scene. He wasn't a small man, so when he approached the fighters, he pushed the dirty man away.

"That's enough. Hold up there, fellows. We'll not have any fightin' in here. What's goin' on anyway?" The men turned toward the owner.

The big muscled man spoke. "This nigger ought not be eatin' in here. Only white folks eat here."

"And who says so?" the owner said to him. "I think I'm the one who makes that decision."

The dirty man said, "Well I'll tell you this; his hide ain't worth a wooden nickel. He come from slaves, and all slaves are good for is work for us whites."

Ben spoke. "Not so. He's a good man and a good worker. He's as good as any of us here."

"That so," he replied. "Well, I want him out!"

The café owner turned to the two fighting men and said, "I think that you two need to be the ones to leave. I don't want your kind in here, so leave and don't come back."

192

"You mean you favor a nigger over a white?" the muscled man said.

He told them emphatically, "I mean, I favor a good man over troublemakers. Get outside right now!"

During the fractious moments, Amos had backed away and moved closer to the door so that in any event he could make a run for safety. Life had taught him self-preservation.

The surly men grumbled to themselves and left. The customers who saw the whole episode began clapping and saying things such as, "That'll teach them," or "Way to go," or "Good riddance!" Ben, Brady, and the café owner shook hands. Ben waved for Amos to come back to the table and sit with them again.

The café owner said to Amos, "You're welcome to eat here. Your food today won't cost you a thing."

Amos was so surprised that all he could say was, "Thank you." He said to Brady and Ben, "I ain't ever had anyone fight for me."

"When men are friends, they take care of each other," Ben replied.

After their meal, Amos and Ben left the café and got onto the wagon. Brady mounted his horse, and they headed back to the farm. The men had several good laughs along the way about what happened at the café. This would be one of many episodes they would experience.

Two days after the trip to town, Ben and Lydia announced that they plan to leave to go back to their home in Kentucky as soon as they could get ready. The news had a saddening effect on all the Patterson family. Everyone helped them gather their clothes and prepared as much food, along with extras, that they could take with them.

The morning sun peered over the horizon, and the kitchen was buzzing as breakfast was served and eaten. Lila Rose and Lilly Anne were seated in between Grandma Lydia and Grandpa Ben listening to the morning chatter. The meal was finished, and the time had come for the good-byes.

Outside, the weather was partially sunny with spotty gray clouds rushing across the morning sky. The breezy air had the cool feeling of fall. The whole family gathered around the buggy. Liza and her baby stayed on the porch, but Jonah and Amos both joined the farewell to Lydia and Ben.

Rose and Lilly grabbed Lydia. "Grandma, please don't leave yet," they both begged. Rose wiped tears from her cheeks as she held Grandpa Ben's hands. "When will you come back and see us again?" she sobbed.

Ben squatted down and held the girls, one on each side, and gave them a squeeze. "I don't know," he answered, "but you can be sure that we'll all see each other again." He kissed both Rose and Lilly on their cheeks, and they kissed his.

Anna Marie and Lydia hugged each other with tears streaming down their faces. "Mother, it has been so wonderful having you here. I'll miss you so much."

"I feel the same, Anna. Our house has been so empty since you left home. We don't want to wait another seven years to be together again."

The men all shook hands. Ben made a point of shaking Pat and Tim's hands. "Boys, I expect you to be like your dad—do the extra to help your friends and neighbors, be trustworthy and honest. Treat others as you would want to be treated, and you'll never be a failure."

"Thanks, Grandpa Ben. I'll do my best," Pat told him.

Ben looked straight at Tim and said, "Tim, I know you like to take chances. Be careful, and think twice before you act."

"Yeah, I know but sometimes I can't help myself. I get a sudden urge, and I do it."

"Promise me you'll try," he urged.

"I promise," Tim said, and he hugged Ben unashamedly. "I'm really goin' to miss you, Grandpa," he said with emotion.

Lydia went back to the porch where Liza was watching the parting of the family she had come to love. Lydia put her hand on Liza's arm.

"Miss Lydia, I thank you for all you done for me. When my little girl was born, you took such good care of me and my baby. I'll never forget you."

"You can be sure that I'll never forget you either. You raise that baby with special care, and she'll grow into a fine young woman." They both hugged and wept softly together. "Good-bye," Lydia told her. Lydia's emotions were about to get the best of her. She could hardly bear lingering any longer. She walked back to the buggy, and Ben helped her to the seat. They both flashed a big smile; Ben snapped the reins on the horses' back and away they trotted down the lane. Everyone waved good-bye to them. It was a bittersweet parting.

Chapter 21

A MONTH HAD NOW PASSED BY SINCE ANNA MARIE'S parents left for Kentucky. Brady and Amos worked on the addition to the barn, with the help of their friends Frank and Jeremiah. Anna Marie truly enjoyed being with Pricilla when she came with Jeremiah. They would relish their time together visiting and laughing and sharing. Their son Joseph was close friends with Timmy. The two boys were the same age and shared the same interests. They would race their horses and explore the creeks and wooded areas within certain perimeters of the farm.

Pat, whose interests were more serious as he was approaching manhood, stayed with the men and helped wherever he could. He had completed the basic schooling that had been available: reading, writing, and arithmetic. His ma and pa had a Bible, the King James translation, which he found difficult to understand each time he tried to read, especially the Old Testament. He had never been around anyone who spoke with "thou art" or "He abideth with thee." But Pat took to heart some verses that he had read in the Psalms: "Then my enemies will be turned back in the day when I call. This I know, that God is for me." He had always gone to church with his family, and he could sing many of the hymns. He thought of the hymn "Trust and Obey"—"for there's no other way"—that always stuck in his mind.

The week passed quickly, and it was now the Sunday after Ben and Lydia had left for Kentucky. The church members discussed whether or not there were enough families living in the community that they could name their town. Many of the attendees expressed their opinion, and the group as a whole agreed they would select a name. Suggestions made were Pleasantville, Happy Valley, or Timber Creek. Other names were of a biblical nature: Bethlehem, St. Peters, Hebron, or Abraham. Of course, no one could agree at the first meeting, so they all agreed to take a vote the following Sunday after a basket dinner.

The following week the topic of most conversations, and some bickering, was choosing the best name for their community. Naturally the word had passed around from one land owner to another and, when the next Sunday arrived, the church was packed. People showed up that had never set foot inside the church before. The pastor was so excited to see so many people in the congregation that his face was flushed and there, were times that he would stammer and stutter as he tried to remember the thoughts he had prepared for his sermon. He could sense the anticipation of all those attending.

A couple was present with one young boy that had moved to the settlement from the east only a year ago. Sven and Helga Jorgensen had immigrated to America from Norway two years before. He was a tall man with a large frame. He sported a full blond beard and moustache, and his curly blond hair stuck out from under his well-worn hat. Helga stood about five feet five inches tall. She had a round face with rosy cheeks and blonde hair, which she had braided and wrapped around the top of her head. She had a jolly nature, so she was always smiling or giggling as she talked. Their boy, Kurtis, was five years old and had, of course, inherited the blond hair and blue eyes that were typical of Norwegians. Helga made sure that he was at her side at all times; consequently, he was quite shy and only smiled when someone made a comment to him.

As the sermon concluded, the pastor stepped down closer to the congregation. "Please stand with me," he urged, and then he offered the benediction. "May the Lord give strength to his people! May the Lord bless his people with peace!"

The air surrounding each person during the meal felt electric. Conversations at times became shrill and excited. When the meal ended, the ladies gathered what was left of their food dishes and stowed them in their baskets. The chattering became more subdued yet contained the edge of anticipation.

Jeremiah stood up before the members, and slowly the talking hushed. He cordially welcomed everyone and said, "You know why we have called this meeting. I think the best way to select a name for our community is to let everyone present their idea. Pricilla will write them all down. When all the suggestions have been made, we will start the vote. We'll vote until the most favored name is agreed upon. I know we can't please everybody, but let us all work together in a peaceful manner. Please raise your hand, and you can announce your suggestion." At least fifteen names were presented.

Jeremiah announced, "This is how we'll vote. Pricilla will read off the three first names on the list. You can vote on only one of the three. The vote will continue till we're down to the most favorite. Is everyone okay with that?" Heads nodded, so the voting began. Vote by vote the names were narrowed down to the last three. Voices became harsh with the few who refused to agree. "We need to approve, or we'll go home without a name for our town. What do we want?"

At that moment the big Norwegian, Sven, stood up and walked up beside Brady and Jeremiah. He said, "I would like to make a suggestion that hasn't been voted on."

"Go ahead," Jeremiah replied. The room became quiet as all listened intently.

"Back in my home country of Norway, we know of a God named Frey. He is the god of good crops, fruitfulness, love, peace, and prosperity. I would like to have the name the Village of Frey." Calmness filled the room as the community listened and digested the suggestion. Suddenly, applause started up and filled the void as many stood and cheered.

Several called out "yeah," "that's good," or "great name." Jeremiah was amazed at the crowd's reaction. He motioned for them to sit down. "Thank you, Sven, for stepping up and stating your idea for the name that seems to be approved by all. Let's make this official. Everyone raise your hand if you want the Village of Frey for the name of our town." The hands flew up into the air, leaving no doubt that it was accepted.

Jeremiah and Brady shook hands with Sven, as did several other men. Excitement filled the church as the men and women spoke with happiness at the results of their voting.

Jeremiah called everyone to order. It took a few minutes for them to settle down. He spoke. "I would like to suggest that we plan to meet on this date next year to celebrate the day that this town was established." All cheered at this idea.

"I also would ask that a volunteer committee be formed ahead of time to see that next year on this date we will celebrate a day for the Village of Frey that will never be forgotten." Again, his suggestion was accepted with great enthusiasm.

The pastor made a point to move among his "flock" as he used this opportunity to invite everyone to attend church again next Sunday. The matter having been settled prompted each family to begin to leave for their home. Within a short time, the church had nearly emptied. The pastor stood with Sven, Brady, and Jeremiah, and their families. His face was lit up with a big smile as he said, "Congratulations to all three of you men for a job well done. You've done a great service to this community."

He shook Sven's large hand and told him, "Sven, it was a blessing that you moved your family here, and it's my pleasure to meet you. Come back and worship with us again." Sven smiled and nodded agreeably and replied, "Thank you. I'll talk with the missus. It was good to see all the people who live around here." He turned toward his wife and son, took the handle of the food basket, and they walked out the door on their way home.

History had been made that day. A community of good, hard-working people came together in peaceful surroundings with the purpose of deciding and agreeing that they would become a town with a name and create hope for their future.

☀

It is now a cool, cloudy day in November. Amos and his son, Jonah, decided to ride over to Frank and Luke's mill west of the Patterson farm. As they rode along, Jonah pointed out how the squirrels were scurrying around gathering nuts and running up the trees with their treasure. Many trees had lost their leaves while the pines and cedars remained green and sturdy-looking. Amos felt the chill of the north wind hitting his face and neck.

As they approached the bottom of the first hill, the two ruffians Amos had encountered at the café came riding toward them. The big muscled man led his black horse directly in front of Amos's horse.

"Well, would ya look who's here? It's the black man that thinks he can sit and eat with white folks," he said sarcastically. Jonah's eyes got big, and he became scared. He didn't like the man.

Amos spoke calmly. "I've done no harm to you, mister. Let me and my boy go on our way."

The dirty, whiskered man dismounted as he laughed loudly, then he said to the muscled man, "I think this fellow needs a lesson in manners. What do you think?"

The muscled man grabbed the reins of Amos's horse as his buddy walked around to pull Amos off the saddle.

"Go for Frank!" Amos shouted to Jonah. Without hesitation Jonah kicked his horse and rode away at full gallop.

Amos tried his best to pull his horse away from the grip of the muscled man. As the whiskered man pulled on his leg, he couldn't manage to break away. He swung at him as he was falling off of his horse, but he barely clipped the side of the attacker's head.

"Whoa now, nigger, you can't win this fight!" he stated in a laughing manner. The muscled man took the three horses over to the side of the road.

Amos struggled as he fought the burly man. He had worked hard all of his life on the cotton farm, and he was a strong man, but he was fifty pounds lighter than Whiskers. The two rolled around on the rough road as Amos wrestled to get loose. The packed dirt and rocks ground on their bodies. He managed to land one good hit on the face of his attacker, and blood splattered out of his nose. He felt the grip loosen on his arm, so he quickly jumped to his feet.

Amos hadn't seen Muscles come over because his attention had been centered on the fight at hand. When he stood up, he felt a hard punch in the middle of his back. Naturally, it threw him off balance. As he staggered from the blow, Whiskers got to his feet and began a series of strong hits all over the front of his body while Muscles beat him from the back. After many punches, he was unable to take any more. He fell down and rolled into the ditch.

The two bullies stood over Amos and laughed. They hadn't seen Frank and Luke come charging down the road until they were close by. They saw the two big men standing and looking down. As they approached the scene, they saw Amos motionless on the ground. Both Frank and Luke began firing their loaded rifles at the men. The attitude of the two bullies quickly changed from laughing and boasting to shock and panic.

One bullet hit Whiskers in his right shoulder, which caused him to spin around and fall down. A second shot echoed and struck Muscles on his left arm. As he grabbed at his arm, he tried to run for his horse. Another bullet hit him on the back of his left leg, and he fell down. As soon as Frank and Luke dismounted, they hurried to check on their friend, who lay quietly on one side. He was alive, holding his midsection and moaning with pain. His face was badly bruised, and blood drained from his nose and mouth.

"We better take him over to Brady's where his wife can care for him," Luke remarked.

"Let's put him on my horse. I'll hold on to him," Frank suggested.

"Jonah, help me get your pa up and on Frank's horse," Luke said.

"Yes, sir," he replied. The two struggled with Amos, as he was barely able to help himself. At last they got the job done.

"I'm on my way right now," Frank stated. He had a good grip on Amos so he couldn't fall off. He said, "Hang on, friend. We'll be back to your home in no time."

Luke and Jonah quickly mounted and followed Frank to the Patterson farm. As soon as they stopped at the lean-to home, Jonah jumped off of his horse and shouted to his ma to come out. Luke dismounted and went to help Amos down to the ground. Liza opened the door to see what was going on and hollered out, "Oh, good Lord, what happened?"

"Hold the door open, and we'll get him inside," Frank told her. Amos groaned as Luke and Frank managed him inside and laid him on his bed.

"Please, tell me, how did he get hurt so bad?" Liza begged.

Luke spoke up, "Jonah and Amos were riding over to our place when he was jumped by the same two men who tried to pick a fight with him in town a while back. He sent Jonah to go get us to help him, but he was already beaten up when we got there. We did manage to get off a few shots with our rifles and hit both of them. We left them where they fell. They didn't deserve any of our help right then; Amos was most important."

Liza looked at both of the men with teary eyes and said, "Thank you both for helping my Amos. We won't forget your kindness."

"We only did what anyone would do to help a friend in need," Frank replied. "We'll leave you to care for your husband now." The two men left but not until they told Brady and Anna Marie about the attack. Meanwhile, the attackers managed to mount their horses and go seek help on their own; they were far from dying.

❋

Amos healed, but it took nearly ten days for him to be able to work. The winter passed without any further incidents against Amos or his family. Liza's baby girl was growing and doing well. Jonah had been accepted by the community, and he did well at the school. It was the best life that they ever had as a family.

Jeremiah and Pricilla continued running the boardinghouse and caring for Foster Browning, whose health had been in decline this past year. Some days Liza would go into town and help Pricilla with meals and chores. She enjoyed the opportunity to go into town to work, and the extra money surely helped her family. Pricilla didn't mind Liza bringing her baby along; in fact, she quite enjoyed seeing her little girl. Pricilla's daughter, Jenny, was seven years old, and she loved playing with Marianne during the day. The customers that frequented the boardinghouse had come to accept them as well.

❂

The next year March came in like a lion. Cold temperatures and freezing rain besieged the land for the first two weeks. The men were miserable trying to take care of the farm animals and to bring in fresh water for the food and washing, as well as finding enough dry wood for the fireplace. The third week brought sunshine and much warmer temperatures, and everyone had a cheerier attitude. The grass began to green-up, and buds started coming out on the cherry and apple trees. Lila Rose and Lilly Anne were outside playing and spotted a pair of red-breasted robins hopping around on the ground. They stood by quietly and watched for several minutes. They quickly ran toward the house as they couldn't wait to go tell their mama about the birds; they were sure that spring had arrived.

A cover had been fastened over the buggy to protect the occupants from whatever Mother Nature decided to pour down from the sky. Tim took Lilly Anne, Lila Rose, and Jonah to school every day in the buggy. One particular afternoon, when school ended, Jonah spotted Muscle Man and Whiskers standing across the road, focused on their buggy. The scowling look on their face had a frightening effect on all the children, especially Jonah.

Jonah said to Tim, "Over there, those two men, they're the ones who beat up my papa."

Tim looked over toward the men. "Don't worry, Jonah. We won't let anything happen to you or the girls."

The two men watched as the youngsters got into the buggy. The men mounted their horses and followed the buggy down the road. Pat made sure that he kept a good distance ahead of them. This particular

ation occurred about twice a week. Of course, all the children kept their dads informed of the situation.

Brady and Amos decided the harassment had to stop, so they decided to take some action. They went into town on horseback as they followed Tim and the girls. While school was in session, the men went about town buying supplies and visiting with friends. Brady made sure to stop at the boardinghouse to see Jeremiah and Pricilla.

Jeremiah looked up the moment Brady walked into his business, and a big smile broke across his face. He took a towel, quickly wiped his hands, walked over to Brady, and grabbed him by the shoulder.

"How in the world are you? I haven't seen you for a month of Sundays," Jeremiah stated.

"That's because you're chained to your cookstove! All you think about is food!" Brady retorted. Both men laughed and shook hands.

"Let's all sit down. I'll get you both a mug of coffee." He chuckled. "I've got time to talk with friends." They reminisced and visited until Jeremiah had to get back to work.

That day at midafternoon the children were all outside playing. The small children were playing tag, using the pump on the well as home base. The older students were running races to see who could go the fastest by eliminating the slower runners on each race. They were all so intent with their fun that they didn't see Muscles and Whiskers standing close to the large trees at the edge of the school yard. Tim and Jonah were lined up for the last race. They decided to run all around the edge of the school grounds before going back inside the schoolhouse. They saw the two men only as they circled near them. Muscles reached out and grabbed a hold of Jonah's arm as he ran past. It yanked him hard, and he fell down.

"What are you doing? Let me go!" he yelled. Tim immediately stopped and looked back to see what happened. With Jonah as their captive, the men had already started hurrying toward their horses.

Tim called to his school buddies, "Come on, Jonah needs help!"

Muscles lifted Jonah up on his horse when Tim threw a hard punch on his back ribs. The big man turned around and said roughly, "You best not mess with me!"

204

Tim pulled on him to get him away from Jonah. By that time, all the older boys came to get in on the fight. Whiskers tried to grab Jonah onto his horse, but the other boys knocked him down and were hitting him. Jonah took the chance to run.

The two bullies were landing some hard hits and getting the best of the young men. About that time Amos and Brady rode up. They jumped off their horses—Amos going toward Whiskers and Brady after Muscles. The young boys backed away as the men fought. Meanwhile, Jonah had picked up a good-sized tree branch about thirty inches long. He came toward Muscles, waited for the right moment, and then hit him as hard as he could. The muscled bully stumbled backward, stunned from the blow.

Jonah was so proud of what he had done that he proceeded to go and give Whiskers the same heavy clunk, which happened to hit his head. The burly man grabbed his wound and shrieked out, "What was that?" and proceeded to fall to the ground, knocked out.

Amos looked at his son, who stood there wide-eyed and breathless. He moved toward Jonah and wrapped his arms around him. "You're a brave young man," he stated. "Those two bullies shouldn't bother us again."

Muscles sat up slowly, rubbing his arm and shoulders where the tree limb struck him. He looked up at Brady and the young men who had circled around.

Brady spoke with authority, "We're here to tell you to leave our children alone. In fact, I think it would be wise for you and your partner to pack up and leave this territory. We don't want you around. If you try to harm *anyone* around here again, I promise you that you may not live to tell the story of how bad you two got beat up!"

Everyone cheered. Amos grabbed Muscles by both ears, pulled hard and yelled into them, "Go git your partner and leave. Don't bother to come back - *Ever!*" He released his grip and gave the bully's head a hard push, a final demonstration of authority.

Whiskers began to moan and move a little. Muscles crawled over beside him.

While all the commotion was taking place, the schoolteacher came outside to see what was happening. The students, along with Brady and Amos, walked over to her. When she heard the story, she said to the children, "We'll close school for today. Go on home."

The students clapped their hands and whistled. They were dismissed for the day.

The two bullies went to their horses and rode off just far enough to be out of sight, and then they dismounted under a grove of trees off of the main road. They were hurting from the blows they had taken from the fight, and it had put them in a bad mood.

❋

Within a few days after the ruckus at the schoolhouse, several men and women began talking that the town needed someone to enforce peace in the town. That next Sunday after church, Jeremiah stood before the people and announced, "This town needs to consider having a law enforcement officer and a place to put anyone who causes problems around here. Do you all agree?"

Many heads nodded affirmatively as others called out, "You're right; we don't want trouble in our town."

"Well, who'll volunteer to be a sheriff for us?" The people looked all around, but nobody spoke up.

Jeremiah looked carefully at the men, and his eyes landed on Sven Jorgenson, the big Norwegian. He asked, "How about you Sven? You're a strong, law-abiding man." Now everyone focused on him. Sven looked toward his wife, and then he stood up.

"You know, I've been helping out at the feed store for a while, and I've become friends with many of you here today. I agree we need to keep our families safe. I'll give it a try and see how it works for a while."

The people began clapping. Jeremiah spoke, "Thank you, Sven. We all believe that you are the man for the job. I'll get some men together, and we'll help you get started." He continued to speak to the

206

people. "Now let's get behind this man and give him all our help. He can't do it all by himself." Everyone clapped enthusiastically.

The Village of Frey continues to grow toward a united community of people.

Chapter 22

ONE OF THE MOST WONDERFUL RESULTS OF THE community becoming a named town was the fact that they now had their own post office. They were more connected to the rest of the country. The people of the Village of Frey won't have to travel several hours to the next larger community to keep in contact by mail with other friends and family that are important in their lives. When the post office was first established it was located in a corner of the mercantile. Most community members went to the mercantile several times a month for various foods, textiles, animal supplies, or tools for their work thus it was quite handy for the locals. It was a main hub, along with the boardinghouse, where the citizens socialized.

Within a short time after the post office was operating, Anna Marie received the long-awaited letter from her parents concerning their trip back home. It seems that they met up with a group of travelers, three couples, in Madison who were going to Lexington. Their journey was safe, and nothing occurred to cause harm or difficulty.

She read the letter alone at first. Tears of joy ran uncontrollably down her face. After she managed to calm herself, she went to the kitchen table and read it out loud to the rest of the family. Lila Rose, Lilly Anne, Timmy, and Pat sat and listened intently to their mother.

Dearest Anna Marie, Brady, and all the family,

We enjoyed being with you so much. My, how the children have grown up! Pat and Timmy are fine young men and so capable of doing things. Lila Rose and Lilly Anne, we were so happy to meet you and spend the special time with you both.

Our trip back home went well. We met up with three other couples when we arrived at Madison. They made our trip interesting. One lady, obviously well-to-do, wore a large brimmed hat that was pinned to her highly piled hair. She had a white french poodle that rode on her lap most of the time. Her husband wore a black top hat and a fancy riding coat. They were really upset when the wind blew their hats off, and we had to stop. We watched them chase those hats for several minutes. They were so flustered. Their poodle ran around with them and got his paws all dirty, which upset the lady. Your grandpa and I still laugh about them.

The other two couples were plain people and hard workers. We visited with them and became good friends. We all traveled together until we reached Lexington. We spent our last night on the road in Richmond at a boardinghouse. It was the nearest place like home that we had stayed, and we rested well. We didn't have any problems or bad weather during our trip. We were glad to get home, and, of course, we were very tired.

It would be wonderful to see all of you again. Please plan for your family to come down.

We send our love to all of you.

Grandma and Grandpa, Mother and Father

When she finished, Lila Rose asked, "Mother, when can we see our grandma and grandpa again?"

Anna Marie, working to hold back more tears, replied, "I honestly don't know. When you're a few years older maybe we'll try to make a trip down to Kentucky."

Lilly Anne clapped her hands and said, "Maybe Lila Rose and I could go and spend the whole summer with them."

"It'll take time to arrange for a big trip like that," she replied.

Lila Rose began to sob. "I miss my grandma and grandpa." Tears poured out of her eyes. Lilly Anne joined her.

Anna Marie said to them, "Girls, I understand you are sad, but be strong. We'll see them again, I promise." She handed each of them a handkerchief and patted them on the cheek. The girls, heads lowered, sniffed and dabbed their eyes and noses. Anna Marie hugged them softly.

☀

A year before, 1844, James K. Polk, Democrat, was elected president of the United States after defeating antislavery candidate Martin Van Buren. Polk had supported the annexation of Texas. While he was in office, he sent troops across the Rio Grande into Mexican territory. After the Mexican troops responded to their presence, he persuaded Congress to declare war. American troops conquered New Mexico and briefly occupied Mexico City. The Treaty of Guadalupe Hidalgo, which ended the war, ceded half of Mexico to the United States. This was important because both the northerners and the southerners wanted any new land to suit their own cause. If slaveholders seized the land west of the Mississippi, they would have more power as landowners, thus more slaves, which was an imperative for the slave system. The northern industrial landowners would have less land and industry than the Southerners, consequently affecting their production for the European market.

From at least 1829 on, many citizens in America opposed the idea of slavery contending that a man should be free to own and work his own land to support himself and his family. An antislavery organization, the American Colonization Society, aimed to end slavery by deporting all free black people to Africa. Others denounced this organization. Frederick Douglass, a black abolitionist, caused many northerners to reconsider their deeply held racism.

The southerners feared that communities of escaped slaves and free black people living beyond the borders of the South would fuel slave rebellions.

Life moved along well for the next two years for the Patterson family and their friends. The children were growing up, happy and healthy, as well they should. Liza had been accepted by the town people at the boardinghouse, not because she was hired help, but because she was a kind, caring individual. Likewise, Amos had acquired friends. He would help his neighbors whenever he could, not demanding pay. Amos and Jonah helped increase the size of Brady's vegetable garden and spent several hours each week to keep the weeds under control and, likewise, gather the vegetables at harvest time.

During this period of time, communication among the states and the towns within each state had increased. Men would gather and discuss the happenings of the nation. More and more people became aware of the issue of slavery. On a few occasions someone would tell that they had seen a black man, or a family of black people, walking through a field or camping beside a stream for a day.

"Those poor people," someone would say. "It ain't right the way they've been treated."

"I hear the landowners down south would whip them mercilessly," another would add, "even if they worked hard all day long."

"This country was founded on the premise of freedom. It shouldn't matter if a man is black, white, or any other color. Those poor people were brought in here against their will and made to work for some big land baron, and then they get punished," another would say.

"I don't blame them for runnin' north. They'd have a chance of gettin' a job and earnin' their own pay to support their selves," Brady stated.

"A man deserves a chance to prove that he can honor himself and his family by providing the necessities for them," Jeremiah would state to others in the boardinghouse.

All this talk about slavery, land barons, and black people quite naturally made Amos nervous. He'd talk with Liza. He'd say, "Do you think that we're safe here? Do you think we should go further north?"

Liza felt secure with their lives now compared to what it was before. She would answer, "I don't think anything will happen to us here in Indiana. I like living where we are. We're gonna be just fine."

✸

Shawn Hennessy, Luke and Lorelei's son, was a smart young man who knew how to work hard, as proven by his well-muscled body. He was now eighteen years old, had learned the craft, and had taken over the wagon and wheel business that Foster worked for many years.

Since Foster lost his wife and still grieved her death, he no longer had the inclination to work, or for that matter, to do much of anything. He spent most of his time sitting around at the boardinghouse listening to the conversations among the patrons who frequented there.

Now Foster had grown to like Liza. She would bring him a fresh mug of coffee or save back a slice of pie and take to him midafternoon. She would smile and say with a lilt in her voice, "Mr. Browning, are you having a good day today?" He would smile back and nod his head to her. She would respond by saying to him, "That's good. We want you to be happy."

Sometimes Amos and Jonah would come in for a meal and to visit Liza. If Foster would be sitting at the table, Amos would join him. Foster enjoyed visiting with him and watching Jonah. He enjoyed listening to Amos tell his stories about growing up, the fun he had before he became old enough to work out in the fields.

He told one story about him and his sister playing in the creek water. "At that time, she was five years old, and I was almost eight. My folks nicknamed my sister Sugar Plum 'cause she sucked her thumb, and they said that she was *so* sweet. She wasn't that sweet as far as I was concerned. I just called her Plum. Anyway, we went to the creek to catch a bucket of crawfish so our ma could make a stew. Course we were barefoot, and the creek bed was wet and slick. Right away I slipped and fell on my rear, slid down the muddy bank, and stopped as my feet hit the water's edge, balls of mud piled underneath. Plum giggled at me, which I didn't care. We looked around for crawfish holes and a little bit later we found some. I took a stick and poked down the holes, hoping one would grab a hold. In a while I started catching some. Plum watched intently. We counted ten crawfish in the bucket and decided to get a couple more. I snagged one and tried for the second. When I flipped it out of the hole, it sailed into the air and landed on Plum's back. She screamed and started hopping around as it started crawling up to her shoulder. She lost her balance and fell into the water. Luckily, the crawfish didn't pinch her. It was so glad to be back in the water that it let go and swam away. Plum splashed around in the water and got soaking wet. When she crawled out of the creek, she had mud all over her arms, legs, and feet. She started crying like a puppy with a sore paw."

"Was that really true?" Jonah asked.

"Sure 'nough," his dad answered. Foster laughed heartily and slapped his own knee loudly. "I would 'a liked to see that!" he stated loudly.

"I'm sure that you have many tales you could tell," Amos said.

"Prob'ly so, on another day," he replied. He looked at Jonah and placed a hand on his shoulder. "When you get all grown up, you'll have stories of your own to tell," he said.

The door of the boardinghouse opened, and in walked two ladies followed by two dapperly dressed gentlemen. You could tell right away they were landowners. The women each wore a fancy, tailor-made dress and had high hair-dos, topped with a store-bought hat. They walked to a table beside the window and sat down. As they chatted, it was clear that they were in their own private world and hadn't looked to see anything else.

Liza went over to their table, "Welcome. Could I bring you something to eat or drink?"

They were used to being waited on by Negros, and it didn't seem unusual to have one come and ask to bring them something. Liza walked back to the kitchen but first stopped to speak with Amos and Foster before getting the food and drink for the customers. The travelers took notice of their waitress's actions.

"That's not usual for the Negro worker to tarry when she's to be working, is it?" one commented.

"I should think not," was the reply. "I certainly wouldn't allow it one bit."

"Do you see that Negro man sitting, eating and drinking with the older white man? Why would that be allowed?" one of the men asked.

"Perhaps we should talk to the proprietor. He surely isn't aware of what's going on out here," the other man replied.

About that time, Liza arrived with their food and drink, politely placed it on the table and said, "I hope you enjoy your meal." She smiled, walked over and picked up her baby, and joined her husband. Of course, they were keenly observed by the travelers.

"That's intolerable!" one man stated. "I'll go talk to the owner back in the kitchen." He quickly stood up and walked directly into the kitchen. He found Jeremiah leaning over the kitchen table chopping vegetables.

"Pardon me," he said, "do you realize your maid and her husband are sitting at a table with a white customer in your dining room? That should *not* be tolerated!"

Jeremiah looked straight into the eyes of the man and noted the look of disapproval that covered his face. "So you think. Are they people like you and I?" he stated.

"Negroes will never be equal to the white!" he said loudly. "They're meant to work for us, help us work our fields and clean our homes."

"Not here in my business. They're my friends and employees and are treated as such. You need to understand that we're living in a time of change. Many who live in this country don't agree with the idea that just because a person is born black that they should be treated as inferior, and I happen to agree. The three blacks sitting out there are free people. I think it would be best if you quietly return to your friends and rethink your actions. The southerner's face reflected the look of unbelief and disgust.

Foster, Amos, Liza, and Jonah had heard the confrontation and saw the man go and join the other travelers. The women were wide-eyed and astonished at what had taken place.

"I don't think I can bear to be here and eat. I'm too upset," one lady said, and she began to fan herself.

"Come now, let's eat. I don't know where else we'll be able to find a meal," her husband said. "Try not to look their way. We'll soon be leaving." They sat eating quietly and only talked with hushed voices. Within a short time, the four travelers had finished and left.

Amos began to quiver inside. He feared that the two couples that left would soon be telling where he and his wife were living and working. When Liza and he returned back to their home, they had a long discussion about what they should do. Amos's pulse pounded, and he mopped the sweat from his face repeatedly. They talked well into the night but didn't reach a decision.

The next morning after breakfast, Amos recounted to Anna Marie and Brady what had happened at the boardinghouse. Brady could tell by the deep furrows in his brow that Amos was worried and in a very nervous state. "What should we do?" he asked. "If we're found, we'll be taken back to the cotton field and beaten."

"Don't run. I'll do everything I can to keep you safe, so will all your other friends," Brady told him.

Amos didn't allow Jonah to go to school the following week, and he insisted that Liza stay home as well. The following two weeks were calm. What Amos didn't know was that the two traveling landowners talked to many people who were southern sympathizers on their trip back to their plantations. They had visited with a group of men who, for a hefty fee, would track down runaways and return them to their owners. Congress had passed a Fugitive Slave Act that would punish fugitive slaves and also those who helped them.

As fate would have it, the two ruffians, Muscles and Whiskers, had also learned that they could earn money by catching runaways. They would sit around their campfire night after night working on plans to capture Amos and his family.

Muscles said, "We best wait until good weather when we do this."

"Yeah," Whiskers answered in a half grunt.

"We'll watch them closely, and when they all get into a wagon to go for supplies, that would be a good time to surprise them. Hell, they prob'ly won't even have a gun with them!" Muscles said jokingly. Both men rolled with laughter as they thought about their scheme and the money they would be paid, up to one hundred dollars for each man, woman, and child.

❄

The winter came with a vengeance and life was difficult for man and beast. By February, the weather began to moderate and even allow a few sunny days with warm sunshine. Long icicles that had formed along the edge of the roof dripped freely to the ground, lending to the formation of large puddles around the cabin. At nightfall, they refroze, as did the puddles. Each day, Lilly Ann and Lila Rose would find patches of ice and slide on their shoes until the melting began. They would return inside the cabin, wet to their knees.

"Look at you girls! Go change your wet clothes right now," their mother would say, "and bring them over by the fireplace to dry." Anna Marie would have a hot pot of tea ready, so she and the girls would have tea and a cookie together. The girls would tell her about slipping and falling. Lila Rose said, "We found a small icicle, broke it off and ate it. It was good." She and Lilly Ann giggled uncontrollably. It was a good bonding time for the three.

By mid-March the worst of winter was over; buds began coming out on the trees and bushes, and the twittering of the returning birds could be heard. Jeremiah and Pricilla were very busy with the increase in business both for boarders and those coming to eat meals.

Foster seemed to be totally focused on visiting his deceased wife's grave, and it was affecting his mental stability. He would get up early every morning, about the time Jeremiah started making coffee. He would sit without talking, twirl his thumbs around, and wait for the coffee. Jeremiah would give him two leftover biscuits from the day before and put out some jam, and he would eat the biscuit, covered with butter and jam, with the fresh coffee. By this time, the sun was up and shining through the kitchen window. Foster would stand up, put on his well-worn hat and his tattered jacket, and then walk outside with only one thing on his mind, to go visit Beulah's grave. He would follow the path from the house to the road that ran in front of the house, cross, and then proceed to slowly walk up the hill, stumbling often, to where she had been laid to rest. He had previously found a large tree limb and had drug it over close to her grave. He would sit, staring downward. His eyes would fill with tears and run down his cheeks, which he didn't bother to wipe away. He was totally engrossed in his grief. Oftentimes Jeremiah would have to go up to the grave site and urge Foster back to the house. Pricilla and Jeremiah both were concerned for Foster's well-being.

It was now April 4, a bright and sunny Easter Sunday. Most everybody in the Village of Frey had dressed up in their best clothes, had packed a large basket of food, and had gone to church to worship. Jeremiah had to persuade Foster to wear clothes that weren't frayed or in need of mending. Jeremiah left Liza and Amos in charge of the boardinghouse so he and Pricilla could go as a family to the Easter Sunday special service.

They left the house, crossed the road, and started up the path toward the church. Foster veered toward the cemetery. Jeremiah caught him by the arm and said, "Now where might you be goin'?" he asked. "This is the day to go to church. Come on now." Foster strained against Jeremiah's grip. "You'll be fine; come on along."

Foster succumbed and walked beside Jeremiah into the church. Everyone inside was friendly and joyful, which encouraged a smile to appear upon his face. Even though he smiled, he had a look of faraway thoughts.

It was a glorious day, this Day of Resurrection, and everyone was uplifted. The sermon was one that made you want to go to heaven immediately to sing with the heavenly choir and see God and Jesus and all the angels, reveling in His glory. Foster smiled, sang, clapped, and moved along with everyone else. When the worship and rejoicing concluded, they were dismissed with a great "Amen" chorus. The people chattered as they opened their food baskets and filled the tables with bowl after bowl of delicious food. Everyone ate as if they were at a great banquet. Cakes, cookies, and pies were left yet untouched. Foster decided to get a piece of bread pudding and take it with him and place it on Beulah's grave; he remembered it was her favorite dessert.

Jeremiah didn't notice him leave the church. He and the others were caught up in conversation, thoroughly engrossed and enjoying it all. Foster made his way over to the grave site, to his wife and friend. He breathed in the fresh spring air and looked at all the beauty that had been created on this small corner of the world where he had lived most of his life. He sat on the familiar tree limb beside his loved one. He took long, deep breaths as he slowly gazed across the grass, almost trancelike, and took in the beauty of the spring flowers, the buzzing bees, and the delicate butterflies that flitted about.

After some time had passed, Foster realized he was still holding the bread pudding. He knelt down and placed the dessert on her grave and said softly, "This is for you, my love." As he laid it down he exhaled a big breath and lay down on her grave.

When Jeremiah and Pricilla were preparing to go home, they looked around for Foster among the others but didn't see him. Jeremiah knew in his heart that Foster had once again gone to Beulah's grave site. When Jeremiah found him, he was lifeless, face down, with both arms extended as if hugging the ground that held his wife.

Jeremiah went back to the church and delivered the news that he found Foster dead. Some of the men helped move the body over to the church. Most all that remained at the church had known Foster and Beulah and were stricken with grief. After they consoled each other, they began to gather their remaining food and baskets and quietly left.

The preacher walked with Jeremiah's family back to the boardinghouse. The moment they went inside, Amos and Liza could tell something had happened. They were so somber-looking that fear began to grip Amos. The adults sat around one of the big tables.

"You need to tell us right now why you came in here like this!" Amos declared. Liza sat with her arms wrapped around herself, as if they would protect her.

"It's not good," Jeremiah started. "I found Foster lying on Beulah's grave. He was dead. I guess he couldn't take it any longer."

"Good Lord, I knew he was in a state, but I didn't expect that." Liza responded. Tears welled up in her eyes.

Jeremiah, still feeling the shock of losing Foster, felt it necessary to approach the subject of his funeral and burial. "We should make some arrangements for a memorial service for Foster," he suggested.

"If we can locate his relatives, we need to notify them," Pricilla said.

Liza spoke. "I believe I've seen some letters on his bedside table. I'll go check to see if I can locate them."

"We don't have much time to have his funeral, three days at the most," the preacher stated. "Let me know as soon as you can."

Brady stood up and stated, "Anna Marie and I will leave for home so we can break the news to Frank and his wife, as well as Luke and Lorelei. It won't be easy." He looked at his wife and said, "Let's get the children and be on our way."

❋

The three days passed. Liza had found some addresses in Foster's room, but the people were located too far away to go tell them and come back within the allotted time.

The day of the funeral was beautiful with sunshine and a clear sky. The trees were budding, and the wildflowers were blooming as the earth continued to come to life for another year. Some remarked that Foster and Beulah would've loved it. Friends from all around filled the church, and several spoke of the many good qualities Foster possessed. An hour later, his body was carried to the cemetery, and he was laid to rest beside his beloved wife. Luke, Lorelei, Shawn, Brady, Anna Marie, Jeremiah, and Pricilla stood for some time in reverend thought about their beloved friend and his wife, gone now forever. These friends felt deeply the brevity of life and the loss of a true friend.

Several friends gathered at the boarding home where they lingered a while, unable to resume their daily routines. The ladies were out of tears, and they now approached the rest of the day with acceptance accompanied with words of hope and the promise of tomorrow. Liza had made an extra pot of hot tea and a pan of cinnamon muffins for the mourners. Liza and Amos also mourned the loss but held it inside, as they had many hurts they had lived through.

Before all visitors had departed, the preacher, who knew the strength that faith in God gave each in the community of believers, stood up to speak. "Dear friends, It is difficult when we lose a friend. I know Foster and Beulah had opened up their home to you. They both acted with a Christian's spirit; they fed you and gave you shelter. They both exemplified how we all should be. The Bible tells us, "Therefore, my beloved brethren, be steadfast, immovable, always abounding in the work of the Lord, knowing that your toil is not in vain in the Lord."

As the day moved along, each family bid good-bye, gathered their children, and left for their own homes.

The next day, Liza agreed to clean Foster's room. It seemed very awkward for her as a black person to have been given access to the private belongings of a white man. She had taken a wooden box to his room to store his possessions. On top of the chest of drawers was a skinning knife, a small vase with dried flowers in it, an old compass, and an oval dish. The green dish held trinkets that obviously had belonged to Beulah. Liza pulled the top drawer of the bureau out and found a well-worn Bible and an old carved wooden box. She was hesitant to take them out but decided to carry them downstairs so Pricilla and she could look through it together.

Jeremiah and Pricilla were quite busy preparing food for the day. Liza carried the two items into the dining area and placed them on a table in the far corner. She said to Pricilla, "I don't think I should handle Mr. Foster's private things just by myself. I'd like for you to look at the old box and his Bible with me."

Pricilla looked at her with understanding, nodded her head and said, "We'll look together as soon as I finish making the pies for today."

Liza went about helping with other chores and waiting on customers until Pricilla had finished the baking. As they sat down to begin the task, they both realized that Foster hadn't made known to anyone of the disposal of his personal effects for the time when he would be gone. The old carved box measured about eight by eight inches square and three inches deep. The hinges were solid copper, although they had turned green for lack of being polished. The eyes of the two women grew large as they looked inside. Such an assortment of treasures they had never seen.

Inside were several Indian arrowheads, stones of flint and quartz, a silver wedding band, a leather strap, an Indian medicine bag, and a coin purse that had been embroidered with seed pearls sewn on it. In the bottom of the box was a yellowed paper, folded and crinkled. Pricilla carefully picked it up and unfolded it.

"Liza, look at this!" Pricilla exclaimed. "This is dated 1782."

"Name: Browning, Chester. Arrived: Virginia From: England

"Wife: Clara, and young boy, Foster."

"This must be Foster's father's papers from when he immigrated with his parents to America. We're holding a piece of history."

"I do say, that's somethin'," Liza said.

The women now set their attention upon the old, leather-covered Bible, which was worn and split on the corners. Pricilla opened the book and saw that the pages were worn on the corners, many stained or torn. In the center were pages titled "Records." Foster's grandparents, his parents, and all their children were recorded with their birth dates. On the next page was written a record of deaths, names, and dates.

Liza said to Pricilla, "I ain't never seen relations' names put down like this. Do all white folks write names and such in their Bible?"

"Probably not all, but many do because it's important to keep good family records."

"I can't read much, you know."

"I'll help you with that. We can do a little bit day by day," Pricilla told her.

The two women continued looking through the Bible, and, to their surprise, they found a detailed drawing of a farm home and a yellowed piece of paper that looked legal.

"I think this might be a land deed. Jeremiah needs to look at it. We must find his children and pass all this to them," Pricilla stated.

The following few weeks were filled with the task of finding Foster's relations. Brady and Jeremiah rode many miles tracing his children but had no luck of locating them. Jeremiah and Pricilla couldn't decide what to do. Should they close the boardinghouse and find another place to live or stay there and continue what they had been doing? It was discussed at great length with their pastor and their best friends. The consensus was for them to stay for the time being.

❋

Muscles and Whiskers had been keeping a close watch on the boardinghouse every day. The time had finally presented itself that the two scoundrels had been waiting for. They saw Amos, his wife, with the young girl, get into the buckboard and head out alone in an easterly direction. The two followed some distance behind for two hours and then decided to make their move.

The family had stopped beside a small creek in order to rest and water the horses. Liza reached back to fetch the basket of food that she had prepared for the trip, and it wasn't in the wagon. She turned to Amos and said, "I can't believe it! We forgot the food basket. I must 'a left it in the kitchen."

"We can't go back now. We'll get more food in town," Amos told her.

"I'm so sorry," she told him.

"Never mind, we gonna be all right. If you're ready, we'll get back on the wagon and go ahead." As soon as they were seated, Muscles and Whiskers rode upon them, quick as a flash with their guns drawn.

"You're gonna go somewhere, all right. We're gonna take you south back to the farm you came from," Muscles announced with a firm voice.

"Whiskers, take your rope and tie this big nigger up and put him in the back. I'll fasten my horse to the back, and I'll take over driving."

"You leave us alone," Liza shouted. "We're free. You got no right to do this."

"You be quiet woman." At that time Muscles tied her hands together and gagged her with a dirty rag he had in his saddlebag. Liza's daughter cried out "Mama, Mama."

He turned his attention to Marianne and told her, "Hush up that cryin' right now." She sobbed quietly. Amos had been thrown onto the back of the buckboard with as much force as Whiskers could muster, and he laughed when Amos groaned. The kidnappers weren't aware that a gun was under the seat. The problem was that it was hidden under some blankets, and, with his hands tightly tied behind him, it would be difficult for Amos to get to the gun and use it. Muscles began driving the wagon.

❖

223

Pricilla spotted the food basket, which had been placed on the floor beside the end of the table. She said to Jeremy, "Look, Liza left without their basket. They've been gone almost an hour. What should we do?"

"Joseph, grab your rifle and come with me, and we'll see if we can catch up to Amos and Liza. Jonah, stay here and help Pricilla while I'm gone."

"Sure thing, I'll take care of her and the home." It made him feel like a grown-up by being given the responsibility. Within minutes, the men were galloping down the road.

They pressed hard for some time and then reined back their horses. "Amos and Liza would've rested after riding a couple hours, I think," Jeremy remarked. "We shouldn't be too far behind their horse and wagon."

A half hour later, they stopped by the same creek Amos had stopped to rest the horses. Of course they didn't realize the circumstance until Jeremy observed many fresh horse tracks. He said to Joseph, "Look at this. Among the wagon tracks are fresh horse tracks. You don't suppose they met up with some others on the road?"

Joseph answered, "I can't figure it out; maybe it's nothing."

"Come on, let's try to catch up. They may need help."

The two immediately jumped on their horses and again took off at full speed. They rode on until their horses were wheezing, and their coats were lathered with sweat.

Jeremy was the first to say, "Whoa, boy," and come to a stop beneath a large oak tree and dismounted. Joseph quickly did the same. "Dad, we need to plan what to do if we find Amos and his family in trouble," Joseph suggested. "We can't just ride up to them."

"You're right, son. We'll ride along more carefully from here on; by doing that, we will be more in control of the situation. If Amos is in danger, we will be able to help him with the advantage of surprise." They let their horses cool down and then resumed their quest.

They rode up a hill, and when they reached the crest, they could see the wagon about a quarter mile ahead. Jeremy and Joseph saw that Amos and his family were in a predicament. The two halted and observed the situation. They saw Liza, but they hadn't seen Amos, and they couldn't figure that part out. The two men looked like the same pair that had been giving Amos and Jonah a bad time. They waited patiently until the wagon disappeared around the bend of the road. After exchanging ideas for a plan, they decided to keep following at a distance and wait until the wagon halted for the night.

Jeremy and his son trailed the wagon as discreetly as possible. There were occasional stops when Muscles and Whiskers got down and walked around, apparently discussing what they were going to do. They had taken a route south, evidently heading for the Ohio River and a place to cross. At sundown, the wagon pulled over, which indicated they were stopping for the night. They waited far enough away to not be seen and watched the activity, and then they saw Amos being helped out of the wagon.

"Look at that! Amos's hands are tied up. They had him down in the wagon bed," Joseph announced.

"We'll wait until they bed down, and it gets quiet," Jeremy told Joseph. They watched the men get what appeared to be food out of their saddlebags and share with their captives. Soon they could see the moon shining occasionally between floating clouds as the sounds of the night overtook the silence. They were thankful it wasn't a full moon. Time seemed to pass in slow motion.

Jeremy and Joseph had walked their horses very slowly to a safe distance from the kidnappers' camp and tethered them loosely. They would make their move. They proceeded with stealth into the area where Amos and his family were. Jeremy went to Amos first and clamped his hand over his mouth, knowing he would let out a yell. Amos immediately recognized who was there. He nudged Liza and the girl.

The five moved slowly so as to not break the silence, and Jeremy signaled for Amos and his family to leave first. They were leaving when an owl flew past Marianne and hooted, which caused her to shriek. Muscles jumped to his feet and reached for his rifle. Before he got it, Jeremy shouted, "I wouldn't do that if I were you!"

Whiskers had awakened with the commotion and looked around for his gun. "Watch out! I've got you in my sights." Amos had come back and retrieved his gun.

"Joseph, get their guns and bring them over here," Jeremy ordered.

"What'll we do with these guys?" Joseph asked.

"Let's tie them to a tree. They can stay there until someone comes along. We'll take their horses and their boots too."

"You can't do that to us. No tellin' how long we'll be here," Muscles yelled out.

"That's better than you deserve, you no good pile of puke!" Amos countered.

"There's one more thing to say. Don't you *ever* come back to our town. I guarantee you, if you do, I will shoot on the spot, without any questions. *Got that?*" Jeremy shouted. The men hung their heads and didn't answer.

"Do you understand?" He asked again loudly. They both looked up and nodded. "Right answer," Jeremy asserted.

The men were bound separately and securely to two separate trees, and their boots were removed and tossed into the wagon. Amos, Liza, and Marianne got back into the wagon, and everyone headed back northward. Joseph had put the food basket in the wagon bed when they had reached their tied horses.

They traveled a couple hours before stopping for the night. They felt assured that the two ruffians wouldn't give them any more problems that night. Just before they lay down, Joseph stated, "It's a good thing you forgot your food basket, or we probably wouldn't ever have seen you again."

"I'll never be able to thank you enough for saving me and my family. God was surely looking out for us," Amos declared.

☀

At dawn, the travelers were up and getting ready to return home. There was little to eat, but they shared what they had, then they started up the road. They arrived late afternoon, weary and hungry, but were grateful to be in secure surroundings. Of course they related the adventure to Pricilla, who was appalled by what had taken place. They all sat together and ate their meal as they talked of the current conditions and changes that were taking place throughout the country.

Jeremy told that he had heard there was a lot of violent fighting in the state of Kansas between those wanting slavery and those who were antislavery. The slavery issue had reached the Congress of the United States, and it was being debated.

Amos looked at his family with such deep concern that his forehead had gone into a deep frown. He said to Liza, "We will have a long, serious talk about all this." Her face reflected his as a pool of tears formed in her eyes.

After the Sunday church service, Brady, Frank, Luke, Jeremiah, and all their families gathered at the boardinghouse with Amos and his family. Everyone had brought bowls of food to share; it was a happy time to share and enjoy their friendships. They laughed as they shared stories from the past times together. After everybody had finished the main meal, Pricilla brought out pie she had made for dessert.

"Pricilla, my dear, you've outdone yourself," Jeremiah told her. "This pie is delicious." Pricilla smiled and said, "Thank you," and then she did a full curtsey, which brought an outbreak of chuckles and giggles from the others. The youngsters ate quickly and left the table to go outside. As the meal concluded, and all were getting ready to go home, Amos spoke up. "Friends, Liza and I have something to tell ya all. You know what we've been through lately when we got captured and taken. The worst fear of our lives happened to us. We can't take another chance of that happening to our family again, so we are going to pack up and move farther north."

The women gasped. Brady said, "Are you sure this is what you want? Nobody else has given one bit of problem, have they?"

"No, but we found that people will do anything for money, whether it be right or wrong. We got to go 'cause the people around here heard 'bout what happened, and someone else will try."

"I just don't know what I'll do without you around here," Pricilla said softly. "Both you and your children are so dear to us."

Liza wept quietly but managed to say, "We don't want to go; we have to go."

All the men told Amos that they would help him any way they could. It was a somber ending to a joyous day. The women hugged each other and asked Liza to keep in touch if possible. Two days later, Amos, Liza, and their family bid good-bye to the Village of Frey.

PART 3

PART 3

Chapter 23

EIGHT YEARS LATER. DECEMBER, 1855. BRADY AND Anna Marie had been married twenty years. Patrick was eighteen years old, and Timothy turned sixteen last September. Both had grown up into fine young men. The twins, Lilly Anne and Lila Rose, were pretty young women nearly fifteen. They had learned to cook and sew, which included quilting and mending. Lila Rose had become a fine horse rider and enjoyed fishing with her brothers and her father. On the other hand, Lilly Anne excelled in the art of baking cakes and cookies, and beautiful needlework . So good, in fact, that she made hand-embroidered satin purses for women and had sold some through the mercantile store.

Jeremiah and Pricilla had their two children: Joseph, age fifteen, and Jenny, age thirteen. Since Joseph was around ten years old, he had an eye for Lilly Anne. He would play tricks on her and tease her about being a tomboy. Many times they would race their horses from the schoolhouse to the road crossing a mile west of town. It was always a very close race. Sometimes Joseph would let her win on purpose so he could see her eyes sparkle and hear her lilting laughter.

Interestingly, Timothy had his eyes on Jenny. He rode his horse into town with any excuse so he could stop by the boardinghouse and have a sarsaparilla. Jenny helped in the boardinghouse by serving the customers and had learned to cook many of the food items that were served. She kept her hair in pigtails because Pricilla told her she didn't want any of her hair to get onto the food. Pricilla kept several brightly colored ribbons for Jenny to wear on her hair, which Tim enjoyed untying when he got the chance. She would say, "Stop teasing me," but actually enjoyed the attention, as most young girls would. He would laugh softly and give her a wink.

Three years ago Frank had a terrible accident when he and Luke were sawing tree trunks. Frank lost his grip on a large log and, as he struggled to catch the log, he lost his footing. His left hand swung around and hit the huge saw blade, which swiftly cut it off. It took several weeks, but his arm healed, and now he copes well with having only one hand.

Patrick was an avid hunter and quite a good marksman. He could shoot a squirrel in its head while it ran across a tree limb. He would often bring home three or more for his mother to cook. She would bake them in a pan with potatoes, green beans, and gravy; to him it was delicious. Pat had always loved the outdoors, whatever it might be. He sometimes would take his gun, walk into the woods, and find a nice cool spot and sit down. He would inhale the sight of the flora and buzzing bees, the animals and birds. He watched the wind rustling the leaves, observing every living thing for two to three hours. What would his life be like if he was an Indian? They live off of the land and are keen on the ways of nature.

He rode into town one day when the weather wasn't bitterly cold to buy ammunition and a new pair of boots, as his had hardened and cracked. He walked into the mercantile and over to the counter where the boots were displayed. He stopped in his tracks the moment his eyes fell upon the most beautiful girl he had ever seen. Her brown hair flowed down to her shoulder blades, tied back with a green scarf. She wore a matching green blouse under her black riding coat, which caused her hazel eyes to sparkle. He looked at her feet, and she wore a pair of tooled leather boots. He could hardly breathe.

"Hello," he managed to say to her.

"Hello," she said back.

"Are you new in town? I don't think I've seen you before."

"Yes, I am. My father bought a farm north of here."

"My name's Patrick, I'm usually called Pat. Uh … it's nice to meet you. What's your name?"

"I'm Catherine."

"That's a very nice name. I came for some new boots; mine started leaking."

She laughed and said, "If your feet get wet and cold, you'll feel cold all over. It's a good idea to buy new boots before yours get worse."

"You're so right," he said, wearing a big smile.

"After I get them, I'd like to buy you some hot tea and a roll, if you want."

"Sure, I'd like that."

Pat felt beads of perspiration on his brow and upper lip. He could hardly concentrate on his task. He watched Catherine walk away to look at other scarves. He stood there as if paralyzed. After a few moments, he brought himself back to reality. Now, maybe he could seriously tend to business. He examined the available boots but kept turning around and checking to see if she was still there. He made his purchase and then turned his complete attention toward Catherine.

"Are you finished shopping?" he asked her.

"Yes, I didn't find anything I wanted," she replied. He took her arm and guided her out the door and toward the boardinghouse. They went inside and sat at a table a distance away from other patrons. Jenny appeared shortly and asked what they wanted to eat at which Pat replied, "We'll have hot tea and some sweet bread." Jenny smiled at Pat, and he gave her a wink as she left to get their food.

The two sat and talked and laughed until they realized an hour had passed. As they walked out the door, Pat took a hold of Catherine's hand and said, "I would like to see you again. Is that something that you would like?"

She replied, "That would be nice. I'll be at church Sunday with my parents," she answered.

"I'll be there, so I'll plan to see you then." His palms were sweaty as he wrapped both of his hands around her hand. "I'm so glad I met you." He gave her a quick kiss on the cheek, then left. It wasn't her

233

first kiss on the cheek, even so it made her feel good. She thought, *He's a nice fellow and good-looking. I can't wait to see him this Sunday.* She giggled to herself.

Pat got home in time to help with the chores. He whistled as he cared for the animals and wore a permanent smile on his face. Brady noticed right away by Pat's demeanor that he was in an exceptionally good humor. It seemed that the chores were completed in record time, and the men were able to go inside early that evening. When supper was over, Pat got up from the table, turned his attention to his mother, and said, "That was a great meal, Mom," and gave her a hug, and then he left the kitchen.

"My goodness," Anna Marie remarked, "he certainly is in a good mood."

"Yeah, he was whistling as he worked in the barn before we were finished," Brady told her.

"You know, something must have happened in town today. I'm a little curious," his mother commented.

☀

Sunday didn't arrive too soon for Pat. He had taken care when he readied himself for church by smoothing out the few wrinkles on his shirt and trousers and got dressed. He brushed his hair, then took scissors and cut away the few stray hairs on his brow and ears. When he finished and came out of his room, he looked clean and neat, a young man at his prime.

"You look quite handsome this morning," his mother commented as he entered the kitchen.

"Naw," he responded, but the remark from his mother gave him confidence. Soon afterward, the family headed toward the Village of Frey for church. As he and Tim mounted their horses, Pat found it difficult to conceal his anticipation. From the moment they rode onto the church premises, Pat's eyes eagerly searched for Catherine. He nearly lost his balance when he dismounted from his horse.

Tim noticed his blunder and remarked, "What's with you, brother?"

"I'm all right, nothing's wrong. Can't someone miss their step once?" he answered defensively.

The church was filling rapidly with all of the families arriving and taking their seats. Pat sat down slowly as his eyes panned over all his friends and neighbors. Then he spotted her, the girl seated across the room smartly dressed in blue, wearing a brimmed hat with a matching blue bow. He couldn't help but stare at her. She hadn't seen him. *She's the most beautiful lady I've ever seen,* he thought. He sat through the worship service—lost in his own thoughts. He couldn't remember one thing the minister said, and then church was over.

Some of the men gathered and discussed the possibility of having a town celebration; after all, it was their town's tenth anniversary from the time it had been named the Village of Frey. The women gathered to talk about their children and their daily lives. This was the time young children could run and play, and the young adults, too grown up for play, stood around and joked, talked, and flirted, usually outside when the weather permitted, away from parental scrutiny.

She saw him, and he saw her. Both smiled, and their eyes lit up. He tried to control himself as he slowly walked toward her. This was not the time to stumble.

"Hi," he said. "You look very nice," he told her softly.

"Thanks," she replied. "I'm happy to see you today."

He took her by the arm and said, "Let's go over by the trees where we can visit alone." She didn't say anything but walked with him. As they got acquainted, they learned more about each other. They couldn't deny that they felt chemistry between them.

Pat looked back toward the others, who stood near the church, and then he pulled her around behind the large maple tree. He took her in his arms and kissed her on the cheek. She looked up at him and smiled, and then he kissed her on her lips. The taste of her lips made him tingle. He held her close, relishing the moment, something he had never felt before.

"That was nice," he said to her.

"It was," she agreed.

"We better go back before my father starts looking for me," she told him.

"Give me another kiss, then we'll go," he replied. She tilted her head up toward him, and they shared another kiss together.

"Okay, let's go," he told her. "We don't want to get your father in a bad humor."

They walked back over to join the other young adults. Some of the other young women looked at each other and giggled, then looked back at Catherine and Pat. It didn't matter at all to Pat; he just looked at Catherine and smiled. By now the parents and older adults were beginning to make their way out of the church and go to their buggies.

Catherine looked and saw her parents come out the church door and said, "I need to go now. Will you be here next Sunday?"

"A herd of wild horses couldn't keep me away. Will you be in town this week?" he replied.

"I'm not sure. We usually come to town on Wednesday for supplies."

"I'm sure that I'll have to come and get hard candy or a hair brush for me," he stated jokingly as he watched her face light up with a big smile. He chuckled and looked deeply into her eyes. "Hope I see you then."

She nodded and said, "Me too."

The following Wednesday arrived, and when Pat's eyes popped open, he nearly jumped out of bed. His only thought was, *I'm going to ride into town today, and, hopefully, I'll see Catherine.* The incentive to see his sweetheart motivated him to complete his chores quickly. Both of his parents noted his cheerfulness that morning at the breakfast table.

Pat and Catherine met every Wednesday and Sunday for the next two months. Their summer romance was growing into love. He wanted to be able to be alone with her, away from watchful eyes at church or in town. He planned to ask her father if he could take her for a Sunday afternoon buggy ride.

Catherine's father, Albert, stood about six feet tall, thin and bony. His dark eyes were set deep into his eye sockets, and his eyebrows were thick and wiry. His moustache and long beard had strips of gray growing in them. His nose, set between his high cheekbones, was thin and went to a point. Sometimes he looked stern, yet when he laughed, he looked pleasant, even likeable.

Patrick had made up his mind. Today's the day that he would talk to Catherine's father when church concluded and the congregation left for home. He and Catherine walked up to Albert, and Pat said, "Hello," and extended his hand to shake his. Albert took the offer, and they looked at each other straight in the eye. Albert said hello back, and a slight smile actually could be seen in the corners of his mouth.

"Mr. McKay, I'm Patrick Patterson, and I would like to have your permission to take your daughter, Catherine, with me for a buggy ride and a picnic this afternoon. I promise to be a gentleman at all times."

"How old are you, Patrick?"

"Eighteen."

"Are you a man of your word?"

"Yes sir."

Albert paused and gave Pat a look-over, then said, "All right, you may see my daughter, but be sure to have her home before sundown. Do you understand?" Albert spoke with a tone in his voice that meant business.

"Yes, sir, you can count on that. Thank you, Mr. McKay." Pat shook Albert's hand once more, guided Catherine by her forearm, and they walked toward his parents' buggy. He could feel the tension relax in his body. He faced toward his sweetheart, looked into her eyes, and they both smiled. He gently helped her to the buggy seat. He went to the other side and climbed up, took the reins, and they trotted away.

How wonderful can the world seem to be when two young sweethearts are alone together for the first time? Everything they see and hear delights their hearts. A feeling of freedom surrounds them as they feel the warm sun on their skin and the breeze brushing their face as they ride down the road. The birds whistle songs of joy as if calling to join with them.

They had left the church, and after having gone a few miles, Brady pulled the buggy over to a shady spot back in behind a grove of trees. He felt his heart rate increase as he turned his face toward Catherine and pulled her close to hug her, then he put his hand to her face and tilted it up toward him. Slowly he put his lips on hers and kissed her gently for several moments as he pulled her even nearer. She wrapped her arms around him as she let his love encompass her.

When they finished their kiss, he said to her, "You make me feel so good. I could hold you all day long."

"I like it too," she responded. "You know, I never had a boyfriend that I cared for before you."

"You are my first girlfriend," he paused, then said, "and I want to keep you."

They enjoyed the closeness, and then Pat released Catherine, and said, "We need to keep going because I have a nice place picked out for our picnic." He flipped the reins on the horse's back. They went back onto the road, and away they traveled. She held his arm as they went along, and she began singing. He looked at his sweetheart, smiled, and joined her. They would finish one song, chat and giggle, and then go into another.

"Here's the place," Pat told her as he guided the horse over to a level grassy spot. Squirrels and chipmunks scurried away when the horse and buggy arrived. A few crows, perched in the trees, scolded the pair when they got off the buggy. It was like they were saying, "This is my home; go away!" Catherine laughed at them and called back, "Calm down. We won't hurt you."

Pat grabbed the quilt out of the buggy and spread it out where they had shade yet a nice view next to a pond, which was framed with wildflowers, cattails, and a few scattered willow trees. They sat down next to each other and held hands. She leaned her head over on his shoulder. They watched and saw an occasional fish jump and swirl the water. They laughed as they told stories of things that had happened in their lives.

The couple lost track of time. Pat suddenly realized they hadn't eaten. "I'm hungry. Let's eat. I'll get the picnic basket out for us." They both stood up and walked to the buggy.

"Let me help," Catherine said. He handed her the small bag, which held cookies and some bread slices, then they went back to the quilt, giggling as the crows scolded and the chipmunks scattered.

After they ate, Pat packed the leftovers into the basket and then lay down on the quilt. "Come here and lie beside me," he told her. It didn't take any coaxing as she quickly obliged and moved close to his side; he immediately held her hand.

"It's very peaceful here even with the twittering birds and other sounds around us," she commented.

"I agree, but the best part is that we finally have some time to be alone." He pulled her hand to his mouth and kissed the back of it. She turned on her side and they were face to face, looking into each other's eyes. He was moving toward her to kiss her lips when they heard a strange sound.

"What's that!" Catherine said as she sat up to see.

"I'm not sure." Pat's horse became nervous and began pulling against his reins and whinnied. By this time both of them were standing up and alert.

They heard it again, only louder. They heard twigs snap and bushes rustle, and then they saw what it was. It was a big black bull. He was tossing his head and snorting. He let out a loud bellow. Quick as a flash, Pat and Catherine grabbed the quilt and basket and ran as fast as they could for the buggy. Of course the bull saw them. He bellowed again and began pawing the ground.

"Hurry, get in the buggy," Pat told her. He untied the reins as fast as possible and jumped onto the seat. The bull had decided to run toward them, his head tossing up and down. Pat snapped the reins hard on the horse's back, and the buggy leaped forward. The horse and buggy nearly ran into some bushes, and Pat pulled the reins hard to the left. They had slowed a little, and about that time the bull rammed the buggy on the rear board. It didn't break, but it jolted the two passengers and caused Catherine to yell out.

Pat hollered out several times, "Giddy up, go," to the horse. He was now up to a full gallop. They were putting some distance between them and the bull. They kept up the pace until they were sure they weren't in any harm. Feeling safer, he let the horse trot slowly all the way back to Catherine's home. During that time, they chatted about their adventure on their first time being out together.

"I thought I had found the perfect place to take you; really, I did."

"I agree, it was quite nice—except for one thing ..."

"Yeah, what would that be?"

"I don't care to be attacked by an angry bull again," she teased.

"I have to agree with you." He kissed her good-bye before he helped her off the buggy. "I'll see you again," he said with a twinkle in his eye.

Chapter 24

THE DATE OF THE TOWN FESTIVAL HAD BEEN SET FOR the first Friday and Saturday of July. The committee members of the various events had been scurrying around making their final arrangements. They planned games and contests for all ages, men and women. Games for the young children had been decided. There would be a long-distance jumping contest, egg rolling on the church lawn, foot races around the church property, and a rock-throwing contest for ages eight through eleven. Children ages twelve and older would have foot races, horse races, firewood throwing contest, and a tug of war. Some of these same contests would be for the older children but would be more difficult.

The women were planning to participate in the pie, cookie, and cake baking contests. The top winners' desserts would receive colored ribbons and would later be auctioned off to the highest bidder. The older members of the community would busy themselves by selling knitted shawls, socks, and lap robes. Others would display their whittling and basket weaving. Some would have to be content with playing checkers, and if someone would win seven games in a row, he or she would receive a ribbon declaring that person a champion checker player. The two-day event would conclude with a hymn sing program followed by a barn dance. Jeremiah listened to the conversations, observed the women bustling around, and saw the men working and laughing together. He realized the happiness and excitement that was building in the community, now his home town.

The weekend of the celebration had arrived. Jeremiah and Pricilla had asked Lorelei, Anna Marie, and her girls to come and help with preparing and serving meals at the boardinghouse. Lila Rose and Lilly Anne were anxious to go spend two whole days in town but only if there happened to be an unoccupied room available. Pricilla had given them instructions about how to approach customers and be polite to them while getting their food orders.

Frank, Luke, and Shawn had split some logs at the saw mill to build a platform on the south side of the church property. For several days, Brady, Jeremiah, and their sons had helped to build it. On the last two days of construction, they decided to nail some solid posts on each corner upon which a covering could be attached.

Preacher Samuel had been watching the men work and even offered some advice when he could. "Are you sure those posts will hold if there should be a strong wind?" he asked.

"Have no worries, a two-ton elephant couldn't knock this down," Frank replied. At that remark, all the men laughed heartily. "You always put your trust in the Lord, and you can put your trust in our building skills today."

The preacher smiled and replied, "I'm glad to hear that. I sure don't want any of God's children hurt on his property. Keep up the good work, boys."

Vic and Lodema lived next to the church. They had volunteered to move their herd of thirty sheep to the church yard so they could eat the grass and weeds down before the end of the week. The herd had been moved in a week ago; wire had been strung to prevent the sheep from wandering away, and, consequently, the task had been accomplished. The bad side that resulted was the manure deposits that were made. The people would have to accept that part.

❋

Pat and Catherine had been seeing each other regularly. Their affection for each other was growing stronger week by week, and their time together led to opportunities for more passionate hugging and kissing, nothing more. They had, however, declared their love for each other.

Catherine's father had been keeping close watch on the two, especially on Sundays. He would watch them hold hands and walk back to the trees at the edge of the church yard. He didn't want the situation to go any further. Albert felt that his daughter was much too young to get seriously involved with a young man, especially one that still worked for his father and didn't have much to offer beyond his affection for her. He made up his mind that he would soon have a serious talk with Pat to let him know that he wanted more for his daughter.

☀

It was a glorious day, the first day of celebration. From the first light of the day, the town bustled as each one went about their appointed round. The children were as excited as if it was Christmas morning, which caused them to run around and shout in high-pitched voices. Jeremiah and everyone who came to work at the boardinghouse had been baking and cooking the past two days for the expected crowds of today and tomorrow.

The whole Patterson family arose earlier than usual, aware that there were many things to do to be gone for the whole day. It was almost a comedy of errors. The men completed the morning chores, but Tim managed to spill half a bucket of milk because the mama cat and her five kittens were wrapping themselves around his feet when he stepped out of the barn, milk pail in hand. Anna Marie had Lilly Anne cook the mush. The pan had been left on the stove unattended, and the mush had scorched, ruining its taste. Meanwhile, Anna Marie was gathering up things that she thought they may need during the day, and she didn't want to forget the cake and cookies that she was entering in the cooking contests. They ate their not-so-tasty breakfast in shifts. They then made their way to the buggy, where Brady, Anna

243

Marie, and the girls were seated while the boys hopped astraddle their horses and rode to town.

Pat, Tim, and Joseph were in charge of the youngsters' games aged seven to twelve. The games were to start at nine o'clock, but most of the children got there an hour early, and they had to be quieted down several times due to some rough playing.

Lorelei had come into town with Luke and Shawn that morning. The men were to help with the games later on that day and generally supervise the activities to help keep all the children from getting hurt. Lorelei joined Elizabeth, Preacher Samuel's wife, who had gathered together the five- to six-year-old children. She was reading stories out of the Bible to them. Most of the youngsters had heard the stories, which made for lively discussions. When the children became restless, they all stood up and played follow the leader here and there around the church, letting the children take turns at being the leader.

Finally, the time arrived for the first round of games for the young adults. Of course, the young men who were more mature and physically stronger were ready to show off their physical prowess.

The log throw began with small chunks of wood and proceeded to larger and larger sizes with each round. Luke and Frank marked the distances of each throw, which was charted on a large board. Each round would eliminate those who had thrown the lesser distances. The game created a lot of enthusiasm, especially when the young ladies gathered to watch the events. Shawn, Pat, Tim, and Joseph were among the oldest and strongest on hand to participate.

Pricilla's daughter, Jenny, begged off kitchen work for a while to go watch Tim try to win some of the games. Catherine and her family arrived in town around noon. Her mother walked into the church with her baked goods for the contest, and her father had wandered over to a group of men standing in the shade.

Catherine wore her riding pants, fastened with a belt, and a loose, long-sleeved green blouse. Her head was topped with a straw hat embellished with a wide green ribbon bow, the ribbon ends falling a few inches down the back of her head. She looked very attractive.

Pat hadn't seen her walk up until suddenly their eyes met. He nearly forgot to breathe; she looked so beautiful to him.

Shawn yelled at Pat, "Your eyeballs are about to fall out!"

"Huh? Oh yeah—she's so beautiful. I can't believe she picked me."

"Well, you better get your mind on the game," Shawn told him, "because you might break your neck looking at her instead of watching where you throw the log!"

Sensing that Pat would probably try his hardest to win because *she* was watching, Tim put the challenge upon himself to win because *his* girl was watching.

Four other boys entered into the contests were young teens who, mostly, hadn't the matured strength of the older young men. However, one of them was tall and bulky and probably outweighed Pat by fifty pounds. The rest of the fellows looked at him, but no one knew him or where he came from. As the contestants were called, they learned his name was Norman.

They were lined up by their height. The smaller guys would throw first, leading to the biggest throwing last. Norman would throw last. Frank and Luke marked every throw, and after the fourth round, Norman was still with the older boys. He would step up to the line, pick up the log effortlessly, and give a toss as if it was a loaf of bread—no problem!

The crowd that was watching the event had grown much larger. They were cheering and saying things such as, "That's a boy," "Good job," "Great toss," and "What a throw." Pat, Tim, Shawn, Joseph, and Norman were the last five in the contest. They'd look at Norman, and he'd just smile a big, dopey smile like "that was nothin' at all." The other four relaxed and tossed the log, then laughed and joked.

"Bet you can't do that," one would say.

"Nothin' to it," said another.

The guys went through the whole pile of wood and had no winner.

"Fellows, we need to figure out a way to get a winner, so this is what we'll do. You will throw two logs at one time. If you all do it, we'll make the distance farther and farther until only one will win. Got it?" They nodded affirmatively.

Shawn went first. He threw his two logs fifteen feet. Joseph matched the throw. Next was Timmy. He threw twenty feet. Pat threw twenty-two feet. Last was Norman. Norman threw and matched the twenty-two feet. Pat and Norman were now the last two in the contest. Jenny and Catherine had moved up to the front of the onlookers to see how the contest would end. Catherine hadn't noticed that her father, Albert, was among those taking interest in the competition.

Frank brought in two extra-large logs and placed them on the start line. He said, "You will each have two chances to see how far you are able to throw these logs. The one that throws the farthest will win." Pat and Norman looked at each other and smiled.

Pat went first. He let out a grunt as he picked up the one and cradled it on his bent arms.

"All right, let's finish this," Frank stated. "Throw the log!"

Pat inhaled a big breath, drew back, and heaved the log with all his strength. It flew high and long. Everybody clapped loudly and hollered out.

Norman was next to get his log. He held end to end and threw mightily, and it landed exactly where Pat's had landed.

Pat took a hold of the big log on each end, began turning as fast as possible and gave a big throw using all his might. It went much further than his first throw. It was now Norman's turn. He gripped the log the same as Pat, rotated his body the same, and just as he heaved to throw, his feet got tangled; he stumbled and fell down, with the log landing only five feet from where he fell. Pat had won the contest.

Catherine broke away from the others and ran up to Pat and hugged him. She turned her face up toward his, and he kissed her unabashedly. Everyone was cheering and clapping. Albert suddenly appeared right beside his daughter and Pat. He grabbed her arm and pulled her back.

"You are not to see my daughter again. Do you understand me?" he said to Pat.

Catherine spoke up. "Father, no. Don't do this!" He glared at Pat and said, "Stay away from her. She's too young to get serious." Albert looked at Pat sternly.

Pat and Catherine were completely surprised at this action. Before Pat could speak, Albert turned Catherine around and led her away. The applause and cheering stopped. Frank walked over to Pat and presented him with the winning ribbon and shook his hand, saying, "Congratulations, nice game."

He presented Norman with the second-place ribbon and said, "Norman, too bad that you fell. You did a good job," and shook his hand. Norman half-smiled after hearing that. He turned to walk away, but some of the young men in the crowd patted him on the shoulder. One said, "You would 'a won if you hadn't tripped." He walked off.

Pat watched Catherine leave town. He felt a pain at his stomach. *What now?* he thought. His head was whirling. Brady approached his son, but as he got close, Pat spoke. "I can't talk to you now, Pa; I need to go." He mounted his horse and rode off.

The next two days were as torture to Pat. He wanted Catherine more than anything. He had a talk with Luke and Frank about the situation, expecting an answer. "You better wait a while before you try to approach Albert. Give him time to cool down," Frank advised.

Pat waited three weeks before he decided to ride out to Catherine's house. He was hopeful that he could persuade Albert that he was a gentleman. As he rode on the lane up to their home, his heart lightened at the prospect of seeing the woman that he loved, almost cheerful.

Catherine was sitting on the porch doing needlework. He waved, and she waved back. He dismounted and tied his horse away from the house. He began walking toward her, uneasy yet alert. He was about to go up the porch steps when the door opened, and Albert walked out.

Pat paused. Albert stood quietly and then spoke. "Don't take another step young man!" He pointed his finger straight toward Pat. "Didn't I tell you to leave my daughter alone?"

"Yes sir. I thought that maybe we could have a talk and work this out."

"There's nothing to work out."

"Please, sir, your daughter is special to me. I have the highest respect for her."

Catherine stood up and took a step. "Papa, please let him stay a few minutes."

"All right, I'll give him a little time, and then he'll have to go." Albert sat down on a chair, watched, and listened intently.

Pat walked up toward Catherine as closely as he dared and told her, "I can't go on living here knowing that we can't be together."

"What will you do?"

I'll see you in a few days when I have the answer. Catherine, I want you to be mine." He kissed the tips of his fingers and placed them on her lips as he told her, "I love you." She touched his hand and whispered, "I love you." He turned and walked away. She watched him go until he was completely out of sight.

She turned toward her father as tears streamed down her face and said, "I hope you're happy. You've ruined my life." She turned and walked to a redbud tree next to their flower garden, sat on a bench, and wept.

☀

Pat lived through the following week as if his body and soul were in slow motion. All of his family felt his sadness even though Pat hadn't uttered a word about what had taken place. Every day he would get out of bed long before the rest of the family, fill the tea kettle with water, and set it on the cook stove. He'd put on his hat and long-sleeved shirt and quietly go out to the porch. He spent those mornings trying to sort out what to do with his life. He breathed in the fresh morning air and listened as the birds began their chirping, announcing another day on this farm that he had grown to love.

The two farm cats crept up on the porch and rubbed back and forth across his ankles. He would stroke their fur and listen to their purring, which soothed him as well as the cats. They'd sense when it was time for the cows to be milked and then scurry to the barn for their warm bowl of fresh milk. As he petted the soft, gentle creatures, he thought about life. *Those small cats, male and female, mated and had their litter every year. They fed and groomed their babies and taught them how to hunt.* It was an existence he now envied, even though he knew by now that life for humans would never be easy or simple.

The darkness of night began to fade when the first rays of light streaked across the sky. It was a beautiful Indiana sunrise. He now knew what he must do.

When Pat finished his breakfast, he spoke of his plans to his family. "Catherine's father has told me not to see her—says she's too young. I'm leaving the farm to make it on my own."

Brady spoke. "Give it time, son; no need to leave."

"It's hard to stay knowing I can't be near her," Pat explained.

Anna Marie felt tears fill her eyes and spill down her cheeks. "Running away can't be the answer," she told him. "Will you wait till Sunday? Maybe your father and I could talk to Albert."

"Ma, I'll wait, but he won't change his mind. I need to tell Catherine I'm leaving." *Maybe she'll wait for me,* he thought.

"Where will you go?" Timmy asked him.

"Don't know for sure. Right now the only trade I know is farming, so I'll find a farm to work on and try to save up some money to get my own place. I might go west and get some property that the government is giving away cheap.

Lila Rose and Lilly Anne couldn't believe all they heard. Lilly Anne said, "Mama, will we ever see Pat again after Sunday?"

"Of course we will," she answered as she hugged them both. Anna Marie had spoken assuredly to the girls, but she did so to convince herself as well.

Sunday arrived. Pat had gathered his belongings: clothes, a rain slicker, a Bible, paper and pen, and other miscellaneous items. On Saturday he had brushed his horse thoroughly and cleaned his hooves, then checked his horseshoes and replaced two. He had achieved peace with his decision and was ready to go. Pa had given him his set of saddlebags. Ma had stuffed a bag full of food, enough for a few days.

Pat and his family had arrived at church about the same time as the other members. They exchanged greetings as Pat's eyes eagerly searched for his love. Suddenly her eyes met his.

Pat couldn't concentrate on the sermon—all he could think of was *her*. She looked at him often. His arms wanted to hold her so much that he could hardly stand it. When church ended, he tried to walk close to her. When they got outside, he touched her arm, and she looked to see who was there. "I have to talk to you," he told her.

"But father—"

"Never mind him; this is important."

Albert was talking politics with a group of men and didn't notice Pat and Catherine as they walked around the church corner, out of his sight.

"You know I can't be with you," she said. He pulled her into his arms and kissed her fully on the lips. He released her but held one hand.

"Catherine, if you can't be with me, I can't stay around. I'm leaving home. Right now I don't know where I'm going. All I know is this: I must leave. Tell me you'll wait until I return, then we'll get married. Will you wait?"

She nodded her head and said, "Yes, I'll wait, but please don't go or else take me with you."

"No, you can't go. We aren't prepared to be on our own. I must go; it's the best for us right now. I'll let Ma and Pa know where I am. You can talk to them. They'll know about me." She began crying, and he pulled her back into his arms and held her. At that moment he wanted desperately to take her with him.

"I better let you go sweetheart. Here, I have something for you." He handed her a handkerchief. "Go ahead, look inside."

She opened the cloth and saw a necklace: a chain with a single pearl hanging from it.

"It means our love is pure as a pearl."

"Pat, it's beautiful. I'll wear it forever," she said. "Wait," and she took the ribbon from her hair and gave to him.

He kissed her again and said, "Wipe your tears, smile, and go to your family, and I'll go to mine. I promise I'll be back." They held hands another few moments, and she walked away.

❂

Fall was in the air. September had arrived. Anna Marie still worried about Patrick. She especially missed him at suppertime. Even though he was tired from a full day of work, he could still make the twins giggle or tell her something entertaining that had happened. Every evening Lilly Anne asked her mother if she knew where Pat was. Brady reassured Anna Marie and the twins that Pat knew how to take care of himself.

PART 4

PART 4

Chapter 25

HE DIDN'T KNOW WHY, BUT WHEN HE LEFT HOME HE had headed south. Maybe it was because his parents had talked so much about when they lived in Kentucky that it guided him in that direction. He had ridden at a steady pace, relaxed, taking in the scenery. He stopped and rested his horse, Buddy, on the road next to an apple orchard. Both man and beast enjoyed eating some of the ripe apples that had fallen off the trees. Pat shoved a few into his food bag before mounting up.

When the sun began its descent, he started looking for a place to spend the night. Within a short time, he had located a good spot. He tethered Buddy where he could graze on the cool grass, and then he went about gathering dry wood for a campfire. Before long, he had flames dancing over the small branches. He took the saddle, saddlebags, bedroll, and food bag off of Buddy and placed them near his campsite. After eating some of his food, he rolled out his blanket and stretched out on it.

As he lay there, he gazed at the sky and took in the beauty of the stars and the moon; it entered his soul. He had never really been as alone as he was at that moment. He closed his eyes and remembered being with Catherine, holding her, kissing her, and feeling so complete. He began to question himself. What am I doing? Why did I leave? His eyes popped open. He spotted the big dipper and the North Star. His conscious reminded him what his purpose was, and he knew it was the right thing, making it on his own. All he could hear were night sounds—owls and a few bird chirps. Sleep overcame him.

Pat awoke as the first streaks of dawn cut through the night sky. He had rested and was ready to continue his journey. He saddled his horse and packed his gear. As soon as he covered his campfire with dirt, he mounted Buddy and headed farther away from home. Pat stopped for a short while in the town of Bedford, where he tied Buddy to a hitch beside a water trough. He stepped inside the mercantile, probably to fend off his loneliness. He looked around a bit, then bought a box of matches and a length of rope, which he had left back home.

The store owner asked Pat, "Where are ya headed, young fella?"

"Guess I'll end up in Kentucky to see my Grandma and Grandpa."

"Ya know, you could go to Louisville and cross the Ohio River there. If you do, be sure and see the big steamboats that anchor there. They're something!"

"Good idea. I'd like that."

"Here, take this hardtack with you and a piece of sweet bread my wife has made."

"Thanks. That's right kind of you. I best leave now."

Pat rode out of town and through the countryside for a long time until he decided he and Buddy needed a break. He saw a small pond and observed only a small amount of brush on the bank. He dismounted and walked Buddy to the edge of the water to drink his fill. The air was brisk, and the breeze caused ripples across the water. Pat drank from his canteen and ate the piece of sweet bread he was given earlier. He looked around and watched the ducks that were swimming around, dipping their bills into the water. He took a few steps toward his horse and bent over to pick up the reins. Just as he reached down, he saw a large water snake crawling close to his hand. He moved back quickly yet cautiously. He wasn't sure if it was poisonous or not, and he didn't want to find out. He took a hold of the bridle beside Buddy's neck, slowly led him up the bank, and mounted up.

The horse and rider pressed onward. He didn't have any idea how far he was from the Ohio River, but he wanted to go as far as possible today. He didn't reach the ferry crossing until the next afternoon. When he approached the river, he was in awe of its size. Steamboats were going both up and down the river while others were docked in various ports. He had never seen such a large expanse of water. Then he noticed the city across the river. Called Louisville, he thought, *it must be the biggest city in America.*

☀

Life on the farm and business at the boardinghouse continued as normal. When she wasn't in school or riding her horse, Jenny continued to learn more about kitchen work and cooking. Timmy was now the older Patterson brother and had to work more to help his pa and keep an eye on his twin sisters. He saw Jenny every Sunday but seemed to come up with a reason to ride into town midweek for this or that, which allowed him to go by the boardinghouse. He and Jenny were quite attracted to each other. He couldn't wait for the barn dance that was coming up next month.

Catherine had become moody since Patrick left. She thought often of him as she hoped that he was all right. She hardly spoke to her father and actually avoided him as much as possible. At mealtime she would look down at her plate and eat in silence. Many times she thought, *I'll pack my clothes and leave in the middle of the night. Pa will be sorry he did this to me.*

In early October, Brady and Anna Marie received a short note from Patrick. They took the letter with them to church and showed it to Catherine. "Dear Ma and Pa, I've rented a room close to the Ohio River docks in Louisville, working on steamboat repair and construction. I am okay and learning a lot. I'm trying to save some money before I come back home. I send my love to all of you. Tell Catherine that I'll be back for her as soon as I can manage it. Love, your son, Pat"

Catherine read the letter and smiled. "Thank you for sharing his letter with me. It makes me feel better." Anna Marie gave her a hug and looked into Catherine's eyes. "I believe that you can trust Pat to do what he tells you he will do."

Catherine said to Anna Marie, "This is the necklace Pat gave me the last time we were together."

"It's beautiful. It'll remind you every day just how much he cares for you," Anna Marie told her. "Stay strong and true," she advised.

It was Saturday, the day of the barn dance. Morgan and Eileen Donahue were hosting the gathering at their farm. Pricilla had asked Eileen to sew Jenny a new dress for the occasion. Jenny was excited to attend the fun evening, for she truly loved to dance. She was sixteen and was growing into an attractive lady. That night Timothy worked as fast as he could to finish up his part of the farm chores. Tonight he wanted nothing more than to hold Jenny in his arms and dance with her.

It was a lively scene inside the building, which had been cleaned and simply decorated. Music was playing, guests were laughing and joking, and children were playing games; it was a festival. Jenny was wearing her new dress. It was made of a pale pink print with wide lace trim around the neckline, accented with pink ribbons. Pricilla had curled Jenny's hair and tied it back with a wide, matching bow. She felt like a princess and, actually, she was as beautiful as one. When Tim arrived at the dance, his eyes immediately started searching for hers. He had seen a group of other young girls, but he didn't recognize her from the back. He had never seen her look so fine. When she turned around, his heart skipped a couple beats, and he started walking toward her.

Tim greeted her, "Hi, Jenny. Wow, you look good!"

She smiled and said, "Hi, Tim. Glad you came."

Tim took her hand and said, "Come with me." He led her away from the others. They sat down together and talked. The band started up a lively tune, and he stood up and said, "Let's dance." He led her to the dance area, where they whirled around together trying to keep up with the fast-beating music.

When the song ended, he once more took her hand, and they walked outside to cool down. The air was crisp, and the sky was clear and bright with moonlight. She rubbed her arms.

"Are you cold?" Tim asked.

"A little, but I'll be all right," she answered.

He wrapped his arms around her. "How does that feel?"

She replied, "Much warmer." He bent his head down and kissed her cheek and continued holding her.

She looked up at him, and he couldn't resist—he kissed her lips. The kiss didn't last long, and he breathlessly said, "Oh my, that was good."

"Uh, huh, I agree," Jenny added. He bent over and kissed her again. When the kiss ended, she pulled back.

"We better go back inside," Tim stated. "I don't want you to catch a cold." They reentered the building and again began dancing and enjoying the festivities. Their parents and siblings hadn't noticed that they weren't in the building.

As the clock ticked closer to midnight, many of the older men and women had already gone home. When the musicians announced the last dance, those that remained led their partners out onto the dance floor. Tim smiled at Jenny, took her hand, and said, "Come with me. It's the last dance."

Their eyes locked as they danced together to the slow waltz music. The song ended, the instrumentalists ceased playing, and the festivity ended. Tim and Jenny walked over to claim his jacket and her shawl, which had been hanging on a peg by the door.

"Thanks, Jenny. I had a great time tonight. Did you?"

She replied, "It was the best."

Pricilla and Jeremiah walked up beside the two. Jeremiah said to Jenny, "Well, the dance is over. Are you ready to go home?"

She nodded, turned to Tim, and said, "It was a fun evening. See you later." He softly squeezed her hand as she walked away. Tim's head swirled, and his insides ached when she left, and he tried to compose himself. He stayed to help clean up the barn before fetching his horse. As he rode toward home, the cool air didn't daunt the warmth he had inside as he recalled the evening with his girl. It was then that he told himself, *I'm going to marry her.*

☀

It is now mid-December. Patrick had settled into his routine, which consisted of eat, work, eat, sleep. He was accustomed to his sleeping room located over McGregor's Coat, Tie, and Barber Shop. McGregor was a short, stocky Scotsman, red-faced and freckled with a thick dull-red curled-up mustache and a short, well-trimmed beard. He was quite a clever businessman with a soothing business line of persuasion that allowed him to convince nearly anyone to make a purchase. He had right away convinced Pat to buy a Sunday dress hat.

The plain room had a small closet, covered only by a single drape. The bed was solid wood, which held a worn mattress of cotton balls and goose feathers. He had to shake it gustily two or three times a week to keep the stuffing from lumping. A small wooden chest sat at the foot of the bed, where he stored his socks and underwear and an extra coat. The inside held a smaller box where he kept notepaper, a hunting knife, the extra hat he had purchased, and a belt. The most special item was Catherine's hair ribbon.

Pat could look out of a small window and see the docks and the varied watercrafts and steamboats. He would watch the workers and fishermen as they hustled about the walkways and docks. He was acclimated to his surroundings, but he also knew he wouldn't be here the rest of his life. The window had a cloth shade that could be rolled up and tied for daytime light, then untied and let down for privacy during the dark of night. Pen and ink pictures hung on each side of the window. One showed couples dressed in their finest attire going aboard a steamboat. They wore fancy hats and carried parasols and canes. The other picture depicted men departing a working steamboat. They walked bent over and tired. Their sagging clothes were dirty and disheveled-looking. They carried ropes, buckets, and overfull, heavy baskets.

Patrick would study the pictures as he lay on his bed. He pondered—a life directed or a directed life. *I'll not be directed,* he told himself. *I will choose my own path.*

The weather had become much colder. The river traffic had nearly halted. Ice had formed around the water's edge as everyday temperatures were freezing or below. He decided he would take two weeks to go visit his grandparents. He might even stop at Lucy and Big Al's place for a day, if he can find it! Even though he was only two and a half years old when his folks moved to Indiana, he still sorta remembered them. His parents had retold many stories about times when they were all together, so that helped with his memories.

Pat went down and talked to Mr. McGregor about the trip he planned. He gave some good advice to Pat. "Be sure to get you a sleeping room every night 'cause it's too cold to sleep out on the ground. If it takes an extra day or two, no matter; you gotta take care of yourself."

"You're probably right," Pat agreed.

"Now I tell you, if you find that you must sleep outside, lay down beside your horse. He'll keep you warm. Let me loan you a warm blanket to take with you, and here's a muffler to wrap around your neck."

"Thanks, Mr. McGregor. I appreciate your help. I've got to go tell my boss about my plans, and then I'll get my bedroll and leave."

Pat talked to his boss, gathered his belongings, and went to get Buddy. Buddy had been stabled most of the time since he had been in Louisville, and Pat didn't plan to push him too hard on their journey. *I need to get some horse feed before I leave,* he thought. The cold weather would use up Buddy's energy as well as his own. Within the hour, Pat and Buddy rode out of town.

☀

Pricilla had been sick for six weeks. Jeremiah, Joseph, and Jenny carried the full load of the boardinghouse. Anna Marie came and worked on Fridays and Saturdays in the kitchen while Jenny was the waitress. Joseph helped keep the kitchen clean and carried some food in to the customers. Jeremiah managed and ordered the food for the meals and rented the rooms while Pricilla spent most of the time in bed. Whenever she ate, the food stayed in her stomach a few minutes and then came back out. The only foods that she could tolerate were mild broths and well-cooked porridge. She was getting weaker and weaker. Anna Marie visited with her and convinced her to go for help.

"Joseph, Jenny, Tim, and I will take care of your business, and Jeremiah can take you to see a doctor," Anna Marie volunteered.

The next morning, amid snow flurries, Jeremiah and Pricilla left for Seymour. They were snuggled under a pile of blankets as their horse and buggy trotted away. Eight hours later, they arrived at their destination and located the doctor's office. Pricilla was so weak that she could hardly walk into the building. The doctor had just finished with his last scheduled patient minutes before Pricilla arrived.

"What can I do for you, my dear," he asked.

"I've been really sick, and I don't know why," she answered. "I'm afraid that I'm dying."

"Come into my examining room, and I'll check you out," he told her. After thoroughly checking Pricilla, he asked her one question."

"Is there a chance that you could be pregnant?" he asked. She looked at him strangely.

"Are you kidding? I haven't been able to have a child for years."

"Well, I can tell you now that you have all the symptoms of an expectant mother." Pricilla grabbed her forehead and nearly fainted.

He continued. "I can give you some medicine that will calm your stomach, and you'll get your strength back."

"Oh, my goodness, I never imagined this!" She walked out of the examining room to see Jeremiah. He looked at her and saw a coy smile on her face.

"Tell me what it is!" he said with concern.

"You better prepare for this," she replied. She then told him the doctor's prognosis.

"You're not serious! That's terrific, another child for us."

"But I'm nearly forty years old, I don't know if I can handle it," Pricilla said.

"You'll do just fine; I'll make sure you are well taken care of," he told her. "Let's go over to the hotel and have something to eat, then I'll get us a room to spend the night. Tomorrow, when we go home, we can surprise the rest of the family and friends.

Chapter 26

IT WAS FIFTY MILES FROM LOUISVILLE TO FRANKFORT, and Patrick planned to make it there the first day. He was truly thankful to have the muffler Mr. McGregor gave him for it helped to keep the cold air from crawling down his neck. He rode into Shelbyville around noon. He watered his horse and took him to the stables, gave him a portion of oats, and searched for a café.

After having eaten, Pat returned to the stables for Buddy, mounted and continued toward Frankfort. The clouds had parted that afternoon, and sunlight warmed both horse and rider. Pat's spirits lifted. He reached Frankfort by late afternoon. Pat made an acquaintance at the mercantile when he stopped to buy an extra pair of gloves. He only knew the man by Chub, but Chub invited Pat to his farm home for some rabbit stew. For two hours, the men enjoyed telling each other stories. Pat opened up and told Chub about his sweetheart that he had to leave. Chub told him, "The trouble with women is that you can't live with them, but you can't live without them!" Pat remarked, "It's the same with having in-laws," a reference to Albert. They both laughed and agreed.

Chub suggested that Pat could sleep in the barn. "Come back inside in the mornin'. We'll have coffee and whatever I find to eat, ha- ha," Chub told him. As they both laughed, Pat replied, Sure thing, I'll be there."

The barn had piles of straw that availed itself to become a soft, warm bed. *This beats the cold, hard ground*, he thought. As Pat lay there, he could hear the rustling of the small creatures that inhabit barns, but exhaustion soon overcame him, and he fell into a welcome sleep.

Come morning, Pat's eyes quickly opened when he realized there were two goats roaming around inside the barn and one was trying to bite the toe of his boot, which he, by the way, was still wearing. He jumped and hollered, "Hey," and the goat jumped on his hind legs at the same time and proceeded to drop some manure pellets right there! "Lordy, goat, git out a here. Go on now." Pat threw off his blanket and stood up as the goats ran around the corner stall. He heard the barn door creak, and Chub came inside.

"Howdy," he called out. "How'd you sleep?"

"All right, but it woulda been nice if you'd told me that the goats slept in here."

Chub chuckled, "Yep, I should'a. Did they hurt'cha any?" Pat gave Buddy some feed and shook his head no. "Let's go on in the house and have a mug of coffee," Chub said and patted Pat on the shoulder. The goats scattered out of the barn ahead of the two men, bleating loudly. It was cool enough that when the men exhaled, their breath looked like puffs of smoke that formed icy crystals and fell away.

"Brrr, it's really cold. You know those goats can be a nuisance 'cause they try to eat everything. You should get rid of them."

Chub brushed his remark off. "Yep, probably should, but you know they keep the weeds down around the house and barn. Come on, now, that coffee pot'll boil dry!"

Pat stayed with Chub an hour or so, then stood up. "I gotta git down the road. I'm goin' to Frankfurt, maybe farther, today. Thanks for the food and the place to sleep." He extended his hand, and the two shook hands firmly.

"We're friends now," Chub told him. "You're welcome here any time you're ridin' by, maybe after you find your grandpa and grandma."

"Thanks again. See you later," Pat said. He watered his horse, saddled up, and rode off. It was a cold ride even with his muffler wrapped tightly around his neck. He knew that he was about thirty miles from Lexington, and he planned to get there by lunchtime, which he did. *This is one big place,* he said to himself. He had no idea how to get through it and find his way to Richmond, his next goal.

He rode a short while and then turned southward on a main street. He stopped where he could tie Buddy beside a water trough, then he walked to a place that had a big sign that said in bold letters "EAT." He didn't expect the little place to be fancy, and he was right, it wasn't! The tables were crudely made of worn, misshapen wooden boards. Food pieces and bread scraps had fallen on the floor and had been walked upon and tracked throughout. Over by the fireplace, a coon hound and two fat cats were sprawled on raveled rugs. They seemed contented and well fed, obviously used to strangers in the room. The air was filled with the pleasant aroma of cooked food while laughter and chatter turned the unkemptness into welcome. He found a place to seat himself.

Pat could see into the kitchen, where he observed one Negro woman standing over the cookstove and another one washing dishes. They were full-figured women with their hair covered with a cloth and tied with a knot in the back. They were talking and smiling as they worked as if they were truly enjoying themselves. A young, pleasant-looking lady approached Pat.

She asked him, "What kin I git ya to eat?"

"I'm not sure," he replied. "What do ya have?"

"Today we're cookin' collard green with chunks of pork and some onion."

"Guess that's what I'll have," he told her, bemused that they offered only one selection.

She slowly walked away, as if time had no value to it. He noticed that the farther south he traveled, the slower everyone walked and talked. He wasn't used to the slow pace, as he had always gone quickly from one chore to another or one place to another all his life. It made him think about the value of using his time more wisely, yet enjoying the things that life offered each day.

266

He turned his attention once more toward the kitchen, and here came the young gal carrying a large, steaming bowl of food and placed it in front of him.

"Will that be all, sir?" she asked in a southern drawl. She placed a large bread roll and a man-sized spoon down on the table.

"Oh, yes, this will do," he replied.

The food was so hot that he burned his lips with the first bite. Some of the other men in the room grinned big when they saw him grimace and wipe his mouth. They knew what had happened because all of them had experienced the same. He looked around and just shook his head and grinned back. He leaned back in his chair and gave the food time to release some heat before attempting to resume. When Pat finished, he went over toward a table to pay for his food. The bewhiskered man seated there was wearing a greasy-looking brown hat and was chewing on a small wooden stick that had been whittled down as a toothpick, even though the fellow didn't look like he had much more than a scattering of teeth left in his mouth.

As Pat approached the table, the man said, "That'll be twenty-five cents." Pat handed him the money and started for the door. "You from around here?"

"Naw, I'm headed for Richmond. Can you tell me how far that would be?"

"It cain't be much more than a two-hour ride on a good horse."

"Thank you. I'm on my way."

"You take care now, and come back an' see us."

"Sure thing," Pat replied, "enjoyed your food." Feeling replenished, Pat fed Buddy two apples from his food supply, untied the reins, and they headed out of town.

❋

Catherine continued to resent her father. If he came into the house and spoke to her, she would merely turn her head away. Her mother tried to talk to her about the situation but to no avail. Catherine would take her sewing to her room, close the door, and stay for hours. She felt she had no more tears to cry, so she would sit in her rocker, hold her pearl necklace, and dream of Pat's return.

As time passed by, she began to plan for spring and summer. She would become eighteen on July 20 and knew she had grown more mature these past few months. Her first plan was to become friendlier to her father and win his trust back. Next, she would be more helpful to her mother. She would work more diligently on making quilts, pillows, dish towels, and knitting socks. What was her plan? She would leave home as soon as she had enough bedding and other home necessities. She could imagine the surprised look on Pat's face when he came back. She was pleased with herself.

✵

Pricilla was doing much better since she got medicine from the doctor. She was careful about what she ate, but all in all, she was feeling normal. The news of her condition had spread around the community, and those who came into their business were constantly asking her how she was feeling. As for Jeremiah, he was still adjusting to the idea of being a father again at his age but knew he would welcome the new little baby when it arrived.

Joseph and Jenny were confused with their feelings about having a new baby coming into their family. Pricilla had several heart-to-heart talks with Jenny, and they shared many private matters concerning life and marriage. Jenny, now more aware of her mother's situation at her age, made sure that her mother would sit down often and rest.

Tim continued to see Jenny as often as possible, and their feelings for each other grew stronger as the weeks passed. Their stolen moments together became almost a game that they looked forward to playing every Sunday. They knew that they were much too young to be serious, but they were completely devoted to each other. Tim was now riding into town at least twice a week to see his girl. When she needed to go out behind the boardinghouse to toss out peelings and food scraps, he would volunteer to help. They would go to the corner of the building and steal a few kisses.

☀

Pat rode into Richmond two hours later as the old man predicted. He wished that he could remember the place, but he was much too young when he had lived there to remember. He stopped at the livery stable and dismounted. He let Buddy drink from the trough and gave him a large handful of oats in his feed bag. The blacksmith walked out as he checked to see who was there.

"Howdy, stranger, what kin I do for ya?" he asked.

Pat answered, "I rode from Indiana to find my grandparents, but I really don't know for sure where they live. I do remember another couple, Big Al and Lucy Bennings. Could you tell me where they live? It's near Reed's Crossing."

"I've heard their name, but I can't say I know exactly where their place is. Your best bet is to go on to Reed's Crossing and ask around. I'm sure someone kin help ya."

Pat felt a twinge of hunger, so he walked across the street to Ester's Pie Shop. He hadn't developed a taste for coffee, but if he bought a piece of pie, a mug of coffee came with it, which made the pie more appealing. When he read the list of available pies, he couldn't decide which would taste the best. He chose chocolate cream pie, which tasted delicious, and he even enjoyed the coffee after he added cream. His thoughts took him back home, and he realized how much he missed his family and Catherine. He had eaten about half of the pie when his emotions took over. His eyes filled with tears that crept down his face. *Catherine, I miss you.* He had never been away from everyone for this long. He wiped the tears away, finished his food, paid, and left. Gathering up the reins, Pat remounted his horse and continued his journey. He didn't have to ride too far until he came upon the wooden sign that pointed the direction to Reed's

Crossing. Thirty minutes later, he arrived there. He questioned, *do I stop at the post office or the mercantile to ask about the Bennings?* He chose the mercantile.

The place didn't seem the same; of course, it had been sixteen years since he and his family had moved to Indiana. He walked up to the counter, where a fellow stood close to the register.

"Afternoon," the fellow spoke.

"Afternoon," Pat replied. "Uh … maybe you kin help me. I'm trying to find some old friends, Big Al and Lucy Bennings. Could you tell me where they live?"

"Ya know, they were in here a few minutes ago. Let's go out and see if they're still close by." He pointed. "There they are gettin' in the buggy."

"Hey there, hold on; I got someone to see ya!" he hollered out.

They waited until Pat and the mercantile owner came over to them. Pat looked at the two of them. He could see that sixteen years had turned them gray and wrinkled, yet they still belonged together.

"Bet you can't guess who I am," Pat asked them. They studied his face and shook their heads no. "I used to be your neighbor when I was about two years old, and then my family moved away from here." Lucy looked harder at his face but couldn't call his name.

"I'm Patrick Patterson," he announced.

They both laughed, and Big Al said, "Really? Good land, boy, you've grown up into a fine young fella! What cha doin' around here?"

"I was lookin' for you," he replied.

Lucy spoke. "We're headin' for our place right now. Come go with us and stay a while."

"I'd like that," he replied. "I'll fill you in on what's goin' on." Pat thanked the mercantile owner and mounted his horse.

The sky had clouded over, and the wind had whipped up, making the air seem icy cold. Pat noticed a few snow flurries as he trotted along. When they all arrived at the Bennings' farm, they felt frozen through and through.

"We might be in for quite a snow," Big Al remarked. "Lucy, hurry inside the house while I put the buggy in the barn. Come with me, Pat."

As soon as the men bedded the horses, they headed directly for the farm home. Lucy had quickly put a meal on the table, and the three sat down to eat. They asked Pat one question after another, and he could hardly answer fast enough. He told them about his brother, Timothy, and his twin sisters, Lila Rose and Lilly Anne and, of course, his sweetheart, Catherine.

"Whoa, now, I can't tell everything all in one sittin'. Tell me, where did all your kids go?"

Al and Lucy exchanged the sort of glances that make you wonder what thoughts were being passed between them. This caused a queried look upon Pat's face. Long moments later, Big Al brought himself to begin telling their story.

He began, "The two older boys met nice young ladies that they married, and they have gone away in search of work and a new home. They come back and see us once a year, and we have a fun family reunion. Each son has two children so far. Oh, they really perk things up around here. You know, we're not gettin' any younger, an' we sure would like to see them more."

"Didn't you have more children than the two boys?" Pat inquired. He immediately noticed Lucy's eyes blinking; she gulped and looked up with tears brimming in her eyes. He knew there was something that she held deep down inside.

Al reached over and took Lucy's hand and looked into her eyes lovingly. "We need to tell him the rest," he said to her.

"You do it," she whispered.

Big Al looked over toward Pat to tell about the girls. "We had two girls, Millie and Mae. Mae was seven years old and Millie was nine. It was when your family still lived down the road, and you were a little tyke. The church people all decided to have a Sunday picnic on the banks of Muddy River. It was a beautiful day, and we all gathered at a nice spot to have the lunch, then the men took their fishing poles and went upstream to try their luck at catching some fish. The

271

children were warned not to go to the sandbar, but they wandered there anyway. Millie got into the water, walked and jumped around, and then fell down." He paused and cleared his throat. "We couldn't save her. She drowned."

"I'm so sorry to hear that," Pat responded.

"Your mother was so nice to both of us. She visited us several times a week and Mae latched right on to her. Your mother even took her home with her to stay a while. Mae improved while she was there. When your folks left for Indiana, it was hard for Mae. Your mother made her a special doll, and Mae played with it for a long time. She began to heal from losing her sister."

"Is that so?"

"Yeah, Mae had her schoolin' and grew up. Her mother taught her to cook and sew and such. When Mae reached twenty years old, she took a job teachin' school in Richmond. The school director took a shine to her, and they were married the following year. They moved to Frankfurt and lived there a few years. She never came back much to see us. She had two boys and two girls; one she named Millie Sue. I think they moved again, but we don't know for sure."

Pat shook his head as he tried to comprehend the whole story. "Have you tried to locate her?"

"We don't get far from home nowadays."

"You good people should be able to see your family. That's a shame."

The Bennings and Pat visited until bedtime. Lucy showed Pat where to sleep as Big Al stoked the fire for the night.

Morning came, and the three were in the kitchen having hot coffee with eggs and some of Lucy's homemade rolls. They talked another hour. Pat stood up and said, "I've really enjoyed being with both of you, but it's time for me to push on to see my grandparents. Thank you for your kindness. When I decide to return back home, I plan to marry Catherine. Do you think that you could come to the wedding?"

The two looked at each other and smiled. Big Al replied, "We'll work our hardest to be there." Al grabbed Pat and gave him a big hug. "Please, come back by on your way north."

Pat and Lucy hugged, and, of course, she cried to see him go. "It's been wonderful to see you. Be careful on your journey."

❋

When Pat left the Bennings' warm kitchen, the cold air outside hit him smack in the face. It had snowed enough that it covered the ground and hung on the trees and bushes. Putting the cold aside, the countryside looked beautiful. He saw two redbirds flitting around a berry bush, seeking a meal. He fed and watered Buddy and threw a saddle blanket across his back, checked his hooves before he saddled him, and then mounted up.

Snow flurries continued drifting out of the gray clouds overhead. He rode at a steady trot for most of the morning. He came upon a farmer that was feeding some cows next to the road. He decided to stop; maybe he could get some help to locate his grandparents' place. He dismounted and walked closer to the farmer.

"Mornin'," he offered.

"Mornin'," the man answered back. "What brings you out this way on such a cold day?"

"I'm looking for my grandparent's place. Do you know an older farmer named Ben and his wife, Lydia?"

"And who might you be?"

"I'm Patrick Patterson, their grandson. I came all the way from Indiana to visit them."

"Well, young man, you're looking at his closest neighbor. He lives on the next farm down the road. I'm sure he'll be glad to see you."

"Thank you for your help," Pat told him as he stretched his arm over the fence to shake the man's hand. Patrick broke out into a sweat; he was so excited that he made it. He immediately remounted Buddy and headed farther down the road. *What should I say first? Gee, I hope they're well.* He reached the front of their home. Questions kept pouring into his mind. He had reached the hitching post close to the porch. He dismounted, paused, then walked to the front door and knocked. His heart was pounding. He heard footsteps, and then the door opened.

A sixty-something-year-old woman with silver hair opened the door and smiled. "Yes, what can I do for you young man?"

"Are you Lydia?" he asked.

"Why, yes, I am. Who are you?"

"I'm your grandson, Patrick."

"Oh my goodness, has something happened?"

"Nothing's happened. I came to visit you and Grandpa."

"Look at you, you're all grown up. Please, come inside." She turned to her husband. "Ben, look who's here; it's Patrick." She couldn't help but pat him on the back.

Ben was sitting in his rocker and was trying to get up, but Pat walked over to him before he could stand. Pat shook his hand, but Ben pulled him close and hugged him.

"Say, if you left your horse tied outside, we should put him in the shed."

The old man and his grandson went out together to tend to Buddy. Ben couldn't help himself as he talked and asked questions the whole time they were outside. When they walked back inside, they felt the warmth from the fire and smelled the food Lydia had heating for a meal.

"This is a good day to stay inside," Ben remarked as he turned his back toward the flaming logs that crackled and popped in the fireplace. Pat joined him for a few minutes as he held his hands out to feel the heat.

☀

Pat stayed with his grandparents a week. He chopped wood and helped with any other repairs or chores that they needed done. He was happy just being there with them. In the evenings, he and his grandpa would have two or three checker games while his grandma sewed and enjoyed their joking around.

Pat tried to relate everything that he could think of about his family and many of the events that had taken place through the years. Before it was time to leave, Pat told them about his love, Catherine, and that he planned to marry her when he went back home.

"I'd sure like for you to be there for the wedding," he told them. "You might even think of going up there to live close to the family," he suggested. They looked at each other wide-eyed, as they'd never considered doing that before.

"My goodness," Lydia remarked. "Where would we live?"

"You could either live with Ma and Pa or take a room in the boardinghouse that Jeremiah and Pricilla have. You haven't seen the twins for a long time, and they're gettin' grown up."

"Ben, what do you think about this?" Ben didn't answer right then.

Pat announced, "I'll be leavin' tomorrow. I must return to Louisville to keep my job. I need to set back as much money as possible."

☀

Everyone was up with the sun, and Lydia started right away to make breakfast. First, she got the coffee pot perking, mixed up the biscuits, fried some pork, and then made a skillet full of gravy. It was a breakfast that would last a man many hours. Both men thoroughly enjoyed the meal, but mostly enjoyed the good times they had shared during Pat's visit.

After the meal, Pat began gathering up his bedroll. Lydia had already packed a bag of food for his trip and handed it to him. Her eyes had begun to fill with tears at the thought of him leaving and not knowing when or if she would ever see him again.

Pat spoke up. "You know, I won't go back home until midsummer or maybe later. If Catherine still wants me, we'll get married when it can be arranged. I'd like very much for both of you to be there. Big Al and Lucy Bennings may decide to come, and, if they do, you four could travel together. I'll write to you and keep you informed."

His grandpa replied, "We'll talk it over and see what we can do to come see all of you." They shared a manly hug.

Pat hugged his grandma and patted her. "Grandma, thanks for everything you did for me. It was a week that I'll never forget. No tears, now, I'll be all right."

"I know. Best of luck to you, and be careful on your trip back to Louisville," she urged.

❂

Pat and Buddy started their journey in reverse that day with the cold air and snow-packed lane that lay before them. As he and his horse trotted down the road, Pat's mind reviewed the past week with memories that he knew he would always cherish. When he thought about the checker games, he chuckled out loud, and he replayed his grandpa's laughter and groans, especially when Pat won the match. And when he thought of Grandma's bread pudding, he could still taste its delicious cinnamon and nut flavor. His innermost feelings told him that he would see them again.

He stopped back at Big Al and Lucy's place. He hadn't planned to spend the night, but they wouldn't hear of anything else. He really didn't relish the idea of a night out in the cold, so he let them talk him into staying. He was glad he stayed there, and they treated him like one of their own. He again invited them to go to Indiana and visit with his family.

Chapter 27

WITHIN THREE DAYS, PAT WAS BACK AT LOUISVILLE.
He felt the lonesomeness, but he also felt refreshed and alive. His mind was set; he would earn his nest egg and marry the woman he loves.

Pat went to work every day. He learned the craft of building the big boats and was also learning to make some repairs on the operation of them. He actually enjoyed his job, even though he got greasy and dirty, and every fiber in his body ached at the end of most days. When it was quitting time, Pat would go with a couple of friends, Tom and Mick, to the tavern for some food. Tom and Mick each would have a stein of dark beer, but they had never before convinced Pat that it was a good drink.

Today was different; he wanted more than coffee or water with his pork sandwich and fried potatoes. He drank one beer, and it went down so smoothly that he ordered another right away. The three men stayed and ate and drank for roughly two hours until they were full. Pat didn't know where his friends lived, but he knew that he was only a short walk away from his room. Mr. McGregor had closed his shop. Pat knocked on the door, their coded knock, and McGregor came and let him inside.

"Come on in, laddie," he offered. McGregor smelled the strong odor of malt brew as Pat walked past him.

"Guess you stopped at the tavern tonight." It wasn't a question that had to be answered. McGregor knew.

"Yeah. I need to clean up now and get some sleep."

"You may feel no pain now, but, believe me, you do this every day, the brew will get you."

"Don't worry; I'll be good as new come mornin'." Pat walked sluggishly up the staircase.

❋

Pat heard McGregor walk up the stairs, and his eyes popped open as he jerked upright in bed. It was full daylight outside, and he had overslept. McGregor called out, "Are you all right?" as he tapped on the door.

Pat's head throbbed, and the taste in his mouth was indescribable. "I'm all right," he answered. "Thanks for the wake-up."

He splashed the cold water from the washbowl on his face and head, quickly dressed, and hurried downstairs. Pat welcomed the hot mug of coffee that McGregor handed him. He gulped it down and hastily left for work. He slogged through the workday. Each task seemed to take every ounce of energy he had. When he left late that afternoon he went to a café near the wharf to have a hearty meal and good, strong coffee. He recalled McGregor's words, which he now knew he would abide by. He would leave the beer to those who enjoy drinking it. He surely didn't want to ever feel this rotten again.

And so, Pat worked steadily through the winter and into the spring months. He kept himself on course to reach his goal.

❋

The Village of Frey came to life when April arrived with showers and days of warm sunshine. The cold of winter had passed, and the earth began to display its raiment of blue irises, purple violets, bright-yellow forsythia blooms, and many more colorful floras. The school year was nearly finished, and some of the older boys had already quit attending to go help their fathers work the land. The hard, frozen dirt roads gave way to water puddles and mud.

Pricilla was now six months along with her pregnancy. She had passed the sick stage and was happy and well. Jeremiah made sure that she rested on her bed every day for an hour while he and their children bore most of the work in the boarding home. Jenny had many talks with her mother about having children. She was learning about men and women, marriage, and the responsibility of having children. She cautioned Jenny to be careful and not be tempted with her relationships with Tim or any other man. Lastly, she told her the same as all mothers will tell their children: "Remember, you are responsible for your own actions."

Jenny smiled and replied, "Yes, Mother, I know. Don't worry."

Tim turned up at the boardinghouse several times a week. He was a good, willing worker, but all the family knew that he was there to be near Jenny. He would touch her hand or brush back stray hairs from her face, and, often as he could, he would steal a kiss. Jenny glowed when he was there. Both Jeremiah and Pricilla observed as discretely and as often as possible the whereabouts of their daughter. After all, she was still too young to get seriously involved with a young man, but Pricilla already knew that Jenny had strong feelings for Tim.

☀

Anna Marie took Lila Rose and Lilly Anne with her into the Village of Frey. She had shopping to do, but she had other motives for being there. She had been out on the farm cooking, cleaning, and washing clothes until she couldn't stand it any longer; she needed to be where she could talk to other women. As soon as she made her purchases at the mercantile, she and her girls went directly to the boardinghouse. Jenny saw the girls first, and all three squealed with delight as they hugged each other. Pricilla came out of the kitchen to see what the noise was all about and was equally pleased to see Anna Marie.

"It's so good to see you, Pricilla. I hope you're feeling well."

She smiled, nodded, and patted her stomach, saying, "We're just fine," and laughed.

Anna Marie and the girls sat down at a table with Pricilla while Jenny went about her work making dishes for the noon meal. Jeremiah poked his head out from the kitchen and said, "Hello. How's the Patterson family?"

"We're taking a break from the farm for a while."

"What are Brady and Tim working on today?"

"I think they went over to Frank and Luke's sawmill. They needed some boards."

"All right, I'll talk to them on Sunday. Say, have you heard from Pat lately?"

"No, I meant to check to see if we had any mail and forgot." Anna Marie turned to the girls. "Would you two go see if we have any mail?"

The girls nodded. Lilly Anne said, "We'll check for you, Mother, and be right back."

"Thank you."

"We have a few quiet minutes now. Tell me what's on your mind," Pricilla said.

"I've noticed that Tim comes into town several times a week. Is he coming here?"

"He does come here often. We know that he and Jenny are sweet on each other; seems he can't take his eyes off of her. Her eyes follow him around. She's only sixteen!"

"Yes, and he's only seventeen, but they'll both be a year older in a few months. I'll talk to Brady about having him work more at home. That should slow things down for a while," she said. She and Pricilla laughed together as they agreed that would be the best for now.

The two women sat and drank hot tea and talked and talked. Pricilla noticed that several customers needed attention, so she excused herself to go help Jeremiah and Jenny. About then the twins came rushing into the dining room.

"Mother, look, here's a letter from Pat!"

"Let me see it," Anna Marie responded. She pulled on the envelope until it gave, and took the letter out.

March 25, 1856

Dear Ma and Pa,

> It's still cold here. I work every day except Sunday, and I've made some friends. Mr. McGregor owns the place where I stay, and he's a good man. I miss all of you, but I can't come home for a while. I'm learning a lot about steamboats and how to fix them. I like being close to the Ohio River and watching the boats come and go. I hope all is well with you and everybody else. I'm sending a letter to Catherine. Please give it to her.

Love from your son, Pat

Anna Marie read the letter three times and smiled. The letter comforted her by knowing her son was well. She reached in the envelope for Catherine's letter. She was curious but didn't look inside. She handed Pat's letter to Lila Rose and Lilly Anne.

Pricilla came back to the table with some pastries for everyone. Anna Marie told her, "I received a letter from Pat. He's all right, but he's not ready to come back."

"I know you worry, but he's a grown man now. He'll come back when it's the right time for him," she consoled.

After they finished their tea time, Anna Marie said, "I think we need to go back home now. I've enjoyed visiting with you. We'll see you Sunday." The three headed toward the door, and who should enter but Catherine and her mother. Anna Marie greeted them. "Hello friends, it's good to see you."

They both smiled, and Catherine said, "It's good to see all of you. How is the rest of your family?" she asked, meaning, "Have you heard from Pat?"

Catherine reached into her purse and pulled out the letter Pat had sent for Catherine and placed it in her hand. Catherine's eyes twinkled when she realized what it was and immediately put in her waistband, where it couldn't be seen.

"I'm so glad we met you here today," Catherine stated. "I'll see you at church."

"Yes, I intend to be there. Enjoy your day today." Catherine gave Anna Marie a quick hug and went over to join her mother. Anna Marie and her girls went to their carriage and headed back to their home. They all felt refreshed from their outing.

❖

With the coming of spring, the farmers were up early doing the chores and working the ground for crops. Mares were foaling, cows were calving, and there never seemed to be enough time for it all. Brady and Tim came in for supper each night completely exhausted from their labor. Tim began to complain that all he did everyday was work, and he never got to go into town. Brady and Anna Marie looked at him and later shared a chuckle together.

Brady would tell him, "Son, that's what farming is about. You reap what you sow."

"Yeah, well, I'm ready to reap some fun!"

"You'll get some time off soon," Brady told him. Brady knew he shouldn't push Tim too hard at this time in his life. "You've proven that you can work as well as any man, and I'm proud of you." Those words helped Tim's self-worth, and he managed a smile and nodded his head when he heard his father's words.

❖

THE LETTER HAD RESTED IN ITS APPOINTED PLACE AT Catherine's waist, and it felt like a hot ember pressing on her side. She couldn't wait to read it but didn't get a chance until she and her mother went back home. As soon as the buggy was unpacked and the items were stored, she quietly went to her bedroom. Her heart beat rapidly against her chest as she opened the envelope and removed the piece of paper.

My sweet Catherine,

> I hope this letter finds you well. Are you and your parents getting along? My work keeps me busy, and I've been able to save some money. Louisville is a very large city, and I'm learning more about it every day. I can see the Ohio River from the window in the room I rented, even at night.

> I miss you every day and every night, but I won't be home for a while. I have your ribbon here with me, and it makes me feel closer to you. I wish I could hold you in my arms right now.

I send you all my love, Pat

Tears filled Catherine's eyes as she held the letter tightly to her breast. Oh, how she ached for his touch and his kiss. She closed her eyes and imagined he was with her, holding her close to him. A few minutes later, she came back to reality and put the letter with the others that he had sent. She picked up her needlework and calmly walked out of her room.

❋

Three months later. Pat and his friends were now working ten-hour days. There were constant repairs to be made on the steamboats. All the men were pressed by their crew boss to work harder every day. The men didn't work on Sundays, but even with resting on Sunday, Pat got out of bed every Monday morning worn out before he began the day. He sat for a moment on the edge of his bed, slumped over and bone tired. His eyes drifted toward the two pictures hanging on each side of the window. As if seeing the pictures illuminated by a higher power, Pat now realizes what he must do. He knows that *he* has been living the *life directed* and he wants to live the *directed life.* He'll stay and work for two more paychecks, and then he'll quit the job and head for everything he loves and cares for back in Indiana.

Pat stood erect, washed his face, and put on his work clothes. He knew, without a doubt, that he could endure the next two weeks. His mind was made up.

✸

Tim was grateful when he heard it raining during the night, for he hoped to go into town and see Jenny. He had only been able to see her at church. His father noticed immediately that he smiled the entire time that they were doing the morning chores. When they finished, they went into the kitchen.

"Good morning, Mother. Isn't it a beautiful day?" he said with a cheerful tone to his voice.

Anna Marie was astonished at his good attitude because he had been grumpy for several days. "Yes, it is," she replied.

"What do you think we should do today, son?" Brady asked.

"Well, I can't see that we can do much at all. The rain has probably set in for the day," he answered with a smile.

Brady and Anna Marie exchanged glances, each smiling slightly. "I think you'll have to figure it out. Myself, I don't care to work out in the rain," he told Tim.

Tim nearly exploded on the inside. *I'll change my clothes and ride into the village and see my sweetheart,* he thought. Tim gave his Ma a hug and said, "Thanks for the good breakfast."

She nodded and said, "You're welcome." Tim went to his room.

Lilly Anne said, "I bet I know what he's going to do."

284

"Me too," said Lila Rose. "He'll go see his girlfriend." The girls giggled and giggled.

Shortly Tim reappeared in the kitchen wearing all clean clothes, his eyes twinkling. "I'm going to ride into the village and visit some friends," he announced.

Lila Rose said, "But, Tim, it's raining hard." Then she giggled.

He gave her a disgusted look. "I'll be all right." He put on his chaps, poncho, and wide-brimmed hat and went out to the barn for his horse.

Tim arrived in town with half-wet britches. They had been splattered with mud that the horse's hooves had thrown up on him. He left his horse and chaps at the livery and borrowed a rag to brush the mud off of his legs and the horse. He walked over to the boardinghouse, his body quivering with excitement to see Jenny. Shortly, he saw her walk out of the kitchen door. He watched her until she looked over and saw him standing there.

"Timmy, why are you here?" she said eagerly.

"We can't work on the farm in the rain," he replied. "Pa gave me the day off. I'm sure glad to see you, Jenny."

"I'm glad to see you too. I have to help Ma and Pa today."

"Would they let me help? I don't need any pay."

Jeremiah had heard the talking and walked into the dining area. "What do you need, Tim?"

"Oh, I don't need anything. Pa gave me the day off, so I came to see if you could use my help. I don't expect any pay. I'm just tired of working on the farm."

"All right, come into the kitchen and peel that pan of potatoes I need to cook for the noon meal." Tim took off his poncho and hat and hung them on a peg and went into the kitchen. He didn't care if he had to peel potatoes; he would see Jenny.

He stayed until evening chore time back at home. He and Jenny talked as often as possible, and he managed to hold her hand and steal a couple short kisses during the day. Before he left he told her, "Jenny, I want you to be my girl. I'm crazy about you."

She replied, "Okay. I care a lot about you too."

285

He left for home that afternoon happy as any young man could be after spending the day with his sweetheart.

❖

Pat decided that evening after having supper that he would get busy and write some letters. To Grandpa Ben and Grandma Lydia, Big Al and Lucy, he wrote basically the same news. The first told he was quitting his job and heading back to his folks' farm. Second, he wanted them to make the trip to visit his folks. Third, he planned to marry his sweetheart sometime in August. Last, he asked his grandparents to again consider moving to the Village of Frey and live out their days with him and all the family. He included a letter to Catherine inside the one for his parents, both stating that he was coming back home.

Before Pat lay down in bed that night, he took another good look at the pictures on the wall. He felt lighthearted, even with his exhausted body. He had turned nineteen while he was in Kentucky, and Catherine would be eighteen this July. He was anxious for the days to pass so he could head home.

❖

Joseph and Timmy got together every Sunday after church. They enjoyed racing their horses, and this Sunday was no different. Tim used to always race with Jenny. It was fun play. Now Tim found it more daring and exciting to race against Joseph. Each race got more adventurous. It wasn't enough for them to race down the road and back anymore. They would now go down the road to a large patch of woods where they had challenging jumps, turns, and ditches. This past week a rain and strong winds had come through. It had done damage to roofs, outbuildings, yards, and trees. That fact had not entered into the minds of the two young daredevils on this one particular Sunday. Neither boy was afraid to take a risk; one was as brave as the other.

Usually Joseph took the lead while racing through the woods. This Sunday it was Timmy. He was so excited to finally be ahead of Joseph. He was galloping through a curved path and turned around to see how close Joseph was behind him. A tree had blown over across their trail. Timmy's horse started the curve, didn't jump over the tree in time, and they both went down. Timmy's horse took a hard fall, and Timmy went flying through the air. He first hit a standing tree with his left upper arm, and when he went down to the ground, his head hit the tree root that had grown up above the dirt level. He was unconscious when Joseph bounded off of his horse and rushed to help him.

Joseph didn't know what to do. He was afraid to try to lift his friend. He decided to mount his horse and go for help. When Jeremiah saw Joseph coming back at breakneck speed without Timmy, he knew something was wrong. Joseph stopped abruptly beside his father. "Pa, there's been a terrible accident, and Timmy's hurt bad."

"Go tell Brady while I get the buggy." Joseph quickly found Brady and told him what had happened.

The three didn't take long to be on their way. They couldn't take the buggy into the woods, but Jeremiah unhooked the buggy and rode his horse on the riding path. When they reached Timmy, he was groaning.

Brady got to him first. There was blood and a large knot on Tim's head. "Son, can you hear me? Open your eyes," Brady told him.

Tim stirred a little, and his eyes fluttered and then opened only a little. "What happened?" he asked.

"You fell off of your horse. We need to take you home," his pa answered.

❋

Big Al and Lucy received their letter first. It had been many years since they had been off of their farm for any length of time. The thought of seeing Brady and Anna Marie and meeting the rest of their children was something that they really wanted to do. They first made plans to go visit Ben and Lydia to work out travel plans.

Ben and Lydia had gone to town to get kitchen cooking supplies, and a length of rope and a saw blade for the farm. Ben stopped to pick up the mail just before they left for home. He had a big smile when he came out of the mail room door.

"What are you so happy about?" Lydia asked.

"Look, we got a letter from Patrick."

"Open it!" Lydia urged. Ben quickly opened the letter and started reading it out loud to Lydia. When he finished, Lydia had tears in her eyes.

"Do you think we should go?" she asked. "I'd love to live closer to them if we could."

"Let's go home and talk this over," Ben suggested.

"You know, I've been thinkin' about this every day since Patrick came and visited with us. I've decided it's a good idea, and I want to go. We won't have to take anything except our clothes and a few other special things."

"What'll we do with the house and farm and our animals?"

"That won't be a problem. We'll let all our friends and neighbors know what we want to do. Somebody will want our home and our animals. We're not young anymore." Lydia used all her persuasion. "We need to be with our family. I want to be with our daughter, Brady, and their children to enjoy the rest of my life."

Ben looked toward her and saw her pleading face and eyes that could melt the heart of any man. She had the same sweet smile that he remembered from days gone by.

"All right, Lydia, if that's what you really want, we'll go home and make some plans."

She grabbed his free arm, pulled him close, and kissed him while he was guiding the team out of town. "What do you think you're doin'?"

288

"I'm kissin' the man I love, any objections?" They laughed together as she squeezed his arm again.

❀

The day Big Al and Lucy read their letter from Patrick they decided right away that they were going to Indiana to see their friends. Patrick had written a special note to them asking them to "please go see my grandparents and arrange to travel with them if possible." Two days later, they were in their buggy heading south toward Ben and Lydia's place. Patrick had told them as best he could where to locate them.

The weather was July hot! They had planned for that and took as much water as possible. They stopped often to rest their horse and allow him to graze in the shade of a tree and drink when possible. Lucy had remarked to Al, "This sunbonnet keeps my head hot and sweaty, but I don't dare remove it; I'd sunburn for sure." He was all too aware of the heat and made sure they stopped in the shade more than he usually would have.

It took several hours, but they had no trouble locating Pat's grandparents. Ben and Lydia were busy sorting what was most important to take with them to Indiana. Big Al and Lucy arrived at their home and stopped the horse and buggy next to the shed in back of the house. Ben was pumping water from the well and watched them ride up.

"Bless my soul, look who rode up!"

"Hello," they both called out. He walked over toward them.

"I can't believe my eyes. What brings you here?"

Lucy began explaining, "We received a letter from Patrick to go to his folks' place for a visit this summer."

"We did too." They both climbed off of the buggy just as Lydia stepped out of the kitchen door. She had heard the talking and went outside to see who was there. She recognized them right away. She wiped her hands on her apron and went over to hug Lucy. "Good mornin', Al," she told him.

"My goodness, it's good to see you folks. Lucy, come on inside out of the heat. The men can unload your buggy," Lydia told her.

After they made themselves comfortable, Lucy explained why they came. Soon the two men joined their wives, and a spirited conversation took place. It wasn't hard to agree to travel together; it was the perfect answer for all of them.

For the following two days, they worked and planned toward their trip. The final decision was this: Ben and Lydia would sell their home and property by auction in two weeks. When that's settled, they would go to the Bennings' place. Within a short time, they would head north. Big Al and Lucy stayed an extra day and then left for their place up by Reed's Crossing.

✹

Pat worked his last day on July 14. He felt so relieved knowing he would never have to go there to work again. He had acquired self-assurance. He had managed his pay well and stuffed any extra money in his saddlebag every week.

At the end of that day, Pat wore a big grin when he entered McGregor's' shop. "Howdy," he greeted Mr. McGregor. "I've finished working *that* job," he declared. The two men shook hands.

"What'll you be doin' now, me lad?" McGregor asked.

"I'll be headin' up to Indiana to be with my family."

"And tell me 'bout the lass you're sweet on."

"If she's still there, I hope to marry her soon as we can make arrangements. Say, why don't you go ahead and close up early today? I'd like to buy your supper. It's the least I can do for you; you've been so helpful to me while I've lived here."

"That's not necessary," McGregor declared.

"Come on now—get out of here for a spell."

"Begora, it may be the last meal ever paid for by another," he declared. The two laughed heartily together.

The evening together passed quickly. While walking back to the shop, the two men talked about the good time they had. Mr. McGregor, being Scottish, had enjoyed telling Irish jokes to Patrick to rib him about being Irish. Pat took it all in stride. They entered McGregor's shop, said good night, and each went to his room.

By eight o'clock the next morning, Pat was packed and eager to leave. The two men had some biscuits and coffee together accompanied by brief conversation. There wasn't much more to say that hadn't been said the night before. They both knew the time they had shared together had ended, and it was likely they would never see each other again.

"There is one thing."

"Well, go on man, spit it out!"

"Those two pictures hanging on the wall in my room, would you sell them to me?"

"No, I won't," McGregor stated. Then he smiled. "I'll give them to you if you want."

Pat's eyes lit up. "Oh, thank you, McGregor. Those two pictures made me realize that I belonged with my family, and I could choose my own destiny."

"You are so right," McGregor replied. Pat immediately went to his room and gathered the two pictures.

Pat set his coffee cup down and shook hands with his friend. McGregor's eyes filled, and he patted Pat on his shoulder. Pat said to him, "Until we meet again, may God hold you in the palm of his hand."

"Get on out of here before I rap you with me stick and lock you inside!" he joked. "Take care of yourself and arrive at home all in one piece."

"I'll be careful. Good-bye." Pat tossed his saddlebags over his shoulder, grabbed the valise that held his clothes and new hat, and walked out.

*****

Brady and Joseph carefully lifted Tim up onto his dad's horse. Joseph mounted behind Tim to hold him in the saddle, and immediately all three retraced the path back to the road. "Hold on, Tim, we'll get you some help," Brady urged. Shortly they reached the buggy and helped Tim onto the buggy seat and headed back to town.

Anna Marie was in a nervous state awaiting Brady and Tim's return. When she saw them appear on the road, she exclaimed, "Here they come!" In no time, the three were at the boardinghouse. A crowd of friends had gathered nearby to see what had happened to Tim. Several men helped to move Tim from the buggy and inside to a bed. Tim was moaning and holding his head. It was plain to see the blood running down from his wound.

"What happened?" several inquired.

Joseph told them, "He hit his head on a tree root, and we think he broke his arm."

When Jenny heard the news that Tim was hurt, she began to cry. "Will he be all right?" she asked Anna Marie.

"Unless he had more injuries than we know about, he should heal fast," she replied.

Jenny gave Anna Marie a hug. "Thank you," she said.

Chapter 28

CATHERINE'S BIRTHDAY WAS ONLY DAYS AWAY. SHE looked through the chest where she had stored the many items that she had made for her future home. She was quite pleased with herself. She took the letters from Pat out of the small bag that was tucked away deep inside the chest. Her heart palpitated as she reread all of them. She ran her fingers over the pearl necklace he had given her and smiled. She knew he was the man she wanted. Catherine's mother suddenly entered her room. "Catherine, I would like for you to sweep—" She stopped. "What's that you're holding?"

Catherine looked up toward her. "These are letters from Patrick."

"How did you get those?" she spoke sharply.

"It doesn't matter. I'm nearly eighteen and a grown woman." Catherine looked straight into her mother's eyes. "We still care for each other no matter what you or Pa think about it."

"Don't be sassy with me!"

"Mother, I'm telling you just the way it is."

Catherine's mother turned around and walked out. It was then that Catherine decided to ride to town and visit Pricilla. She dressed for the ride and went to get her horse. Her father saw her and called out, "Where are you going, young lady?"

"I'm going for a ride. I'm tired of being inside all the time."

"I'll go with you if you want."

Catherine had regained his trust back. "No, I won't be gone too long." Within thirty minutes, she was riding into the Village of Frey and directly to the boardinghouse. She dismounted, tied the horse next to the water trough, and went inside.

Jenny saw her walk into the dining room. "Hello, what are you doing in town?"

"I'd like to talk to your mother if she's not too busy."

"She's always busy, but I'll go get her."

Pricilla came waddling in, as she was heavy with child.

"Come. Let's sit beside the window where a little breeze can come inside. What do you have to talk to me about, anything serious?"

"Matter of fact, it could be called serious. I'll be eighteen on the twentieth of this month, and I plan to leave my parents' home." Pricilla's expression became somber. "They don't approve of Patrick and me being near each other. Fact is, we're in love."

"I understand that Pat left home and went to Kentucky."

"That's true, but he's coming home soon, and I want to be where I can see him. We plan to get married. Father will never agree—especially now."

"Why's that?"

"Mother caught me reading the letters I'd gotten from him since he left. She was angry, and I know she'll tell Pa. I don't know how he'll be when I get back home. I'd convinced Pa that I had gotten over Pat. I'm not a child anymore. I know what I want, and I won't have my father telling me that I can't see Pat."

"Would it help if I talked to your parents?"

"I don't know. I think I would like to stay here. Could you have Joseph go to see my parents and tell them that I'll be staying here tonight to help you?"

"Yes, if that's what you would like."

"Yes, I think that would help me sort this out. Thank you." Pricilla called Joseph and asked him right then to ride out to Catherine's home and tell them that she's staying till tomorrow.

Joseph left immediately to see Catherine's folks. He saw Albert as soon as he arrived. Joseph dismounted and walked over to the corral where Albert kept his horses.

"Hello, my name is Joseph. My ma and pa run the boardinghouse in town. I've come with a message for you."

"What would that be?"

"Catherine, your daughter, she's at the boardinghouse. She'll be helping Ma and spending the night. She wanted me to let you know."

"Thank you, young man."

"I'll be goin' now; so long." It was obvious that Albert had not talked with his wife for he showed no signs of being upset.

❖

It was Sunday morning when Patrick left for home. He knew he should be in church, but his desire to reach home as soon as possible drove him to leave regardless of the day of the week. Once he got off of the ferry on Indiana soil, he jumped on Buddy and began retracing his path back home. He rode most of the day, stopping only to rest his horse and eat from his food sack. About sundown, he began to wonder where he would spend the night.

Tall thunderheads were moving in from the west and the wind was picking up. *Could be a storm headin' this way,* he thought. He hadn't even seen a barn for a while. As he rode along, conscious that he needed to find shelter, he noticed how thick the pine and cedar trees were. He rode off the trail into the wooded area. He chose a place in the midst of a grove not far from a water supply and led Buddy over to it to drink and graze while he worked on some shelter.

Pat found some downed trees and large branches and started cutting them with his hatchet. The sky had darkened further, and the wind began blowing in gusts. Pat perspired as he worked, swiftly constructing a lean-to under the thickest stand of trees. When he finished, he brought Buddy over to the site and removed his saddle, bedroll, and his other belongings. Lightning flashed, and thunder rolled, and then the skies opened up and poured down rain. He had barely completed his task when he crawled under the shelter. The storm worsened, and it began to hail. Buddy began to pull at his rein and prance around. Pat talked to him to try to calm him down.

Crack! The lightning hit close by. **Crack!** It struck again. A tree popped hard, and a ball of fire went out its top. Buddy whinnied loudly and reared up on his hind legs. The hail stopped and the wind quit blowing as it became eerily quiet. Pat went to Buddy and untied his reins and brought him over close to the lean-to. With some encouragement, he managed to get him to lie down.

Noise, a roaring like a huge whirlwind, moved overhead. He watched the pines swirl and sway. Some of the treetops twisted off and sailed away. Pat soothed his horse and talked to him during the storm. Then, in minutes, the roaring faded away, and the rain began pouring down again. Pat knew that he was in for a long, wet night.

As morning arrived, all the clouds had moved on, and the sun shone brightly. Buddy had gotten up before Pat and was grazing contentedly. Pat decided to remove most of his clothes and lay them about to dry while he went to the water that had pooled and wash off. It took him a while to light a campfire before he could make hot coffee, something he had learned to drink in Louisville. He didn't know how far he would have to travel before he reached the next town, but he knew he was ready for a good meal.

Within two hours, the sun did its job of drying, and Pat got dressed. He brushed Buddy's back and mane before placing the saddle on him. He loaded the bedroll and saddlebags and after putting the fire out, he mounted up and headed out. It was only four or five miles when he rode into the small town of Brownsburg. He found a house that had a sign outside that read, "Ma's Place." There was a hitching post on the side of the house under a big elm tree. He dismounted and hitched Buddy, walked up on the porch, and rapped on the door

"Take off your boots and come on inside and have a sit down," a voice hollered out.

Pat obeyed but entered the home cautiously. As he looked around, he knew this was a place where, whoever lived here, there were plain people, no frills, and hopefully, good food. It looked like embroidered white tea towels were used for curtains at the windows. A bouquet of wildflowers placed in a tall brown crock sat in the center of the long dining table. On each side of it were salt, pepper, sugar, and a larger crock that held silverware.

A tall, thin, gray-haired woman walked over to Pat. He could tell that she was a hard worker, and life had been a struggle for her. He observed her thin, heavily wrinkled face and her well-worn hands and fingers. She approached with a smile. "Are you ready to eat?" she asked.

"What's on the stove?" he asked smiling back.

"I made some laripen good sausage and biscuits this morning. And if you like, I got some apple pie."

"I'll have some of all of it," Pat told her.

"Shore thing," she replied and walked back to the kitchen. Within two minutes, here she came back with a big plate of food, covered with milk gravy, and a piece of pie. She made another trip with a glass of water and a cup of strong coffee. Pat slurped up the sausage and biscuits in record time but took his time on the pie and coffee. He felt much better.

"Did you have a storm come through here last night?" he inquired.

"Whooee, we shore did. It took some trees down and damaged some people's buildings," she said. "Were you in it?"

"Yeah, I was. I didn't have much shelter, and just got soakin' wet. Got my clothes dried before ridin' out this mornin'." Pat paid his bill and thanked her for the food.

"You come back and see me anytime, and be careful as you ride," she advised.

❖

Big Al, Lucy, Ben, and Lydia had crossed the Ohio River and had spent the night in Madison, Indiana. They had been on the road three days and calculated another three to their destination. It was a long, hot trip, and it was close to half over. The four travelers were holding up well considering their ages. The trip bonded the two couples as they told about their lives and laughed at the many fun things they had experienced.

As they continued on toward their northward destination, they observed that the storm that had passed in the night had definitely caused some wind damage to homes and the countryside. The road was muddy and already had deep ruts. This would slow their progress. By lunchtime, they arrived in North Vernon. Both Lucy and Lydia were feeling weary from riding over the rough road. The men weren't doing much better.

They pulled over under a shade tree and got down from the buggies and walked around to stretch their tired legs. The horses were left to nibble on what green grass they could find. After sharing some food, they resumed their trip. It was about twenty-five miles to Columbus, where they planned to rest for the night.

❂

Albert had gone into the house to see his wife, and he learned about the confrontation she had with Catherine. At first they were both concerned about their daughter's actions, but, after much discussion, they decided that after all, she would be the same age that they were when they fell in love. They would wait to talk to her when she came back home.

❂

Catherine and Jenny both fussed over Timmy so much that he had nearly forgotten how much his head and arm hurt. Jenny went to his room once an hour to put a cold cloth on his head and, if she could, steal a quick kiss. However, at bedtime Timmy moaned and held his head until he fell asleep. By the next morning, he was able to sit up in his bed. He rubbed the large knot on the side of his head and felt it throb as he touched it. Around ten o'clock, his pa came to take him back home.

"Mornin', son," his pa spoke. "How's the horse racer feeling today?"

"I still hurt."

"Yeah, you'll probably have a sore head for several days. Do you feel good enough to go home today?"

"I think I'll make it home all right; just don't make the horse run too fast," he joked.

"Okay, we'll take it nice and easy. Your mother sent a pillow for you to rest your head on in the buggy. If you're ready, we'll leave now. Let me help you walk out to the buggy."

Timmy stood up slowly. His pa held his good arm and helped him balance as they walked out of the boardinghouse. Brady thanked everyone for their help as they left.

☀

Pricilla didn't feel up to par this morning. She asked Catherine to take over her place in the kitchen while she rested. She sat in her rocker and rubbed her large stomach, every once in a while uttering a moan. "This baby is kicking like a mule today!" she would tell Jenny and Catherine. "It will surely be here soon." Of course the girls hadn't experienced that. They would look at each other wondering what it was like having a baby inside. They coddled her all day long.

Catherine decided that she needed to ride back home and get more clothes. She knew that she was needed at the boardinghouse. She dreaded going, though, knowing how upset her parents would be with her, riding off like she did, then not coming back home. She told Jeremiah and Pricilla that she would be back as soon as she could.

It was sundown as she arrived back home. She fed her horse and went inside the house. Both her ma and pa were sitting at the kitchen table finishing their evening meal.

"Hello. I'm home," she said cheerfully.

"Hello, Catherine. I'm glad you're back," her ma spoke softly to her. "Have you eaten?"

"Yes, I'm doing all right. I'm only home for the night. I need to go back first thing in the morning. Pricilla's time for having her baby is close, and she needs my help. I hope you don't mind."

Her pa spoke. "It's the thing to do to help someone in their time of need." She couldn't believe that they weren't upset with her.

"I know I left hastily yesterday. I'm sorry."

Her pa spoke again. "Your ma and I talked things over, and we understand. It's hard for us to recognize that you're a grown woman now. We don't plan to keep you from being happy. If Patrick comes back, you may see him whenever you please."

She went to him and threw her arms around his neck. "Thank you, Pa." She then hugged her ma as well.

"I must clean up and gather my things for tomorrow. I'll probably stay there several days. Jenny and her pa can't do it all." She then turned and walked to her room.

☀

Pat continued northward with Buddy, trotting along at a steady pace. He chuckled to himself as he thought how amusing the whole scene was where he had just eaten. However, there was a lot to be said about an honest, wholesome meal in more than comfortable surroundings. The gal, Ma, used the phrase laripen good, which he had never heard in his life. It must mean that it's so good you lap up every last drop. He laughed out loud; fact was, he *did* eat every bit.

The two were making good time. Pat noticed the storm had washed the road and damaged the countryside. He had become preoccupied with thoughts of Catherine and had loosened his grip on the reins. He imagined her long, flowing hair tied up with a pretty ribbon. He thought of her hazel eyes and her sweet lips, how they made him tingle down to his toes. *I hope to have my arms wrapped around her soon.* Pat's mind was so preoccupied, the next thing he knew, Buddy lost his footing where rushing water had dug a ditch, and they both pitched forward and hit the ground with a thud. Pat's right leg was pinned under his horse, and it hurt something terrible with the weight of his horse on it. What could he do? He tried to get Buddy to move by smacking his rump and saying, "Come on boy, get up." Buddy lay there and grunted as he struggled to finally get his hind legs under his body. It took some time, but inch by inch Pat managed to wiggle his foot until finally relief came as his leg found freedom. He tried to stand, but it wasn't possible.

He crawled around to check Buddy's front legs. "Easy boy," Pat said as he felt the horse's joints. Nothing seemed to be broken; however, when Pat examined the left front ankle, Buddy jerked and whinnied. Pat could tell that the ankle was swollen and sprained. The horse finally managed to get up on his three unharmed legs. "Well Buddy, looks like we'll be here for a spell until you can walk on all fours," Pat spoke out loud. He looked around for some shelter where he could rest. Because of the heat and humidity of the day, both man and beast were lathered with sweat.

Pat took a hold of the reins and halter to balance himself as he and his horse hobbled over to a shaded area. He managed to get the saddle and all else off Buddy's back and tie him close by. First, Pat had to decide how to wrap Buddy's ankle and second, how he would make some shelter for the night. He decided to rip the sleeve out of a shirt to use for a bandage for his horse. He dug through his saddlebags and found that he had a small bottle of horse liniment. Within a matter of thirty minutes, he accomplished that task.

Next, he crawled around and gathered sticks enough to start a fire for the evening. As he sat and wondered what he would have to eat, he noticed that several squirrels were running around. He took his rifle and waited patiently—then fired. "Yes indeed," he said out loud, "squirrel for supper tonight." He would dress it and then put it on a stick, where it would slowly roast for his supper.

Pat limped around as he went about doing his tasks to get him through the night. He fed Buddy, and soon the horse lay down to rest. His lean-to wasn't much, but it would have to do. "Tomorrow," he told himself, "I'll get ready to head north as soon as I'm able. I'm not sure how far I have left to travel, but I know it'll be a long walk."

�֍

The two Kentucky couples had spent the night at a boardinghouse in Columbus. The next morning, they chattered together as they walked to the large dining room. The room was busy as people were ordering their meals, and the two waitresses moved in and out of the kitchen delivering the food to their waiting customers. They sat together at a big round table, which would easily seat eight.

The ladies looked around at the unique pictures and artifacts hanging on the wall. Green curtains trimmed with white lace hung at the two windows, and table runners matching the curtains went down the center of each table. White lace doilies placed in the center held the sugar bowl and salt and pepper shakers.

Lydia remarked, "The curtains and table decorations look nice. Don't you agree, Lucy?"

"I sure do." She laughed and said, "I never had time to try to decorate my kitchen like this."

A waitress approached. "We have fried potatoes with scrambled eggs, biscuits, and coffee or tea for breakfast," she told them.

The four looked at each other. Big Al spoke. "Sounds good to me. How does that sound for the rest of you?" They all nodded affirmatively.

Another couple had walked up to their table and asked if they might join them for their meal. Ben said, "We'd be glad to have you join us. Come and sit down."

The three couples visited and shared stories while they enjoyed their meal. Time had passed quickly. Ben suddenly realized that they had been there for over an hour. "By golly, we'd best be goin'. We want to reach our daughter's place today if we can."

Lucy told them, "It's been real nice meeting you all."

"You folks take care now. We've all enjoyed your company," Big Al told them. The men all shook hands and the Kentuckians left to get their belongings and resume their trip. Soon they were in their buggy and wagon and headed west. The two women were full of talk because they were so anxious to get to Brady and Anna Marie's place.

Ben spoke up urgently, "Oh no, we need to go back to town. I forgot to buy some horse feed; we're completely out." He began turning the wagon around and headed back toward Columbus. Big Al and Lucy decided to stay by the side of the road and wait until Ben came back.

"It shouldn't be too long till we get back," Ben told them.

Big Al replied, "Shucks, it's no problem. We'll sit here and rest until you get back." They watched as the wagon headed back east.

The two occupied their time watching all the activities of the birds and small animals. They reminisced about times when Anna Marie and Brady lived just down the road from them in Kentucky. About an hour or so later, they sighted the wagon coming back their direction. They all waved at each other. Big Al and Lucy climbed back into their buggy and joined up with Ben and Lydia and all resumed their westward trek.

☀

Pat and his horse had been limping along together but hadn't made much distance. In fact, with his sore leg, he was ready to stop. He led Buddy over beside a water hole to drink while he sat in the shade to take a short rest. He felt of his right thigh, and he cringed when he rubbed his hand on it. He took a chunk of hardtack out of his food bag and chewed on it. *I'll sure be glad to be home and eat some of Ma's good cookin'*, he thought. He allowed Buddy to graze a few minutes and then decided they should get back to the road.

They crippled along for some time, stopping and resting from time to time, and eventually arrived at the crossroad he recognized where he would turn west. That would take him straight to the Village of Frey. He stopped again for another short rest. His right leg was thumping with pain, and he was sure his horse's ankle hurt also. He checked the injury and found it still swollen and tender. He rubbed more liniment on the sore limb and encouraged his friend to lie down. He talked softly and rubbed Buddy's head and neck to soothe him.

The July weather was mercilessly hot. Both man and beast were soaked with sweat. As they lay on the grass, the flies and bugs were constantly pestering them. He gazed skyward. *Lord, I know I haven't prayed like I should have, but today I could use some help. I don't know if I can make it home. Please send help.* He drank from his water bottle and leaned back against the maple tree. As he sat on the hard ground, his hope of getting home soon had faded. He had never been so depressed in his life. Tears filled his eyes and ran down the slope of his face. Soon he drifted off to sleep.

☀

Pat awoke when he heard the loud sounds of horse's hooves. He couldn't believe his eyes. He saw his grandparents riding up in their buggy. He looked skyward and watched the clouds as if he saw a host of angels, and spoke from his innermost being, "Thank you, God."

"Look over there," Lucy spoke loudly. "Let's stop under the shade trees and see if we can help that man. Something terrible might'a happened to him."

Big Al pulled over right away and got out of the wagon. Ben followed, and they both walked over toward him and his horse.

"Pat—is that you?" Ben asked.

His eyes popped open. "Yes," he answered spiritedly. "Papa Ben and Big Al, how in the world did you find me?"

"We're on our way to your ma and pa's home," Big Al responded.

Lydia and Lucy had come off the wagon and buggy, nearly running over toward Pat. Lydia grabbed and hugged him tightly. Lucy rubbed his shoulder and said, "Are you all right?"

"Buddy and I had a little accident yesterday afternoon. He stepped into a hole in the road, and we both fell over. He sprained his left front ankle, and when he went down, he landed on my right leg."

Ben said, "We can help you. You can ride with us, and I'll tie Buddy behind the wagon. We'll go nice and slow. Big Al and I'll help you to the wagon. Come on now."

The two men put Pat between them as they went toward the buggy. Pat rode the wagon with his grandparents. The next few hours were spent with conversation as Pat related his months of being away. The group stopped toward late afternoon. They realized they wouldn't reach their goal at the rate they were now traveling.

Chapter 29

IT WAS JULY 19. TO SAY THAT THE BOARDINGHOUSE was in a state of confusion would definitely be an understatement. Pricilla was showing definite signs of going into labor, so Jeremiah jumped on his horse and went across the road to get Eileen to come help.

"Eileen," he yelled out, "I need your help." She quickly came to the door.

"What do you need?"

"It's Pricilla; she's gone into labor. Could you come over and be with her?"

"I'll be right there," she replied. Her husband, Morgan, had joined her at the door.

"If I can help you, you just let me know," Morgan told Jeremiah.

"I thank you," Jeremiah told him. "I best go back to the boardinghouse now." He hastily rode off.

As Pricilla lay on the bed moaning, Catherine tried to comfort her. Within minutes, Eileen rapped lightly on the door and entered the room.

"Oh, Eileen, I'm so glad to see you," Pricilla called out. "I think my baby's coming."

"You need to relax. Catherine and I'll take good care of you."

Jeremiah and Joseph worked frantically to prepare food for their noontime customers. Jenny kept busy greeting the men and women, taking their orders, and bringing out cups of steaming hot coffee and glasses of water. The heat of the day was affecting everyone. The next two hours went by in a flash. Jeremiah had broken two plates and spilled a half a pan of cooked beans during the time he was filling the meal orders.

It happened to be that Anna Marie and Lilly Anne had come into town for a few items and went over to the boardinghouse to see their friends. Of course they heard the news that Pricilla had started her labor. When Lilly Anne realized that Jeremiah could use her help in taking care of the customers, she was more than willing to help out. When Joseph saw her, he went over to her table, smiling broadly.

"Lilly, would you like to help out today. We sure could use you," he said.

"Oh, Mother, could I?"

"Of course you can. They may need you more than just today," she answered. "We'll have to wait and see how Pricilla gets along."

Jeremiah came over and asked Lilly Anne, "Could you help out the rest of today?"

"Yes, I believe I can," she replied. Soon afterward, Anna Marie went home, and Lilly Anne stayed.

Around four o'clock in the afternoon Pricilla stopped having labor pains. She got out of bed and went into the dining room with Eileen and Catherine, where they had tea and biscuits.

All the workers at the boardinghouse had finished cooking and serving the evening meals. About seven o'clock that evening Pricilla moaned heavily and rubbed her belly.

"Oh, Lordy, the pains are back. Help me to the bedroom," she told Catherine. She immediately took Pricilla by the arm and led her out of the dining room. Pricilla was bent over with the pain. Eileen had gone back home to be with Morgan, but as soon as Joseph rode over and told her what was happening, she came right back over.

Jeremiah had filled the lamps with oil, thinking they would burn all night long. He was so right. Pricilla's labor continued until eleven thirty that evening. She was becoming very tired. Catherine wiped Pricilla's brow with a cold cloth and held her hand. The labor increased.

"Why can't this baby come out?" she asked Eileen.

"You're gonna be all right. It won't be long now."

❖

July 20. The Kentuckians and Pat arose with the sun that morning. They hadn't rested well, and they were moving very slowly. There were screech owls calling out half of the night. Then the campfire went out; consequently, the rest of the night they swatted mosquitoes. They went ahead and built another fire to make their coffee and warm some bread slices to spread honey on; that would be their breakfast. Afterward they kicked dirt over the fire and readied to leave. Pat checked his horse's leg. He applied liniment and massaged it. It didn't feel as swollen as before.

It took a while to get everything back into the buggy and wagon. They were on the final part of their journey. Pat and his grandparents talked about all the things that had taken place this last year. They were all anxious to be with their family. The time passed quickly, and before they realized where they were, they saw the sign that said, "WELCOME TO THE VILLAGE OF FREY."

❖

The baby arrived at 12:45 a.m. on July 20. He was a large, healthy boy, perfectly formed, with a head of reddish-brown hair. Eileen handed the baby to Catherine. She smiled broadly as she gazed at the wonder of the newborn child. Eileen finished cleaning up the afterbirth and told Catherine to place the baby into Pricilla's arms.

Eileen said to her, "Pricilla, God has blessed you and your husband with a perfect child. As sure as the sun rises each morning, he will bring you both much joy in your lives." Pricilla gazed at her child, and her face glowed with the look of a mother's love.

Jeremiah was seated with his head resting on his arms on the dining room table. Catherine left the room to tell Jeremiah the good news. He immediately got up and went into the bedroom to see his wife and newborn child. He took her hand and kissed her on the cheek. He told her, "I'm so proud to have you for my wife. Thank you for having this beautiful baby for us." He lightly kissed her on the lips and sat there and watched Pricilla with their new child.

☀

The morning arrived, and the boardinghouse was bustling with activity as they prepared for the day. Catherine was devoting her time tending to Pricilla. Joseph, Lilly Anne, and Jenny were doing all they could to help Jeremiah cook the food for the noon meal as well as take care of the customers who came in for their breakfast. Whenever the baby cried, heads turned as ears heard the sound. Jenny went in to see her mother and new baby brother at least twice each hour. She still couldn't quite comprehend that her mother had another baby.

Lydia and Lucy entered the dining room without making any noticeable noise or actions and sat at an empty table. Lilly Anne walked over to serve in her usual manner. Her eyes made direct contact with her grandmother's, and for a moment was unable to speak until she realized who was sitting there.

"Oh, my goodness, Grandmother, it's you!"

"Yes, we came into town a few minutes ago. Are you Lilly Anne or Lila Rose?" Lilly Anne bent over and hugged her.

"I'm Lilly Anne, Grandmother." Lilly Anne looked around. "Where are Grandpa and Big Al?" About that time they walked in, followed by Pat.

"Oh, my gosh! Everybody came all at one time! I can't believe you're here. Tim, Jeremiah, come here!"

They immediately stopped what they were doing and rushed into the dining room. As soon as they saw who was there, they smiled, and everyone broke out in joyful laughter. The men shook hands and patted each other on their backs. Everything came to a halt at the boardinghouse.

Lilly Anne told Pat, "It's good to have you back."

"I'm sure glad to be here," he replied.

After things settled down, Pat and Lilly Anne's grandparents, Lydia and Ben, told Jeremiah that they would like to live in the boardinghouse for the time being.

Jeremiah replied, "It'll be a pleasure to have you here. I have space right now."

"Did you hear that, Al? He has room for us."

"I've got news to tell. Pricilla had a new baby boy early this morning."

"What?" Pat said, astonished by what he heard. "You mean you and Pricilla have another young'un? Gee, lots happened while I was gone." That caused another ripple of laughter to go around.

"Come on now, we've got food to fix for today's meal. Customers are waiting," Jeremiah stated. As Jeremiah went toward the kitchen, Pat happened to notice a young woman walk into the dining room. It was Catherine.

At first neither could speak—only stare at each other. They started toward each other. She walked briskly while Pat limped.

"Pat, is it really you? Do you have something wrong with your leg? What happened?"

"I'll tell you later. Catherine, I'm so glad to be back. Come out back behind the kitchen for a moment."

"I've missed you every day. I've got so much to tell you."

"And so have I missed you all this time. I haven't been home yet to see Ma and Pa. I'll see you Sunday at church, and we can spend the day together if you'd like."

Catherine hesitated and then said, "Pat, before we go back inside, I want to tell you; Pricilla had her baby today, on my birthday. I'm now eighteen years old."

"I never once thought about it, as I was so glad to be back and to see everybody. Happy birthday, my sweetheart," he responded. He squeezed her hand and kissed her lightly.

"Father and Mother both agree I am old enough to see you anytime I want," she told him.

"I'll see you Sunday. I have something very important to tell you." He drew her close again and kissed her longingly. They held each other a few more moments, and then they went back into the dining room.

As soon as the Kentucky travelers ate their meal, the women went to see Pricilla and the newborn. Oh how they ooed and aahed over the baby. Of course, the three talked and talked. The men became anxious to leave.

Ben spoke firmly, "Lydia, come on out. We need to go." Right away Lydia and Lucy bid Pricilla good-bye.

❋

Anna Marie and Lila Rose were outside sitting under the shade of their large maple tree enjoying the breeze that drifted by and rustled the leaves above them. Lila Rose hummed softly while she stroked her favorite cat, a calico, which she named Callie. Not very original, but she liked it. Anna Marie was sipping on a cup of clover tea as rambling thoughts of herself and her family ran through her head.

They both saw the buggy and wagon coming up the lane. At first they didn't recognize who it was. As they trotted closer, Anna Marie realized who had arrived. She jumped up so quickly that she spilled her tea all over the ground. It didn't matter; her mother and father were there.

Lila Rose yelled out, "Look, Mother, it's Grandma and Granddad. They're here!" As soon as the horses halted, both Anna Marie and Lila Rose ran toward their visitors.

Pat got off of the wagon and limped to his mother and immediately hugged her. "I'm home, Ma!"

She squeezed his hand and said, "It's so good to have you home. What's wrong? You're not walking very well. Are you all right?"

"I *sure* am."

Brady had heard the talking and came from behind the barn. "Bless my soul, look who made it here." He extended his hand to the men and greeted them.

"Good to see you, son," Ben told him.

Big Al grabbed Brady and pretend arm wrestled him as he laughed loudly.

Brady teased, "Well, old man, glad to see you came all this way to see us." Big Al grinned from ear to ear. He was so tickled to see the friends that had moved away so long ago. He turned toward Anna Marie. He drew her close; they both hugged and hugged. She had missed the family that she left behind so many years ago.

Anna Marie energetically hugged both her mother and Lucy. The women's voices were at a high pitch as they talked about how each one looked so well and how happy they were to see each other. Meanwhile, the four men, including Pat, were equally excited. The happiness of the reunion continued through suppertime as they all reminisced with stories of past days.

As sunset approached, Ben and Lydia were feeling the weariness of their day. They exchanged glances, and then Ben told everyone, "It's been great being here with you folks. I don't know when we've had such a good day, but Lydia and I need to go back to the boardinghouse to rest." They stood up and said good-bye. Brady walked with them to their wagon.

"We'll see you after you've relaxed and feel refreshed from your long trip," Brady told them. He stood and watched them leave his lane and head toward the Village of Frey. When he returned inside the cabin, it was filled with lively chatter of the children, Lucy, and Big Al. Anna Marie's face was aglow as she listened, interspersed comments, and giggled at the stories and reactions of her family.

Lilly Anne and Tim had arrived at the cabin after they helped finish up the work at the boarding house. She sat near Lila Rose, a normal move for her, the twin connection. It was obvious that Tim and Pat were genuinely happy to see each other. Pat noticed Tim's arm injury.

"What happened to you? Did you trip and fall on a pile of chicken feathers?" Pat asked teasingly."

"No, I hit a tree when my horse tripped as I raced through the woods."

"I told you horse racing was dangerous. Are you going to quit?"

"Probably not. I like riding my horse as fast as he can go."

"Well, brother, best ride with caution, or you'll have more accidents," Pat advised.

"Now, tell me how you hurt your leg! Did you fall over a rock while kissing a girl?"

"To tell the truth, *my horse* caused *my* injury."

"Sure it did!"

"Listen, I was riding toward home. It had been raining and washed ruts across the road. My horse stepped in a hole and fell, and that caused me to go down with him. He landed on my leg, and I was pinned underneath. I liked to never got him to move so I could pull my leg out."

Everyone had stopped talking and was listening to the boys tell how they got injured. Big Al spoke up, "Sounds to me like you two are ready to blame your horses for your injuries." He laughed uproariously, a laugh that rolled through the house, which caused all the others to join. They all enjoyed the moment.

More stories filled the house 'til both young and old needed to find their beds for the night.

Chapter 30

JULY 24. PAT THOUGHT, *IT'S FINALLY SUNDAY.* **HE WAS SO** anxious to get to church and see Catherine that he could hardly stand it. He planned to sit with her and her parents and afterwards—who knows.

Anna Marie and Brady both observed the sparkle in his eyes. They gave each other a knowing look and smiled. Tim tried to talk to Pat about taking care of Buddy's lame leg, and he realized that Pat wasn't hearing a word he was saying. Tim punched his brother's arm and said, "Where are you? Have you lost your hearing or what?"

"Huh? What did you say?"

"What's wrong with you?"

"I'm thinking how good it'll be to see everybody at church."

Tim punched him again. "Sure, you can't wait to see your sweetheart, right?"

"You are *so* right," he admitted.

"I think you'd better leave Buddy in the barn and ride another horse."

"Will do," Pat replied.

❋

The boardinghouse had bustled with excitement from the time that Pricilla gave birth to her baby boy. She and Jeremiah named him Matthew. He was long and strong with a touch of red in his hair. At first Pricilla had trouble coming to her milk, but after the first twenty-four hours, she was able to feed him well. Jenny and Catherine doted over her as if they were his aunties. Timmy wasn't quite sure how to handle a little brother who was nearly seventeen years younger than he was. He couldn't believe such a thing could happen to his parents!

Catherine woke up Sunday morning with such enthusiasm that she nearly jumped out of bed. She had gone through her clothes a half dozen times the night before trying to decide which dress to wear to church. She carefully had laid it out so she could dress quickly and have time to brush her hair and put in her new hair ribbon. *I will look my best today for Pat,* she told herself. She knew deep inside that today would be special.

Pat, along with his family, Big Al, and Lucy, arrived at the church earlier than usual. Soon afterwards, Ben and Lydia came with Jeremiah and his family while Pricilla stayed at the boardinghouse with her baby.

It was a beautiful Sabbath day. The red rose bushes that had been planted along the front of the church were in full bloom despite the July heat. Today the weather was mostly agreeable with partially cloudy skies and a lilting breeze. Pat dismounted off of his pa's horse and tethered him under a tree as he waited for Catherine and her parents to arrive. Joseph, Lila Rose, and the others went on into the church while the other young people that came stayed outside. Tim went over and took Jenny by the hand and walked her away from the others to talk alone. Pat watched as the two hugged each other and quickly stole a kiss.

Hoof beats and squeaky wagon wheels made Pat look out toward the road. There she was. *Lord of mercy she's beautiful,* he thought. As soon as they stopped, he began walking toward the buggy.

"Mornin', good to see you today," Pat spoke to all of them. He shook hands with Albert and tipped his hat to his wife. As they began coming down off the buggy, he helped Catherine while Albert helped her mother. The mere touch of her hand sent shivers through his body.

"Good morning," she said with a big smile. Her heart began to flutter as he lightly squeezed her hand.

He said to Albert, "May I sit with you and your family in church today?"

Albert looked at his wife, and she nodded ever so slightly. "That will be all right," he replied. The four proceeded to go inside and sit together. Pat sat next to Catherine, but not too close; however, neither could keep their minds on the songs or sermon or anything except each other.

Tim and Jenny noticed that nearly everyone had gone inside the church. They laughed as they walked quickly toward the door and proceeded to sit with their own family.

The final song, "God Be with You," was sung, indicating the church service had ended. The usual light chatter filled the building, and the people slowly exited, making sure to give the pastor a warm handshake and compliments for his nice message.

After Pat, with Catherine and her parents, were outside, Pat asked permission to come to their home during the afternoon to take her for a buggy ride. Albert nodded a yes.

"Thank you," Pat told him. "I'll see you after dinner," he told Catherine.

"I'll be ready," she said. Her eyes were twinkling as she looked into his eyes.

☀

The Patterson family, Ben and Lydia, along with Big Al and Lucy, arrived back at the farm. The shared meal and afternoon was a joyful time of reminiscence and new memories for everyone. Pat excused himself to keep his appointment with Catherine. He readied his pa's buggy, climbed on, and guided the horse down the lane.

Today will be a day to remember, Pat thought. He felt as sure as the sun comes up in the east that Catherine loved him. Why was he nervous? Was he ready to make a commitment? After all, he wasn't twenty years old yet and still learning about life. He didn't have a job, but he had saved some money this past year. He felt his heart pounding in his chest. He had lost track of where he was or how long he had driven the buggy while his mind raced through all the possibilities of this day. He jerked back to the real world when he realized that he was guiding the buggy down the lane to Catherine's home.

His eyes scanned then stopped when he saw her sitting on the porch. His heart pounded as he admired her beauty. He guided the horse and buggy to a shady spot under a tree, jumped down, and looped the reins around a tree branch. She waved at him. He smiled as he began walking toward the porch. Her mother, Della, was sitting across from her. Pat politely said, "Hello."

"Welcome," she said. "Please, sit down with us."

"Thanks," he managed to say. He felt as if his throat and mouth were cotton. He sat in the empty chair beside Catherine. It wasn't long until Catherine's father, Albert, walked up to the porch. Large drops of perspiration formed on Pat's brow. The four engaged in small talk for a short time, and then Pat stood up and turned to Catherine.

"Are you ready to go for a buggy ride?"

She rose and looked at Pat. "Yes, I'm ready." She picked up a small bag to take along.

He turned to her parents and said, "We'll be back by sundown."

He offered his arm and guided her down the steps over to the buggy. He was the gentleman as he helped her up on the buggy, knowing her parents were watching their every move. They made their way away from the farm home. She sat close and laced her arm through his. He noticed that she was wearing the pearl necklace he had given her last year.

The two traveled a couple miles when Pat guided the buggy into a shaded grove of elm and maple trees. He couldn't stand not holding her for one more minute. He drew Catherine into his arms and kissed her fervently. When they parted both were breathless.

"Please stop," she said. He held her as he softly caressed her hair. His emotions overwhelmed him. He turned to face her and looked deeply into her eyes.

"Catherine, I love you so."

"And I love you."

They embraced in another long kiss. He released her and laughingly said, "We'd better go along; we have all afternoon."

She giggled and said, "I agree," and patted his arm. They trotted down the road content to be together in this moment of time. Pat led the horse through some rolling hills to a secluded, quiet place close to a stream. He looped the reins over a low branch, then walked back to help Catherine out of the buggy.

"This is a beautiful place," she told him. He took her hand and walked her to a level, grassy spot where they sat on a braided rug that he picked out of the buggy. Wild daisies sprinkled along the small riverbank swayed in the breeze and flashed their bright yellow colors. Catherine pointed to a blooming honeysuckle vine that was growing up and around a wild mulberry tree. The honeybees were feasting on the fluted blooms.

Pat said, "Look, two turtles are swimming right in front of us." They watched as the small creatures swam to the edge of the water and climbed upon the rocks on the bank. Pat threw some small pebbles into the water beside them, but it didn't seem to bother the calm pair. The two lovers were one with nature, mesmerized with the flowing water and all that complemented the scene. Time drifted by.

"I brought gingersnap cookies for us. Would you like some?" Catherine asked.

"That'd be good. Let's get them right now," Pat replied. They walked hand in hand into the shade where the buggy sat.

Pat waited anxiously as Catherine reached for her bag. They relished the snack while exchanging light talk about the day. When the bag was put away, Pat again took her into his arms and kissed her lovingly. When they parted he said, "I have something to say to you." She gave him her full attention.

He dropped on one knee and looked into her eyes. "Catherine, my love, will you marry me and spend the rest of your life with me?"

She had been waiting until this time happened. "Yes, I will. I want to be your wife."

He stood up and gave her a short kiss. "How soon do you want to be married?" he asked.

"I'm not sure. What do you think?"

"I'd like to be married while my grandparents and friends are here visiting. Big Al and Lucy should be here another two weeks before they head back to Kentucky."

"We should talk to your and my parents to figure out the best time."

"You're so right. When we go back to your home, we'll talk with them first. After all, you are the bride," he said, smiling.

The lovers stayed another hour in their serene surroundings. Pat had his arm around Catherine the whole time, unable to put any space between him and his lady love. They talked and giggled, watched and pondered, as they savored the world around them. As the sun began to lower in the west, they made their way to the buggy and left this special place.

They rode up the lane to Catherine's home as the shadows began to lengthen across the countryside. "Do you want to talk to my parents tonight?" Catherine asked.

"I'm not ready. How about I come over on Wednesday afternoon? You can get it all arranged, all right?"

"Sure, I'll tell them that you want to visit with them." Pat walked Catherine slowly to the porch, told her once more how he loved her, and then walked to his buggy. They exchanged a quick wave as he headed down the lane.

☀

As Pat guided the buggy toward the barn, he detected that something was awry. It was chore time, which was usually busy and noisy. It was too quiet. Pat hastily unhitched the horse and left the buggy sitting. Tim was telling something to his pa.

"I don't know. He's got a fever and panting. He may not make it through the night."

319

Pat walked through the barn door and saw Tim and his pa bent over Buddy. They both looked up at him.

"What's wrong?" Pat asked.

"Your horse is sick. He's running a fever and breathing heavy. His sore foot is swollen and hot. He'll need water through the night."

"I'll stay with him. Let me fetch a pail of water from the well and get some towels. Do we have any turpentine?"

"I'll go see," his pa said as Pat headed for the well.

Tim took care of the chores while Pat put cool rags on Buddy's head and rubbed his neck. Pa returned with the turpentine and clean rags. Pa immediately poured the turpentine on a large rag and wrapped it around the swollen ankle. Buddy neighed softly as he tried to express his agony. Pat felt a knot in his stomach as he continued trying to soothe the animal that he had grown to love these past years.

The night grew longer and longer. It seemed Buddy would settle down, and Pat would try to rest, only to wake up minutes later by his horse kicking or groaning. Neither man nor animal rested. However, Pat kept the vigil that he assigned himself by applying the cold rags on Buddy's feverish head and watering him often. Daybreak was approaching when Buddy's fever broke and his breathing eased.

Pat heard other barn noises as the world was coming to life in the new day. The other horses began rustling in their pens, barn swallows flitted from rafter to rafter, and he heard the rooster's crow outside to welcome all. Pat stood up and stretched. The barn door rattled as Pa and Big Al came inside, eager to see how Buddy felt.

"We came to check on you and your horse. How's Buddy doing this morning?" Pa asked.

While the men were talking, they noticed Buddy struggle to pull his feet underneath and he stood up. He gave his head a toss and whinnied.

"I think he'll be all right now. His fever broke early this morning," Pat told them as he turned toward his horse. "Hey, boy, good to have you back." Pat looked into Buddy's face and rubbed his forehead. He answered by nodding his head and nuzzling Pat's shoulder.

"It's a good day. Last night I wasn't sure he'd make it through the night," Big Al stated.

Pa put a scoop of feed in the trough and gave him half a pail of water. Buddy immediately took a drink and began eating. "He's on the mend," Pa stated.

The men heard Anna Marie call out, "Breakfast time." Ben, Big Al, and Pat started toward the kitchen door. The smell of cooked bacon wafted out when the door was opened.

"I'm hungry as a bear!" Pat stated as he went inside the kitchen.

"Tell us how Buddy is," Lydia asked.

"Yeah, tell us," the girls both ask.

"He's much better. His fever broke, and this morning he got up and started eating and drinking."

"I'm happy for both of you. Let's hope he stays well," Anna Marie added.

☀

Wednesday arrived quickly, and Pat was getting more nervous by the hour. He kept as busy as possible all morning, hoping to fend off the jitters. It didn't work! He stayed quiet during the noon meal, only speaking when spoken to. It was then that he announced that he would be going to see Catherine and visit her parents. He gave no explanation. Each one at the table exchanged questioning looks but didn't ask any questions. Pat excused himself and proceeded to wash his face, comb his hair, and change his clothes, making sure his shirttail was firmly tucked in. He took a rag and tried to wipe the mud and manure off of his boots but decided he'd better wear his Sunday boots. When he walked back through the kitchen, everyone in the room took notice of his neat appearance and that he was wearing his new hat. He had a package tucked under his arm. Lilly Anne and Lila Rose looked at each other and covered their face as they began giggling.

"Pa, is it all right to take your horse today? I don't think I should ride Buddy yet."

"Of course you can," he replied.

"Thanks. See you later today," he said to his ma and pa as he went out the door.

Minutes later, Pat was headed down the lane on his way to see the woman he hoped to be his wife. As he rode toward Catherine's house, he tried to think how to talk to her parents. The more he thought about it, the more worked up he became. He was jolted back to reality as he realized that he had turned up the lane, and he saw her house. There she was sitting in a chair, pretty as could be. She began waving to him, and he waved back.

After tethering the horse, with the package again under his arm, he sauntered slowly toward the porch and went up the steps. Catherine stood up to greet him. She radiated with joy as they held hands. His hands tingled the moment they touched, and his heart was beating like a drum.

"Hi, you made it," she commented.

"Yeah."

"Don't worry, Pa promised not to bring his rifle out," she teased.

"That's good." He laughed nervously.

"What's the package?"

"I thought I'd show you and your parents together."

"Oh, all right, come over and sit here beside me. They chatted together, not really saying much when Catherine's ma and pa came out on the porch. She had put a tablecloth on a small table upon which she had placed a plate of cookies and four of her nicer glasses. Pa carried a pitcher of cooled milk and put it beside the glasses.

Pat stood and said, "Afternoon," and shook Albert's hand, then nodded to his wife.

"Afternoon," they each replied. Albert added, "Let's sit a spell and visit. Della plans to serve us refreshments shortly."

For the next thirty minutes they talked of ordinary things and laughed about funny things that had happened to them. The light conversation ran out, and it became awkwardly quiet. Pat wiped the perspiration from his brow with his shirtsleeve. He cleared his throat and stood to face Catherine's parents.

"I came today for a special reason." He paused. "Your daughter, Catherine, is a beautiful woman. I loved her the first time I saw her. We have come to know each other very well, and she has agreed to become my wife, but I would like to have your permission to marry her." He turned and looked at her. She stood up beside him, and they looked at each other, both wearing a big smile.

"Well, somehow I suspected this would happen. You're both full grown and old enough to know what you want. Her ma and I don't have any reason to deny you happiness. I want you both to be sure that you are ready for this big decision."

Pat and Catherine held hands, looked at each other and nodded their heads affirmatively. Albert and Della both stood. Albert shook hands with Pat as Della hugged her daughter and then turned to Pat and said, "You both have our blessing."

"I'll fix our drinks now," Della offered. Catherine went to help her ma. The once tense feelings of the four became lighter and family-like.

Albert started talking seriously to Pat. "How do you plan to support our daughter? Where do you plan to live?"

"Honestly, I don't know. I've got some money saved up from when I worked in Kentucky. There's no room for us to live at home. I'm a good worker, and I know I could find work somewhere."

"You know, Della and I have this big house here with land and cattle. We're getting older, and we don't have any other children to take over our place. Would you consider living here and working with me?"

This was something that took Pat by surprise. He ran his fingers through his hair and inhaled deeply. "I'll talk this over with Catherine before I answer. It works for me if she agrees."

They had their cookies and milk, and Pat decided it was a good time to open the package he brought and show it to his future wife and in-laws. He reached and brought it to his lap.

"This is something I want to share with all of you. These pictures hung on the walls of the room that I rented the months I lived in Louisville. When you see them, I think you will understand why they mean so much to me. He had Catherine help take the wrapping off. She looked at them first.

"Nice pictures but so different-looking. Do they mean something?" she asked. She showed them to her parents. They looked intently, not sure how to respond.

Pat began to explain. "The one picture has the tired, slow-walking men, who labored all day on the steamboat, leaving from the day's work. The other has the well-dressed men and women walking onto the boat, enjoying their life to the fullest. I call the first picture *A Driven Life* and the second *A Life Driven*. It was when I realized that as I labored every day and came off the boat, bone-tired, that I was living the driven life; in other words, driven according to the will of others. I wanted the feeling from the second picture, where I would be living a life driven. I wanted to live the way *I* wanted to live, doing what *I* wanted to do and living where *I* wanted to live."

"Now I understand," Catherine stated happily. Albert and Della nodded in agreement.

Albert told both Catherine and Pat, "You know, as we mature, we come across certain things or events that make a distinct impression on our lives. Those cause us to rethink our decisions and help direct us to the next level we will live. I commend you for realizing that which helps you decide what you want for yourself."

"I wholeheartedly agree," stated Della. "Unfortunately, many people don't think about that."

"These are wonderful pictures. We'll treasure them always," Catherine told him.

Della asked Catherine, "When do you two think you want to get married?" Catherine and Pat turned toward each other. They hadn't decided for sure.

Pat said to her, "I'd like to have the wedding while Big Al and Lucy are still here. Would a week from Sunday be too early?" She squeezed his hand.

He asked Della, "How would that work for you two?" Albert and Della were surprised that it might be so soon.

"I already have a new dress," Catherine quickly announced. "We could get married right after church. All our friends will be there. What do you think, Mother?"

"Oh, my, could you give us two weeks? That would make the wedding about Sept. 14."

Pat and Catherine looked at each other, smiled, and nodded yes.

Chapter 31

IT WAS AT THE BREAKFAST TABLE THE FOLLOWING day that Pat broke the news to everyone. "I've got something to tell all of you." He paused and looked toward his parents. "I've asked Catherine to marry me, and her parents agree. We want to get married two weeks from this Sunday."

"That doesn't give us much time," his mother said rather out-of-sorts sounding.

"Listen, we want to have the wedding before Big Al and Lucy leave for their home."

"But you don't have a place of your own. How do you plan to earn a living?" she pursued.

"Catherine's father and mother have offered for us to live in their big house. Also, Albert asked if I would work on their farm. They don't have any other children, and Catherine would inherit the place someday anyway."

"This is so exciting!" Lilly Anne nearly shouted. "My big brother is getting married!"

"I'm so happy for you," Lucy told him. Big Al stuck out his hand toward Pat and said, "Put it there, my man. Thank you for letting us in on your plans."

Lucy got up from her chair, walked over to Pat, and wrapped her arms around him lovingly. "Thank you so much for planning your wedding so we will be here."

"You're welcome," he said as he returned her hug.

Anna Marie turned toward the twins and said, "Girls, we've a lot to do in the next two weeks." Smiling, they both nodded affirmatively.

Tim couldn't resist saying, "Brother, are you sure you are ready for married life?" He laughed loudly. "I don't know about you, but I intend to look around at a corral full of fillies before I let myself get reined in!" He continued laughing.

"Yeah, we'll see about that," Pat responded.

☀

The Village of Frey was all a-twitter with the news of a wedding. Pat and Catherine talked to the preacher and arranged for the wedding to be in the church. Pricilla and Jeremy agreed to have the reception at their business with their daughter, Jenny, offering to bake the wedding cake. Pat told her, "You should talk to my ma. I don't know what she has planned." The wedding seemed to be moving along in the right direction.

After Pat took Catherine back home that day, he went back to town to the mercantile store to buy a wedding band. Naturally there weren't many to choose from. He chose a silver ring set with a small ruby with ivy leaves carved all around it, like a flower. He thought, *this will be perfect for her.* After paying, he stuck the ring box in his pants pocket and headed for home.

☀

The days seemed to fly by for both families and their friends. Pat's grandparents were exceptionally happy that they had come to live in the Village of Frey and would see their first grandchild get married. Ben and Lydia made a point to be at the Patterson family farm more than usual. Lydia helped Anna Marie work on dresses for the twins by sewing buttons and lace on them. Ben cared for the horses and spent time trying to clean and check the buggy. He decided to construct a better cover for it, "spruce it up," he would say, should it happen to rain on the wedding day. Lila Rose and Lilly Anne decided it needed some fancy trim, so they engaged their grandmother to help them with making it. She happily agreed. It made her feel more like part of the wedding preparation.

Pat wasn't able to make the trip over to see Catherine every day as he would've liked, but he managed to see her about three times a week. His last time to see her was the Friday before the wedding. As he rode past the school yard, he looked over toward the well and saw two men and their horses. He didn't think too much about it at the time. It wasn't an unusual occurrence. Travelers often stop off to rest for the night and then soon continue on their way.

Pat could hardly contain his want for Catherine. He watched her open the door as he walked up the porch steps, and his heart pounded in his chest. He pulled her over between the door and the window and held her close, then kissed her lovingly.

"You're so beautiful. I'm so blessed that your family moved here where I could meet you."

"I'm happy that you found me," Catherine replied as she smiled. "We should go inside and visit with Ma and Pa for a while."

"All right," he agreed and then gave her another quick kiss.

Della proceeded to tell him all about the food that she had prepared for the wedding meal.

Albert said teasingly, "She wants me to butcher half our flock of chickens just to feed those who attend the wedding!"

"Now, Albert, you know that's not so!" she retorted. They all laughed together.

"I'm sure that the food you make and what all the others add will make a great feast for everyone," Pat inserted. "I was wondering if I could come Saturday morning and bring some of my clothes, since I'll soon be living here?"

"Of course you can," Albert answered. "Bring what you'd like." Have you two decided if you plan to make a trip somewhere?" Catherine and Pat hadn't given that a thought. The two turned and looked at each other curiously. They both began to laugh. They were so concentrated on getting married that the idea of a trip never entered their minds.

Pat looked into Catherine's eyes and replied, "I guess we'll have to talk about that, won't we, sweetheart?" Pat stayed and became more acquainted with Catherine's parents, and then he turned to Catherine and said, "Let's go for a walk together." They both stood up; he took her hand and led her down the porch steps and out into the yard. She took him over by the flower bed and pointed out what all the flowers were and plucked out a couple of weeds. He looked at her and asked, "Would you agree for us to spend our first night after our wedding at the boardinghouse?" She smiled bashfully and nodded yes. He replied, "That's good."

They sauntered to the outer edge beside a large willow tree. Pat took her into his arms and whirled her behind it, pressed her back against the trunk and kissed her fully and longingly. When he released her, they both were breathing heavily. He put her face between his hands and looked into her face, saying, "I can't wait until we are married and truly together. I promise to always be there for you and love you."

"I promise the same to you."

He kissed her a softer, loving kiss and started walking her back to the porch. "I need to go back home now. I have things I must do." They walked hand in hand to the porch steps. He gave her hand a squeeze. "See you soon." He waved good-bye to Albert and Della.

As Pat retraced his way toward home, he again looked at the school yard for the strangers. He thought he counted more, maybe four men this time. They were huddled around a small campfire. It all seemed calm enough. *Don't worry about them,* he told himself.

❋

Saturday morning arrived. Pat had awakened at the crack of dawn with no chance of going back to sleep. His mind was alive with thoughts of Catherine, the wedding, and moving away from his family to begin his new life. He swung his feet out and felt them touch the cold floor. The birds were beginning their twittering, a sound he always enjoyed during the early morning hours. He stretched his arms widely and sucked in a deep breath. His brother was still asleep in the bed next to him. He pulled on his trousers and socks and crept over to his washbowl. He poured some of the cool water from the pitcher into the bowl and then proceeded to splash his face and neck to wash the night's sleep away. He began to hear noises coming from the kitchen. His mother, Lucy, and both of his sisters were up early. The kitchen was bustling with activity as the women were making and baking food for the upcoming event. He threw on a work shirt, picked up his boots and walked quietly toward the kitchen.

"Mornin', Pat. This is your last day as a free man," Lucy said and chuckled.

"Yeah, last day," his sisters echoed, giggling loudly.

"Your days will come, and I'll torment you both 'til you holler." He turned toward his mother, "Mornin', Ma. I'm on my way out to help Pa."

"Mornin'. See you in a while," she replied.

❋

The chores were finished, and the men had come into the kitchen for breakfast. They ate their fill of hot cakes and fried eggs. Tim turned to Pat and asked, "Do you need any help today, or do you have everything under control?"

"I guess most everything is ready, but I'd like to ride in to the boardinghouse to arrange a room for tomorrow night. I don't have enough money to take Catherine on a trip, not now anyway."

"I'll ride in with you whenever you're ready," Tim offered.

An hour later, the two brothers had saddled their horses and left for the Village of Frey. Pat had gathered up some of his clothes to take along with him. The brothers shared their time together, some of it serious, some bordered ridiculous, as they moved along the familiar road. Next thing they knew, they approached the school yard. Pat looked toward the place where he had seen the men the night before, and they weren't there. For some strange reason, he felt relief.

That relief was short-lived. He and Tim went into the boardinghouse. There sat four men that they had never seen before. He had a feeling in his gut they were probably the same four that camped in the school yard. He glanced their way as he went toward the kitchen to talk to Jeremiah about having a room Sunday night. He tried his best to not catch their eye. He could tell that they hadn't cleaned up for a good, long while. Two of them had spittle on their whiskers around their mouths. In fact, they smelled so rancid that when he took in a breath, it made him cough.

Jeremiah had taken some food out to the strangers just before Pat reached the kitchen door. "Hi there, Pat. You surprised me. I didn't expect to see you here today. What can I do for you?"

"Would you have a room for Catherine and me tomorrow night?"

"Sure thing; you'll be my guest, a wedding present."

"That's right kind of you. I brought my bag. I'd like to leave it here in your care."

One of the strangers spoke up, "Hey, fella, are you getting married?"

"Yeah, I am—tomorrow—to the most beautiful woman I've ever seen."

"Where's the wedding?"

"It'll be in the church."

"I shore hope it goes good for ya both," he stated as he turned toward his buddies with a sly grin across his face.

"Well, I don't expect anything to go wrong," Pat said with assurance. He turned his attention toward Jeremiah and Tim, where they continued visiting about the wedding.

The men eavesdropped to learn as much as they could. When they finished eating, they sauntered outside. The people walking and riding past didn't notice anything unusual about them. They talked with hushed voices before they mounted their horses and rode away.

Tim and Jeremiah joked with Pat about getting married. Jeremiah's wife, Pricilla, came over and said, "I wish you and Catherine the best on your wedding day. You both deserve the best life can offer."

"Thanks. If we can be as happy as you and Jeremiah, that'll do." She smiled pleasingly.

☀

Catherine's mother was so nervous about the upcoming wedding that she found herself walking from room to room, not knowing what she was doing. Albert came into the kitchen expecting to eat the noon meal, but nothing was fixed. He called for Della. She didn't answer. He walked through the house and found her mending tears in an old winter jacket of his. "What in the world are you doing?" he asked.

She told him, "I decided that I needed to fix this today." She had a faraway look, and tears brimmed in her eyes. They spilled out and down her cheeks. "Oh Albert, the idea that Catherine is getting married, I don't know, I guess I'm not ready for it."

Albert walked over and pulled her into his arms as her tearing face wet his shirt. "Come on now, you have no reason to cry. She's like any other young woman who falls in love. Do you agree that she chose a hard-working, honest man?" She nodded yes into his body. "Well, then, be happy. She'll be all right, and so will you. You don't want Catherine to see you crying. Let's go into the kitchen and set out some food to eat."

She looked up toward his face, smiling slightly. He looked into her eyes and said, "We'll get through this just fine. Before long, he'll fit right into the family." Catherine entered the room just as he gave her a quick kiss. They jumped apart and chuckled when they saw her, and she joined in the laughter. "Sure glad to see that you two still like each other," she said jokingly.

During the meal, the three discussed the wedding and decided it was well under control. Pricilla and her daughter had baked the wedding cake. Her mother's friend, a seamstress, had made

Catherine's wedding dress. Several women were preparing food for the meal after the ceremony. From all that they had done, they all decided the wedding should go off without a hitch.

❂

That evening, the four wandering men were still camped at the edge of the school yard. They began talking about the conversation that they had overheard about the wedding that is to take place the next day. They began hatching up plans to catch everyone off guard after the ceremony and help themselves to what valuables they had.

The gang leader, a burly man, spoke with experience. "They'll be like sitting ducks! All dressed up in their finest, why they won't know what to do when we show up." He began laughing. "They'll be watching the bride and groom, and we'll circle them. I'll fire a shot to the ceiling and tell them to turn over all their money and jewelry. You boys can start gathering everything they have into your hats; then we'll make our getaway."

Another gang member said with a snarly voice, "Yeah, it'll be as easy as taking candy from a roomful of babies." They guffawed and slapped each other on the back.

"We'll be long gone by the time they figure out what to do," the leader announced.

❂

Sunday morning, the third day of September, the anticipated wedding day arrived, and it couldn't have been more perfect. The sun shone brightly, while a few puffy clouds drifted across a heavenly blue background, giving its blessing to all below.

Timmy, Pat's brother; Joey, Jeremiah's son; Luke's son, Shawn; Sven's son, Kurtis; and Norman, the guy that nearly won the log-throwing contest, had gathered together before church starting time. They were plotting what trick they could play on Pat after the

333

wedding. They decided they would leave the church immediately after Pat and Catherine were pronounced man and wife.

The church was full. Not another spot was left for anyone else to sit. Voices were at a high pitch as the people of the Village of Frey anticipated the wedding and the celebration to follow. The children fidgeted in the pews, and the parents exchanged whispers while the pastor, already nervous and strained, addressed this full chapel.

He incorporated today's sermon with the message he would express during the wedding, love. He quoted from the Gospel of John, chapter 15, verse 9, which says, "As the Father has loved me, so have I loved you. Now remain in my love." When his talk ended, he drew in a big breath, wiped his brow with his kerchief, then said, "Our people, our church, and our town should all unite together in peace and care for each other with God's love." The congregation joined by saying, "Amen."

The pastor continued. "Now is the time that many of you have been waiting for, the marriage of Catherine McKay to Patrick Patterson. Would the bride and groom, with their witnesses, Jenny Whitmore and Timothy Patterson, come forward and face me." Pat handed Catherine a bouquet of fall flowers tied with green and gold ribbons.

☀

The four gang men that had camped at the school mounted their horses and rode over to the church, where they saw many buggies and wagons hitched in the church yard. They dismounted and tied their horses close to the road where they would make their getaway. The head of the gang reminded the others to stay quiet until he gave them the signal to enter the church.

Anna Marie and Brady, with Albert and Della, sat at the front of the church. Anna Marie's eyes started tearing as soon as Pat and Catherine approached the minister with Tim and Jenny alongside. She took a hold of Brady's arm and squeezed. He placed his hand on hers and patted. They looked at each other and smiled a knowing smile. She knew everything would be all right.

Preacher Samuel began the ceremony. "Pat and Catherine, you are about to enter the wonderful life of matrimony; it is not to be entered into lightly. God created man, and from man he created woman to be his companion in life. God wants both of you to honor, respect, care, and love each other through all of life's trials, both good and difficult, no matter what. Hold hands and look at each other. Do you agree to love, honor, and cherish each other the rest of your life? If you do, say yes.

Pat looked into Catherine's eyes and she into his, and they both said, "Yes."

Preacher Samuel said to Pat, "Do you take Catherine to be your wedded wife? If so, say, 'I do,' and then place the wedding ring on her finger."

"I do."

"Catherine, do you take Pat to be your wedded husband? If so, say, 'I do.'"

"I do."

"I now pronounce you husband and wife. You may kiss your bride." The people all clapped heartily as Pat gave Catherine a short sweet kiss.

Preacher Samuel spoke again. "Jesus was quoted as saying to his followers, 'This is my command: Love each other.' I leave you with these words." He looked at all the people and said, "I present you Mr. and Mrs. Brady Patterson. May God bless them all the days of their lives." Everyone stood, clapped and cheered. All began moving forward to greet the newlyweds; all, that is, except the five young men who had other plans for the newlyweds. They worked their way outside, chuckling at the pranks they planned to do.

The four rogues watched the young men come outside and go over to the buggy. They didn't know what was going on, and they really didn't care. They were ready to make their move. They kept still a few moments until they were sure they could enter the church unnoticed.

The young men were so busy with their orneriness that they didn't see the gang men make their move. Timmy began tying some old cooking pans on the back of the buggy so they'd flop and bang as the buggy went down the road. Sven and Norman brought a burlap bag in which they deposited fresh horse droppings and placed under the buggy seat. Joey gathered dried cocklebur stems, which they put on the seat, while Timmy scattered leaves and dried flowers throughout the buggy. About that time they heard a shot, and people screaming.

"Hey, fellas, there's trouble," said Shawn, the oldest one of the five. "Grab something to fight with. We'll take care of this. They're not going to ruin the best day of the year for Pat." The five gathered rifles, a knife, and some solid tree limbs and headed for the church.

It was mayhem inside. The robbers were so intent on fleecing the captives that the young men were able to enter the scene and begin whipping on the gang members immediately. There was no escape. Now Sven, without a doubt the biggest man in the room, had worked his way near the gang leader, who was wielding his gun. The women were shrieking, and the children were crying. When the counterattack started, the lawman overpowered the unscrupulous thief and socked him so hard that he hit the door and spilled outside. By this time, every able-bodied man joined in the battle, and, in a short time, the four gang men had been overcome. Sven went out and picked up the one gangster while Albert, Brady, Shawn, and Norman herded the other three outside. They were taken immediately to the lockup building to be dealt with later.

Preacher Samuel called out to the people, "Let's all settle down now. I must admit, that was the most exciting wedding that I've ever ministered!" They laughed loudly. "Every one of you will have this story to tell your families for years to come. The best part is this, not one of us was hurt. This is truly the House of God."

Della stood and announced, "You're all invited to Jeremiah and Pricilla's boardinghouse for a meal and a piece of wedding cake."

Pat and Catherine walked out followed by Tim and Jenny. Tim held Jenny's hand as they walked, sneaked a quick kiss, and said, "Soon you and I'll be the bride and groom." She looked at him with wonder.

Pat and Catherine approached their buggy. "Oh, no, what's all this?" she hollered. "We can't sit on all this stuff!"

About that time Kurtis and Joey appeared. "What a mess. How did this happen?" Joey asked. Kurtis added, "I can't believe anybody would do this!" Both Kurtis and Joey were giggling as they spoke.

"No, I guess you wouldn't know anything about this, would you?" Pat said, irritated.

"Not a thing. We'll see you over at the boardinghouse," Joey said as he and Kurtis were leaving.

"Don't worry, it'll come back around," Pat told them.

"Thanks for all your help," Catherine said loudly. Pricilla and Jenny had the food all set up on one side of the dining area. A white lace tablecloth covered another table, which held the wedding cake. Green and gold bows and streamers flowed outward from the cake, and on one side was a bowl of homemade candy. On the other side, Pricilla had placed a pair of crystal candleholders with flaming tapered candles. The scene was breathtaking.

The boardinghouse eating room filled, and the topic everyone discussed was the attempted robbery at the wedding. Big Al and Lucy sat at a table with Ben and Lydia. The women wiped tears as they talked about Pat and Catherine and how they looked so in love. Lila Rose and Lilly Anne sat with their parents, Brady and Anna Marie. Tim and Jenny came in and went into the kitchen to help Jeremiah and Pricilla with the meal. Finally Pat and Catherine walked inside and to a space saved for the newlyweds with each set of parents seated with them.

Everyone could see bits and pieces of leaves, stems, or weeds on their clothing. Della stood up beside Catherine, "What happened to your dress? Let me pick these pieces, whatever they are, from your dress. How did that happen?" she inquired.

"I'll tell you all about it later. Tricksters decorated our buggy." It was time to cut the cake. Tim called out, "Pat and Catherine, come to the front of the room." As they walked up, all the guests clapped and cheered.

Tim said, "Ladies and gentlemen, we're here to honor this couple as they begin their lives together. We want to wish them many happy days, success in their endeavors and a wagonload of children." At that everybody in the room laughed and cheered.

"What do you have to say, Pat?"

"First, I say thank you all for coming to our wedding and for all the good wishes. We'll be living with Catherine's parents; please come visit. Enjoy the meal with us." He turned to Tim, "Tim, you're an ornery brother, but I know you would help us if we needed you. Remember, I'll get you back!" Tim reached and shook hands with Pat, and they laughed together.

Pat turned toward Catherine and said, "I will love you forever, Mrs. Patterson."

"And I will love you as long as I live." Pat took Catherine in his arms and kissed her full on her lips. The crowd clapped and yelled at them.

Tim spoke loudly above the noise, "That's enough, you two. You've got the rest of your lives to hug and kiss each other."

THE END

Glossary

arduous—Difficult to do; using much energy; strenuous.

besieged—Press with requests; cause worry or distress to.

bittersweet—North American climbing woody plant having clusters
of small greenish flowers succeeded by yellow capsules that open
when ripe and disclose the scarlet aril.

brevity—Shortness of duration.

brown Betty—A baked pudding of apples, bread crumbs, and spices.

buckboard—A four-wheeled vehicle with a springy platform.

burly—Strong and heavily built; husky.

crevice—A narrow opening resulting from a split or crack.

coverlet—Bedspread.

cuffed—To strike with the palm of the hand.

dapperly—Neat in appearance, stylish.

deterrent—To discourage, prevent from acting.

eulogy—A speech giving high praise.

executed—To carry out fully; put completely into effect.

flanked—To be placed at the side of or on each side.

guffawed—A loud burst of laughter.

hardtack—Bread made of flour and water.

hovered—To move to and fro near a place.

jerky—Preserved meat in long, sun-dried slices.

lanky—Ungracefully tall and thin.

lilting breeze—Move in a lively spring-like flow.

mayhem—Needless or willful damage or violence.

mesmerized—Hypnotic appeal.

mired—To cause to stick fast; to hamper or hold back.
moonshine—Intoxicating liquor, especially illegally distilled corn whiskey.

pristine—Free from soil or decay; being fresh and clean.

prowess—Distinguished bravery; extraordinary skill.

reminisced—Recall to mind a long-forgotten experience or fact.

retorted—To say in reply; to answer back, usually sharply.

rivulet—A small stream, brook.

sarsaparilla—A sweetened carbonated beverage flavored with sassafras
    and oil from a European birch.

spider pan—A pan to cook with that sat on tripod iron legs that could be placed over a campfire.

succumbed—To yield to superior strength or force or overpowering appeal or desire.

unabashedly—Not abashed; not destroy the self-confidence of.

Printed in the United States
By Bookmasters